THE MOST HIGH

MAURICE BLANCHOT

# THE MOST HIGH

Le Très-Haut

University of Nebraska Press : Lincoln & London

Translated and with
an introduction by
ALLAN STOEKL

Publication of this translation was assisted by a grant from the French Ministry of Culture.

⊚ The paper in this book meets the minimum requirements of American National Standard for Information Sciences – Permanence of Paper for Printed Library Materials, ANSI z39.48-1984.

LIBRARY OF CONGRESS CATALOGING IN PUBLICATION DATA
Blanchot, Maurice.
[Très-haut. English] The most high = (Le très-haut) / by Maurice Blanchot ; translated and with an introduction by Allan Stoekl. p. cm. — (French modernist library) Includes bibliographical references. ISBN 0-8032-1240-2 (cloth : alkaline paper) I. Stoekl, Allan. II. Title. III. Series.
PQ2603.L3343T713   1996      843'.912–dc20      95-31873 CIP

# INTRODUCTION: DEATH AT THE END OF HISTORY

*I keep asking myself what these events are that people miss. — Sorge's stepfather, in The Most High*

Why read a novel like Maurice Blanchot's *The Most High* (1948) today, in the 1990s? What does the immediate postwar period mean to us, and why does it continue to fascinate us? Now, when the century and the millennium are about to click over; now, when the great opposition of monolithic blocs is finished; now, when we seem at an end that refuses to end, locked as we are in economic decline, cultural irony, despair, and ecological ruin; now for some reason we are most intrigued by that distant period of smoldering rubble and witch hunts. Why?

First, the late 1940s and early '50s seem distant, more distant even than the 1930s, another strongly cathected period in this century. The '30s in one sense are more like today, for that decade, like our own, presents the horror of nationalistic fantasies and the threat of ever expanding ethnocentrism and genocide. The post–World War II period, on the other hand, in its very dance on the edge of the nuclear abyss, reminds us of the security of the Cold War. Already people are nostalgic for the Cold War. The 1950s are mourned. History then seemed to be going somewhere: for the Communists it was moving toward universal liberation, by way of many Koreas and Vietnams. For 'our' side, it meant the bracing challenge of fighting an evil empire: it gave us purpose. We would win. Or we would lose; not a pleasant thought, to be sure, but one that still presented an easily comprehensible definitive end: apocalypse now, or soon. And the Cold War also meant that we had to stay strong to fight the bad guys: we had, for example, to enact progressive social legislation, to counter the charges hurled from Moscow and Peking. Would the Civil Rights Act and Medicare/Medicaid ever have come about without the menace of Communism?

But the more we think about the differences between the present period and the immediate postwar years, the more we are struck by their similarity. We miss the opposition of blocs, but each bloc saw itself as the culmination of history, beyond which nothing else was conceivable. In that sense the Cold War was necessary to the blocs' self-definition, but at the same time it was fundamentally irrelevant. Each side, in its more rational moments, saw the other only as an aberration that could not be directly confronted—for that would lead only to nuclear annihilation—and so had to be lived with, for the time being. World War II was the last war to the death; the wars of liberation that followed were fundamentally wars of negotiation. Implicitly, then, each side recognized, in the practice of treaties and trade, that the other would eventually have to fade away, even if its rhetoric proclaimed the opposite. Or—and why not?—that in its posthistorical pretensions the other side was very similar, perhaps even the same. The other was identical, yet so aberrant that it would disappear by itself. As a working hypothesis, each side had to proceed as if the other did not exist. The other was a double located in the blind spot of historical vision.

It is no surprise, then, that the postwar period, seemingly so historical, was at bottom posthistorical. And the uncanny feeling of recognition we have when meditating on the postwar comes from the realization that nothing has happened since 1945, that the postwar is the posthistorical is always already the postmodern. (The most distant, the most foreign, is the most intimate. We can't get away: there is nowhere else to go. Hence our fascination, horror, and desire.) At the end of history, different historical options, different blocs, become simple questions of style; micro-oppositions, in other words, that are automatically subsumed by the larger endless end, which is fundamentally indifferent to them.

We are, after all, still *in* the postwar. Our cult of the postwar is a form of narcissism. We return to writings of the immediate postwar period because they help us to reflect on, and grasp, the paradigm that is constantly recycled, the paradigm of constant recycling: the collapse of blocs, of neat oppositions, through the end of history, through the end of historicism. Our paradigm. In the yellow, brittle pages, more yellow even than those of seventeenth-century books, we literally see the shortages (of paper, in this case), the black markets, the ice. But on these pages we also read what we have been living every day: the entropy of historical paradigms, plenitude as absence. *The Most High,* more than any other work I know, allows one to think about this distant period, this outmoded question of the end of history, and to recognize the unrecognizable—that this period, in its remoteness, is what is most near, and to conclude that this question, in its extinction, is what is most alive.

\* \* \*

Blanchot is an enigmatic figure, a shadow floating over French letters. Perhaps, if indeed he actually 'exists,' he would like to be one of his characters, magically cleansed of all biography: 'I have kept "living proof" of these events,' his narrator writes in *Death Sentence.* 'Once I am dead, it [the "proof"] will represent only the shell of an enigma, and I hope those who love me will have the courage to destroy it, without trying to learn what it means. [. . .] If these details are not there, I beg them not to plunge unexpectedly into my few secrets, or read my letters if any are found, or look at my photographs if they turn up, or above all open what is closed.'[1]

Blanchot the 'author' has long since disappeared into his text, but as he is transformed into paper and ink, and into the 'unavowable community' of his readers,[2] his myth grows ever stronger. Of course at some point enterprising biographers may root out some details of his life; his convoluted politics and his ignoble and noble gestures are in any case already well known.[3] But his larger stance is one of withdrawal, and the disappearance of his 'person,' in the end, while perhaps covering many sins, may also be necessary: for once, in Blanchot's case, we are forced to look more closely at the author's writings and to forget about the author's heroism (as in Malraux), his cowardice and duplicity (Céline), or his inflated public persona (Sartre). Indeed, it seems that anyone attempting to write a political biography of Blanchot would be forced to forego the 'intimate details' of his life and confine him or herself to the paper trail of Blanchot's writings. Would that all biographers were so constrained.

As Blanchot the author withdraws, the mythical persona of the autobiographer inflates to infinity, but it also becomes infinitely fragile. *The Most High* is a kind of diary of a civil servant and compulsive scribbler who is utterly insignificant and, like Blanchot, faceless, but who is nevertheless the incarnation of the reason and truth of his society, the embodiment of its simultaneous perfection and radical failure, of the force of its law and of the consequences of that law's transgression.

*The Most High,* written in the same years as Albert Camus's *The Plague* and George Orwell's *Nineteen Eighty-Four,* has much in common with those works. Blanchot's novel nevertheless presents a world in which the author, the intellectual, and the functionary—key figures in the other two works as well—is not simply a figure among others, a hero (Camus) or a cipher (Orwell), but the very *raison d'être* of a society that is perfect, beyond history, and is at the same time caught in the grips of an all too historical entropy that is all the more entropic for its inability to be fully historical. Blanchot's autobiographical myth (or his mythical autobiography), that of the absent writer, leads, in *The Most High,* to the conundrum of the endless end of history, and to the concurrent end of the end of history, as refracted and constituted through that writer's writing.

In spite of these seemingly abstruse paradoxes, which I discuss in greater detail later, large parts of *The Most High* show a high degree of verisimilitude. The year the novel was published, 1948, was a time of severe crisis in Europe. Europe had been destroyed in the war, and virtually anywhere one traveled, with the exception of neutral countries like Sweden or Switzerland, one found rubble. Large portions of northern France and Italy and virtually all of Germany, Poland, and Ukraine had been destroyed. It is a cliché, but one that must be repeated, to stress that the Europe we take for granted today—powerful, complacent, jealous of its threatened prosperity—was inconceivable in the five or so years after the war. Blanchot's novel contains, to my knowledge, some of the strongest images of this postwar reality, a reality that in its very strangeness seems, for some reason, familiar to us: the collapsing buildings; the omnipresent checkpoints, police, and prisons; the ruined idealism of the inhabitants; the epidemics; the subculture of shattered, homeless 'ex-' prisoners; the prostitution and black markets; the entrenched civil servants, guilty to the bone, who cannot conceive of a civilization lacking their invaluable services.[4] And, in the figure of Bouxx, the revolutionaries waiting in the wings who hope to topple once more the fragile 'legal' underpinnings of civil society—institutions which themselves are hopelessly compromised.

Beyond this first-order verisimilitude, as we might call it, there is a second, one that will be evident to those readers familiar with such authors as Arthur Koestler (*Darkness at Noon*), George Orwell, and others. Here we have not a simple description of a state of affairs but a presentation of a moral bind, one that had become evident in such countries as Stalin's Russia and Hitler's Germany: in a perfect revolutionary society, all crimes and suffering that have led to that society are retrospectively justified. Ends justify all means. But in this way, crime itself is redefined as law, anarchic violence as the necessary and coherent functioning of the State. We see this in Koestler, whose hero, based on Bukharin, is led to denounce himself at a purge trial so that the revolution can make use even of his extinction. And we certainly see it in Orwell, where the posthistorical society feels itself justified not only in rewriting history but in rewriting all laws, including mathematical and natural ones. For the Party, $2+2=5$, if necessary. In Blanchot, the State at the end of history, in and through its very universality, recognizes that all violence, all death, must lead not to the State's downfall but to its permanence, its immortality. Universality, in its immanence, becomes invisible and evaporates: the State is everywhere and everything, and therefore every act, no matter how 'illegal' or hostile to that State, inevitably acts to reinforce it and further its goals. Indeed, every act *is* the State. Not only is the violence of the past recuperable: with history ended, *all* violence is immediately recuperated, in one way or another. Bouxx, the revolutionary, ends up simply starting another administration, another bureaucracy, another system of repression (based, interestingly enough, in the health care system). We are back in the realm of 'doublethink' as put forward by Orwell: postrevolutionary peace is nothing but omnipresent violence; the social is the antisocial; the universal, embodied by the State, becomes a multiplicity of microdegenerations, a society of marginalized and invisible citizens living and dying in open graves. And the civil servant, that embodiment of the health and efficacy of the State, becomes, in the person of Henri Sorge, a kind of living death, a suspect in the eyes of the State, a figure who is either God or yet another plague victim — or both.

I call this state of affairs a 'second-order verisimilitude' because one can take it as still representing a 'state of affairs' in the world — the goal of works such as those by Koestler or Orwell. Law as crime, universal harmony as chaos and entropy, the glorious end of history as a rebirth of barbarism — these are all things we associate with actual regimes that justified themselves by referring to the necessary movement of history. But Blanchot's novel goes further in that it also presents what we might call a theoretical meditation on the possibility and meaning of ending an end state. Unlike Koestler or Orwell, Blanchot's novel never implies that the specter of the end of history can be done away with, and that we can or somehow should return to a blissful, democratic time when bureaucracies simply did their job and were not tied to a logic of plenitude, truth, and universal satisfaction. But if one *recognizes* that history has ended — that something definitive has happened and that events can never have the grave significance they once had — how then can an unjust regime be ended?[5] And how does one even go about distinguishing between a just and an unjust regime, let alone *ending* one that is terrible, terrible to the point of identification with the plague? Sorge, the novel's hero and diary keeper, has a stepfather high in the State administration. In a reversal of roles (discussed later), Sorge poses the obvious question: with the plague, with the crisis of institutions, won't the State collapse? The stepfather replies, 'How could it end, if it's the one that gives meaning to all the regimes that have ended, and if, in its absence, it would no longer be possible to imagine that something could end? In some ways it itself is finished, it's found its end, it's put an end to everything, and itself. Yes, from this point of view you're right but I'm not scandalized: one can't associate it too much with ideas of death, endings, or collapse; but its stability expresses death, and its endless duration is its fall.'

These remarks, coming from a character who is untrustworthy to say the least, nevertheless pose what is one of the crucial problems of the novel: if the end State is the very thing that gives sense to the word 'end'—if without it nothing could really be said to be over, to have ended for good and to have taken on its ultimate historical meaning—then how could this State itself ever end? Its end would mean endlessness; but endlessness is also its end. Same difference, in other words. Its end, put most simply, would merely mean its replacement by another, and any difference between the two would be one of degree, not kind. But, paradoxically, as end this State is also its own end: it itself cannot escape the generalized ending its arrival mandates. If all significant activity is over, then the State as locus of significant action is over as well—dead, in other words. The State cannot die, cannot end, yet its very life, its eternity, is a function of its status as always already dead.

But why would Blanchot write a novel in which the end of history is simply accepted as such? Other writers such as Orwell and Koestler were happy to point to the apparent fallacy of a notion of history that supposes an end state that justifies retrospectively and gives meaning to all previous events—at least to all events that are determined, again a posteriori, to be significant. Blanchot, through his character and narrator, does not do this. We are never really given a space outside the end; Sorge's stepfather is never fundamentally challenged when he considers the ineluctable nature of the end.

I think that there are a number of explanations, and to grasp them we must plunge deeper into the postwar *Zeitgeist*. First, on a purely practical, historical level, it was not at all clear in 1947–48 that a Communist government would not be taking over in France. Blanchot, writing in a mode of cultural pessimism, simply assumes a society that takes for granted the logic of the necessity of the end of history. He is already, so to speak, writing under a regime that posits itself as the culmination of all of history's struggles. Blanchot's friend Georges Bataille was already doing the same even before the war: in December 1937, in a letter to his friend and mentor Alexandre Kojève, Bataille wrote, 'I grant (as a likely supposition) that from now on history is ended (except for the dénouement). However, I picture things differently (I don't attribute much importance to the difference between fascism and communism; on the other hand, it certainly doesn't seem impossible that, in some very distant time, everything will begin again).'[6] For Blanchot, as for Bataille, the central question was not whether history was ended but the nature of a negativity left 'without a job' in a posthistorical State. Bataille posed eroticism and mysticism as an outlet for the destructive and excessive power that had expressed itself not only in labor but in revolutionary events; Blanchot, on the other hand, focuses exclusively on a problem that for Bataille is only one of several: death.

*The Most High* demonstrates Kojève's importance in the postwar years and the fascination he continued to exert on the left. Kojève's inescapable influence is the second factor that explains the centrality of the end of history in this novel. As has been pointed out by a number of scholars,[7] Kojève's 'explication' of Hegel's *Phenomenology* at the Ecole pratique des hautes études in Paris, starting in 1933, signaled a major shift in the emphasis of French philosophy and intellectual life. There was a move away from neo-Kantianism and atemporal rationalism toward Hegelianism and historically based truth. By 1948 it was hard to find anyone of importance on the intellectual left—the right had for all intents and purposes ceased to exert any influence at all—who was *not* a Hegelian: Sartre, Merleau-Ponty, Lacan, Bataille, Hyppolite, Queneau.[8] And these authors, writing in different genres—philosophy, psychoanalysis, social analysis, the novel—all assumed that history was going somewhere, that it had an endpoint, a goal, already here or just around the corner, that would justify and give meaning to the struggles and pain of all the preceding years. Ironically enough, Kojève, the godfather of this Hegelian wave, himself withdrew in the postwar period from the 're-public of letters' to become a civil servant, a French negotia-tor with the GATT talks.[9] After all, if history was ended, not only was negativity out of a job; the philosopher was too. The philosopher, or even the Hegelian 'wise man' (*sage*), is, in effect, downsized into a civil servant (like Sorge).

This is not the place for an extended analysis of Kojève's arguments in his *Introduction to the Reading of Hegel;* nev-ertheless, a brief summary of some of them, especially those relating to death and indifference, is useful. Kojève bases his entire reading of Hegel on the master-slave dialectic; this is a struggle for recognition, and indeed Kojève sees all of human history founded on the desire for recognition of each by an-other or by all others. The master and slave fight for recognition; the master wins, since he is willing to risk death; the slave, unwilling to take the risk, surrenders, recognizes the master as human, and thus becomes subordinate to him. The human is precisely the willingness to 'stare death in the face,' to risk one's own life in order to be recognized as free by another. The most fundamental desire, then, is the desire to be recog-nized as free—free to risk one's own life in struggle, which no animal could ever do. The slave, afraid of taking this risk, is consigned to the realm of materiality, of working, 'creatively destroying' nature in order to produce everything the master needs.

Of course in the end it turns out that the slave is the one who is really free, or is at least on the way to freedom, since the labor of the negative, its creative destruction, is the true mastery, the truly profound relation with death and destruc-tion, and it is the means not just to a one-sided recognition—what good is it to be recognized by a being who himself is not free, not human?—but to a State in and through whose medi-ation each person's desire to be recognized as free is recog-nized by every other. For the creative destruction of labor is also the destruction of historical processes—war, insurrec-tion, revolution—leading to such a posthistorical State.[10]

Kojève saw this end State as one of plenitude and the full satisfaction of desire (for recognition)—a kind of secular paradise, really.[11] But it was a paradise whose origin and end

xv

were not in eternal life and immortality, but in the risk and action of death. Death arises in Kojève's scenario in another way as well: at the end of history, 'man' himself will die— 'man' defined as the temporality of labor, the bearer of creative destruction, the subject and agent of history. With history closed, time will cease and therefore so will 'man.' But what will remain? Kojève is indifferent: perhaps 'man' will once again be an animal, with a language like that of bees.[12] The State at the end of history will be a kind of higher order nature, lacking all the elements that make for a human ex-perience—history, progress, conflict. But no, Kojève later cor-rects himself: negativity, destruction in labor, will remain; only now it obviously cannot serve a purpose. All humankind will engage in purely formal exercises, like (Kojève claimed) the Japanese.[13] Tea ceremonies, the Noh theater, the specta-cle of formal dress will replace useful labor in 'the struggle.' We will all be dandies, in other words. But all this is a foot-note—literally—in Kojève; the important thing is arriving there, as if the actual details are of little significance. But this indifference is more than a personal quirk; in some sense it is inscribed in Kojève's view of his own project, 'after' the end. For he sees the *Phenomenology*—and no doubt his own com-mentary—as a Book that will be Spirit, but which necessarily will also be dead.[14] Presumably people will read it, but since its status as Truth will be definitive, the process of reading and interpretation as well will also be in a strange way dead. There is, or will be, literally nothing more to say, and that nothing will be restated endlessly. The sense is given once and for all, and the Concept, in its fulfillment, will rest there, inert, wood pulp and ink. Its 'reading,' if we could call it that, will be mere mechanical repetition, taking place, perhaps, in the midst of the games and ceremonies of the living dead.

Blanchot, rewriting Kojève, also gives us a revolutionary (or postrevolutionary) State founded, in a sense, on the death of its own inhabitants. Mortality, finitude, is no longer a func-tion of risk taking or labor, but of universal indifference in the midst of universal dying. The State is *in principle* indif-ferent: its verbiage, its Book or Books, can bear no relation to the horror and tragedy taking place everywhere. For that negativity is discounted as irrelevant, or it is immediately recuperated, which amounts to the same thing: revolution is either no longer possible, or it has become a permanent function of the State. This is the posthistorical 'Reign of Terror': 'People [like Henri Sorge] cease to be individuals working at specific tasks, acting here and only now: each person is universal freedom, and universal freedom knows nothing about elsewhere or tomorrow, or work or a work accomplished. At such times there is nothing left for anyone to do, because everything has been done,' Blanchot writes in his crucial essay 'Literature and the Right to Death.'[15]

First there is indifference, then, freedom as indifference, the indifference of total freedom. Sorge's stepfather says, 'Maybe there will still be a lot of historic dates, strikes, like you say, earthquakes, upheavals of all kinds; it's also possible that the years to come will be empty. What difference does it make—because what counts isn't that I'm walking around in your room right now, or that I'm working in my office, as I should be doing, and from now on wars and revolutions will have neither more nor less importance than my little daily habits. What counts instead is that with every step I take I can recall, from beginning to end, the movement, filled with hardship and triumph, which permits all of us to say the last word by justifying the first.' And then, a little later, comes recuperation. Sorge's stepfather continues, 'And then there was a time when this return of an anachronistic spirit [the spirit of revolt, of nonconformity] was repressed: those who fell short of their tasks were condemned. But today condemnation is no more, because there are no more lapses. The inside and the outside correspond: the most intimate decisions are immediately integrated into the forms of public usefulness from which they are inseparable.' (chapter 6). Unlike the historical State analyzed by Michel Foucault in later years, Blanchot's posthistorical State is not concerned with the inner reform and recreation of the individual: now even violent revolt, no matter how nihilistic, is recoverable, or it is a priori recovered, *as such*.

The deaths of men, and the death of man, are the plenitude of the State: the two are identical before the blind gaze of the master bureaucrat. Since, as we know, the State cannot end, cannot die—but is already ended, already dead—the plague, public death, will always again be put to use by the State, but *as* pointless death: the days of simple progress, of transformative labor, are over, after all. Roles are reversible, since every social role is purely formal. The stepfather and his stepson can and do change places. After contemplating the possible future annihilation of his stepson by the State—an annihilation that nevertheless would sanction the son's position as a correct civil servant—the stepfather remarks, 'I'll go, but my leaving won't change anything. You could take my place and I yours. Maybe you're already in my place.'

It is important to stress that, at this point in the novel, Sorge has been using against his stepfather the same sorts of arguments that were used before and that will be used later, by Bouxx. Roles here are so fluid, then, that not only are those of stepfather and son reversible, but those of violent revolutionary and correct civil servant are as well. All these reversals 'mean' nothing. Indeed each role in itself is unstable: Sorge, ever correct, nevertheless cannot keep himself from scribbling a note that indicates he wants to resign his function and regain his 'freedom.' In other words, everyone tacitly or openly agrees with the stepfather in his or her assessment of the State but at the same time is in revolt and opts for freedom. Yet that leads back into the State again, because no freedom is conceivable outside it. 'You could take my place and I yours.'

Because of this immortal mortality of the State, and the perpetual Statehood of dying death (the State itself is constituted in and through death), it is futile to suppose that the plague and the State are somehow in opposition, albeit a nonlogical one. Some critics have argued that the plague, as a movement of non-recuperable death, is equivalent to the 'general economy' of expenditure and gift giving analyzed by Bataille, and that the State, with its coherent structure and rigorous notions of utility, is equivalent to a 'closed economy' of conservation.[16] This view also implies that Sorge eventually moves away from a position as champion of the State to one of a fiercely opposed critic, acting not out of Bouxx-like revolutionary motives, but out of ones that would favor the 'general economy.' But this view of the novel raises as many questions as it seems to answer. Why would Blanchot choose a thoroughly negative image of the 'general economy'—the plague—to represent (for lack of a better word) a movement that is positive in the sense that it, and it alone, finally escapes and undoes the power of the State? What then of all the indications that the plague and the State are inseparable, that the plague is a function of the State, and that any attempt (such as Bouxx's) to fight the State only leads to its reappropriation? That, in other words, there is no 'space' outside of, or beside, the State-plague combine? And, finally, where is there an indication that Sorge has definitively turned his back on, or separated himself from, the State?[17]

This way of considering the reversibility of the end of history—as State and plague, as truth and death, as death at the heart of truth—can also be seen in the figure of the law. Is the law another instance of the repressiveness of the State? Or does it have a much more problematic status?[18] If so, what is that status? Perhaps we have an indication when Sorge's stepfather tells him, 'What you'll do to escape the law will still be the force of the law for you.' The law, then, may encompass both the harsh laws of the State and their transgression, the double movement whereby the State enacts its rules and the citizens rebel, in any way whatsoever, in fury, in sickness, in death. It also encompasses the movement whereby citizens of the State (which means everyone) change position, sometimes realizing their embodiment of the State, at other times engaging in relentless warfare against the State, and (like Sorge, at one point at least) pointing out the State's cruelty, blindness, and hypocrisy.

What we might call Sorge's silence—his inability effectively to defy the State, even when he is most opposed to it—is also the power and impotence of his speech. Like the Kojèvian version of Hegel's Book, Sorge's journal—the text of *The Most High* itself—is circular: Sorge is finally able to speak in the last line of the novel, the point at which he dies, when he is radically silent—but it is his death that generates the novel, just as it is death that generates the State. Like the

Book, the novel will be repeated indefinitely, read endlessly, but it and its reading, its interpretation, will never change; its changelessness is both its eternal life (its inability to die) and its death as human experience, and even as simple organic matter (books are dead trees). The structure entails the repetition of the same words, the same silence, the same void.

It is very hard, then, to read the novel as a kind of *Bildungsroman* in which Sorge comes to an awareness of the tyranny or injustice of the State.[19] What law, outside of the reversible law of the State-plague, could he appeal to? What economy is outside the State's? And how can Sorge be said to change, to realize anything about the State, when he is always back there again on the first page, just 'anyone,' being knocked down and yet holding forth on his own, and everyone's, true position in the State? If Sorge really could come to a definitive conclusion about the State, about its cruelty or insufficiency, such a realization would be historically important—it would change everything and lead to another understanding of the State and history. In that way, however, it would be just another historical event, and it would be fully recuperable by the logic of the State, as yet another final chapter in the history of its development. It would hardly be a break from the State, a realization of its tyranny and an embrace of some elusive 'general economy.'

Perhaps the most puzzling aspect of this novel is the divinity of Sorge. At several points characters 'recognize' him for what he is—the Most High. When Jeanne Galgat, his nurse, shoots him at the end of the story, it seems she is carrying out a kind of sacrifice but its purpose and effects are less than clear. In fact, as we have just seen, Sorge does not 'die,' cannot die, since he is the already dead *scripteur* of a repetitious text; he is reborn as dead text each time he is 'killed.'

In this context an early article by Pierre Klossowski, 'Sur Maurice Blanchot' published in *Les Temps Modernes* in 1949, might prove of interest.[20] Klossowski stresses the idea of the 'mystery of the anteriority of the word to being, founded in the relation of the word and nothingness [*de la parole et du néant*]' (300). Language itself is fundamental to this theological 'mystery': language is no longer seen to reveal being, but rather, in mystery, it 'gives rise to an experience of non-being. This experience belongs essentially to the domain of language which, by this fact, is no longer supposed to reveal in the name of being, but in the name of the nothingness of things' (299).

Language in Blanchot's view derives its reality precisely from the destructibility, the death, of what it refers to. '[M]y language,' writes Blanchot in 'Literature and the Right to Death,' 'means that this person, who is here right now, can be detached from herself, removed from her existence and her presence and suddenly plunged into a nothingness; [. . .] my language essentially signifies the possibility of this destruction' (42). Yet the converse is true as well: 'the word as inexistence becomes objective reality.' Not only does it become objective reality; as death it takes on power, immortality. Blanchot writes, 'Whoever sees God dies. In speech what dies is what gives life to speech: speech is the life of that death, it is "the life that endures death and maintains itself within it"' (46). Hegel again.

Whoever sees God dies. But God sees Himself in and through others, and He dies too. He is the naming, the speech, the constituting word that, as Klossowski writes, 'constitutes the subject in death, in the survival of his death' (301). For speech becomes a 'dying without end' that 'thereby permits one to conceive of death as the source of perpetual temporalization' (301). Thus Sorge's death at the end of the novel can be seen as the death of God as recurrent naming, a death that, through language and through the novel itself, becomes 'the survival of his death'—He survives His death in the repetition of the novel, and His death survives, *as* the repetition of the novel.

The end of God, like the end of history, is a repetitious end, an end as death that nevertheless as death survives itself, endlessly. So Sorge always again survives, writing the book, written in it. And Sorge as God is also 'anybody': 'j'étais un homme quelconque,' 'I was anybody,' he states at the outset. God, the highest, the relation of infinite distance between the speaking self and the other negated in language, the relation, in other words, between Jeanne and Sorge, between 'Man' and 'Woman,' is also every God seeing Himself (or Herself) in the other, it's the relation of everyone to everyone else in the State, of every person who necessarily embodies the wisdom and accomplishment of the State, its institutions, its reason, its madness. The Kojèvian recognition of each by each and of each by all therefore becomes, in Blanchot, the endless death of God at His own hands, in His own words, which are the words of the other. This recognition in the words of the State, in the State as word, as 'anybody's' word, is also the naming of the person, of God, His death and maintenance in and as death in official language. 'Now, now I'm speaking.'

Sorge—what an odd name. Of course one thinks of Heideggerian *Sorge,* usually translated as *care:* Klossowski goes from there to see Sorge as a kind of personification of an 'existence without essence,' or, as he puts it, a 'negative theophany' (306). But one should recall another Sorge who was well known in the postwar period: Richard Sorge, master spy, Soviet agent in Tokyo during World War II, who made the full defense of the Soviet Union against the Nazis possible by revealing to Stalin in 1941 that the Japanese had no plans to attack in the east. Sorge, double agent, triple agent, Nazi journalist, working under his own name, an early student of the Frankfurt School, finally executed by the Japanese just before the end.[21] In the novel the details drop away, but we are left with a figure who represents the other to everyone and who is nevertheless anyone; in his very otherness he is the same, and yet he is the same as distance, difference, elevation. A triple agent, in other words, the same, a nobody, unrecognized, yet God, but God in the same way that everybody, anybody, nobody, is God. God as He is not seen, but God as He is recognized, put to death in His unread writing that is there for everyone to read—that you will read—recognized as dead, always again inhabiting the empty space between the end as beginning and the beginning at the end.

But Sorge is also Orestes to Jeanne (and Louise's) Electra.[22] The important reference here, I think, is both to the classical tradition of Aeschylus or Euripides and to Sartre's *The Flies.* Flies abound in *The Most High,* settling on faces, buzzing, flipping over, making strange sounds. Sorge, a near anagram of Orestes, and his sister/nurse Louise/Jeanne can be seen as doubles of the figures in the myth, and especially of those in the Sartre play, not because they murder anyone overtly, but because they too are locked in a struggle with official, ruling figures (Sorge's mother and stepfather) who represent, on one level at least, the weight of officially generated remorse and cyclical retribution.

Blanchot, in an important early essay, 'Sur le mythe d'Oreste,' sees a strong difference between the classical version of the myth and the Sartrian one.[23] In Aeschylus's tragedy, according to Blanchot, the conflict is not a 'personal' one between Orestes and a 'blind and incontestable order.' Rather, it is between 'subterranean [. . .], dark powers of fear and blood [and] higher powers whose sovereignty presupposes a true subjective union with man' (73). Orestes commits matricide on the orders of Apollo, but he is spared through the intervention of the 'higher' gods. Orestes thus regains his innocence and the entire order of the vengeful dark gods is replaced by 'the youthful power of the new gods'; unlike the old ones, these new gods are close to mortals, and act out of friendship with them: a new equilibrium is thus created, which is beyond the 'powers of the night' (73).

The Sartre play, on the other hand, rewrites the myth by putting Orestes forward as someone who acts on his own initiative, and who takes responsibility for his own acts. The reign of the flies is one not so much of dark evil as of bad faith: it is, according to Blanchot, 'the ransom through which men, unable to tolerate what is horrible, trade it for a feeling of repentance; it's the abject transaction that drives them, in the hope of being delivered, of being satisfied, no longer to accept themselves, to transform the movement of time into a perpetual falling back of the past onto themselves' (76). Orestes, far from doing away with remorse and escaping the consequences of his acts, after his act instead faces them more clearly. He is free of all 'consolation' but is 'weighed down with the heaviest weight, which is innocence in evil.' His act 'links man to anguish [angoisse] with a purer connection: that of liberty; [he has] substituted for the Furies of revenge and remorse, the Furies who reign only in an empty sky' (76). Blanchot's only regret is that the Sartre play does not convey the heroic nature of Orestes' struggle; instead Orestes is a mere rationalist, the only kind of opponent 'appropriate to combat a rigged regime [. . .] founded on hypocrisy and the crude exploitation of credulity,' one that is 'mediocre and petty' (77).

Here one can read *The Most High* as a critique not only of the Greek vision of the new, human-oriented gods, but of Sartrian existentialism as well. First, there are no gods that are distinct from humans; it is not that the gods are more friendly to them, but rather that god *is* anyone, if not 'everyman'—but this fact does not guarantee a new, comfortable position for anyone. On the contrary; 'man' as god (or God) is subject to a radical difference from 'himself,' a noncommunicability in speech, or the word, grounded in death but also in the deathlessness of that death. Beyond this, the plague is never lifted in the novel; the plague, if anything, is only internalized when, in the final chapter, the external crisis dies down but a crisis of perception and naming, on the part of Sorge but also Jeanne, intensifies. If indeed the novel is circular, then the plague too is recurrent, moving through various phases: latency, crisis, social collapse, inward virulence, and back again.

The most human God—the God of the State, the perfect civil servant, Sorge himself—is himself the carrier of the recurrent plague. At one point (chapter 5) he wanders around the streets without having been vaccinated; he is stopped at a checkpoint on the street, taken to the police station, but is inexplicably let go, despite the fact that he is clearly carrying the sickness. One has the sense that he is *supposed* to circulate, that the State or its shadow is letting him go so that he can infect the maximum number of people possible. And there he stays, in the dispensary, strangely alone in his room, but going out and perhaps infecting others. Perhaps infecting his nurse as well. And that infection is also the infection, the sickness, of human violence, for everywhere the plague spreads we see massive social dislocation, bombardments, imprisonment, social chaos leading to the point where the living are indistinguishable from the dead. Sorge does not lift this violence, he embodies it, he dies through it (and is reborn in it);

it is a death that only maintains the death of human conflict, the indelible residue of the historical violence of time and progress. But this death is also a maintenance, a deathless-ness, because it is the end: the end ends but cannot end, and so we see a speech, a communication, arising in and through death. Jeanne shoots Sorge: he dies—perhaps—but he speaks, and she does too.[24] The radical distance between them, the 'height' of the separation that is human society, is also the death carried in language, a death that cannot be covered over in bad faith, but also one that cannot be defeated through a heroic albeit self-defeating gesture. Blanchot, in his review of the Sartre play, mentions the 'rancor' of Electra ('Sur le mythe d'Oreste,' 74). If Louise/Jeanne, the Electra figure here, is rancorous (see Louise's 'oath' at the end of chapter 3), it is only as a double of Sorge: she is his other, his possibility of speech, but also his inability to extirpate a universal resent-ment, an incessant bad faith. For, as we see throughout the novel, the violence of revolt in the State—as epitomized by Bouxx—is the *ressentiment* of a revolt that can never hope to be revolt. Sorge, arguing with his stepfather, also reveals him-self to be a carrier of this virus, as no doubt everyone else is as well. His inability to conquer bad faith only underscores his total lack of heroism: how ironic it is, then, that Blanchot at the end of his review of *The Flies* called for a more heroic figure in Orestes.

There is more: *The Most High* reenacts not only the story of Orestes, but that of the dreaded Furies, the Erinyes, of Greek myth. 'Greeks believed the blood of a slain mother infected her murderer with a dreadful spiritual poison, *miasma,* the Mother's Curse. It drew the implacable Furies to their victim, and also infected any who dared help him,' writes Barbara G. Walker.[25] Another version has it that the Furies 'represented the Scolding Mother. Whenever a mother was insulted, or perhaps even murdered, the Erinyes appeared.'[26] It is not far from this to the story of *The Most High:* the 'scolding,' in-sulted mother could be not only Sorge's shadowy but ines-capable mother, but the nation itself, wounded, insulted, al-ways on the point of death. And the *miasma* is everywhere: the black water dripping, seeping into everything, through walls, into and between bodies locked together in incestuous embrace and combat. Just as there were three Furies (Tisiphone [Retaliation-Destruction], Megaera [Grudge], and Alecto [the Unnameable]) so too there are three women in the novel (besides Sorge's mother) who can be identified with the Furies just as easily as they can be with Electra: Louise Sorge, the sister, bent on monumental revenge; Marie Scadran, the distrustful photographer; and Jeanne Galgat, the killer, whose name itself is a pseudonym, and whose identity is as unknowable as her mad father's.

Perhaps this all sounds *too* allegorical; the novel starts to appear as a lament on the decline of the great nation as mother, and as a strange affirmation of the just punishment of everyone responsible for that decline (the entire population, in effect).[27]

But then again, by going Sartre one better and writing an even less heroic Orestes, Blanchot may be pointing up the decline of the possibility of allegory itself. For allegories need heroes, larger-than-life figures who can confront the Furies and foil the plague. Sorge is anything but. One thinks here too of Camus's *The Plague,* published a year before *The Most High.* In that novel we have heroic figures fighting a battle and winning it. It was not all that hard for postwar readers to see, and find comfort in, an allegory of their own resistance, or imagined resistance, under the Occupation. Stable allegory is dependent on the very characteristics of language that Blanchot would question. In a world where the signifier is the death of the referent, and the carrier of a deathless death, the stable certainties of story and moral erode very quickly. If anything, *The Most High* is an allegory of the collapse of political allegory, the awareness that heroes who conquer death, who stand up to the gods of bad faith, are no longer tenable. That is why as a fiction it is so slippery, so hard to pin down, so . . . well, difficult. Orwell, in *Nineteen Eighty-Four,* seemed to want some reassurance that 2+2 really does equal 4. His dystopia, at least on a first, naive reading, seems to attempt to demonstrate the necessity of a realm where such certainties do exist, if only outside the fictional space of the novel. Blanchot offers us no such hope because the collapse of allegory in *The Most High* is also the collapse of the possibility of all equation, of all correspondence-in-opposition between inside and outside, life and death, truth and fiction. For clear-cut political allegory would depend on a law with a definable inside and outside—but here not only inside and outside but all stable identities collapse: God is everyone; the State is dissolution; the perfect civil servant is a terrorist, a triple agent; the end as end cannot end.

All this does not mean, however, that allegory is simply eliminated. The novel contains an allegory of its own collapse as allegory. Allegory becomes heavier, more monstrous, death-bound. When they visit the cemetery, at the end of chapter 3, Sorge and Louise see two tombs; one is light and gay, the other 'heavy and massive, a kind of barely elevated tower squashed at its summit by a gigantic allegory.' Later, this allegory is referred to as a 'monumental accusation, a dull and mute stone rancor.' Entering a room, 'just a simple tomb, clean and cold and empty,' Sorge is brutalized and forced to repeat an oath of 'resentment and revenge.' And over it all is the crushingly heavy allegory of two people, a microsociety, united, frozen in death. Allegory itself presides over the descent into resentment, into the tomb. It stands 'for'—or is it 'on'?—death. But it keeps standing, in its impotence, in its downward push, its endless collapse. Allegory endures death and maintains itself within it.[28]

As we see in this passage, allegory in *The Most High* is unstable. Like the State, like the law, it is always being reversed, affirmed at the moment of its evident destruction. Its collapse is also the collapse of language, and of literature. But for Blanchot, literature remains: it has a unique, even privileged, mission, even as it doubles, in the universality of its mortal negation-affirmation, activity within the posthistorical, 'revolutionary,' State.[29] In 'Literature and the Right to Death,' Blanchot writes, 'Now, nothing can prevent this power [of death]—at the very moment it is trying to understand things and, in language, to specify words—nothing can prevent it from continuing to assert itself as continually differing possibility, and nothing can stop it from perpetuating an irreducible double meaning, a choice whose terms are covered over with an ambiguity that makes them identical to one another even as it makes them opposite' (61). A double meaning of allegory too, of terms spinning in death—like Louise and Sorge, like the stepfather and Bouxx, like God Himself and a wretched, mad civil servant dying alone. But there is also the double meaning of and as literature, for the 'original double meaning, which lies deep inside every word like a condemnation that is still unknown and a happiness that is still invisible, is the source of literature, because literature is the form this double meaning has chosen in which to show itself behind the meaning and value of words, and the question it asks is the question asked by literature' (62).

\* \* \*

I would like to thank my friend and colleague, Jean-Claude Vuillemin, whose patient advice helped me to get through more than a few rough spots. Thanks as well to my indefatigable copyeditor, Adrienne Mayor, who made a huge number of useful suggestions. This translation is dedicated to my wife, Nan Moschella, and our two offspring, Bruno and Ricky, who endlessly put up with my deathbound subjectivity.

*Allan Stoekl*

#### NOTES

1. Maurice Blanchot, *Death Sentence,* trans. Lydia Davis (Barrytown NY: Station Hill, 1978), p.3.

2. See Blanchot's essay *La Communauté inavouable* (Paris: Minuit, 1984).

3. Blanchot wrote for right-wing reviews, such as *Combat,* before World War II. After the war, his politics seem to have changed: he is the reputed author of the 'Manifesto of the 121,' which proclaimed the right to insubordination as a means of protest and resistance against the French prosecution of the war in Algeria (1961). Politically, like so many other leading authors of this century (Orwell, Céline, Bataille, Foucault, Derrida, and even Sartre come to mind), Blanchot seems to have been fundamentally an anarchist, distrustful of all unified authority and codified doctrine; among figures of this type, political commitment, as understood in conventional terms, is always in flux and sometimes takes a dangerous or sinister turn (to the far

right, early on, in Blanchot's case; to the Stalinist or *gauchiste* left, later on, in Sartre's, etc.). What remains constant is the anarchism, the *opposition*.

4. On life in Paris in the mid-1940s, see Antony Beevor and Artemis Cooper, *Paris after the Liberation, 1944–49* (New York: Doubleday, 1994), especially chapters 9 ('Provisional Government') and 16 ('After the Deluge'). Germany shortly after capitulation is explored by Stephen Spender in *European Witness* (New York: Reynal and Hitchcock, 1946); 'zero hour' is presented with a most rare and withering honesty in Victor Gollancz's *In Darkest Germany* (Hinsdale IL: H. Regnery, 1947).

5. Perhaps this loss of a 'grave significance' explains the subtle and dry humor that runs through the first few chapters of the novel. See, for example, Sorge's discussion of public ceremonies and sports with his concierge in chapter 1.

6. Georges Bataille, 'Letter to X., Lecturer on Hegel' in *The College of Sociology, 1937–39,* ed. D. Hollier, trans. B. Wing (Minneapolis: University of Minnesota Press, 1988), p.90.

7. Most notably, and influentially, by Vincent Descombes in *Le Même et l'autre: Quarante-cinq ans de philosophie française (1933–78)* (Paris: Minuit, 1979). See especially the chapter on Kojève, 'L'Humanisation du néant' (pp.21–62).

8. Several recent books have charted the impact of Hegel in twentieth-century, and above all postwar, France. See Judith P. Butler, *Subjects of Desire: Hegelian Reflections in Twentieth Century France* (New York: Columbia University Press, 1987), and Michael S. Roth, *Knowing and History: Appropriations of Hegel in Twentieth Century France* (Ithaca NY: Cornell University Press, 1988).

9. See the biography of Kojève, *Alexandre Kojève: La philosophie, l'Etat, la fin de l'histoire,* by Dominique Auffret (Paris: Grasset, 1990). GATT refers to the General Agreement on Tariffs and Trade, an ongoing set of agreements whose larger purpose is to lower trade barriers and increase commerce worldwide.

10. On the master-slave dialectic, see chapter 2 ('Summary of the First Six Chapters of the *Phenomenology of Spirit*') of Alexandre Kojève's *Introduction to the Reading of Hegel,* ed. Allan Bloom, trans. J. H. Nichols Jr. (New York: Basic Books, 1969), pp.31–70.

11. On the posthistorical State as a secular paradise founded not on immortality but on mortality, and in which Christ is replaced by the 'Napoleon-Hegel dyad,' see Kojève's revealing essay 'Hegel, Marx et le Christianisme,' in *Critique* 3–4 (1946), pp.339–66.

12. See Kojève, *Introduction to the Reading of Hegel,* p.158 n. 'Man

remains alive as animal in *harmony* with Nature or given Being,'
Kojève writes (158).

13. Kojève, *Introduction to the Reading of Hegel,* 2d. ed., p.159 n. 'But
in spite of persistent economic and political inequalities, all Japanese
without exception are currently in a position to live according to
totally *formalized* values' (162).

14. The passages on the Book in Kojève's *Introduction* are not
contained in the English edition. See *Introduction à la lecture de Hegel*
(Paris: Gallimard, Collection 'Tel,' 1980), p.394: '[The] empirical existence of Science is not historical Man, but a Book made of paper, in
other words a natural entity' (my translation).

15. 'Literature and the Right to Death,' in *The Gaze of Orpheus, and
Other Literary Essays,* ed. P. Adams Sitney, trans. Lydia Davis (Barrytown NY: Station Hill, 1981), pp.21–62; the quote is from p.38. Blanchot's
discussion of the end of history as absolute freedom—and absolute
indifference—can be found on pp.37–41. It should be noted that for
Blanchot the end of history first shows itself, so to speak, with the
French Revolution and the Terror. Thus while his argument throughout the essay is informed by Kojève's reading of Hegel, Blanchot
nevertheless presents his reading of the end of history as a dystopia,
rather than the rather flat utopia of Kojève (for Kojève, the personification of posthistory is Napoleon on his horse at Jena, witnessed by
Hegel —or even Stalin, but not Robespierre). Blanchot can therefore
cite the example of the Terror, via the *Phenomenology,* as the indifference of the gesture by which heads are cut off 'the way you cut off
a head of cabbage' (40). But the Terror certainly did not embody the
end of history for either Hegel or Kojève. Blanchot here seems to
appropriate an old *idéologème* from the right—the Terror as matrix
of modernity—while turning it on its head, to the extent that he goes
on to valorize the Terror, stress its inescapability, and identify it with
literature in general. Rewriting Jean Paulhan's argument in *Les Fleurs
de Tarbes, ou la terreur dans les lettres* (Paris: Gallimard, 1940),
Blanchot states, 'Literature contemplates itself in revolution, it finds
its justification in revolution, and if it has been called the Reign of
Terror, this is because its ideal is indeed that moment in history, that
moment when "life endures death and maintains itself in it" in order
to gain from death the possibility of speaking and the truth of
speech' (41). 'Literature and the Right to Death,' first published in the
same year as *The Most High,* can be read as a detailed commentary on
the novel (or, conversely, the novel can be read as a commentary on
the essay).

16. Two excellent pieces on *The Most High* seem to present the

relation between the plague and the State as one of simple opposition, rooted in the irreconcilable difference between a 'closed' (or 'regional') economy and a 'general' one. See John Gregg, 'Writing the Disaster: Sorge's Journal,' in *Maurice Blanchot and the Literature of Transgression* (Princeton: Princeton University Press, 1994), pp.72–126. See also 'Le Très-Haut: The (N)ever Present God(dess),' in Larysa Ann Mykyta's 'Vanishing Point: The Question of Woman in the Works of Maurice Blanchot' (Ph.D. dissertation, SUNY-Buffalo, 1980), pp.18–43. Mykyta's work is the only thorough investigation of one of the most fundamental questions in Blanchot.

17. Gregg suggests that Sorge has separated himself from the State when he claims, for example, that Sorge at a certain point is 'no longer an active representative of the State' ('Writing the Disaster," p.113). But when was Sorge ever an *active* representative of the State?

18. For a discussion of the figure of the law in *The Most High,* see Michel Foucault's 'La Pensée du dehors,' in *Critique,* 229 (1966), pp.523–46.

19. This is implied by Gregg, when he states, for example, that Sorge's 'language festers and grows out of control, and [he] *is transformed* into a spokesman for the neutrality of the epidemic' (p.125, my italics).

20. Pierre Klossowski, 'Sur Maurice Blanchot,' in *Les Temps modernes* 40 (1949), pp.298–314. Translations are my own.

21. See the biographical sketch of Richard Sorge in *Who's Who in Espionage,* by Ronald Payne and Christopher Dobson (New York: St. Martin's Press, 1984), pp.160–61.

Sorge's letter, in which he declares his 'freedom' (chapter 6), also has a precedent. The Soviet foreign agent Ignace Reiss, tiring of his employment, wrote Stalin a letter in which he declared: 'I cannot stand it any longer. I take my freedom of action.' Reiss was machine-gunned by a Soviet hit-team in Lausanne, Switzerland, in September 1937. (See Richard Deacon, *Spyclopedia: The Comprehensive Handbook of Espionage* [New York: W. Morrow, 1987], p.233. This book also has a section on Richard Sorge, on pp.241–43.) This leads to an interesting idea: perhaps Jeanne Galgat, in shooting Sorge, is acting as an agent of the State (if not of Bouxx).

22. Blanchot, in a letter to me (20 Feb. 1984), states about *The Most High,* 'The political meaning (if in fact there is one) effaces itself before the metaphysical and ethical meaning: the relation with others [*le rapport à autrui*], the ambiguous appointment of Electra [*la nomination ambiguë d'Electre*], etc.' Foucault, in 'La Pensée du dehors' (536–37) also notes the rewriting of the story of Orestes in *The Most High.*

23. Blanchot, 'Sur le mythe d'Oreste,' in *Faux pas* (Paris: Gallimard, 1943), pp.72–78. All translations are my own. For an understanding of the figure of Louise/Jeanne in *The Most High,* the next essay in this collection, 'Le Mythe de Phèdre' (pp.79–85), is of great interest.

24. But there is this tantalizing phrase in *Death Sentence,* first published in the same year as *The Most High:* 'A year or two earlier, a young woman had shot at me with a revolver, after vainly waiting for me to disarm her. But I did not love that young woman. As it happened, she killed herself some time after that' (6).

25. Barbara G. Walker, *The Woman's Encyclopedia of Myths and Secrets* (San Francisco: Harper and Row, 1983), p.327.

26. Brian Branston, *Gods of the North* (London: Thames and Hudson, 1955), quoted in *Woman's Encyclopedia,* p.327.

27. Thus *The Most High* can be read as an expression of postwar right-wing cultural despair, an elegy on the loss of the very possibility of nationhood. Civil society might go on, but cultural pride, the strength of a people in and through its language and literature, is over (see, for example, Sorge's evocations of crowds, political rallies, and blaring radio propaganda). All that remains are right-wing collaborators and left-wing terrorists (Bouxx, Dorte, and the rest) in not so secret complicity.

28. An optimistic, politicizing reading of *The Most High* has nevertheless been attempted. See Georges Préli, *'Le Très-Haut* de Blanchot: Loi, épidémie et révolution,' in *34/44, Cahiers de recherche de S. T. D.* 2 (Spring 1977), pp.67–85. In this context see also my own essay, 'Blanchot and the Silence of Specificity,' in *Politics, Writing, Mutilation: The Cases of Bataille, Blanchot, Roussel, Leiris and Ponge* (Minneapolis: University of Minnesota Press, 1985), pp.22–36.

29. See Blanchot, 'Literature and the Right to Death,' p.38: 'Revolutionary action [i. e., the Reign of Terror] is in every respect analogous to action as embodied by literature: the passage from nothing to everything, the affirmation of the absolute as event and of every event as absolute' (translation modified). In this respect every one of Sorge's acts, even the most seemingly insignificant, is fundamentally *literary* (by Blanchot's definition), since Sorge holds each to be absolute in relation to life within the State. There can be no distinction between the minor events of everyday life and the most imposing political decisions. See also note 15.

# THE MOST HIGH

'I'm a trap for you. Even if I tell you everything—the more loyal I am, the more I'll deceive you: it's my frankness that'll catch you.'

'Please understand: everything that you get from me is, for you, only a lie—because I'm the truth.'

# 1

I wasn't alone, I was anybody. How can you forget that phrase?

During my sick leave, I used to go walking in a neighborhood downtown. What a beautiful city, I told myself. Going down into the subway, I bumped into someone, who shouted at me brutally. I yelled back, 'You don't scare me.' His fist was released with fascinating speed; I collapsed on the ground. There was a crowd. The man tried in vain to lose himself in the mob. I heard him protesting, in a rage, 'He was the one who pushed me. Let me alone!' I wasn't hurt, but my hat had rolled into some water. I must have been pale, I was trembling. (I was getting over a sickness. They had told me to avoid jolts.) A policeman came out of the crowd and calmly invited us to follow him. We went up the stairway, separated from each other by a group. He too was pale, even livid. At the police station, he exploded in anger.

'It's very simple,' said the policeman, interrupting him. 'He went after this man and let him have it on the chin with his fist.'

'Are you going to press charges?' the captain asked me.

'Can I ask my . . . this person one or two questions?'

I went up and looked at him.

'I'd like to know who you are.'

'Any of your business?'

'Are you married? Do you have any children? No, I want to ask you something else. When you hit me, you felt that you had to do it, it was a duty—I was challenging you. Now you're sorry, because you know that I'm a man like you.'

'Like you? That'd make me sick!'

'Like you, yes, like you. If you have to, you can beat me. But kill me, crush me—could you do it?' I got right in front of him. 'If I'm not like you, then why don't you crush me under your heel?'

He stepped back quickly, awkwardly. There was a commotion. The captain grabbed me by the sleeve. 'He's . . . all worked up,' he exclaimed. The policeman led me off. Going out, I saw cold, frozen faces. My assailant looked at me, snickering, but still his face was pallid.

* * *

Having a family—I knew what that meant. Sometimes I had no idea, I worked, I was useful to everyone, we were all close to each other. But suddenly something happened—I could turn around. My mother and sister were sitting in the waiting room of the clinic. What a sleazy place! Armchairs, couches, carpets, a piano, and a cold light, a perpetual half-light. Still, the hospital was modern. But it was a question of atmosphere, of silence: the doctor had explained it to me. I was uneasy. I hadn't seen my mother in a number of years. I felt that she was watching me.

'You don't look so good.'

She asked me why it had taken so long to let them know.

'As soon as I could, I wrote you. I had a high fever, that was all. They were waiting for other symptoms, but there weren't any. I was delirious, I think. Deep down I didn't feel so bad. Instead, it's now that I'm tired and depressed.'

'Your surroundings are bad. Your place, I've heard, is a tomb. Why don't you come back home?'

'My apartment? Yes, my place has a lot to do with it. Have you seen the doctor?'

'No, he had left, but we saw the nurse.'

'I have to get back to work. I can't stay outside of collective life. They're replacing me at my office. But I miss work.'

Both of them looked at me.

'It's ridiculous, I know. I have such an unimportant job. But what difference does that make? I have to do my part.'

My mother must have said something like, 'It's up to you alone to find a better job.' At that point I had an uncomfortable feeling: both of us were lying. We weren't lying, it was worse than that. I said what was necessary, but suddenly I was torn out of the moment. I realized that all of this could have taken place at some other time, thousands of years ago,

as if time had opened and I had fallen through the crack. My
mother became openly disagreeable. I was disoriented and, at
the same time, I understood better why she was so distant,
why I hadn't seen her for years, why . . . This went a long way
back. My mother now was someone from before, a monumental person who could lead me into totally crazy things.
That's what the family was. The recollection of the period
before the law, a scream, rough words from out of the past. I
looked at my mother, who was staring at me with a look of
discomfort.

'Go home,' I said. 'See you tomorrow.'

'What's the matter with you? We just got here.'

She started to cry. Her tears deepened my uneasiness. I
apologized.

'You've become so indifferent,' she said crying, 'so foreign.'

'Not at all. It's life that gives you that impression. A person
has to work, get through each day. You give yourself to everybody, but you're separated from your own.'

'So come home for your convalescence.'

'Maybe.'

'You're a lot thinner. This sickness worries me. Did you feel
it coming? Were you feeling tired before?'

I looked at my mother without answering.

'Come on, mother,' Louise said drily. 'Don't torture him.'

\* \* \*

At noon I had lunch in a little restaurant near city hall. The
tables were arranged so that they faced each other, the whole
length of a narrow room. There weren't many places, so I
chose a table where someone was already seated.

'Anything new since I've been gone?' I asked the waitress.
'In any case, the menu hasn't changed.'

'That's true, we haven't seen you around lately. You had
some time off?'

'No, I was sick.'

She grimaced.

'Excuse me,' I said to my neighbor, 'I've seen you a number
of times, you're a regular. You work around here?'

'Around here, not exactly.' He looked at me closely for a

3

moment. 'A few years ago I was a salesman in a store in the neighborhood. I've changed neighborhoods, but I still come here a lot.'

There was plenty of noise, the noise of things clinking, of spoons scraping the bottom of dishes, of liquid being poured into glasses. Across from me, two women at adjoining tables were talking to each other. 'She's spying on me, she's harassing me.' I distinctly heard these words. I ate without gusto.

'The food's not really that great.'

He rolled a cigarette.

'It's not expensive, and there's a lot of it.'

The plate in front of me contained a number of vegetables and a big hunk of boiled meat.

'The ingredients are there,' I said, tapping the meat with my fork. 'But they wreck the merchandise.'

'Hey! — A good soup's on the way this evening.' He went on praising the restaurant, exaggerating. 'And you?' he asked. 'Where do you work?'

He was a rather small, very neat man. He spoke with authority. 'Talk to him frankly,' said the woman across from me. — 'No, I'll never speak to him again.'

'I work at city hall.'

'A civil servant? The job has its advantages.'

He wanted to add something. But the woman had started to cry; abruptly she stood up and walked to the back of the room.

'So what's going on?' I asked the waitress. Without answering, she took my plate, then pushed a meager cake at me. She seemed to be saying, Why ask me? It was none of my business.

'She works in a dressmaker's shop. She doesn't get along with her supervisor.'

'And you — you get along with the management?'

She shrugged, smiling.

'Very well,' she said, walking off.

My neighbor had been listening attentively, but as soon as we were alone he plunged into his newspaper. The woman came back, her face calm and bright.

'What's in the news?'

I read the headlines on the page he showed me: A Woman Falls Accidentally from the Sixth Floor. New Hygiene Service Regulations. Another Fire on the West Side (my neighborhood). A Flood of the. . . . I felt impatient and a bit feverish.

'Did you read this story: "On Center Street, a woman falls . . ."?'

'Yes, I read it.'

'What do you think—was it an accident or a suicide?'

'I've no idea. An accident, if you believe the headline.'

'But,' I said brusquely, 'a suicide too is an accident. Read the story. According to the doctor's testimony, the woman was mildly ill. She suffered from overwork, and her superiors gave her some time off. Note that: time off. There was no fault on the part of her employers. As soon as an employee shows signs of fatigue, the doctor recommends rest, prescribes medicines, the system functions marvelously. But it so happens that the sick person has dizzy spells, she needs air. She goes to the window and feels sick. Now what happens? Why does she fall? Why does she fall precisely from the side where it is the most difficult and the most dangerous to fall? And then too maybe she voluntarily threw herself into the void, because . . . because she felt sick, because she was ashamed not to be working, who knows? You can imagine that and plenty of other things as well. In the end, who's responsible? The author of the article implies that the doctor really didn't do his duty, that he should have sent the sick woman to the hospital.'

'So?' said the man. Elbows on the table, he was looking at me fixedly.

'Well, it's clear.'

'What's clear?'

'I don't know,' I said, feeling a bit tired. 'A little while ago you blamed me because I was being critical. You think one shouldn't criticize?'

'Me? I blamed you?'

'It was about the restaurant.'

'You're funny. I think this restaurant's not bad, that it's as good as the others. I have no interest in the place.'

'But,' I insisted eagerly, 'criticize? Well, you don't like that.

Criticizing all over the place—you think it's wasteful, messy, doubt invades people's minds, it's unhealthy, backwards. In your profession, you criticize, but only in the right departments, according to the prescribed methods. You don't like it when I say that this is a sloppy restaurant, just as you hold it against this woman for complaining about her boss. Is that it?'

I looked at him: even though spoken only half aloud, I had the feeling that my remarks were out of place.

'Excuse me. I really feel these things. I don't disapprove of your way of seeing. But look—the article backs me up. The author didn't say, "It's nobody's fault." Not at all—he doesn't hesitate to accuse someone, there'll be an inquiry, reforms will come out of it. That's all I meant.'

The man took back the paper and looked at it attentively. Then he folded it.

'You can criticize as much as you like. Personally, I couldn't care less. You don't want to read it?' he added, offering me the paper. He got up and called the waitress. 'I know, as well as anybody else, how to see what's not working,' he said sullenly. 'I can be outspoken too. But I don't complain to just anybody, in an irresponsible way, surrounded by irresponsible people. There's no shortage of impressionable people.'

He gestured as if to say, Enough on this topic. The waitress brought him his change. 'Will we see you tonight?' she asked him. —'Yes, sure, tonight. Here, take the paper; it's a gift.' It was my turn to ask for the check. There were still a lot of people. Submissive, passive patrons waited, standing, patiently eyeing tables. The waitress didn't come. 'Miss!' I yelled. She walked past without seeming to hear. 'What a dump!' I said aloud, and went to the counter to pay.

\* \* \*

Coming home, I found a man I didn't know waiting at my door.

'I'd very much like to get to know you,' he said eagerly. 'I've heard very good things about you. And I live right nearby. I'd like to be on good terms with you.'

I looked at him and didn't answer.

6

*imprudent*

'You've been sick, I believe?'

'Yes.'

He observed me silently. He was very tall, his face was extraordinarily massive.

'I learned that from the concierge. When I moved in I was afraid of bothering you, but she told me that you were being treated in a clinic. You've recovered completely?'

'Completely.'

'Health is a strange thing. I'm naturally robust myself, as you can see. I've never really been sick; I'm very strong. And yet, on some days, I don't feel like getting up, I don't want to do anything, I don't even sleep. I feel as if my blood has stopped leading me and that I'm waiting for it to get around to giving orders again. Your place is fairly cramped,' he said, looking first at the room we were in, and then at the other room visible through the glass door—obviously my whole apartment.

'I'm a bachelor, it's enough.'

He laughed.

'Sorry,' he said. 'Your tone says a lot. You lead a solitary life, I think. You don't like to see people much?'

I stared at him; he looked at me.

'It's possible,' I said evenly. 'In other words, I see everyone willingly, I have no preferences, particular relationships seem useless to me.'

'Really, that's what you think?'

He sat there silently, his hands on his knees, his back against the window; he looked like a half-hewn block of stone, cut straight from the mountain.

'You're a civil servant?'

'I work at the registry office.'

'Exactly what kind of work is it?'

'Office work, naturally.'

'And . . . it suits you?'

'It suits me just fine.'

'I was indiscreet a few days ago,' he said abruptly. 'You were walking down the street, the day before yesterday, I think. I was behind you, I knew who you were. I was watching you carefully.'

'You were watching me? Why?'

'Why? Really, it seems rude to mention it. But I knew you were my neighbor. I was well aware of your position. There's nothing wrong with that. So I followed you. You were walking quickly down the street, not looking around. You were, probably, coming home from work?'

'I come home every day, at the same time. Every evening's the same.'

'It was fairly dark that evening. Do you remember that a man . . .'

'Yes, so what?'

'He came up to you, right?'

We looked at each other; I saw his eyes trained on me, half curious and half approving; then they lost all expression.

'He was a panhandler,' I said.

'I did have the impression that you gave him some money.'

'You saw that too? You really were watching me closely.'

'Yes, sorry about that.'

'Listen, if you're interested in this incident, I can give you even more details.'

'Please, let's drop it. I got carried away by my curiosity.'

'Wait, this story seemed strange to you. If not, why did you come to talk with me? Maybe you'd like to know what he said to me? Sorry, but it was typical. He said what's usually said in those situations. And I no doubt could have sent him back to an Agency or asked him why he had stopped working. I should have asked for an explanation. But I didn't do anything. He got his money, nothing more.'

I saw a drifting expression on his face, as if he wanted to disguise himself with a far-away emotion.

'Do you want me to describe the man in a precise way? You noted, no doubt, that he wasn't badly dressed, that he wore a heavy leather jacket. That's how it was, I'm sorry to say. It's clear that if he'd been in rags my act would have been easier to understand.'

'But how? Your act seems completely natural.'

'I don't know. Maybe,' I said, staring at him intently, 'stories like these are made up from beginning to end. My impression is that some of these people who stop passersby and ask for handouts aren't really in need, as they claim. And they're not trying to take advantage of the public's generosity, either. They might have a completely different goal: for example, to give the impression that everything's not going perfectly well, that the system, in spite of the finer and finer safety net, always lets a fine dust of pathetic and miserable cases fall through, or even that for some people work is no longer possible. Why? It doesn't have to do with health, or good will, or faith. They want to and they can, but still they can't. It all makes you think.'

He looked at me with an expression of interest; I felt how my face must have seemed tense and somber to him.

'Do you think that, as a civil servant, I feel obliged, out of loyalty, to defend official points of view? I don't feel obliged to do anything. I'm completely free, like everyone else. And furthermore my opinion is nothing, it's only an allegory, I don't believe in it.'

'Still, you gave money to the panhandler?'

'Sure, but so what? I did what I felt like doing. I was afraid—that's the truth of it. I'd been bothered. To cut off the explanations, I gave him a little money. You also have to take personal reactions into consideration.'

'You're a nervous type, aren't you?'

'If I had refused, I would have had to invite him to some special Office or interrogate him closely on the nature of his difficulties. I would have tried to convince him. Of what? It's absurd. By going along with him, I ended the thing at the least cost.'

Leaning on my desk, he observed me silently. I noticed then how much his face fascinated me and seemed different from the others. It was a face that had too much color—his cheeks were almost red—and yet it was, in certain areas, too white: his forehead was white as paper, as were his ears. There was something authoritarian and disagreeably imperious in his expression, a casualness that would stop at nothing. And suddenly I also read in it a distrust, an underhanded and clumsy spirit that rendered suspect his enormous calm.

'Don't hold it against me,' he said, 'but you seem different from other people. You're young; I'm certainly older than you are. So I can tell you, even though ordinarily one conceals remarks like this. I'm struck by . . . is it your way of talking, or your ideas, or some of your gestures? Sorry, my straightforwardness is becoming ridiculous. You aren't by any chance a foreigner?'

I shook my head.

'I've been a doctor, I need to catalog people. Unlike yourself, I don't look for subtle explanations. And, on the whole, nobody worries about theories or doctrines. Have you already heard about me?'

I indicated that I hadn't.

'I've lived in foreign countries for quite a while. You know how it is: the customs are different, they eat this instead of that; the landscape is different, at least up to a certain point, because big cities naturally look alike. And then, the language . . . anyway, there's no point insisting. All in all, everything's different. And from one country to the next, everything is always fairly different. Still, if you discount the feeling of strangeness and other similar impressions, you realize very soon that crossing a border isn't much and that foreign countries hardly exist. You feel strongly that the country you're leaving extends to all the others, that its surface covers other surfaces that are a thousand times bigger, that it itself is also all the rest. And if the traveler feels this way, then the native, who sees his city as the center, as the equivalent of the world, does too, and all the more so: he's happy to dream vaguely about something else.'

He stopped and fixed on me for a moment his small, vacant eyes—eyes that were too little for his massive face, I noted queasily.

'I don't see any value in going back to fantastic interpretations to account for commonplaces like that. Some people feel they have the ends of the earth at their fingertips. That's an exhilarating feeling, but what does it finally mean? It's just the way clever theorists see things.'

'Why do you see me as being different from the others?'

'No, you're not very different. You've gotten tangled up in general ideas and you're starting to feel dizzy. You have the vague feeling that these ideas are perhaps nothing at all, but if they collapse, what's left? Just the void, and then again they can't be nothing; in that case they're everything, and you stifle. Do you know,' he said with impudent naiveté, 'that you sometimes talk to yourself while you're walking? You move your lips, you even make a few gestures. One has the impression that you don't want to interrupt the stream of aphorisms and maxims, not for a second. Your frame of mind has been firmly molded by your public duties!'

At this point I had the feeling that something like a rift had opened in our conversation, and that my interlocutor was just talking nonsense; I didn't listen to him, I listened to something else, and yet what he was saying couldn't have been very different from what I thought I heard. I made an effort to look only at him. He examined the room carefully.

'You have a lot of books,' he said. 'Do you like to read?' I followed the movement of his eyes, which seemed to turn like tiny wheels. He got up and read a few titles. 'I don't have the time to read,' he said, coming back and sitting down. He looked at me for a long time, absent-mindedly. 'When I was abroad, I studied a lot, and wrote, too.'

'You were a journalist?'

'Yes, I wrote for a few newspapers. I've only been back in this country for a little while,' he added. 'I'm what you call an émigré, even though words like that don't mean much any more. Since I've stopped being a doctor, I've been concerned with a variety of questions.'

I made another effort.

'You've been a doctor? You left the profession?'

'I was expelled.'

My eyes fell on his suit, his hands; then I looked through the window and I saw the somber, incredibly somber mass of the avenue.

'I was given a leave of absence,' he replied calmly.

I heard my neighbors' radio shouting. From floor to floor a violent, obtrusive song, a real collective voice, traveled with irresistible power.

'I can tell that I've surprised you,' he said, suddenly smiling. 'Maybe it's unusual to say, I've been fired, I lost my job. It's not polite to say that. But I wasn't really a doctor, just a doctor's aide; I worked at a number of places. Really I was only in training, the work didn't agree with me.'

'You've traveled a lot,' I said stiffly.

'Yes. Yes and no. I lived abroad, but I didn't travel there. I lived in a hotel room.'

'But . . . in what capacity did you live there?'

'On what grounds?' He stared at me. 'I thought I'd made it clear,' he said coldly. 'I got mixed up in governmental matters. At a certain point, I had to leave the country.'

'What! What are you trying to say? Why are you telling me this?'

'Calm down,' he said, getting up too. 'What's so unusual? I think you're a trustworthy man, I can have confidence in you.'

'What are you saying?'

'I have a regular position here. You don't have to get upset. My affairs are in order,' he insisted.

I felt him standing near me; I drew back against the bookshelves.

'It's an unimportant story, of no consequence. Nothing dishonorable happened, I assure you. I wasn't prosecuted. I went into exile on my own, because that seemed preferable, and because I wanted to try to understand a few things. Right now I have a job, I work. Are these answers enough?'

'But why did you talk to me about this?' I said, half to myself.

'You asked me. Sooner or later you would have heard the story, and then you would have held it against me for being so reserved. My name is Pierre Bouxx.'

'Bouxx,' I said. 'And that's why you quit your job?'

'Yes . . . well, yes. And I have to say again, I wasn't cut out to take care of the sick under those circumstances. I understood very quickly that I couldn't continue to be associated with all that.'

'You're alone? You have a family?'

'No, no family. You know, I'm already old; my parents are gone. I got married abroad, but my wife is dead. I married her in the city of Basel. At the time I lived very much alone. My fellow exiles had, for the most part, trades or occupations.

After her death, I really got down to work; I clearly saw that, even if by marshaling all my strength I only managed to change a single thing, move only a wisp of straw, it wouldn't be useless. And maybe I could do a lot more, too.'

He opened the door and waited a few moments.

'Are you leaving?'

He didn't move.

'I saw that what I said upset you. Don't think that I'm used to jabbering. I got carried away by friendship. It seems to me, like I told you, that there's something really special about you—well, not right now, maybe it's yet to be born. I know that in this city there's no point in talking with just anybody. There's nothing to say, nothing to learn. That's what a city's like. On the other hand, right away I felt compelled to speak to you. I followed you. So I got worked up about you. But naturally if I bore you, I won't insist. The fact that we're neighbors shouldn't enter into it.'

After he left I was surprised to feel extraordinarily disgusted. I had the feeling that something shameful had happened. Nevertheless I wanted to see him again. I summed it all up by saying, What an actor!

\* \* \*

The next day Louise came by to clean up the apartment. I heard her sweeping and wandering around. She did the carpets, pushed stools, overturned chairs. 'What are you doing? Want to go to the movies?' I took a paper and sat down on the bed. 'Let it go, you're boring me with this sweeping.' She started straightening the blankets; I wanted to grab her by the arm and send her packing, but I held back. 'What did mother say after seeing me? Come on, talk.' —'She didn't say anything special.'

Once outside, I was sorry I'd left. It was warm, humid. The subway dumped us out at O. Square, where I breathed in the smoke and noise. The racket was extraordinary. 'What noise,' I yelled at her. 'On Saturday everybody goes shopping.' I took her arm and led her into a side street. There were a lot fewer people there; the whole crowd went by a few steps away from us, in front of our eyes.

13

'Do me a favor,' I said. 'Describe everything you see.'

'What?'

'Yes, really, what do you see?'

We stopped a while to watch the people who came slowly down the boulevard. Sometimes a girl would separate herself from the crush in order to slip toward the store windows. She'd come forward hesitantly, with a stingy and forced movement, stay there a moment until, running, hurrying with a trembling step, she was once again lost in the crowd.

'You really want to go to the movies?' I asked Louise.

The café was packed. There was a holiday feeling, everybody seemed overexcited and feverish. Louise chose some ice cream, tasted it, pushed it away. 'It's bad?' She smiled. A newsboy went by our table, offering us a half-opened paper. 'Strange,' I noted, 'another fire.' The patrons followed all the comings and goings with a passionate, almost painful gravity. No one said anything, but still there was a deafening noise of voices, shouts, of musical instruments out of tune and in again, and there was even yelling coming from the back room—a row had probably broken out between the waiters and head waiters.

'Well, they talk a lot about me at home. Couldn't you repeat a conversation, at the table for instance, word for word?'

'A conversation? Mother wants you to come back. But you know that, she told you.'

'And would that make you happy?'

'I think sooner or later arguments would start.'

'Arguments?'

Music broke out. It came from an orchestra of big, strong women wearing white blouses with red embroidery. They did a resounding and wild opening number; at every crash of the cymbals voices yelled and burned. I felt tired. There was a general torpor. When Louise opened her purse I thought she was going to take out her lipstick, but then I saw from her face that she wasn't, so to speak, made up. I saw her eyes, her lips; I looked her straight in the face.

'Poor Louise, you're really badly dressed. Why doesn't Mother buy you another dress? You look thirty years old.'

She opened her coat, and her gaze descended to the black cloth of her dress, a dirty and faded black.

'What's going on? Now I realize that all afternoon I've been bothered by this impression. I couldn't look at you; I had the feeling of something disagreeable, painful. Why do they make you dress like a beggar?'

She gazed at me blankly, with an almost contemptuous look.

'You're exaggerating,' she said.

'You're acting strange. Are you sick? Do you blame me for something? You're there but we aren't talking to each other.'

'We don't necessarily see each other in order to talk,' she said curtly.

I wanted to tell her how her entire attitude expressed a humiliating reticence. She looked at me, affecting a righteous expression, as if I had acted improperly and reprehensibly. That was what made her old, made her seem of another time. She seemed backward, and she expected me as well to look backward. I called over a little girl who had a flower basket and bought a bouquet of violets.

'We would have done better at the movies,' I remarked as we walked out.

\* \* \*

I woke up tired. Sundays are terrible, I thought. The concierge knocked and entered. From her glance I understood that she disapproved of my appearance, of the disorder of the room, of the still closed shutters. She had brought my lunch in two tightly sealed plates.

'Should I open it?'

She pushed on the window. I was undressed; I felt dirty, my hair a mess, my eyes half open.

'Boy, how you sleep!' she said, irritated.

She hesitated, probably to study me, before arranging my clothes and pushing the chair with the tray next to the sofa. I lay flat, exhausted.

'You would have been better off going for a walk outdoors. At least try to eat.'

As she was going into the corridor I called her.

'Was there a march this morning?'

I had heard in my half-sleep the enormous rumble of a crowd—cries, distant music, the pealing of bells. These noises weren't echoing from the street, but came from a nearby radio.

'Sure, they were celebrating the anniversary.' She mentioned a date.

Thinking about this ceremony, I could imagine the main images: whole streets empty, shops closed, entire sections of the city plunged into silence, and, on the other hand, downtown, the crowds, bodies packed together, people standing around, their eyes fiercely trained on the other crowd, the one carrying the placards and banners and coming forward solemnly, as if it were demonstrating the certainty that there was nothing more to life than this moment of collective peace.

'I like these ceremonies a lot,' I said. 'I heard them all morning on the radio. If I felt better I wouldn't miss a single one.'

'I like them too,' she said.

'And there are still other interesting ways of getting together. For a lot of people, Sunday means participating in sports: they meet, get excited, everybody yells. How can you reproach them for that? Those are perfect moments.'

'Sports are a good thing,' she said.

'Yes, it's a duty to raise young people who are strong. But movies are also good clean fun. Really, all get-togethers are good.'

She let out a kind of laugh and lowered her head. I too started laughing. 'What is it?'

'But you don't go out much!'

I looked at her, and suddenly I wanted to explain to her in detail how I saw things. I felt that she'd understand me: she was straightforward, a strong, young woman. We were on the same level. But she said, 'The problem is your poor health.'

'Thanks, I'm steadily getting better. You know, I'm a bachelor, but that's not the point. I'm no more alone than anyone else; I don't live alone at all. I take part in everything that goes on, my thoughts belong to everybody. I don't need to get married or take part in group activities in order to be a good citizen.'

'Oh! I didn't want to hurt your feelings,' she said hastily. 'Everybody in the building sings your praises. We know you're conscientious and hard working.'

I looked at her silently. 'Sure, I'm conscientious, but still not enough: if only one could constantly remember that the least impression, the least word, is important! I'm also sick too often.'

A little later I heard the door close. I thought that I would be alone all day, with these crowd noises, these sports reports, coming from above my head; I'd see the trees in the street, I'd sleep in my armchair. Thinking about sleeping stirred up an odd memory. For a moment I saw the clinic again, the nurse. I recalled that I was in a deep torpor there; the slightest thing woke me up. I knew I hadn't slept; I was convinced that there was playacting, illusion, and also temptation, in sleep. At no point was I lost, that's what my delirium and fever were claiming, and I repeated it because in spite of everything one has to defend oneself. And now this idea was coming back to me and hounding me. But I didn't have to think about it: I counted the window panes of the door, I looked at the table. And was this really an idea? I uncovered the dishes and ate.

As the evening came on I could hear noises on the other side of the wall. Music from a record player started to whine. I heard the floor creak and the vague rhythmless steps of a crowd that seemed to be stamping around deep in a cave. From time to time a shout came through and was answered by interminable laughter. For a few hours I listened to this racket, but when it got dark I put on my bathrobe and went into the kitchen. Without turning on the lights, by the light from the rooms across the way, I drank a glass of water. The disorder—the mess on the table, the smell of very ripe food— hit me hard. I went slowly down the corridor and after having noted, a little further on, on the left, the door to Bouxx's apartment, I turned right and faced the wall from which music flowed as if from a kind of grave or torture site.

I knocked loudly. A few seconds later, instead of the young woman I was expecting, a young man in shirt-sleeves, with shiny hair and a round and perhaps flushed face, opened the door. Beyond the hallway was a light-filled area. Suddenly the music stopped.

'I'd like to speak with the lady of the house.'

'What do you want?'

'I live in the building, I'm a little tired. This noise . . .'

The blonde woman came forward.

'Excuse me for bothering you,' I said, looking at her.

'Are we making too much noise?'

She was lit from behind, and yet there was a kind of phosphorescence around her face that came from her complexion, something radiant and pale. She was wearing a loose housecoat, which was fairly fancy but seemed to me to be well-worn and made of cheap material.

'It's Sunday,' said the man. 'It isn't even nine o'clock. We have the right to play music.'

'It's nine o'clock? Sorry.'

'But didn't you say you were sick?' she asked.

At this point she turned on the light in the hallway.

'Sick? No; I've been unwell, I'm still a little tired. I tried to sleep this afternoon and I heard the reverberations from your little party. I thought you were a whole group. Since you're alone, I shouldn't have come.'

The man turned to the young woman, and his look said, What's this all about? What a character! She looked at him for a second.

'It's not important,' she said mechanically. 'In fact we were about to leave. You can relax in peace and quiet.'

I kept looking at her: in the light, her face seemed bony and a little coarse, but her skin displayed an appealing health—youth and life.

'But don't go out on my account.'

'Come on, it's OK,' said the man after a moment. 'We hope you'll get your health back.'

I went down the hall. Coming into my place, I turned the lights on in all the rooms. I'd have liked to write a report on the day, and, moreover, on my whole life—a report, by that I mean a simple diary. That everyone was equally faithful to the law—ah, that idea intoxicated me. Everyone seemed to be acting only in their own interests, everyone performed obscure acts, and yet there was a halo of light around these hidden lives: there wasn't anyone who didn't see every other person as a hope, a surprise, and who didn't approach him knowingly. So, I asked myself, what is this State? It's in me, I feel its existence in everything I do, through every fiber of my body. I was certain then that all I had to do was write, hour by hour, a commentary on my activities, in order to find in them the blossoming of a supreme truth, the same one that circulated actively between all of us, a truth that public life constantly relaunched, watched over, reabsorbed, and threw back in an obsessive and deliberate game.

# 2

I got up early. I was tired and nervous. The wind, a kind of autumn wind, had blown all night; the rattling windows kept me from sleeping.

On the stairs the wind was still blowing, and the windows were shaking. I caught up with my neighbor who was going down the stairs as well.

'Let me walk with you a bit. I want to tell you something.'

Outside the wind was so strong that sometimes you had to stop and walk backwards. She had tied a scarf around her hair.

'What do you have to say?'

'The other night I was acting rude. All afternoon I had been deafened by the music. I imagined a happy get-together, and that I found rather pleasing—there were the sounds of steps, the bursts of laughter, and all of it a few yards away, just on the other side of the partition. But suddenly my nerves gave out.'

'Drop it; it's unimportant.'

'Right, it's no big deal.'

We walked side by side, now protected by the trees. At the end of the avenue I saw the subway station.

'You work at City Hall Square? Maybe you know that I work in that neighborhood too. I often see you in your store.'

She didn't answer. Around us everyone was in a hurry, and we too were hurrying.

'Still, I'd like to thank you. You could have given me a worse reception. When a neighbor comes to say that you're making too much noise, you don't want to hear him out with kindness.'

'But did we treat you that well?'

'Yes, definitely. At least you did, I think. Back at my place I got really carried away. It seemed extraordinary that peoples' relationships could be so easy, so complete. Think about it;

it's almost crazy—I come and knock on your door, you don't know me, you didn't even know I existed. And in spite of that you understand the reasons behind my move, you welcome them, you give them a hearing, as disagreeable as that might seem.'

'It's customary between neighbors!'

'Listen, I know perfectly well that if you were nice to me it wasn't because you had already noticed me or because you had suddenly found me likeable. For you I'm nothing—I'm anybody, a neighbor. But that's exactly what excites me: I don't need some special recommendation. I was of no interest to you and yet you welcomed me. Don't you find it surprising that we can understand each other like this? I talk to you and you answer; maybe I bore you, but the conversation takes place as if nothing separates us, as if we had what's essential in common. I'm sure you see what I'm getting at.'

'You're . . . you're enthusiastic. Beyond that I don't see where this conversation is headed.'

'On the contrary,' I told her, looking straight at her, 'I think you've seen right through me.'

We got to the station and had to follow the other commuters. A man slipped between us, then another; I saw her red scarf floating through the crowd. On the platform I found her near the gate. During the ride, I tried to look closely at her face: she was really quite ordinary except for her bright white skin—maybe she wasn't really that young, but her features, her cheekbones conveyed health and vigor.

'I've got to hurry,' she said, leaving the subway.

'I still have something to tell you. I swear, it's very important.'

'Please, let me go.'

All morning I couldn't work. They sent me two representatives who asked for a copy of a lost document. Their attitude irritated me. They were awkward and timid; they spoke to me as if I were their superior; I treated them harshly; it was all downhill. After they left I called home. Why? To overcome my agitation, since talking to my sister would have calmed me down? But somebody else answered; when I heard the voice, I thought it was the concierge. And yet I knew it was my mother. I hung the phone up gently and went out. After going into Iche's office I had to wait, so I inspected the line of pedestals on which sat sculpted heads—beautiful old-fashioned heads—representing historical figures. I admired them, but not without uneasiness: I had remembered them as being completely different, less solemn, even less immobile—as real living persons, instead. But these heads had a funereal gravity.

'Really, why do you keep all these busts in your office?'

Iche looked at the statues with interest, the carpets, the decorated ceiling, the whole room—then his gaze faded.

'I've been gone for a few weeks and I've come to apologize. I haven't gotten into my routine yet. But being gone also opened my eyes to a lot of details that had escaped me before.'

Even though he was my head, I could look at him and his chubby, clean-shaven, almost hairless face—young, but nevertheless worn out. I spoke to him as an equal. Hierarchy had no effect on the meaning of my words: we spoke the same language.

'While I was sick I thought about all kinds of things. I noticed that I hadn't had the right idea about our times. It was a kind of revelation: I learned nothing, but I glimpsed the importance of what I was wearily living. Until very recently people were only fragments and they projected their dreams onto the sky. That's why the past has been a long series of traps and wars. But now man exists. That's what I discovered.'

'Well, well, my boy,' said Iche, kind of wheezing.

I smiled.

'I'll speak frankly. While I was sick, I suffered from not working. I suffered all the more because I didn't really feel sick. My idleness was intolerable. I would have liked to do something useful, but rest was the absolute rule. I realize that sometimes I must have acted strangely. Sometimes I grabbed a broom and swept the corridors, or I hurried to help because I heard a patient's buzzer go off. These pranks made me the nurse's bête noire. But still, even if I did stir up trouble and act like an undisciplined maniac, my behavior demonstrated a justifiable aspiration—the feeling that work is the basis of existence, that you don't exist as long as you live in a world where, by working, you only humiliate and destroy yourself.'

23

'What's wrong with you?' said Iche. 'You're talking philosophy!'

'I'm quite aware, of course, that these are well-worn ideas.'

I saw him take a sheet of paper and, his eyebrows raised, start to jot things down at random.

'Before'—I went on, even though I would have liked to stop—'I didn't much like this office work. Please forgive me— but I didn't like it. Maybe there was too much idle time, or the bureaucracy . . . anyway, I hated it all. But I noticed that, even in this position, I performed a service. And then, what is working? It's not only being in your office, writing something in a register, giving the secretary something to copy. I think— and this is my discovery—that, whatever I do, I work usefully. When I speak, when I reflect, I'm working—that's obvious. Everybody can grasp that. Even if I look . . . at anything at all, at this office, these busts, sure, I'm still working, in my own way. Because there's a man there who sees things as they should be seen—he exists, and all the notions for which we've been struggling for so many centuries exist with him. I'm perfectly aware that if I changed, or if I went off my head, history would collapse.'

'You're reasoning too much,' said Iche after a moment of silence.

Through the window I could make out the bridge and the trees along the quai. The river was flowing rapidly, and the barges and boats followed its flood-stage swirling. Fishermen were waiting on the shore. I went to the window. The trees and houses appeared in a soft light. It was all so true! What a quiet scene. This really was our river, and not just any river. So was I starting to wander? Were my explanations perhaps sterile? Suddenly Iche's words—'you're reasoning too much'—struck me.

'You're right—one shouldn't speak so generally.'

But I saw that he was signing his mail. The secretary, standing, turned the pages of the file for him and watched him read. 'You don't know my new secretary—Suzanne.' She smiled at me weakly. 'This poor girl's the victim of an accident: her house burned, she lost almost everything.' She continued to smile, her face glowing as if the recollection of the disaster were enough to turn it into an infinite blessing.

24

'Your house burned? They couldn't put out the fire?'

'A combination of unfortunate circumstances,' he said, accompanying me to the door. 'I saw your stepfather, you know. If you need another leave, don't hesitate.'

'No thanks, not right now.'

The wind was still blowing, but now it was a hot wind, the wind of noon. My neighbor's shop seemed very small and laden with all kinds of objects. A bright light illuminated the walls on which innumerable portraits were shining with frozen smiles. The girl came out of a small booth.

'I need some identity photos,' I told her.

She raised the curtain and had me sit in the cubbyhole. I met with sudden light, on and off in successive bursts. The operation over, I looked at the portraits hanging from the walls, portraits of men, mostly, who all looked like each other, in spite of the differences in features: bold faces, open and yet reassuring. In the middle a blowup caught my eye. It was her, her shoulders set, her head thrown back, her expression both naive and provocative. I could never have imagined her that way. It was her life, her air of health, that struck me and now there she was, like her own ideal—like her law, which nevertheless was not separate from her, and which I was certain to rediscover on her face as soon as she turned around, but which had been isolated for some strange reason, in its pure form, within the frame. Really it was only a publicity photo, but it was no less interesting for all that. It certainly was—the fact that her face had become public, that she had a face for the public, led me to think about all sorts of things.

At that point my pictures were ready. She wiped them off, cut them, and handed them to me. I barely looked at them. She put them in an envelope and I paid.

'If you have something to say,' she stated belligerently, 'please say it and don't beat around the bush.'

I sat down, but she remained standing by the door, with a look of profound irritation.

'I don't know if I can talk to you now. I see you in a new light. Have you worked here long?'

'A few years.'

'Are you an employee, or management?'

'I serve as the manager.'

On a corner of the counter splendid flowers were blooming—flowers that evoked not the countryside but the greenhouse, the appealing luxury of cities. The store was very modern. I went on in the most confused way. I had already, on other occasions, spoken haphazardly, without wanting to. But while in those cases something more calm and more general than me had come out of my mouth, this time a drunken, incompetent, useless individual held forth. Still, what I explained wasn't unreasonable. I had suddenly noticed that people came to see her above all for official documents—identity cards, passports, and so on. From that perspective, our duties were almost the same: we collaborated with each other. Thanks to us, individuals had a legal existence, they left a lasting trace, it was known who they were: in short, I wanted to show her that, in the eyes of the law, we performed analogous functions. All this was silly, not incoherent. But what I said must have seemed muddled and out of place—she kept staring at me in amazement. I wanted to stop talking, but if I stayed it was because I was understanding her better: she was neither original nor subtle, but there was something superior about her, she had a strong, common nature, the character of a true woman of today who knows everything and rejects the singular, the cumbersome remnants. Fortunately a customer came in, also to pick up some identity photos.

'Do you have an archive?' I asked after he had left.

'An archive? We have a few photos of famous men.'

'Every time you take a picture, why not keep a copy? You could paste it in a big book, with the name, the address, some dates, some observations. That would be a splendid source of documentation. If all of your colleagues did the same thing, we'd have a true archive, almost as complete as the one the police have.'

'But why?' she said, thinking about it. 'What good would it do? Exactly—other agencies take care of it. And what value would our information have?'

'You could demand proof in writing, like they do at the post office, or elsewhere. Maybe these formalities wouldn't be that useful. Yes, in the end it'd only mean more paperwork.'

'Is that what you wanted to tell me?'

'No, not at all. I've been sick, a number of weeks ago. I live alone. Last night I didn't feel very well, I was overexcited, almost feverish. My earlier bouts of sickness also started with a high fever. Suddenly I was afraid of getting sick again. And I had an idea. . . . Listen, you're not going to like this, but it's because of my visit on Sunday. I realized that we live right next to each other: all I have to do is knock on this partition, I told myself. Well, would you allow me to knock, if something very serious happened to me—if, for example, I became paralyzed or was unable to get up?'

'You're afraid of becoming paralyzed?'

'I'm not particularly afraid of paralysis. I'm not even afraid of being alone and sick. No doubt it's a painful situation to be condemned to stifle at night, without a drop of water, calling in vain, but this solitude also has its advantages. Anyway, such a situation should be tolerable. What I'm afraid of is completely different. At night, I sometimes feel really alone. I wake up and remember everything: my family, my friends at the office, some face I've seen. I recognize my room, beyond it there's the street, other houses, everything is in its place, everywhere someone is with me, and still that's not enough. At that moment I would like a person in flesh and blood to be at my side or in the other room, and to answer if I talk—yes, that's it, I'd like to know that I've also spoken for her. But if there's no answer, if I raise my voice and realize that I'm speaking all alone, I suddenly almost start trembling—it's worse than anything. It's an insult, a real offense. I feel as if I've committed a crime, I've lived outside the common good. And besides, am I alive? Life is elsewhere, amid these thousands of people packed together, who live like that, who get along, who have attained law and liberty. Maybe you can't grasp what crazy ideas take hold of me at times like these: shameless, degraded ideas, I can't recount them. Last night, I remembered something that took place the day before yesterday, which at first didn't make an impression. In the subway, a woman started shouting 'Thief!' —somebody had taken her wallet and she pointed to the guilty party, a fairly imposing and well-dressed man who was standing a few steps away.

*impossible*

The man scornfully objected, but the woman threw herself on him, stuck her hand in his overcoat pocket, and triumphantly pulled out the wallet. At the next stop they got off: both were emotional, yelling. They were followed by quite a few witnesses; I suppose the whole crowd headed over to the police station. Well . . . yes, that's all.'

I looked at her.

'Does this story seem strange to you?'

'No,' she said, thinking about it, 'I don't see why it should.'

'No, that's true, and still, that evening, it struck me as almost incredible. I asked myself: why did this man steal? He took something—supposing he really took it—and he didn't have the right to do it—that's obvious. How could that be? For a few minutes, I was lost, I couldn't understand anything. I was obsessed with the idea that if I was wrong on this point, I was wrong about everything. And suddenly the light went on. I remembered that there was no real offense, the man had stolen but for all that he was still a man; and the police could easily throw him in prison, but beyond that there wasn't a real conviction. It was just a sham, a kind of game to make the law circulate, to recall to everyone the depth and intangibility of liberty. You've got to understand—it's the same man, both here and there: so yelling "Thief!" means nothing, at least it has less meaning than you imagine, since it only signifies "We possess truth, peace, law, and this person steals, not because he's outside of justice, but because the State needs this example and from time to time it's necessary to create an interruption through which history and the past can rush."'

She turned and looked at the little electric clock; it was past noon. I asked if she wouldn't have lunch with me, in the neighborhood, before coming back to the store. Around this time the square was busy and noisy. Cars went by slowly. People waited on the sidewalk, saying nothing, with a resignation that came from the inevitability of the rules. When I saw her sitting at my side, ready to eat the same things as me, to gesture in the same way, to look at the same people, I was amazed. It was more than surprise. I had always sensed what was going on there; I knew that we all lived together, that each of us reflects the others in himself; but with her this existence in common became a vertiginous and frenzied certainty. First, I had proof of it, I could talk to her. What I said thus conformed perfectly with public opinion, with the wisdom of the newspapers that sometimes passed before my gaze like stories from another time. But then a very different idea grabbed hold of me. The law was always in movement, it passed ceaselessly from one person to another, it was present everywhere, with its even, transparent, and absolute light, illuminating everyone and everything in an always different and yet identical way. Ordinarily everything made me aware of it and, sensing it, sometimes I got carried away, felt drunk, and sometimes I asked myself if I weren't already dead. But at present, in other words right now, when I looked at her hand—a fairly pretty hand, with well-done nails, big and strong like the rest of her—when I looked at it I couldn't imagine that it was like mine, and I didn't believe it was unique, either. What bothered me was that by taking hold of it, by touching it in a certain way, yes, if I managed to touch this flesh, this skin, this moist swelling, along with it I would touch the law, which was there, it was obvious, and which, perhaps, would linger there for a moment in a mysterious way, held back for me from the world.

When I became aware of this thought, I made an effort to look around the restaurant: as usual, there were a lot of people. I knew quite a few, some by sight, others from having talked a bit with them; there was even a colleague from the office. But something strange happened: nobody looked at me or seemed to have noticed my presence, just as if no one had been there, as if around us there was only a noisy void, a true desert, vulgar and sordid. Beyond this there was our silence, which had been making itself felt in an irritating way ever since we had sat down at the table. My neighbor had a good appetite, and even ate voraciously: she looked straight ahead and masticated, her face serious, her eyes indifferent. I had a strange feeling as I watched this: she became an impersonal mouth, chewing and rechewing, with no apparent satisfaction and yet out of a deep and irrepressible need that came from deep in her guts. The more I watched, the more I saw the strange image she conveyed. But seeing was nothing, it wasn't a question of something visible, but of a deeper modification, in some ways still to come, and whose realization required more than a glance: for example, the approach of my hand. It seemed inevitable. An impending change was on her face, one that would be produced with me and thanks to me, as soon as I moved. I half closed my eyes. I gently leaned toward her. Yes, now something was going to happen. She rocked a bit, and then, looking straight at me, she smiled. I was covered with sweat, I hugged myself tightly, I was trembling so much. She probably said a few words: 'You're not eating.' Then she kept on talking to me, about her work, the customers she had; I distinctly heard the word 'family.' Again I myself wanted, desperately wanted, to talk to her.

'I'm on bad terms with my family,' I said, staring straight at her. 'My father's dead, my mother remarried. I see my sister fairly often. When I got sick, my mother came to see me at the clinic and offered to let me stay with them. My relatives live on the south side in a house that has a yard with trees and a lot of space. It's a beautiful house, enormous, at least as I recall, since I haven't been back there for a long time. Do you have a family?'

She told me her mother was still alive.

'Your mother? Does she take care of you? I mean how do you get along with her—are you two close? Do you tell her everything you do?'

She shrugged. 'No, of course not.'

'I knew it. You lie to her, it's inevitable. Listen, I mustn't return to the house, and my mother is going to force me to go back, I'm sure of it. She insists too much. Already she's gotten my sister involved in her game. She's authoritarian and opinionated. It's a terrible prospect, you can't understand why. Promise to help me stay in my apartment.'

'Really,' she said, 'what's the big deal? After all, you're free.'

'Sure, I'm free, but what if I get sick? You can't imagine how afraid I am of getting sick again. Have you ever been sick? What happens is strange: it's a permanent temptation, you don't know what's going on anymore, you don't recognize people, and yet you understand everything infinitely better.

There's no more beginning, everything's displayed in a peaceful and full light, the points of view of all people coincide, they've disappeared—do you understand?'

'Are you all right?' she said, nudging me with her elbow. 'Be careful, you're getting too excited.'

My eyes were fixed on hers, it was a moment of hope and extraordinary strength. I really felt that, by saying this, I had, once again, reached a crucial moment of my life.

'It's delirium,' she said.

'Yes, delirium,' I said, stopping. 'What's awful is that later, when it's over, you think that you've blanked out and become a tomb of silliness and incompetence. You get out of your bed, the nurse told me, and keep going around a table. How stupid can you get? Still, it had a meaning, I swear, it was even an extraordinary symbol. But that doesn't prevent sickness from being a disastrous accident, a catastrophe: you don't grasp the law any more, you contemplate it, it's bad. At times like that, my mother could easily have me brought to her house.'

'Are you ready?' she said cordially, even gently. 'Shall we go?'

'Aren't you going to ask why I won't visit my relatives? That seems natural to you, doesn't it?'

'Let's go.' And she got up, pulling me by the sleeve.

Then a ridiculous thing happened that had all sorts of consequences. I followed her, my mind absorbed by everything I wanted to tell her, without noticing that I hadn't left any money. The waitress caught up with me at the door. 'The check!' Her reminder made me furious. The tone was cutting: she suspected me of not wanting to pay, and my forgetfulness in front of the young woman was oafish, a real blunder. To get the upper hand over this scullery slave, I yelled, 'Next time!' I must have shoved her, too. Then she grabbed hold of my arm, as if I were a thief, and started screaming in a piercing voice, squealing insults and shaking me. It was intolerable and grotesque. I no longer knew what was going on. I saw myself slipping into a disgraceful business: everybody was watching me. What had I done? Maybe a menacing gesture—only the suggestion of a blow, to cut her down to

31

nothing. But she responded incredibly quickly, slapping me with all the strength she had. I stood there half blind; then I threw my wallet at her and left.

In the street, with the fresh air, I became calm again. I didn't see anything, I didn't see my neighbor whose absence seemed a distant and normal event. When she came back, handing me the wallet that she'd picked up after I left— disciplined and methodical person that she was—her return seemed just as natural. Perhaps we walked around a bit. Then it was time to go back to work: she held out her hand in a lively and friendly way.

'Are there marks on my face?'

She said no. I had the feeling that she wanted to say something else, but the crowd drew her away, enveloped her, and then she disappeared. At the office I could go up via a service stairway that spared me from having to go through the typing room, which was open to the public. I went there for no reason. I wanted to spend the afternoon in darkness, dust, and forgetfulness. No doubt I was also ready to work. At the office there were some co-workers with whom I had cordial but superficial relations—typical office friendships. They were young people without ideas, fairly common, and for this reason they pleased and displeased me. In general I paid little attention to their comings and goings; I had no idea what they did, and I myself was one of them when we were together, and that's all. That day, I had started to draft a letter when a young man named Albert came in to ask me to reread with him a long list of names that he had to check meticulously. He gave me the papers and took a seat. I glanced at them and, with a quick movement, brushed them off the table. Albert greatly enjoyed this little prank. He burst out laughing, slapped me on the shoulder, and jovially picked up the scattered sheets. He had barely reorganized them when, again, with a flick of the fingers, I sent them to the four corners of the room. To make my gesture seem more serious, I announced, 'I'm not going to work any more today'—the wrong words, because they in fact seemed to prolong the joke. Albert, very satisfied with this game, ran around the room, hunting down the wretched sheets. But, after getting back up, standing near the door, he looked at me, became sullen, and went off shrugging his shoulders, without saying anything. Fifteen minutes later a tall, puny youth came in. They called him 'the cripple' because his left arm, after a number of seizures, had become paralyzed. He interested me because we shared the same first name and also because, seeing him motionless at the table on some days, bent over registers in which he was writing nothing, I imagined that we had the same problems, and that he was struggling to overcome the difficulties of his work. Still, I should note that every time I had offered him some help he had rejected it in the coolest possible way. On my desk he opened an enormous dossier, bulkier than a Bible, and asked me to spend a few minutes helping him organize it. I immediately grasped the plot against me that this guy was involved in. I stood up slowly, I looked at him hard: there was a lie on his sickly, closed, and ceremonious face, a lie that turned the playacting into a dubious and repugnant scene, with a vague odor of snitching. Then I had another idea. Maybe he wasn't up to anything. Hopelessly overworked, he really needed me: the administrative work had caused his equilibrium, always shaky, to give out just at that moment; he was like a hulk going down. By helping him I'd save him and myself as well. What a coincidence! Something like that had been done on purpose. I shook my head. 'I'm not working today,' I told him. He turned, and I heard him murmur, 'Excuse me.' Basically, it was probably playacting. The others didn't come, as I had expected. Still, I had imagined the scene: a parade of scribes who brought me their dossiers and statistics every fifteen minutes and to whom, obstinately, I would reply . . . with my line. Well, they didn't come. My victory was complete, too complete. Maybe there was something pleasing in having convinced them, but now their idiocy stopped at the door. What were they saying and doing? I remembered another co-worker who, back at the café, had seen me get slapped, and who wouldn't hesitate to joke about it. And so what? I got up and went out.

The street was extraordinarily bright, the wind had died down. A kind of luminous stream went from one passerby to

33

the next, from one car to the next. With my finger I brushed a wall, then a window, then a door with iron bars, and then again the rough grain of a wall. At that moment I saw a white square, a real brilliant image, carved out of a darker horizon. I crossed the square and recognized the pretentious paint job of the photography studio. Naturally, I didn't go in. I didn't want to, I had no desire to see anyone in particular loom up before me, and I even thought it was impossible. I followed one street, then another. I walked straight ahead, nobody followed me, the day was radiant, one of those days that explain completely why, through the different seasons, beyond the vicissitudes of day and night, there remains an indelible horizon of light. Every passerby gave me the feeling that all my secrets were known to him, and that all of his were known to me: his secrets—in other words that he walked, that when walking he had an idea and that nothing strange about him could surprise me. I started to run. Why? In a city you don't run. But, precisely, I could act like an eccentric. Really, I could: there I was, everywhere, outside, everyone could see me, passing by the buildings, passing by the policeman's white glove, passing by the banks of the river, and still I ran, and besides I didn't run, I was swept along by a feeling of triumph, the definitive certainty that the sky as well belongs to us, that it's our responsibility to administer it along with everything else, that at every moment I touched it and flew over it. I reached the river. It was remarkable that I had come there, because such a calm view intimidated and disturbed me. The impression of serenity was perfect. Water flowed, on the banks people fished, others read, in the distance a tugboat pulled some barges. A scene like this was full of menace. It demanded something, but what? The feeling of a plot here was stifling, I sensed an intermingling of motives and episodes whose lines slipped through my fingers—such was the voice of the river, the comical meaning of this calm, and of these immobile images, connected with another time. This whole neighborhood was very old, and not only old, it gave the impression of never having changed, and the river as well seemed to have flowed through time, affirming with its vast tranquility that there was neither beginning nor end, that

34

history constructed nothing, that man still didn't exist—who knows? From this assurance there arose, like a suffocating deception, the recollection of a lie, of an endless fraud, an insinuation carried out in order to degrade noble feelings. Besides, it could only be dishonest stupidity.

I walked along the quais, then took another route. My excitement had passed. The day seemed revolting, it was so bright. A strange and painful spasm shook my throat, as if I wanted to cough up the day, as one sometimes vomits very pure water. I was returning with the feeling of disgust for what least merits disgust. I was contaminated with it. This couldn't go on, and besides it wasn't disagreeable, even a spasm can be appealing. I knew where this street was headed: to her store. Still, I didn't want to see her. Going through the door, I saw her from behind, half turned to the back of the store and most likely speaking with someone in another room. At the time I was unfamiliar with the layout of the place: besides the cubbyhole, there was a little studio for 'artistic photography.' At certain times a technician came; one door of the studio led to a corridor of the building; and, on the other side, crossing the corridor, you reached the door of another room, used for storing junk, and also by the manager. I went in, I didn't even look at her. I recognized the place, the frames, the enlargements, the little armchairs. I was extremely tired, I had the feeling of having come here a hundred times, and I'd only dropped in once before. I was overwhelmed by this feeling throughout my visit.

She was sitting down, maybe because it was late and she wasn't expecting any more customers. There was a visible difference between her attitude in the morning and her be-havior now. You could explain it in a number of different ways: she was getting used to me; she felt sorry for me be-cause of the fight in the restaurant; and, finally, she had some plan in mind. She talked about some of the tenants in our building. I didn't know them: I was wary of them. I couldn't recognize a single one when we met on the stairs. She insisted on telling me their stories. A family on the seventh floor was much talked about because the older daughter had come down with a serious, probably infectious, disease. A few

1) waste away
2) shapeless

weeks earlier the youngest child had died. They asked my neighbor to take her picture, and she showed me the prints. It was an unpleasant sight: a dead child lacks both beauty and youth; this one was horribly emaciated and made you think of a pile of bones found by accident in a pit. According to my neighbor the older sister had contaminated the younger one. The apartment had seemed clean, but an overwhelming sense of stale air and sweating walls turned it into a pigsty. Everybody was amazed by the fact that the sick girl had been released from the hospital, and that, even after the younger one's death and the findings of the doctor, the hygiene office still hadn't done anything. The story ended like this: one of the sons was in the police. Since he was young—in his uniform he seemed like an adolescent, even a girl—he only had a tiny bit of authority. But, they claimed, his interference nevertheless caused the bending of the rules that favored the family and put them all at risk.

An unimportant story, I thought, just gossip. 'What's your name?' —'First name or last?' She took down her portrait and I held it in my hands: her face seemed to look at me from far away with a promising and agreeable smile, and yet it also looked beyond me, replacing me with somebody else—I don't know who. At the bottom of the portrait she had signed, in large handwriting, the name Marie Scadran. I put the picture down on a chair. She was working out the receipts behind the counter. Through the window the square changed, it became a gray platform crossed by lights: cars, passing quickly, fanned out through an amorphous confusion.—'This photograph was . . . a long time ago?' She leafed through her book. 'Six months,' she said, 'more or less.' I got up and looked through the door: a few people had stopped in front of the display window, summoned by any number of brilliant and delicate, clean, and elusive faces, which left no trace. For a moment they leaned forward, then slipped lightly away into the haze of the street. Turning around, I saw that the portrait was still staring at me with its calm familiarity, as if for six months I had continuously been there for it, saying yes to this paper light and, behind it, to the promise-laden image that claimed to be there. 'I'm going,' I said.

*1) overwhelm*

The subway entrance was still only dimly lit. There was daylight, a daylight no less sparkling, through the fog, almost more penetrating, more radiant, than at midday. At the edge of the sidewalk a policeman watched over the flood of cars. A few yards away another policeman, his hand on the signal switch, let the crowd spill over onto the street in an imperceptible inundation, until, anticipating his gesture, the stampede rushed into the street in black, opaque waves at the very instant the light changed. I didn't move, and for a minute people accumulated around me, then slowly and irresistibly plunged in, and went to the other side. Then I started to run. She was still in the store, her overcoat over her arm, the store lights turned off. 'Couldn't you have your own picture taken?' —'Now?' She smiled in a vague way. I had gone into the little studio and was looking for the switch. 'There's no help here now,' she said behind me, turning on the light. Nevertheless she showed me a device with which you could take your own picture, given the correct exposure. But suddenly she became cross. 'Not tonight, I'm tired, it's too late.' She still had to go into the storage room to put away a frame. It was the only badly lit room: there were a lot of things in it, pieces of furniture, filing cabinets, even an old sofa. I sat down while she rummaged around. We heard someone buzz at the door. 'Just a minute. Maybe it's my boss,' she said. While she was gone I found in a filing cabinet rejected photos—botched prints—of every possible size. They made a shiny pile. I stuck my hands in; I threw images by the dozen onto my lap. This vast number of faces gave me an extraordinary feeling—I had perhaps a hundred, two hundred there. I piled them up in front of me. All these photos looked alike, as is often the case with the work of professional photographers. The poses were the same; the clothes, Sunday clothes, went from one person to the next; the difference in features was hidden by the identity of expressions; in short, tremendous monotony. They were the same, but the same in an infinite number. I stuck my fingers in, I pawed them, I got drunk on them.

At this point my neighbor came back. Her mind was on her boss, and she talked about nothing but him. He was a remarkable man: he had a lot of character, and he knew all about technical things, he'd invented a new kind of camera, etc. All these strengths got him onto the Economic Council. The praise seemed excessive. That's why I too started heaping praise on my superiors. Generally I didn't think they were that good—neither good nor bad. I never judged them; I had my job, they had theirs, we got along for the most part. But now I separated them from their duties and started heaping exaggerated praise. But I couldn't do it—to describe Iche as an energetic man, one of those new-style administrators who are interested in every case as if it's unique but who still never lose the overview, to say that he examined reports scrupulously, that he listened to everybody with the same attentiveness, that he left his office late, well after the official time—I just couldn't do it. First of all, it wasn't true: he was crude, rather inattentive, negligent; when I tried to connect him with precise facts, I had the impression that he didn't act like a model official (besides, he was criticized openly at work). Nevertheless I was forced to recognize all his good qualities; his faults meant nothing. It would have been necessary to discover even vaguer characteristics, ones that could have been applied only to him and would also have suited everybody. So I talked of his punctuality—it was unimportant, it defined him.

After this speech I noticed that she was across from me, sitting on the sofa. She rocked back and forth with her hands clasped around her knee. 'Should we go?' she asked. She looked at me, and I came over and sat next to her. —'Whenever you want.' Her hand was lying on her dress, its large, thick palm up, its fingers flattened in the backlight, the third finger swollen by a red ring. I wanted to take that ring off. She leaned back a little, continuing to look at me, her head resting on the sofa back. She raised her hand slowly to her shoulder, then reached behind her neck and unfastened a chain from which hung a tiny silver pendant. 'I have a friend,' she said. In a false, emotional way she gazed at the pendant, blowing on it and making it swing. 'The young man I saw at your place?' She didn't move her head, she didn't signal anything; then her eyes rose to my face, first skirting it, then touching it, with a kind of surprise, a basic surprise that I in turn felt, as if the two of us, at the same moment, had become aware of my presence. 'I'm only an employee,' she said. 'But I do my best. You shouldn't have come here during working hours.' —'Yes.' She kept her eyes on me. She got up, then I did too; I grasped her hands. I held her, roughly. She was rigid with a rigidity that called for a hammer. Suddenly the cloth of her dress came to life under my fingers. It was strange—an irritating smooth surface, a kind of black skin that slid, adhered and didn't adhere, billowed up. It was then that she was transformed—I swear, she became different. And I myself became someone else. Her breathing grew deeper. There was a change in every part of her body. It sounds strange, but up to this point we had had the same body, a true common body, impalpable and light. With a shattering suddenness this body broke in two, dissolved, and in its place a burning layer formed, a moist and strange greed that was blind, urgent. Yes, I swear it: I had become a stranger, and the more I held her the more I felt her become a stranger, determined to show me someone and something different. No one will believe me, but, at that moment, we became separated, we felt and breathed the separation, we gave it a body. That was obvious; finally we were no longer touching.

Now I want to try to understand what happened afterward. She got up and flipped the switch. Then she shut the door. A little later we left. At my place, on the bed, I bundled up and clung to the wall. It was very cold. At eight, or maybe after eight, the concierge knocked and brought me my tray. Now night had really fallen. A few minutes later there was another knock and I thought it was the concierge again. I bumped against the tray opening the door and I made out, in the hallway, the shadow of a visitor. First I thought it was my neighbor's friend, but even before turning on the light switch I recognized Pierre Bouxx. I found this extremely disagreeable. It was insane for him to show up at that hour.

'Are you feeling sick?' he asked. 'I've come as your neighbor; if I'm bothering you, let me know.'

I let him sit down, and I got back into bed.

'I didn't tell you the truth the other day. I'm not concerned with politics. A long time ago one of my friends got mixed up in that sort of thing, but I lost sight of him. Right now I'm

nnected with a medical establishment: I've got a minor
 ough decent job.'

He spoke very softly; the bedside lamp barely lit his face.

'Even though I work in a clinic, I'm looking for a good
doctor. Lately I've been tired. I think I'm suffering from insomnia.'

I made a gesture that indicated I knew nothing about it. He
remained silent. A little bug was circling the light; suddenly
it fell so heavily that I shuddered: it was then that I realized
how cold I was.

'I have no idea what kind of people live in this building.
Probably they're like all the others. That reminds me of something you said the other day, which really made an impression. *I see everyone willingly, I have no preferences.* When you
said that you said something really important.'

I looked at him without answering. Then a thought came
to mind with so much force that I believed I had expressed it.
'It's the official doctrine,' I said. 'Besides, even when you prefer someone, you prefer anyone.'

'Ah,' he said, 'if you took that maxim literally! I'm struck by
your attachment—no, it's more than that, your real veneration of the authorities. In every one of your gestures you
express that veneration. And you put it into words. Sorry, but
at first that seems almost like servility: one gets the impression that you're a functionary and that you want to get ahead.
But don't be offended; I dropped that idea right away. I even
wonder if you don't harbor completely different thoughts—
you talk too much, you think too much: it's not natural.'

Yes, I thought, I've heard this before.

'I'd like to tell you something. At the hospital there's a
cashier with fifteen years of seniority: he's a very honest and
very hard-working man. He's got a big family, but a lot of his
children work and so they live comfortably. This cashier has
won a number of awards but, after a few questionable incidents, he fell under suspicion and had to give back his decora-
tions. Since then he's been carefully watched and they became
convinced he was stealing. So—I read the report written by the
higher-ups: they didn't accuse him of theft, but of plotting
and sabotage.'

'Why are you telling me this?'

'I'm going to tell you another story. Again, at the clinic, there's a waiter who's almost a fool—he's really simple-minded. He sweeps up, does little errands, but everything he does is half botched. Naturally his salary is very modest. And yet he's a good fellow, kind of a dreamer; still, it would be better to let him skip the work entirely. Do you know why they keep him, then? The director told me himself: he makes himself useful.'

'You made these stories up,' I said right away. 'I hate this way of talking. Besides, I'm unwell, I have to sleep.'

He got up and looked at me sympathetically.

'You really do seem to be suffering. Pardon me, I shouldn't have come in. I saw you go up the stairs with the young woman who lives on this floor. I had the impression that my visit would be less of a bother today. And in fact I came in order to ask you a question about the young lady.'

'What!?'

'I don't know her; I know she runs a little photo studio. I have a special kind of job for her to do. You're something of a psychologist—can I trust her?'

'What are you saying?'

'It's very simple: can she help me put together some fake identity cards?'

I looked at him.

'I understand you perfectly,' I told him. 'You're trying to irritate me with outrageous stories. But they don't bother me. You want me to tell you something about your cashier? He's guilty of plotting because nothing's higher than the law. Really, all offenses are plots against the law: you'd like to disobey it, but since that isn't possible, you have to rebel against its legitimacy. A long time ago you could steal and leave it at that; now you're committing through the theft an infinitely more serious crime, the most terrible of all and, besides, a crime that can't be carried out, that fails. Of that crime there remains, precisely, only an insignificant trace—the theft. This is all obvious. And why did you remind me of what I said about specific relationships, why after that did you mention the young lady, using a ridiculous pretext? It's too clear—all

41

your words are allusions. Believe me, maybe I'm delirious, but your remarks are superfluous: you aren't teaching me anything, you're only expressing what I think, and when you speak, it's not you, it's me who's speaking. So you don't intimidate me.'

'Excuse me, please,' he said, 'it's truly a mistake. Really, I do like you a lot.'

'It's not a question of liking me. Anyway, that's not important. Maybe I am servile, like you say, but the word servility doesn't offend me. To whom would I be servile? On the contrary, I'm proud and independent—that's why I'm servile. You yourself are servile.'

'Please calm down. I'll leave right now, if you like. But let me tell you something. I don't know how you see the world— you express yourself strangely. There's another point of view, though. You think this society is perfect. Why? For me, this is nothing but an unjust system, a handful of people against a mass of people. Every day, in the lower depths, a nameless class, with no rights, grows by thousands of individuals— individuals who, in the eyes of the State, cease to exist and disappear like mold. Once it has crossed them out, effaced them, the State can then act as if everything that exists glorifies it and serves it. That's its hypocrisy. It is profoundly sly and hypocritical. The State has pressed into service everything you say and everything you can do. There isn't a single thought that doesn't bear its mark. All governments are like this.'

'You don't surprise me,' I told him. 'And you don't shock me. You're nothing but a dated and dateless book, that's all. Leave me alone now.'

'One more thing. I told you that I like you. You don't know me, but our relationship may be about to change. A little while ago, when I came, I wanted to do away with my earlier assertions and deny my political activities. Now you see what's happened: my words have decided otherwise. I'm not hiding.'

'Yes,' I said. 'What could you be? An imposter, a spy, a loser? I hear you buzzing around me, like a fly. And everything you say is crude. Why this *I'm not hiding*? You're perfectly free to conspire out in the open, the State won't take offense. You're just reinforcing what you think you're knocking down. *I'm not hiding!* As if you could hide! Now, good night; I'll end up believing that you really visited me.'

He went into the corridor and I waited five minutes, ten minutes. Now I was very calm. The wind shook the windows softly. Night too had its softness. I knocked on the wall a few times, but since I was waiting she didn't come. Then I was forced to ask myself why she hadn't come and why he had. A little later, completely awake, I saw there was light in the room; my eyes were fixed on something on the other side of my bed, a stain that moved around a little. I knew this stain well. I saw it for the first time at my parents', quietly resting on the wall behind the sofa. It sprawled on the clinic wall, across from me, in a place hidden by the door, when the door was left wide open. Here it was the result of water leakage. This stain was unusual in that it was only a stain. It represented nothing, had no color, and, except for dusty permeation, nothing made it visible. Was it even visible? It didn't exist under the wallpaper; it had no form, but resembled something dirty, spoiled, but clean as well. I had looked at it a lot; I had no reason to avert my gaze. Since it was only a stain, it absorbed me; it never looked at me; that's what made looking illicit. I got up and, feeling my way, went into the corridor.

'Is it you?' he said.

He was still dressed, but he must have been resting, stretched out on a reclining chair. The room was vast, much bigger than the ones in my apartment; it seemed almost empty, there were no carpets and almost no furniture. It wasn't poverty, but something much worse: a poverty due to the abandonment of life, a dirtiness without dust or lint, the sordid wretchedness of dispensaries and clinics that are free of scattered paper.

'I thought,' he said, 'that it was one of my friends.' He looked at me without asking me to sit down. 'He lives in the building, a guy named Dorte. Maybe you've met him?'

'Why do you like me?'

'It's really late. It seems to me you shouldn't have gotten out of bed. You want me to take you back?'

43

'Answer me. My questions might seem abnormal, but I have reasons for not putting them off. Did you or did you not say, *I like you*?'

'I did.'

'Why?'

'But don't you realize, my boy? Aren't you making too much out of a word?'

'It's a polite phrase?'

'ok, polite.'

I turned my back on him and went into the hall.

'Please, don't go away like that. Why did you have to ask me that?'

'Your liking means something to me, something dangerous. You're like me, and you're telling me your plans. You aren't taking into account the revulsion they inspire in me. You speak in the most uncalled-for and most shocking way. And, in fact, you're speaking to me. Why to me? You answer: because you like me. I want you to explain yourself candidly on this.'

'With pleasure. First, I'm sorry, but I don't like you *that* much. I had hoped to be on good terms with you, but that seems to raise too many problems in your mind, and finally we end up with unpleasant remarks.'

'Why don't you stop buzzing around me?'

'I'm not buzzing. I don't even know what you mean by that. Maybe you don't realize that your attitude is bizarre, that you seem to be suffering from some kind of phantasmagoria. To put it simply, you like to complicate things and you're extremely thin-skinned. The way you are aroused my curiosity, that's all.'

'The way I am. . . ,' I said, looking at him.

'Your ways and your words are sometimes surprising. Well—it's two in the morning, and here you are at my place. Why? "Because I like you." It's very strange, it's crazy.'

'There's nothing strange about my behavior. Why tell me your plans?'

'Sorry, I don't think I've told you anything—what do you mean by plans?'

'I'd rather not go back to words that hurt and disturb me. I wish I'd never heard them.'

44

'You really are thin-skinned! Are you like this all the time? You've got a fever; maybe this is the beginning of a serious illness. Besides, it's very cold. Take this blanket.'

I sat down and he handed me his blanket.

'I'm not sick. I'm cool and calm.'

He looked at me while I carefully wrapped myself up; then, getting up, he slowly walked across the room.

'Why do you say, *I'm not sick*? One gets the impression that you're scared of sickness. There's nothing dishonorable about being sick or feverish.' He added, 'This Dorte I mentioned also has bouts of fever. He used to run a garage, a very big garage, with a lot of employees, and very modern repair facilities—he's a technician, he's studied a lot and read a lot of books. And then something collapsed. He let his business go. On some days I give him huge doses of quinine, but the attacks vary in intensity: sometimes they're weak, sometimes they're violent. Don't you ever take medicine?'

'Did you tell me that you suffer from insomnia?'

'Yes, insomnia. In other words, I have to watch my blood. My blood is too strong; at night, it circulates freely, in a real frenzy, it's my master, and then it calms down. Nevertheless, I had a sleepless night.'

'And your friend has the same ideas as you?'

'Let's drop it. . . . These sleep problems are very strange. Some years ago, around the time when I had to quit my job at the hospital, I had the same dream a number of times. I dreamed that I went before a magistrate, at some ungodly hour in the morning. Naturally the servants refused to let me in, and on top of that I was very badly dressed. Still I went in, I got as far as the door to the bathroom, and then I shouted, "I'm guilty." I think I had a stick in my hand. The judge, who was shaving, turned around and, very surprised, said a strange thing: "Guilty? What's that? I've never seen a guilty person." I was aware that this remark made my case much worse. Still, that was only an impression. The judge was very welcoming: he gave me something to eat and drink, let me stay in his best bedroom; in the end, he sent me away. From that time on, the dream became a nightmare, because it was recurrent; and since it was repeated every night, I knew in advance in my

45

dream everything that was going to happen, so that I couldn't even find the strength to dream it. At each new trip to the magistrate I knew how I'd be received and why I was treated so well. Courtesies of all kinds, fine meals, parties, all that had only one goal, to make me drop my appeal to justice, to make me forget the word *guilty*: this intention was obvious everywhere. But I couldn't make out what was hidden behind it. Was it a trap? A chance for salvation? Maybe they hoped to see me disappear, so that they themselves could stay out of this bad business. Or were they waiting for a signal or for a moment of forgetfulness on my part—in order to strike and ruin me? These doubts were exhausting and, besides, they accomplished nothing: I had nothing to decide. Scenes followed each other mechanically, the end approached, announced by signs that couldn't fool me. The judges were always more obsequious, they became my servants, I was showered with honors, treated with vile respect. The lights shone, there was music, a ball: at that moment my dread reached its high point and suddenly I understood everything. I'd been searching, for days, with these judges, and what I couldn't find, even at the ball where there was a huge crowd. . . . It was . . .'

'Well?'

'Sorry, I think it was a woman. I needed a woman. But even at the ball there weren't any. For that reason the world of justice is stifling. Acquittal could only mean the presence of a woman, but I could only seek acquittal in prisons where there are no women. That was the punishment.'

'Your dream proves that your thoughts are unhealthy and perverted. And you talk too much. My sense is that you're also sick, that you're not quite yourself today.'

'I've told you a dream, which I had a number of times. In other words, the dream really did go this way, but often the ending was different. You want me to tell you how it ended then?'

'No. I understand your allusions. But this obscure chatter has gone on too long. If it's my neighbor and my walk with her this evening that's behind your puzzles, don't bother.'

'Look here, Henri Sorge, I'm a very busy man, I've got major responsibilities. I work day and night. I assure you that you can spend time with whomever you like, and I'll think nothing of it: I couldn't care less.'

'I know you're interested in what I do. Besides, you're wrong, this young lady is very respectable. She runs her little shop very competently, and she takes care of her mother, whom she supports. I've seen her two or three times, that's all.'

'Wouldn't it be better if I told you the end of the dream?'

'What dream?'

'Yes, let me finish. I've told you that I was a helper in a clinic. And the last of my judges was the director of the clinic. And, soon enough, without even knowing what I was saying—and precisely because before him I felt innocent and determined to affirm my innocence—he mixed me up with my earlier confessions, gagged me, kept me from protesting, taking me at my word with a hypocrisy that made me sick, even in my dream. I was suffocating, I felt like I was gagging: so this is what they were concealing, that's why they entertained me with that incredible servility—because I had confessed without being aware of it, because I spoke imprudently and too soon, losing the right to speak at the only time that would have required my sincere and true words. It was mean and it was dirty.'

'So they threw you out of the clinic?'

'What difference does it make!'

'Do you think,' I said slowly, 'that one can meet . . . a woman, for example, look at her, approach her and little by little feel that everything you have in common with her is disappearing? Who's there? Something else. It can only be a trap! For a few moments, you touch something foreign—believe me, you really feel it. It's not just a sensation, it's indisputable, it's horribly clear. It can only be a temptation.'

'Yes. Aren't you getting tired? If you like, you can spend the night in this chair. I'll turn the light off.'

I saw him take some blankets from a corner, spread one on the reclining chair, then wrap himself up to his chin in the others.

'But,' I said, 'aren't you going to bed? I'd be better off going back to my place.'

e'd already turned out the light. After a moment the cur-
ess window let in a little clouded light.

...e you really going to ask her to do that kind of job? I
don't know her; I don't know who she is.'

Now I was speaking in a low voice. He didn't answer, but
through the darkness I felt him turn toward me and listen
carefully.

'I know,' I said, 'that there are still a few organizations that
distribute tracts against the State. They have meetings and
cause incidents. Be careful—the government knows everything, and everything that happens does so with its complicity, and at its instigation.'

He was obstinately silent. I seemed to make out his two
eyes shining like an animal's, but their gleam expressed nothing but an anxious and frightened presence.

'I don't think you're spying on me,' I said. 'I even have a
certain trust in you. Up to a point at least, because I seriously
distrust you as an individual. But my opinion of you, in any
case, has changed. You're irritating, you make me queasy with
your evasions, and yet I'm here. It's strange, sometimes I even
doubt that you exist. I think it's because you're sick.'

'Would you agree to be in one of our organizations and set
up a little group in your department at city hall?'

'No.'

'Why not?'

'It's against my ideas.'

'Can your ideas allow you to live with a system that crushes
people under the pretext of liberating them, and which reduces
the people who slip through its cracks to nonexistence?'

'I've already read all that in the tracts, and it's stupid: the
State doesn't crush—you can't crush yourself. The truth is
that all these criticisms are prompted by the law itself: it
needs them, and it's grateful to you for them; otherwise,
everything would come to a halt.'

'And those outside the law, the underclass?'

'What?' I waited a moment; I could make out his face,
although only vaguely. 'I've heard talk of all that. But you're
crazy,' I suddenly exclaimed. 'It's a story from a long time ago,
a vague memory. You're a book; you don't exist.'

'Don't talk like a fool. You know perfectly well that I'm outside the law myself. Right now you're struggling for your class, the huge class in your mind that encompasses everything. You sing the praises of your administration; you don't even see that outside yourself there's also something, but sooner or later you'll slip up.'

'Never. It's not possible. Turn on the light.' I was tossing around; the light went on.

'Why did you talk to me? Where did you get that idea?'

He barely looked at me and said rapidly, 'I don't know, it was an impression. Besides, I'd like to compromise your stepfather. Now, go back to bed.'

I got up. Near the door, I tried to tell him something; then I forgot it or I got mixed up. I returned to my place and went to bed.

# 3

As soon as I stretched out on my bed I fell into a state of fatigue that wasn't sleep, but inert lucidity. Yes, death, I told myself. The next day Louise brought me to the house. I went back to my old room, and then everyone started spying on me to see if I would come out of my inertia. How ridiculous! I knew I would come out of it when I wanted, since I wasn't sleeping. I kept quiet while I waited. One morning, before anyone was up, Louise came into my room. She was wearing a red dress—a strange dark and violent red. Walking right in front of me, she led me across the room, into another, bigger one, and then into the hallway. I followed her, watching that strange red. In the hall, she pushed me toward the stairway, and we went up in silence. On the second floor there was a vast antechamber, with two entrances on each side; in the back, there was also a door. She pointed to one of these doors and went up to it and pointed to it again, staring at me in a furtive and insistent way, with such dark eyes—ah, with very old eyes, eyes which seem always to have looked at me with this air of waiting, reproach, and command. Her hand moved to the doorknob and grasped it. I looked at it with all my strength; there was such a strange intention in her gesture. There was, as well, an incredible memory of having come with her here once before, and of her looking at me once before with tired and gleaming eyes as her hand moved to the door, so that I trembled not only in the present, but also in the past, and perhaps only in the past—and so that the sweat that I felt on my skin signified only another, already proverbial sweat, a water of death that had flowed and would flow from me, again and to the end.

She led me along brusquely and made me go up another stairway. She pushed me into a room. Barely in it, I turned around, gripped by an extraordinary sensation of coldness, dampness, and decay, a feeling so strong that I was disoriented and even repelled. There was something excessive in it, as if the decay and dampness had separated themselves from the room in order to become visible—more visible than the walls, the window, and the floor. 'Let's go back down, before mother gets up,' said Louise. —'Is this your room? Why do you live in a place like this?' —'But I've always lived here.' She was standing next to a huge portrait that was enthroned, alone, on a table. Behind it an old tapestry was spread out, with worn-away figures and faded colors. It struck me that this relic, which still had a certain majesty, explained by itself the poverty of the room.

'Do you want to show me this portrait?'

She had trouble lifting it and carrying it to the bed: it was a real monument. The frame looked like a granite table, thick and smooth on every side; it had a crushing mass, which was almost ridiculously impressive for the normal-sized photograph it surrounded. I looked at the long and bony face; it expressed little, except for the eyes which had a fierce steadiness—quite striking in this featureless face. A dutiful man, no doubt; he seemed to be about forty. Louise held up the frame from behind and, along with the portrait, I saw her own face, and her equally cold and sharp gaze which, from above the frame, and with a jealous haste, slipped down to the image as if to verify its physical identity. I remembered then all the other photographs, behind which there was also something to look for—all of them seemed, today, to return me to this face with its fierce gaze, this face whose only penetrating feature was the eyes.

The frame weighed down on me so heavily that my thigh seemed to be alternately burning and turning to stone. But as soon as I moved, Louise, without letting me take hold of it, quickly carried it off. From afar, on its pedestal, it was a real icon. The room began to lighten up. It was fairly long, narrow, and low; the daylight, starting at the bed in the back of the room, only got about halfway in, stopping just at the wall hanging. From there on the shadows made a kind of alcove. In other words the room was like a strongbox.

'It's the same room as when you were a little girl,' I remarked. 'Come on,' I said, seeing her still motionless next to her portrait. 'Come on!'

I took her hand and moved it toward my forehead. She touched it, not in a caressing way, but roughly. She noticed a scar on my temple; she examined it slowly, exploring the mark meticulously; then she fiercely fingered it, probing it with an almost maniacal insistence.

'Why are you lowering your eyes?' I asked after pushing her away a bit. 'It's not like you. How old were you when you left the house?'

'Twelve.'

'Twelve! So at twelve you threw the rock at me,' I said, pointing at my temple.

She shook her head.

'What do you mean, no! I was digging a hole. You stood at the edge. You took a rock, a piece of brick, and you threw it at me the moment I stood up.'

She kept on shaking her head.

'You know perfectly well,' she said, 'that when you were small there was an accident; mother let you fall.'

'Mother? Yes, mother. Still, it's true—when we were little, I was the scapegoat; I satisfied every one of your whims. Right here you forced me to lie flat for hours under the bed while you swept up, whisking dust and bits of dirt on me.'

Her look became even more severe; she didn't smile at my wild talk. I grabbed her hand and kissed it, hoping to brighten her mood. And, in fact, it seemed that her face relaxed, that something like a smile passed over it—but then suddenly she grimaced, her mouth contracting horribly; I thought she was about to burst into tears. For a second she was motionless, and then she threw herself on me and embraced me, violently. I was overwhelmed. She had never shown affection, except through silence and despotism. I was stunned, I almost felt terror, I babbled something—and when I saw her with her arms crossed, and with the same fierce look as before, I hated her for it.

'Now,' she said, 'we have to go down.'

I had forgotten my stiff leg. For a moment I had to take hold of her arm, and I glanced at the tapestry. It certainly was a relic—it was threadbare, and even the threads were in tatters. I thought I'd go up to it and blow on the wool; soon I was surrounded by fluffy bits of dirt, dozens of tiny moths— my eyes were full of them, I spat them out.

'It's filthy,' I shouted, covering my face, 'a real bug nest!' Disgusted, I thought of the thousands of worms, mites, creatures of all kinds that were proliferating in it. 'How can you keep a piece of trash like that?'

She too had ducked her head under the cloud.

'It's very old,' she said in a low voice.

'Very old, very old!' And as I was repeating these words I suddenly saw before my eyes, coming out of the wall and hurling itself into the room, the image of an enormous horse that reared up to the sky, that had gotten worked up in the craziest way. The head was tossed back and had an extraordinary appearance: ferocious, with wild eyes, it seemed to be battling against rage, suffering, and hatred. This fury, which it could not comprehend, was turning it *more and more into a horse:* it burned and bit, and all in the void. The image was really crazy, and it was enormous as well: it took up the entire foreground, it was all you saw, I couldn't even see the head distinctly. Nevertheless, in the background there were surely still a lot of details, but there the wear had obliterated the colors, the lines, and even their imprint on the weft. Stepping back, you couldn't see anything more; getting closer, I mixed everything up. Standing stock still, I sensed a glinting light behind this chaos in rags, skimming over it. Something had moved; the design was held up from behind, it looked at me, and I looked at it. So what was it? A ruined staircase? Columns? Maybe a body lying on the steps? Ah—a false, perfidious image, vanished and indestructible. Ah—certainly something very old, criminally old. I wanted to shake it, tear it apart, and, feeling enveloped in a fog of moisture and earth, I was gripped by the obvious blindness of all these people, by the crazily unconscious movement that turned them into agents of a horrible and dead past in order to lure me as well into the deadest and most horrible past. I looked at Louise with real hatred; she fiercely clutched my arm, not wanting to let go, holding on, no doubt forever. Ah—woman, cursed

1) acquired by stealth

woman—and suddenly, the words I had spoken before, when she embraced me, came back: 'I'll always obey you.' I had said that, I was sure. This memory immediately calmed me down. I was stunned, I stared at her. I heard her murmur, 'Come.' She opened the door. I saw her already on the stairs, turning her red dress to me and waiting. 'Come,' she said, 'come quickly.'

That afternoon I withdrew into the garden. Usually I refused to go there; I would lock myself in my room instead.

It was already fairly hot. I sat down on a bench, near an arbor. This modest garden was enclosed by enormous walls, walls of an excessive height that cast much too much shade. And the trees? Too many of them, and too tall and powerful for such a small enclosure. And the earth? Black, even at the surface, sterile but black, poorly hidden by the gravel. I scraped aside the stones: it really wasn't any color, not gray, or yellow, or ochre, and still it appeared to be as black as if, from deep in the earth, a layer had shown through the surface, with the dull appearance of an entirely fossilized earth, where things could no longer even rot, but were maintained eternally as eternally dead things. I imagined the hole I had dug, probably next to the biggest tree: a deep hole, almost as deep as I was tall. I was in the hole, she was standing at its edge, I saw her legs, her arm; I was sure she had aimed at me. Why? What did she want to do?

'It was a good idea to come out here,' said my mother. 'In the old days you liked this yard a lot.'

I watched her come down the stairs, slowly, one by one. From afar, she had an extremely majestic, almost sublime appearance. I recalled that Louise always spoke of her as the queen.

'I still like it a lot,' I said.

Sitting down on the seat, she threw me a quick, sidelong glance—exactly what I couldn't stand. I could put up with anybody looking at me, even Louise, but with my mother, I couldn't stand it, I lost my composure; and she, because of my obvious discomfort, dared observe me only surreptitiously, with an uneasiness and suspicion that increased my uneasiness. I heard her talk about the pool they filled in after

I left and whose place was marked, between a line of trees, by a little mound: it was trimmed with flowers. It was the only slightly cheerful spot in the whole yard.

'Are you getting along well with your sister?'

'Yes.'

'Well, that's all to the good. She's kind, but she has a difficult personality. She's withdrawn. When you're together, does she talk, do you talk a lot?'

'Yes, it depends.'

'I respect her, I think I even admire her. But perhaps you don't know how she hides things. When you got sick, I'm sure she got rid of the letters sent by the doctor. She wanted to be the only person who knew you were sick. She didn't talk to anyone, she only spoke up at the last possible moment. Did she come to see you at the clinic?'

'No, I don't think so. I don't recall.'

'She claimed she went to see you and that you asked her to keep me from coming. Why? But she's the one who didn't want us to meet: out of stupid jealousy, to brush me aside again. What a personality! She never loved me,' she said suddenly, violently. 'When she was little, I'm sure . . . well, I can barely say it, I think she hated me. When she was three years old she hated me already, she scratched me, she slid under the table to peek at me and hit me. Nowadays she's a little nicer. But on some days—have you noticed?—she's sullen, almost shriveled. She doesn't talk, she doesn't seem to hear. In fact she hears everything, doesn't miss a thing. When I see her like that, totally unresponsive, I get out—she tortures me.'

I heard her crying. Her tears too infuriated me. I would have liked to spare her the tears or see her cry more. Louise had never shed a single tear: I held this against both of them. At that moment, I suddenly recalled something, a scene. It came back to me with such force and I had so completely forgotten it that I seemed to be seeing it only now. It happened around four in the afternoon. I had opened a door and I saw Louise standing in the middle of the room, her hands behind her back, terribly thin, a thin five-year-old ghost— and a few feet away my mother threatening her, her fist

56

raised in a gesture of spite and rage. I saw it for a second, maybe two seconds; I saw Louise, her face somber, pitifully thin and implacable, with an ageless and timeless impassivity, and in front of her my mother with her fist in the air, the majesty of my mother reduced to this threat. She was pitiful, more powerless in front of this patch of red cloth than she was before the mask of her own crime. Then she noticed me, she noticed her raised fist; an expression of horror passed across her face, an expression the likes of which I'd never seen on any face, which I never wanted to see again and which turned me away from her face now, as she turned hers away from mine, allowing us only the exchange of furtive, suspicious glances.

'Why are you afraid of me?' I said.

I felt her eyes turning to mine. Quite beautiful eyes, it seemed to me, eyes from another country, pale, of a distant blue that summoned light. Right now all I could perceive was their troubled, weak movement.

'Why do you say that? Sometimes I'm afraid for you. It's true—you scare us. You're alone too much, you're sick so often. Recently I learned that you spent a few weeks at the clinic.'

'I'm not alone, I lead the same life as everyone.'

'You need to be watched, cared for. When you're feeling better, would you be willing to spend some time in the country?'

'I don't know. . . . I haven't thought about it.'

'I'm upset, I know. Maybe I'm being too rash, but look: you disappeared for so long. I don't know much about you. The only news I get comes in bits and pieces from your sister. I leave you alone a lot, because I get the impression that my presence . . . Yes, I'm afraid of being in the way—isn't that sad?'

Her tears were coming through her voice again, making it shameful, old, the voice of a hired mourner. 'Why did you ask if I was afraid of you? Who gave you that idea?'

'Nothing, I was mistaken.'

Without looking at her, I held out my hand. She took it gently, though with some embarrassment.

'You have a pretty hand,' she said, 'a girl's hand.'

As she said this, I heard something. Near the biggest tree, almost hidden behind the trunk, you could see the red splotch of a dress, immobile, just positioned there as if it had fallen from the tree, barely showing itself and yet too visible, as if by seeing it you had seen too much. I wanted to take my hand back, but my mother, who hadn't noticed anything, tried to keep hold of it, stroked it, calmed it, but when she too understood who was there she did more than let me go—she quickly pushed me away.

'Well here you are,' she said. 'So did you finish working?'

The red cloth drew itself up a little, then dissolved into this cold, imperturbable apparition, which no threat could push back or thrust aside, maybe because it was already infinitely remote.

'It's Saturday,' said Louise. She stayed near the knoll, not looking at me, not looking at my hand—which I didn't know what to do with—as if all this had already been erased, crushed by her granite judgment.

'Did you take him into your room this morning?'

'Yes.'

'I see that he's allowed to penetrate into your sanctuary. And why did you choose that time?'

'Because he asked me, and to avoid any remarks about this incident in case it may not have leaked out.'

'What a strange person you are,' said my mother, confused but calm. 'You say nothing, except what everyone else would be ashamed to say. Is it pride—the better to look down on me? And you don't even tell the truth.'

'I knew,' said Louise, 'that you wouldn't be happy to see him go back there.'

'Why? You can do whatever you want. I've been resigned to your behavior for a long time now. You always kept me at a distance. Sure, I was close enough to be snubbed. I've only been your mother to be hurt, offended. You made me ashamed, and that's the truth: thanks to you I know what shame is. But you'll be punished, I feel it, we'll all be punished together because of the wickedness of this . . .'

'Be quiet,' Louise said softly.

I stopped up my ears. It seemed to me that my mother was calling her a spider. It's true that when she was younger she looked like a little red spider. I had seen one long ago on a box tree or maybe a cypress branch. It was a minuscule spider, barely a spot; I had observed and examined it for a long time. Taking shelter on a wet leaf, it didn't move, it didn't seem capable of spinning even the smallest web; I found it extremely strange and even pretty. In the end, wanting to touch it, I crushed it.

'Always secrets,' said my mother, 'and really, what secrets? Nothing at all.'

'You did what you wanted with your own life.'

'My life! What can you tell me about my life? Naturally, you're in a hurry to judge me; you don't know anything, and you judge with your ignorance, your heartlessness. And you, you think you're better than everyone else, you alone are just, faithful, virtuous in every way.'

'Be quiet,' Louise said softly.

'You don't have to say "be quiet." Maybe it would be better for you if I were to be quiet, or if I were to forget certain things. You're not virtuous in every way, far from it; I'll tell you something, not out of meanness but sadly, because it is sad, you have a bad disposition. There's something in you that's bad, and what went on up there, really it's better not to talk about it. But at least leave your brother alone today—he needs consideration. What's on your mind? What are you looking for? I don't even want to think about it.'

'Be quiet,' Louise said softly.

The red cloth, once again visible, passed with a small sound from tree to tree. A strange sound, this rustle of cloth. It was leading me away. I got up to follow it.

'You're leaving,' said my mother, fearfully.

'Yes, I think I'll go home.'

'Stay for a while—just for a moment. I'm sorry about all these scenes, they're so unfortunate, but one shouldn't exaggerate their importance. Louise is crazy with pride, she's passionate. When you talk to her about her bad personality, she answers, "I'm cold and a hypocrite," because one day I reproached her for her hypocrisy and coldness. But she's more like fire. Basically, I don't understand her. She thinks like a little girl, that's all. Does she talk about me sometimes?'

'Sometimes.'

'And up there, how's it set up? I haven't gone in once in the last ten years. Not me or anybody else. Nobody has the right to go in, not even the cats. It's childish, it's crazy.'

'Not even the cats?'

'Yes. What do you make of it? On that topic I can tell you something, it happened two or three years ago. Back then we had a gorgeous cat. You remember it, your . . . well, we've always loved cats here. Surprisingly—most animals don't like her—this one attached itself passionately to Louise. In spite of her, it followed her; as soon as it saw her, it got off its throne and ran after her. She, as usual, didn't notice. One day it disappeared; nobody saw it again. What happened to it? It wasn't stolen, it never went out, it never left the house, it barely went into the yard. What I think, though I've no proof, but . . .'

'So?'

'I'm sure that, because it prowled around her, it managed to slip into her room. The concierge claims he heard horrible caterwauling one night.'

'She killed it,' I said flat out.

'How? Did she tell you something? Has she talked about the cat?'

'Here's what happened. One night she woke up, feeling that there was someone in the room, near her. She didn't get up, didn't move, even though she was certainly very scared. She didn't think of this animal, or of anyone from around here: how could someone from here get into her room, which is always locked and which is a wasteland? For hours she stayed like that, motionless, only feeling the presence of someone nearby who couldn't have come in the usual way, who came with the shadows and as a shadow, whom she had awaited, perhaps, for a very long time. Who was it? In whose presence did she think she was lying that night? I don't know yet. In the morning she saw the cat and smashed it with an axe.'

'She told you that?'

'That's how it happened. She told me.'

60

I went back to my room. Toward evening, I opened the door softly, I listened to this strange sound, a murmuring, papery speech that was cautiously crumpled and torn. I crouched in the darkness. The sound had stopped, but something continued to brush against the silence: the rustle of cloth, the faint sound of water or rather the approach of a voice, yes, a timid and patient effort to arrive in the vicinity of speech. This wasn't alarming, and if I felt a slight apprehension, it was because there was something too calm in this sound, something so soothing it was unheard of—it was so calming, more restrained than all restraint: a story, complete and finished, of all the events of an interminable day. Suddenly the sound cracked, and I glimpsed an almost open mouth, eyes half open as well, still unfocused and unable to see, up to the moment in which the sound, completely stopping, turned into a precise gaze trained on me, a gaze which had the same calmness and the same seriousness as the sound—an accommodating air, reserved and cordial, but nothing more.

'Well,' he said, without taking his hand from the lamp. Then he straightened and stood up.

He was almost small, I noticed. He must have been very sturdy, and even his large and thick head seemed dangerously solid. He came forward, dragging his leg.

'Excuse me,' I said, 'I heard a noise and I was listening.'

He held out his hand.

'It's nothing, it's my fault.'

I didn't get back up; I looked at this perfectly white hand. It had a singular distinction and slenderness, especially if you thought of his brutish appearance.

'When I have to work in the evening, I try to sleep a little before dinner.'

I looked at him again.

'But maybe . . .'

'Yes,' I said, getting up, 'I recognize you.'

'Well, I'm happy to see you.' He stared at me quietly. 'We haven't met, and I think you're looking well.'

'Yes, thanks, I do feel better.'

I had the impression that the other door opened. I caught

myself thinking: what a meeting! Everything was going just fine! And, as if this thought had gotten out, Louise came up quickly and shot me a cruel glance.

'The day before yesterday,' he said, 'I had a conversation with Iche. Don't worry: your sick leave's all set up.'

'Iche?'

'Yes, your department head.'

'Yes, thanks.'

'I was going to bring you your dinner,' said Louise.

'Go ahead and eat,' he said brusquely.

I ate; Louise said nothing and didn't leave. After dinner, she didn't clear off the table, so that my mother, coming in, saw the disorder of dishes and silver. 'Louise isn't here?' She saw her at the back of the room, sitting on the floor, on a cushion and looking, as well, at the little table with its tray and dirty dishes. My mother came up to the table; Louise got up and came over as well. I looked at their hands, which slid next to each other, they brushed and met without touching. Louise, who was carrying the platter, made an odd backwards movement, looking at the door. As it opened, she shifted her weight without budging, all the while holding the platter, petrified.

'Have you finished eating? Can I stay for minute?'

He sat down without seeming to notice the strange apparition, looming out of the dark recesses of the house, posted behind him and studying him with a metallic inflexibility.

'Look at them!' he said, gesturing toward the two cats who came and went, disconcerted and startled, their paths crossing. They didn't feel at home yet. He grabbed the smaller one, examined its bandaged paw, and stuck his nose in its horrible yellow fur. But right away he grimaced and, taking it by the scruff of its neck, set it down some distance away; it wobbled and steadied itself with difficulty. 'It's strange,' he said, turning toward me. 'We've washed them, we've put them through all kinds of disinfectants, they've even been in a sterilizer, but nothing helps, they still give off this scorched smell.' He bent down again to sniff the yellow fur. 'I don't know what exactly it smells like: the stench of burning, of gamy fire. I can't put my finger on it, it's strange. I picked them up on one of our

1) false appearance

visits, in the rubble of a gutted building. Have you ever been in one of those houses? What an odor! Kind of a sickly smell I can barely stand. You get the impression that in these piles of embers . . . But apparently not; it's only the fermentation of fire, of debris of all kinds that steeps in the smoke. In any case, what a stench.'

I heard my mother ask if lingering in such places wasn't unhealthy. He started to laugh, a little reserved laugh.

'But we hardly linger! The way things go on our visits, when we go in somewhere we come out again in a few seconds, or sometimes we just look from the street at the blackened façades. Even if the plague were in there, it wouldn't have time to catch us.'

'Still, they're talking about an epidemic.'

'Sure, the newspapers are talking about it—maybe ten suspicious cases. But you have to read between the lines; these are, instead, administrative cases, a way of getting rid of the filth of the old neighborhoods and getting backward areas to toe the line. Anyway, the technicians are taking care of it and even these little animals have gone into the laboratory.'

'So where do these fires come from?' I asked abruptly.

'The fires . . . but you've read the newspapers. Some are caused by one thing, others by another. The security service is having a hard time. Socially, the fires are a very strange, very complex phenomenon: it's something very old, and collective. When you see a house burn, you always get the impression that it's something from long ago, that an old feeling, an old bitterness started the fire, or more precisely that it's a small forgotten fragment of a distant time which is suddenly coming around and wants to cast some light. Notice how strange firelight is: it illuminates and doesn't illuminate; it smothers itself; it feels illegitimate, threatened, impossible. That explains its suffering, its hatred. It's crazy when you think about it. Nowadays fires are hardly in favor, but in the old days the capital was burned a number of times. And even now, you know, if a fire starts somewhere, all of a sudden there are a thousand people who want to watch—you get the impression the sight of it gets them high, they're drunk on it. And the result is that sabotage comes back, the old ideas start

63

smoldering again. But it's basically a good thing—it wears us out, but it also performs a service. In the end what burns will be exactly what must burn.'

I was half sitting up on the sofa—I knew I was looking and listening too hard.

'Maybe we should let him sleep now,' said my mother.

'You want to sleep?'

'No.'

'I relax by talking,' he said as if apologizing. 'When I'm real tired I have to talk. On the council it's gotten to be a joke. If I make a nice speech, the guy sitting next to me looks at my color, stares at the whites of my eyes. "You're speaking too well," he says, "you're resting." Really, it's true. I speak or I sleep. In my chatter the overly strong impressions that I've registered during the day come out, then they come back to me, then they go out again. Finally they pass on to somebody else, they no longer belong to me: I feel fine. You don't talk much yourself?'

I stared at him without answering.

'During our inspections I've seen your neighborhood and I think even your street.'

'It's very unhealthy,' said my mother. 'The conditions are awful where he lives.'

'It sure is a dirty neighborhood, not very attractive. Houses there like to burn. Wouldn't you like to live somewhere else?'

'Did you go past my building?'

'Yes, I think so. You know how official processions are—we don't hang around. Why are you smiling?'

'It's nothing.'

'Maybe these ceremonies seem ridiculous to you? But we can hardly do without them. You know, the newspapers are there, photographers, movie cameras. Everyone takes part and, as soon as everybody sees that we're there, the ruins are no longer exactly ruins; they become the start of a new house.'

'What do you mean?'

'Besides, you're not wrong—sometimes these events do have a comic side. As a matter of fact something ridiculous happened today. On our route, at the end of the street . . . not

64

far from a building we were supposed to visit, we saw a good-sized crowd overflowing the sidewalk and getting in the way of traffic. So what was it? No doubt people from the neighborhood who, having heard about our visit, were waiting for us out of curiosity, a taste for parades, or some other reason—in short, it was abnormal and disagreeable. The police patrol shot ahead: our cars approached slowly. One of our colleagues, standing, shouted, 'Hey—it's a little fair!' And the crowd really was standing around a little street orchestra; there were boxers and, I think, dancers. But a few people in the crowd sensed something new: they recognized our cars. They started yelling, cheering, singing patriotic songs. You know how our crowds are, they like life, spectacles—what a magnificent crowd! Unfortunately, the regulations are strict. The police intervened using their methods. They wanted to empty the square, but there were only a few of them, there was resistance, people became impatient and booed. I think fighting broke out then, there were screams, insults. Finally, after we waited in our cars for an hour, calm returned and the ceremony could take place according to the rules.'

'What's so funny about that? What does this incident have to do with laughter?'

'Well, maybe it isn't so funny,' he said, giving me a serious look. This serious look went right through me. I was certain that this man, who was so important, understood me. More than that, he took me seriously.

'I think I saw you limping,' I said.

'That's an old story! It's just a slightly troublesome rheumatism.'

'Let me tell you, I think this incident is extraordinary. Yes, I understand why you talked about it as something ridiculous. You had to disperse the crowd, chase the people away, create a void: no one has the right to be present at your ceremonies, and yet they're carried out for everyone. It's strange, but it's there that the profundity of the law appears; everyone must withdraw, one mustn't be there in person, but in general, in an invisible way, like in a movie theater. And you yourselves come, but to do what? It's an official gesture, a simple allegory, it's ceremonial. Before you arrive, anybody, by coming to examine the rubble, has already started a new building, has turned these shattered remains into rebuilding materials. And even the arsonists, simply because they've watched the building burn, have already extinguished the fire and restored the house. That's why the newspapers can go ahead and print articles but, basically, you can't talk about fire: there never have been any real conflagrations, and certainly never any ruins. That's the truth.'

'I had no idea you spoke so freely. Your observations would please one of my colleagues, who wouldn't miss asking his favorite question, the one he always has on the tip of his tongue: "Which fly is it today?" The fly is any reflection that's too strong or too delicate, it's the spirit of truth or depth when it takes off and tries to separate itself from its own movement: it buzzes, it hears itself vibrating. So you see, there's another allegory.'

I knew that I had spoken with a laughable fervor, and I was still burning—so what. I felt that, even if he judged me to be slightly ridiculous, he approved of me. There was such a perfect benevolence in his way of speaking, his tone was so calm and so just—everything he said comforted me.

'Who were you just talking about?'

'You must have heard at some point about Etienne Agrove. He's a very distinguished man, who performed some great services: he directs the Office of Records, and all the important reports pass through his hands. Unfortunately, he's getting on in years, and he's almost blind; he always knows everything, but he has also always forgotten everything, and in fact his department has been severely criticized.'

'Why does he talk about flies?'

'His adversaries call his department the Fly Department, which amounts to a crude joke. But when you know the man—small, thin, not very well dressed—when you imagine him walking crookedly because he's nearsighted, bumping into chairs and looking for someone he can ask, in his shrill little voice, "And have you found your fly today?"—the name makes you laugh, because he's a . . . fly himself.'

He spouted this with an odd, almost impudent good-naturedness. In contrast to everything about him that was

66

rough, authoritarian, and even ferocious, this boundless benevolence ended up being irritating; it almost made me shiver.
He got up, with the two cats in his arms; I saw he was wearing
casual clothes. Standing for a second, two seconds, he looked
at me in a neutral, almost dead way—in a way so welcoming
and so foreign that I became shamefully embarrassed. Even
though he hadn't extended his hand, I grasped it and stammered, 'I feel only sympathy and confidence. One ordinarily
doesn't say this, but I'm sure you'll understand my thinking.'

'Thank you—I understand you very well.'

He continued to look at me in that neutral, dull way.

'Are you satisfied with your work at the office? You don't
have anything to complain about?'

Finally I let go of his hand.

'No, nothing.'

'Go rest now. Here,' he added, leaning over unexpectedly
and sticking the yellow fur under my nose, 'smell this.'

First I sensed only the slight stink of a wet animal, and it
was out of courtesy that I agreed with a gesture of my head.
But after he had left, when everybody was gone, and just after I turned off the light, I started to suspect that there was
something to smell. The odor arrived softly, I breathed it on
the sofa, on my sleeve, and then it withdrew. At a certain
point it came to rest in the darkness, waiting, monumental, a
few steps away from my face: I sensed it there, and even when
I inhaled deeply it didn't approach, it observed me in some
way, gathered up in a single point and from there it watched
me as an odor will do, in a sneaky, dirty way. During part of
the night it stayed that way in front of me, at a distance.
Upset, I decided not to think about it, and it didn't get any
closer but made itself felt insidiously, like an odor that's refused to let itself be inhaled, a base, humble, and prideful
odor, a funereal stench, beyond, always beyond, with a subtle
pharmaceutical taste.

The next morning I thought back without pleasure on the
previous evening. I noticed that during the night I had taken
as plausible the idea that, if he was dragging his leg, it was
because of a hatchet blow I had landed when I was younger. It
was just an after-dark fantasy, because he limped. The news-

67

papers said that he had received a fairly serious injury to the hip in an attack. And yet my explanation seemed true and made me happy. I was gripped by another idea: why had Louise agreed to work with him, to serve as his secretary at home? Why, instead of leaving, had she incrusted herself on the house? Now, even if she had been removed for one reason or another, she would certainly have managed to bore a hole from below in order to come back and continue, in the darkness of the cave, her endless ratlike labor. She hated him, it was obvious, you could smell it—and still that scene from before remained, I'd never forgotten it, unlike the other one with my mother. One day he took her on his lap, he stroked her face, kissed her hand, and she neither scratched nor slapped him. She stared at him in a remark-able way, profound and silent, even though she was already twelve years old, even though she had never been a girl you could put on your lap without risk, and at this age less than ever. And she looked at him, maybe without gentleness but without anger, in a serious and profound way. Seeing me, she didn't move, but he let her slip down fairly quickly, after softly touching her hair. I turned my back on them, I was horrified, distraught: at that moment, for sure, the axe blow would have been a pleasure, and I would have gladly stran-gled her, too. But even after this incident she still dominated me. She seemed neither uncomfortable nor ready to be more courteous, so that I'd forgive her. Not at all; she seemed to hold me more in contempt, and even to hate me, as if I alone had been guilty. It was shortly after that that she threw the brick to punish me, she who had willingly been kissed and stroked.

One afternoon they decided I could go for a walk. 'For no more than fifteen minutes,' my mother said. The street was almost empty and it was very hot. Instead of heading for the park, we took a route that led to the big boulevard. Louise gripped my arm tightly, then let go and ran on ahead. I saw her slip off to a store window. Water was flowing, streaming, against this window: it came in hazy sheets, oozing from everywhere, and it gave the impression that it was seeping out, little by little replacing the solid transparency of the glass

1) building ; abstract structure
2) dirty
3) able to be touched ; noticable
4) ~~tready~~ ~~directly~~

with a moving and disturbing transparency of water. Through the open door I breathed in a cold smell, a stench of wetness and earth mixed with a stifling exuberance.

The taxi carried us along; houses started to pass by, always the same ones, and sometimes, when the car stopped, brilliant dresses floated back and forth, faces with long and brilliant hair—and all this, barely gone, reappeared. 'We're in a hurry,' said Louise, tapping on the glass. The same cold perfume, the same smell of earth and basements, came from her now; again her dress was dull, and she herself had seemed to age, immersed in a mood that came from deep in the earth. We got out and, having crossed the portal, I stopped to look at the silent infinity, not a desert but rather a boundless expanse of structures, of rows of stone. No emptiness. There wasn't a corner that didn't have its piece of marble, not a meter of earth that wasn't covered and built up as if, for all those who had entered, there was only one watchword: construct, construct, raise up, pile pedestal on pedestal. All this resulted in a monstrous tangle of edifices, and yet it was a desert, but a desert that was afraid of itself, that had bewitched itself, and now tried sordidly to make a city spring from the ground, in the hideous form of these specters of construction, a city of holes, basements, and pits, summoned to last forever. We followed a huge avenue. On each side flowers bloomed; rare were the ones that had faded and dried; and everywhere the same odor—of candles, turned earth, and stagnant water. I wanted to slow down, but Louise, so close to the goal she had relentlessly been approaching through so many zigzags, by walking in an infinite circle, now could only run at it straight on; it drew her forward almost palpably, it forced her to go forward without looking around, without any detours. We went past mounds, stepping over cups and vases; we slipped behind columns. I felt her hand gripping mine so tightly it seemed that she was pulling me into the earth and that she wanted to pass her sweat off into my arms, onto my body. Her life was fleeing down the lawn, groping over the fissures, and it was already three-quarters swallowed by the earth.

When we arrived at the wall and the gate opened, I saw the

path with its two great cypresses and, a few meters beyond, the two tombs, one an arrogant little palace, with sculpted traceries; mawkish, delicate little columns; and overly brilliant stained glass. The other was heavy and massive, a kind of barely elevated tower squashed at its summit by a gigantic allegory. I was not surprised. I knew I had already been here with her, under the same sun, that I had met her, wearing the same dress, her hair hidden, insulting the sun with her disgrace. We proceeded past the box trees, approaching the two monuments—the one, brilliant, with its light funereal coquetry, young, lovable, almost happy, as if love here had been exclusively feminine, had sought to perpetuate charm, dreaming, and even betrayal and crime in the form of cheerful ideas and the perfectly gay heart that had held them—and the other, endlessly rising out of a black and tormented void, with naked virile pride, a regret, a monumental accusation, a dull and mute stone rancor. Then, before this couple slowly raised to the daylight by the madness and the patience from below, I knew that Louise, rejecting any reconciliation between these two pasts, would walk, with hatred, on the sentimental, ring-laden hand which kindly reached out to her from under the earth, and that she would revere, in horror, cursing, only the dark side of death.

She took a key and opened the door. She went down three steps, and I followed her. The darkness made me stumble. I couldn't see anything. It wasn't really black as night, but I couldn't distinguish anything. I couldn't see her. I went forward slowly, holding out my hand; I thought I would find her near the cenotaph at the back of the vault. I took a few more steps, I tried to see her in the half-light, but there was nothing in front of me, nothing next to me. I called her; I whispered her name, and I felt the name dissolve in my mouth, become anonymous, disappear, and I said no more. Then, gripped by a strange foreboding, I thought, she's killed herself, she's killing herself now, it can't end any other way. And, strangely, I was trembling, but not only from fear or horror—desire also made me tremble. At that moment, as I turned back, I saw her and was petrified. She was three steps away, set back into the wall, immobile in a kind of niche, stiff, arms flat against her

et. Her face, so often
d on me; there was no
ace. And yet her eyes w
ge, frozen way that I didn't
r that behind them there was some-
ing—doing the looking.
rd, I didn't go back, I just stood there,
denly I saw her mouth move, heavily
down,' she said. I turned around, with
e voice was coming from someone else
ned, I saw clearly the entire vault: it
row room, without a cenotaph, with-
oom, just a simple tomb, clean and
down,' she said. I knelt down and
 face against the stone. In this void
my breath, I rejected it, I pushed
ng, and the void itself made me
. was suffocating and, suffocating, the void filled me
with with a substance that was heavier, fuller, more crushing
than me. 'Stretch out,' she said. I stretched out. I heard the
sound of her steps, the sound of her dress, moving forward
and fluttering. Then she crumpled some paper and it fell to
the ground. Now she was near me, almost above me, and it
was my face that drained of blood, and my eyes were trained
on her and looked at her, and not my eyes but rather someone
was looking at her behind them, someone and perhaps nothing. I heard her murmur rapidly, 'As long as I live, you will
live, and death will live. As long as I breathe, you will breathe,
and justice will breathe. As long as I can think, there will be a
spirit of resentment and revenge. And now, I've sworn it:
where there was unjust death, there will be just death; where
blood has become crime in iniquity, blood will become crime
in punishment; and the best will become darkness so that the
worst will lose light.'

I heard this disordered low voice because I had already
heard it; and the words foaming on her mouth and, like foam,
moistening the corners of her lips, flowing, becoming sweat
and water—I had heard them. Suddenly I caught my breath,
and I stood up. I saw her distinctly: she came forward and

71

*shes*
*, irrelevant*
*3) overbearing*

leaned over. For a second she remained bent over me, and I saw her undo an enormous spray of flowers; their odor floated out and it was the very one that I had breathed during the night, smelling of earth and stagnant water. She scattered the flowers, leaned over further and, bowing her head, she undid her scarf, spread out her hair which cascaded, poured forth, touched me, buried me in a mass more black and dead than the earth of the garden. My feeling was nameless. I smelled that hair. I saw her hands approaching, slip the point of a shining blade into it: I heard the scissors open and bite. And what happened?

I saw that she too was running. I took a route that cut across, then another; sensing that she was gaining on me, I left the path and returned to the stones and columns, but in a second she was on me. We stood still, breathing painfully. When I raised my eyes I saw her hair falling down onto her shoulders, in beautiful intact layers. I have no idea what she read in my look. Her eyes became ashen, something snapped, and she slapped me—a slap that crushed my mouth. She had to take her handkerchief and, while we were rushing to the exit, wipe off my bleeding lip.

\* \* \*

'Where are you coming from? Where did you go?' asked my mother. Louise led me into her room. 'What have you done? You've been gone for nearly two hours. What happened?' She looked at her, then at me. 'Look at your brother: he's exhausted. He's had a choking fit. He must have been lying down for quite a while.' My mother approached me suspiciously; my fingers touched my lip. 'What happened to your mouth? Did you fall? It's swollen and puffed up. Somebody hit you.' She turned to Louise who, motionless, mute, was looking at her, her eyes bright, too bright, and nasty. 'You're lying,' she screamed, 'I'm sure you're lying.' Louise stepped aside, took off her scarf and went to the mirror, shaking her head. 'Yes, I'm lying,' she said. Her hair fell, she combed it—it was intact. —'What an impertinent girl—what insolence!' My mother struck the floor violently with a chair. Louise came away from the mirror, her scarf in her hand:

walking past, she threw me a profound, complicitous glance. 'Stay here, I order you to stay!'

Later, I had a slight fever; it was a strange and restless night. In the morning I went up to Louise's room and told her I couldn't stay at the house.

'I'll get dressed,' she said. 'I'll get a car.'

# 4

The fog was lifting. I asked myself why I had had trouble recognizing my apartment. Because everything was impersonal? Hadn't I come back to my place? Through the window I saw the trees coming up out of the fog: they lacked all subtlety, they showed themselves too clearly, they tired me out as if they were screaming. Further on, still a little hidden by the fog, I knew there were houses; I could barely make them out, but they were there, just like mine, maybe a little different—so what? They were houses.

I quickly closed the curtains, and, like every time, there was a slight stirring that gave me hope: something tried to fade away, as if I were about to lose the ability to see behind me, as if the back of my neck and my shoulders, now blind, were willing to rest. I waited a moment. How stupid! Again, the light was everywhere, an ingratiating, suspect light, which, moreover, I saw, disclosed itself. Maybe this was an advantage: the other flowed into a sickly sweet clearness, an invisible blankness, it showed everything; it showed itself, I saw it at work, I thought it would attack and drown things, and that there would finally be a little disorder. I waited a moment. How stupid! There was neither darkness nor disorder, everything was in place, as clear as day. I went back to lie down. Despite the darkness, Louise was still reading. Angry, I ripped the book out of her hands and tore it up; all these pages and pages, these volumes. I threw it in the corner.

'Sorry,' I said, turning to the wall.

A little later dull music started outside, perhaps coming from a nearby house. It reached me softly and expressed nothing; little by little it escaped the neighborhood; elusive and sad, it went from one place to another, from one world to another. Then suddenly it broke out and became public. Why hadn't I recognized it? There must have been national mourning, and the funeral march went looking for each of us, in houses and streets, it unified us in common sadness, where pain meant something for everyone and became a celebration, a funeral celebration but a celebration nonetheless. This music was slow and solemn; it had always carried me away. I saw the huge catafalque, set up above the crowd; the fog too had lifted; the army marched, delegations paraded; in the neighboring streets, thousands of people, packed together, heard from afar the cadence of marching. I was surely there, I couldn't be distinguished from them; my face, like theirs, raised up to the monument, was a face among thousands of others; it didn't count, and still it counted. That was what was terrible—even absent, it counted; I was part of the procession, I was taken up in a stifling mass, I couldn't budge or find any support. I heard the sound of a single distant and interminable note, rising up against the sky. Didn't I hear it? Didn't I see my own sadness on the others' faces? And weren't they sad with my paleness, my fatigue? Short cries resounded. I hesitated; I was motionless and I floated; something came loose in my chest. I distinctly saw the faces fade away, becoming chalky and dirty; a wave came up into my mouth. As I vomited I told myself that my vomiting too expressed their sadness, that everyone was going to feel himself vomiting with me in a common feeling that would make my seizure pointless.

Louise, after wiping my face, stood still for a moment, her forehead moist. I felt fine, but now she was disturbed; she too participated in my attack; nothing had been missed. She went into the kitchen, came back with water, and washed me. The music had stopped. Somebody was talking in long monotonous sentences. I suspected that Louise had completely misunderstood this incident; she explained my retching in her own way—she must have thought I was sick or overcome by last night's flight. But it was hardly important. In any case, unfortunately, she explained it.

\* \* \*

A few weeks ago I would have been scared by misunderstandings. Now they gave me a moment's rest—a moment, a very short moment. Even looking at Louise and forcing myself to believe that she wasn't Louise but instead, for example, a nurse, I couldn't forget how slight the difference was: she was a nurse for me, she took care of me, that was all. (Besides, I didn't believe in this nonsense.) It was necessary, I thought, to slow down this flow of reflections passing through me with incredible speed. Everything's going too fast, it's running, it's as if I always had to walk faster, and not only me but also other people, things, dust; everything is so clear; these are the reflections that never get confused, the thousands of infinitely small and distinct shocks. For a whole night I listened to the window rattle. It was a neutral vibration, always faster, always closer to breaking: and now I *am* this window that rattles. I looked at Louise, I would have liked to have spoken to her, but it was strange—I asked myself if at this very moment I wasn't talking to her. She looked vaguely around the room; what she saw, I saw; she was in front of the wall, as I was, in front of the spot on the wall, as I was; what she was thinking was also on the wall, or it was somewhere, in the city, perhaps at my parents'. Yes, certainly, she was thinking of my mother, she was waiting for a phone call, or whatever; it wasn't mysterious, all she had to do was say it to give me some idea. How would we have been able to understand each other if I hadn't first talked to her in a certain way? I did speak to her, that was obvious if only in the way she stayed next to me, in the same room and with the same thoughts. It caused a buzzing, a muffled and indefinitely sustained note, which called out to her and permitted us to stay together.

I wanted to listen to this sound, and only to this sound. It had the regularity of the ringing of a bell, quite close to me, quite far away. I ran down the hall; it was there and it had even carried along Louise, who was in front of the door, looking at me. So was I right? It was as close as my own voice and probably, like my voice, there was nowhere in the world I couldn't have heard it. Only I never shut up. Louise, taking me by the shoulder, quietly brought me back. What did she think? That I was still sick, that I was going to take off? As soon as she imagined that, I had the proof that she had heard me and that she was listening: something was flowing from me, something I couldn't hold back, something I had mastered, and which I hadn't completely mastered. That's why I suspected I was speaking without really hearing myself speak: most of the time I made the distinction easily, sometimes it seemed that the words took off by themselves, I let them go in order to rest. Really, it was my right to do so. None of this was new. It was so natural that it was explained by the very fact that it took place, and it always took place, so that everything was continually explained.

During the night I started suffocating again. Louise quickly left to find help. I saw them come back together and they faced each other behind the glass door, under the lamp. I looked at him calmly; he was embarrassed and disconcerted.

'I was expecting to see you,' I said, 'but not at this hour. Louise was wrong to bother you.'

'Louise?'

'Yes, my sister.'

He turned to her slightly.

'Your sister? But she was right; I go to bed late; I had just gotten home.'

He stayed a little while and when I saw he was about to leave, I motioned.

'You see how things are. A few days ago, I would have done everything to avoid you. I even left so I wouldn't have to see you again. Now I've come back, you still live in this house, and you're the one who's bothered at night.'

He looked at me in a strange way—disconcerted and interested.

'You left in order not to see me?'

I nodded.

'Why? You find me so disagreeable?'

'Not disagreeable, not much, not all the time. You bothered me, I told you. Right now . . .'

'Right now?'

'I have the impression that you don't bother me any more. I think I'd even enjoy speaking with you, at least right now; I mean that's the impression I have right now, with you here. Maybe it won't last. Maybe I'm simply happy to be able to speak, and before you were here I wasn't calm enough to do it.'

78

'You feel upset?'

'I'm not upset. I remember one of the things that drove me away from you was that in my mind you were associated with the idea of sickness. You treated me as if I were sick, and I was afraid that you would take advantage of my condition. And for me, on the other hand, you were the one who was strange, abnormal. Whereas now . . .'

'Now?'

'I don't know. I see it was foolish, naive. It makes no difference whether I'm sick or not.'

'You certainly aren't seriously ill. I'll come back to see you soon. This is your sister?'

'Yes, Louise.'

'I hadn't suspected. There's no resemblance.'

'Yes there is. We look a lot alike.'

He didn't come back. I only had Louise to look at. She tidied up, walked around the room: her movements were all predictable. You would have said that she had lived her whole life with this same furniture: her hand knew all the pieces in advance, and took hold of them in a knowing way. That's surely why she managed to be so perfectly quiet. She disappeared in what she was doing, she slipped away and things slipped away too.

Still, eventually, once again I felt myself on fire. One day I told her I was going to go out. My impatience was too great, it was so great that I could also not have gone out, it was becoming a kind of patience. I took a little walk in the street. I wanted to breathe the air outside, see other people, especially passersby. I looked at them eagerly: everyone, from afar, closer, then another glance. For the whole time I watched them coming, I knew that I wasn't seeing them, neither their clothes nor their features, not even their manner, and still they showed themselves completely, they were at my disposal, I was looking at someone. It was a little different for the women, at least for the ones who arrived through something, a color for example, the color red. I didn't see them better than the others: on the contrary, much less. They refused to appear, and that's why I stared at them.

Arriving at the square, I was struck by the furious movement of the cars, whose paths intersected; they hurtled out of the darkness of the avenue, suddenly slowing down; the pedestrians crossed as best they could. Everything came and went crazily; it was as significant as an official parade: cars, bicycles, people, the procession was infinite and always the same. I was exhausted by it, but I could no more turn away from it than one can move away from a demonstration as long as it keeps going. I was part of the parade as soon as I looked at it, and as long as I paraded I couldn't keep from looking at it. On the avenue, I felt a little tired. It was still dark; the streetlights hadn't been turned on yet. I saw that one of the little streets leading into the shopping area was blocked, with a barrier of the kind one sees on roads being repaired, but more solid and forbidding. A little farther on, at the start of West Street, the same kind of barrier was set up, with policemen. I hesitated before approaching. Cops and rifles kept me from getting to the sidewalk. The blocked-off street seemed calm; the storefronts had disappeared; a few windows were still open; on a little balcony, aligned in a naive way, six geraniums in pots appeared, the last two with red flowers. Craning to see, I made out at the end of the street piles of rubble which must have come from a house being razed — the whole width of the street was filled with it. This is bad news, I thought. I felt discomfort, as when one confronts a tricky and hypocritical idea; it was unhealthy; it came from the street, but also from the cops. This area must have been one of those condemned to a demolition made possible by the threat of the epidemic. The entire street, with its questionable appearance, its run-down façades, its look of a sick man struck down suddenly, seemed to be calling for its own condemnation. It accepted it passively, and I, looking at it, saw this condemnation displayed, painted on the walls. Seeing it, I associated myself with it, and anybody else who participated in it with me was as responsible as I was. All you had to do was walk by: the passerby fulfilled a duty. Wasn't it extraordinary? I had gone out for a few minutes with Louise, I wanted to take a walk — and what was I doing? I was making the law circulate, I was contributing to the application of a public decree. This should invigorate me, I thought, and help me live. And still, I felt very uncomfortable. Knowing that everyone was grateful for my glance and that even those on the other side of the barrier, those condemned to isolation and destruction by this glance, were grateful—what could I do? I couldn't stand it; it bored a hole in my sight. In other words I really tolerated it, in spite of everything; for this hole changed nothing, I didn't even go away. I continued to look according to the rules, seeing what everybody saw, and the discomfort itself, also absorbed by the rules, became an honorable feeling of sadness provoked by the spectacle of common misfortunes.

The walk ended. In front of our building a boy, who was hanging onto a male nurse's white coat, came out of a taxi and was drawn too quickly toward the wide-open door. After we crossed the street and entered the foyer, I heard the elevator going up, maybe to the fifth floor—maybe my own. Rushing into the stairway after them, going up and seeing nothing, I was suddenly stopped and pulled backwards, brutally and violently. I could hardly breathe. I saw a hand, a bare arm, a boxer's arm. I let myself be led, I had the feeling that we were going up together, that he was pushing me into the room, that he was telling me to wait. I was barely aware that he was leaving. Even before I got back up I felt annoyed and offended by such a lack of formality. He took no notice—he threw me there, and then he left; he was acting as if he were my guardian. I felt so distrustful that I thought he was hiding behind the door; I ran over to open it. No one was there—he was completely ignoring me! And why, I wondered, was he in shirt-sleeves, one of them pulled above the elbow? But when I saw him come back, go to a coat rack, take a jacket, and put it on in an absent-minded way, when I saw this face, still so amazingly large, coming up and going back, finally coming to a stop above the desk and turning to me, he seemed so tired and so faded that I again felt a slight sympathy for him, even though such a monumental fatigue must also be very dangerous.

'Who was that injured person? Why was he brought here?'
'An injured person?'
'You know,' I said, 'I can guess a lot of things. One day you

told me, "You think too much." Maybe that's not your expression, but you said something like that. I don't believe I think too much. Still though, sometimes I do get the impression that at some point there *is* a "too much." Even when I don't think, I think too much. Well, maybe this too much is for you.'

He looked at me with his exhausted, expressionless horse-face.

'You seem very tired,' I remarked.

'You mean, Let's chat, or do you really have something to tell me?'

I was sitting on his sofa; this room seemed so different from the one I had visited before—it had been repainted and refurnished, rather luxuriously.

'Coming here, I noticed some changes. I ignored these changes, I acted as though they had nothing to do with me. But I could just as easily have taken them into account.'

'Changes—what changes?'

'It doesn't matter. But I wanted to let you know that, even if I close my eyes, even if I seem to be mistaken about things— if, for example, I take you for someone else—it would be wrong to see this as a serious misunderstanding. Whatever I do, I still know who you are.'

'What do you mean? What are you talking about?'

'A little while ago I took a walk in the street. I wanted to see some new faces. Maybe this seems childish to you, but I take a certain pleasure in looking at passersby. And everybody's like that, everybody likes to look, they look at each other, it's striking. Coming into a little square, and having seen someone, I suddenly had this idea: you're in the street now, I've just met you, because you're only a passerby, like the others. For a few seconds the impression was so strong that I couldn't resist it, I really did see you, I did more than see you, because I didn't see anyone else. Why are you making a face?'

'Did you really see me?'

'Yes, I saw you. In similar cases, it's not exactly called seeing. Does one *see* a passerby? After all, you were only a passerby.'

'Do things like this happen to you often?'

'Sometimes. I'll tell you something else. A year or two ago I shared an office with a co-worker, a young man who was highly rated. He worked hard but was taciturn. He was taciturn to an extraordinary degree. For days on end he didn't say a thing, not once—he just said hello or shook my hand. Eventually the situation became intolerable. I couldn't look at him, I was afraid I'd hit him. I took steps to change offices; my boss asked me why, and I couldn't hide it: it was impossible to get along with this guy. You can imagine my surprise when I learned that he too had asked for an office change, and for the same reason: I had never said anything to him. Then it hit me like a bolt out of the blue. It wasn't true, but didn't this happen because I was the same as him—and how could I make it clear that my silence was perhaps only the echo of his own?'

'Is this a tall tale?'

'No . . . why? It's not a tall tale, it happened when I was younger. I see that you've put in new furniture. Have you settled in for good?'

'No doubt about that.'

'First I thought that this would only be your pied-à-terre, that you had to move a lot. But it's natural that you've given up such precautions. You're a strange man.'

I looked at him.

'You'll have to take this into account,' I said with all the strength of the thoughtless sympathy I felt. 'I'm a trap for you. Even if I tell you everything—the more loyal I am, the more I'll deceive you: it's my frankness that'll catch you.'

He started laughing. His laughter struck me as insolent and sullen.

'Don't worry about me,' he said. 'How do you come up with ideas like that?'

'I don't come up with ideas. I think what everybody thinks. Maybe it's because you're everyone's enemy, because you've already become a reformer, a schemer, that you don't notice it. I can hardly be wrong about you, you know.' I let him come closer. 'Even if you aren't,' I said, grabbing him by the jacket, 'it would still be . . . well, really it could only be you.'

'Why are you laughing?' he said, looking at me nastily.

Then, abruptly, he grabbed my wrists. 'Let's wind this up. You know perfectly well that I'm not any of those things, but only your doctor. I'm taking care of you. You've got to trust me.'

I tried to get loose, but he held on.

'Why are you acting as if I'm someone else?' he shouted. 'Why do you talk about reforms and schemes?'

I felt him trembling; I too was trembling.

'Watch out,' I yelled, 'not a step closer!'

He certainly wanted to throw himself on me. Finally he stepped back to the door. He's going to call out, I thought, he's going to . . .

'What difference is it to me that you're a doctor? You are, you aren't. I know all that. And this building could easily be a clinic. What difference does that make? It's stupid.'

'All right,' he said. 'Let's stop fighting.'

'It's almost unbelievable the way you try to cling to your persona. You stick to your gestures, your words. You throw just about anything in my face to get recognition. You lean against the wall, as if you want to leave your traces. And your profession? You find it intolerable to have been rejected, to be there only halfway, you want to belong to it completely, to be one with it, to leave no gap and to never be in someone else's place. Don't you notice it yourself? It's almost crazy. That's where my earlier dislike came from, you raise my hackles. Listen—I don't want to hurt you—I'd like to enlighten you. Really, this need not to be taken for another, this violent instinct, for you've suddenly become violent. This rage should not be confused—don't you realize it gives you away? Even if you had a different face, if your face was only a mask, just about anybody could recognize you, you who don't want to be just anybody, you who cling desperately to yourself in order to distinguish yourself, to be someone special, an anomaly, an exception to the rules, an exception that does not know, that crushes, the rules. Calculation shows through in every one of your gestures; even if there were, right here, right now, a pile of papers proving your illegal activities, I could know a thousand times more just by looking at you. Really, since our first meeting I've studied you, I haven't stopped looking at you: your way of being, of walking, of behaving, it's what is in you that works against the law, it's a desperate effort to scheme, to conspire, an effort—but not even an effort because suddenly, as you yourself are finding out, no scheming is possible, everything's already gone out the window, you are anyone, a doctor, and you start shouting, "I'm your doctor, you mustn't take me for another," so that your protest, at that very moment, betrays you again, and again it's scheming, the hope of scheming, and it all starts over.'

I was scared, I'd gone too far: he was so perfectly immobile there in the middle of the room, he seemed so distant that I had the feeling he was going to kill me. And when he turned to me I stood there, frozen.

'Let's stop fighting,' he repeated.

'Why . . . why did you force me to talk this way? I don't want to hurt you. On the contrary, at times I feel the need to help you. Enlighten you, sort things out with you, loyally—with the others it's useless, but with you it seems to me I'd find relief doing it. I've got too much understanding and it bothers me, since I haven't found real ignorance to <u>dissipate</u>.'

We looked at each other steadily.

'How did you get there?' I said. 'Was it tempting? Dizziness? Unless you were simply ordered to spy on me?' I still was staring at him. 'It's no secret there's no shortage of spies. The best citizens need to feel they're under suspicion. It's a duty to make them uneasy: you bother them and at the same time you watch them.'

'And if I am a spy?'

'Unfortunately, you're not. So what do you want to do? Do you want to stand up to the State . . . weaken it?'

'Does that scare you? It's a crime, isn't it?'

'No, not a crime, a deception. It's useless, impossible, even stupid.'

'Stupid? That's a good one.'

'You're not taking what I say seriously. According to you I'm sick, and what I say is only of interest as a symptom linked to a disease. Is that it?'

'Perhaps. But do you yourself have another opinion?'

85

'No, I am sick, I know it. I'm overworked by my ideas—in other words, I don't think about anything, and yet I can't get rid of what I think.'

'You have this feeling? Do you really think you're sick?'

'Yes, I am sick. My ideas smack of sickness.'

We just looked at each other. He sat down next to me on the sofa.

'Which ideas, exactly? What's bothering you?'

'Personal things.'

'Do you have some problems? Maybe I can help you: you should trust me.'

'Thanks. . . . But why you?'

'I don't know. I listen with interest. Basically, you impress me.'

'You're flattering me to get my secrets. Well, why not? I left my family when I was very young. My father died suddenly, when I turned seven. A little later my mother remarried. She had two small children to raise, mind you. Since she was young—she had an extraordinarily youthful look for a long time—a second marriage was inevitable. She married one of my father's colleagues, a very remarkable and important man.'

'Why did you leave your family?'

'Why? I ran away. Yes, one fine day I disappeared, out of bravado, to amaze my sister. You know her. I'm very attached to her: she's a terrible girl, she does exactly as she pleases, she's passionate, headstrong. She's strange. Besides, she's not strange, she's someone out of the past. By the way, did you really tell me once that you wanted to compromise my stepfather?'

'What makes you laugh all of a sudden?'

'Nothing; anyway, that's my story. What do you think of my sister?'

'Your sister . . . she seems very devoted to you.'

'Yes, she despises me; she's nasty and hateful. When she was little she burrowed into cabinets or even into the trash can, and she stayed there for hours on end—she wanted to feel bad and look like a slut, that was her ideal. Since then she's grown up, but her ideal's the same.'

'What behavior! But aren't you exaggerating? Why did she act like that?'

'To bother my mother, I suppose, to punish her. Or out of modesty, or a taste for purity. And that too was part of the story.'

'The story?'

'Look at this scar. One day she threw a brick at my head. Why? Because things had to be that way, I had to bear this mark. She's always loved to lie. Even when she was very small she slipped in everywhere, she spied. You've seen her, she's small, dark, ugly. Whenever my mother thought she was alone, alone or with someone, this black thing was there too, in a corner or under a table, spying. As for punishing her— how would you do it? She chased after punishment, she wanted it above all.'

'Did she make you leave?'

'She didn't make me. She holds me in contempt, but she doesn't see anything beyond me. I ran away to make her see that I was capable of something exceptional. Besides, the initiative also came, perhaps, from my parents, who wanted to get me away from this bad influence. Anyway, I spent part of my childhood in the country. None of this is important.'

'But haven't you just visited your family? You've made up with them now?'

'Yes, made up; I've rid myself of this whole business.'

He looked at me morosely. It was already getting dark.

'Does my story seem banal? You've put your finger on it: it's banality itself. Listen,' I said suddenly, 'a lot of situations repeat themselves, no doubt about it. They recur: yesterday, today, a long time ago. They come back, they come from the dawn of time, it's happened once, ten times, and in spite of changes of detail, it's always the same event. Don't you find that strange?'

'Why are you shaking? What does that mean?'

'It means . . . Now you're listening! Now you're paying attention. You know my family?'

'Naturally; your stepfather's name is in the papers.'

'Are you aware that he's a perfectly superior man, first rate? He works constantly, he directs everything, he's everywhere.

He doesn't seem to be just one person but a great many, more than a great many, and at the same time unpretentious, almost unassuming. My sister hates him.'

'And you?'

'Not me.'

'You don't hold it against him at all? After all, he replaced your father.'

'Yes, my father. You know, I never knew him very well, I can barely remember him. He was like you, big, strong, but more severe, almost stately—you know?'

'I see. Still, you speak of him with veneration. Deep down you're quite proud of your family.'

'Not at all,' I said sharply. 'For me they're cardboard characters—I can't quite think about them. I get the impression that they still don't know what exactly they are: they're waiting. And me, I wait with them.'

'What could they be waiting for?'

'For me to decide, maybe. Think about it: all the events of history are there around us, just like the dead. From the beginning of time, they flow back to today. Sure, they've existed, but not completely; when they were produced, they were no more than incomprehensible and absurd outlines, terrible dreams, a prophecy. They were lived without being understood. But now? Now they're going to exist for real, now's the time, everything's reappearing, everything's being revealed clearly and truthfully.'

'But your family?'

'Hollow statues. Whenever I see Louise, it's not her that I see but, behind her, other, more and more distant faces, some well known, others unknown; they stand out as her successive shadows. That's why she harasses me, she doesn't give me a moment of peace; it's a spiral. And my mother can't even look me in the face, she coddles me and spies on me—but she never faces me. That's how scared she is that her gaze will call up from behind me some terrible figure, a vague memory that she mustn't see. Listen to me now: the darkest bloody horrors, the earth's worst convulsions come down to us, come down to me, from the dawn of time. Books talk about it, but I don't have to read them, I know them. All these stories stand in the background, daunting, motionless—and they wait: they wait for me to do something, so they can take shape through my life. Listen—listen well—nobody knows yet what they'll be, for they haven't really happened yet, they've only been a first, dreamy try, groping, starting again, century after century, before the true completion others will give them today. Now is when we're going to understand the truth about all the horrible things, now is when this long-ago life, suspended for so long, rotting and contaminating our houses, is going to show itself as it should be. It's going to be settled and judged once and for all, according to the law.'

A second later I saw that he had stood up and was pacing. He passed silently in front of his desk, glided past the chairs— and suddenly his steps, resounding now, struck the floor powerfully, like a hammer of stone and lead; then, once again soft and smooth, they faded away.

'These are the kinds of ideas that are tormenting you?'

'They aren't ideas.' I listened to his step hammering the floor and then suddenly enter a region of sleep, a dead region. 'Have you always suffered from insomnia?'

'Sometimes. You'll have to be more honest with me: are you projecting something?'

'Like what? You think I'm fixated on something, that I'm an obsessive. You're observing my behavior? You've got it all wrong—I'm not feverish or delirious, I'm not sick. And I have no desire to be frank.'

'Didn't you say a little while ago that you yourself thought you were sick?'

'No doubt about it, it's true. When you listen to me, I'm a sick person. In coming to you, my words come to sickness; it's through sickness that they reach you. Otherwise they wouldn't even make it to your ear, you'd pay no attention to them, or they'd mislead you even more. Aren't you still a doctor? Well then, I must be sick. For the time being, that's how we relate to each other.'

He took a few steps, then started laughing.

'You're tiresome,' he said, continuing to walk.

He laughed again, a humiliated, awkward laugh. I heard him walk away; with all his weight he crushed thousands of tiny shells, a thousand living, frightened noises. Then he came back and, without noticing it, penetrated softly into the dead part of the room. He kept going and once again rolled along, sending out a cloud of sand and dust. I thought that during his sleeplessness he must have walked like this, up and down, through the drowsiness of his blood summoning sleep in vain.

'I suppose you've heard,' he said, 'that the building is going to be turned into a dispensary. We've already taken over the first two floors. The other floors will become a reception center for people from the neighborhood who have had to leave their homes and who are sick. So you can't stay here.'

'Are you serious?'

'In any case, you'll have to leave. Your place is not here. The sanitary conditions are bad. Any number of unpleasant things could happen at any time.'

'The building's going to be requisitioned?'

'Maybe. In any case, circumstances have already requisitioned it.'

I was listening so hard it hurt; I even felt a sharp pain in my thigh.

'A dispensary? But if it's going to be a dispensary, why couldn't I stay? I'm sick, I'll be treated on the premises.'

I heard him laugh again.

'We'll take in other sick people, those in a special category. So you see, Henri Sorge, contrary to what you believe as a member of the ruling class, everything isn't perfectly fine everywhere. You walk around in the streets, and what you see pleases and comforts you. You go into houses, and everybody you meet seems satisfied, good citizens, workers, rich in the public good, sometimes poor but nevertheless very rich. But I personally don't go into houses, I don't walk around in the streets. I go underground and there I meet people who are very different. I see walled-in people, people who've fallen into the depths of humiliation and shame and who turn this shame into pride, people who've fallen out of official life and who, in order not to go back, prefer to live outside of life, without name, daylight, or rights. For them, what you call true enlightenment is the depths of the pit, and your freedom

90

is their prison. And they are neither devoted workers.
good; they have no civic spirit, they give nothing away, .
they don't go around constantly repeating, like you, "Ah! I'd
like to help you, I'd like to enlighten you." They're not demanding wealth, only to be poor against you, to be criminal
against you. And through your trickery and your spirit of
domination, you're trying to take that away from them as
well. Do you want to know why I became interested in your
case, why I ended up spending a lot of time with a satisfied
and talkative young man? Because of your name? Perhaps.
But above all because you're so devoted to this world that
even when your thoughts become really bizarre they're still
prompted by it, they reflect and defend it. Even your sickness
wants to indoctrinate me. Sure, you've taught me that. It's
impressive. It's worth the trouble.'

He kept on walking; his walking was killing me.

'You're satisfied,' he said, 'but a lot of people don't share in
your satisfaction.'

'But it doesn't come from me! It's a universal satisfaction! I
find it everywhere: when I breathe, when I look. It's here in
this room, I feel it, I can't get rid of it, it enters every pore.
Even when something goes badly, I feel it like a halo around
evil, it doesn't leave me; it was in your words as it's in mine. If
you hadn't lost the spirit, you'd know that it's there, and that
it's spying on us.'

'That's enough!' he shouted.

'And you say you're poor, that you give nothing? But what
are you doing right now? I see you in the darkness, you're
walking, leading me along, I know everything about you; I
see right through you; I understand you from every vantage
point, I grasp you, and it's you that you're explaining. Thanks
to you this night is bright, incredibly bright. You're enlight-
ening me, you're helping to make me a good citizen, you're
incessantly putting me back on the right track. What do you
think? Isn't it marvelous?'

'That's enough!' he shouted.

'Yes, I'm satisfied. And this satisfaction isn't mean-spirited;
it's noble. I feel noble and true, I can't help it. I'm obviously a
nonentity, a helpless fledgling. In any case I'm only a zero

because the law is everything, and that's why I'm satisfied. And I'm everything because of the law, and my satisfaction is measureless, and for you it's the same, even when you think the opposite, and *especially* because you think the opposite.'

I suddenly noticed that he'd turned on the light. For a few moments I continued to stammer; I still wanted to talk, I had to, or write. I was about to ask him for a piece of paper when he indicated that he had to leave. Following him, I entered the dead part of the room, whose boundaries were marked by a thick red carpet. In the hallway, the door facing his apartment was half open; he pushed it open and brazenly went in.

'But,' I said, 'isn't this where the young woman lives?'

'Look around.'

He flicked the switch and made me go in. It was a total mess; the wall between two of the rooms had been knocked down, leaving a fairly large single room.

'When the wall separating this place and yours is knocked down,' he said, 'then we'll have a real room.'

'So she must have left?' I asked timidly.

That thought took hold of me and it made the future look very dark indeed.

# 5

I left without incident. The smell started to invade the house. It wasn't confined to the lower floors: it came up the stairway, wafted down the hallways. Until now my room hadn't been affected, but I often smelled it on me. The street had its inscrutable morning look, which made you think it was lit in plain daylight here and there by weak streetlights. Squads of police were stationed at street corners. When the cars, with their calm mechanical benevolence, gently stopped between two subway stations, I noticed in the general immobility that the train held four times as many people as usual. Nobody moved, I didn't move; singular, brilliant, and frozen, a few faces stood out only to disappear again in the enormous, immobile mass. The lights went out. Through the window the tunnel was still lit; it had a flickering radiance that seemed to come from deep underground. Then those lights went out. Nobody talked; I didn't talk. The black of the arched roof still glistened, like the heat of black skin. Then that glint faded out. The train softly penetrated the darkness with its calm mechanical torpor. Nobody seemed to breathe; I didn't breathe.

At the station the crowd carried me along: along passages, on stairways, outside, the same crowd, immobile, shot through with sudden shivers, then falling back to inactivity, then again shaken with shivers, not advancing yet always going forward en masse, so that the streets rose up like nearand distant ramparts, endlessly raised and strengthened by those who tried to cross them. I was hardly surprised when I reached the shop, since during the journey I vaguely understood where this crowd was leading me, with its dreary patience which made it stagnate for hours in narrow streets and then suddenly burst through with a torrential speed toward a goal it had suddenly discovered—and all this to reach the brilliant shop window against which fog streamed. I entered and the fog came with me, the fog that replaced everything. I pushed the door open. 'What happened to you? Did you fall?' I heard these words come from beyond the fog, spoken by a disembodied voice, a voice that itself possessed a body, completely different from mine, fertile and eager—ah, a really beautiful voice. Then, suddenly, the fog was swept away. The room shone in all its brilliance. I saw her standing there, big and strong, like a vigorous peasant. Dozens of portraits sparkled around her, all with the same eyes, all looking out from a calm realm of luxury. The flowers on the counter were still radiant, flowers that could never wilt, as if time did not pass for them.

'The subway's on strike,' I said. 'I got caught in a crush of people. I think they're fighting in the streets.'

I didn't leave the door; she didn't come up either—her eyes focused listlessly on my clothes, which were probably dirty and rumpled.

'You're feeling bad?' she asked.

In spite of the sympathetic tone, I didn't sense in her expression the voice that had come from behind the fog, the bodiless voice, itself corporeal. This one was perfectly helpful and good, but it came from anywhere, and I didn't see why I should get any closer. I'll take things calmly, patiently, I thought.

'Why did you come back? You mustn't come here any more.'

She turned her back on me. I looked at the relaxed shoulders, the red embroidery around the collar of her blouse. Small freckles formed a little constellation on her neck. 'Don't move,' I murmured. She turned around; my pallor must have scared her.

'You're white,' she said, pushing me into a chair. 'Do you want some cologne?'

She came back with her bottle and swabbed my face with the alcohol. At that point some customers came in; she got up on a chair and chose a frame, which she held up; she spoke to them with her kind and perfectly good voice. Back at the counter, she leaned over to write unhurriedly in the register, with meticulous, steady motions devoted entirely to their task. But the fact that she was an excellent employee also pleased me.

1) extravogent
2) boldness; brass

'Why did you move out of the building?'

'The neighborhood was too far away.'

'It was too far? So you left because of your work?'

'Yes. For a long time I'd been looking for an apartment: I wanted to get out.'

'Where do you live?'

'Around here,' she said, vaguely pointing the way.

She turned back to the door, as if to stand in front of another customer. Again the little spots on her neck showed up with a certain profligate self-confidence. They seemed to expand—they let themselves be seen as completely as if there were no one to see them, as if they were invisible, so brazenly did they show themselves. 'What is it?' she said. 'A parade?' She opened the door. I was jolted by the noise of motors, of loud cars in endless procession. Because she was standing in the doorway, from my chair I saw nothing but the fog and the mass of people. The whole store was shaken by the noise, there was a powerful vibration, a solemnity that forced its way through to reach the smallest objects and take them over with an incontestable authority. 'Close the door, please!' I cried. She had gone out on the sidewalk: the spectacle fascinated her. She would gladly have let everything go in order to join the crowd.

'They're huge military vehicles,' she said. She looked at me absent-mindedly. 'It's a big parade.'

She stood behind the shop window; from time to time she yelled to let me know that the police had signaled—and when a particularly impressive vehicle went by, making the windows rattle and the mirrors shake, she was up on her feet, enthusiastically clapping her hands and joining in with the cries of the crowd. 'Listen,' she said, suddenly turning around, 'horses!' I got up; I was breathing with difficulty. 'There've got to be fights,' I said, without coming closer.

'Do you feel better?'

She came back with a look that reflected her excitement of a minute ago. Her cheeks were shining, she looked so much like her photograph that I felt a pain in my chest. 'I have to talk to you,' I said, touching her. I held her away from me a bit; I looked at her; I wanted to see . . . I don't know what, maybe her face, but I only saw her smile and her nice appearance. 'So look at me!' I had to hold on to her more tightly, I was overcome with anger; by squeezing her I thought I could make her come out from behind this look shared by everybody and transform her once again. —'What's wrong with you? Are you crazy? Let me go!' She struggled; for a second her dress clung to me, she twisted her wrists, but I barely moved: yes, it's true, maybe it was going to happen again. 'I have to,' I said. 'Right away, right away.' She hit me again. 'Please,' she said, 'not here. Imagine if a policeman . . .' 'Yes,' I said, 'in the store.' But, as if these words had made her much stronger, she broke loose.

I sat still, breathing, waiting; she had gone into the next room. A moment later I found her looking at herself in the mirror.

'Please forgive me. I was acting like a demon.'

Without saying anything she raised her wrist a little in the mirror, as if to make me see the slight bruise.

'Did I hurt you much?'

'You almost broke my arm,' she said caustically, but with a certain conciliatory tone.

That moment I saw my own face in the mirror, behind hers; for a second we looked at each other. 'Ah!' she cried. Her cry rang in my ears while she led me, pulled me, along; I still heard it when I reopened my eyes, and it made me come to. I was on the sofa in the storage room, which had been completely transformed and redone and now looked like an attractive bedroom.

'Do you live here?'

'You frightened me,' she said. 'It was so sudden. I thought it was an attack. Is it epilepsy?'

'No, it's nothing. It's being annoyed, the lack of air. Can't you open the window? I only cause problems,' I said as I saw her move a table to get to the window.

'Really, your visits aren't that much fun.'

She left because someone was at the door. When she came back I got up to go, but I wasn't very steady on my feet. 'If you still need to rest for a few minutes. . . ,' she gestured as if to say; Stay, since you're here already. 'I have to go back to the store,' she added. 'Be reasonable and stay calm.' She went into the hallway, then came back.

'Do you want me to call a cab to take you home? You shouldn't have gone out. Have you been sick lately?'

'You're very nice. No, I'm not sick; just shaken up. It'll pass.'

'Your eyes are burning with fever,' she said, coming up and examining me with a kind of interest. 'You know that right now there are sicknesses going around—and especially in your neighborhood. Maybe it's the vaccine that's affecting you. You have been vaccinated, haven't you?' I indicated that I hadn't. 'Haven't they given you a shot? Everybody should get one—you're showing signs of the epidemic! For a week now they've been imposing harsh measures: the public's been put on notice. Hasn't the doctor come to your office? Haven't you been examined?'

'I haven't been to the office lately.'

'Why not? This is very disturbing. You're sweaty. Your pupils are dilated,' she said, looking at me closely. 'It's almost digging a hole in your eyes. The papers have mentioned that symptom. Maybe someone should be notified . . . your family.'

'My family?'

We looked at each other; her hand, reaching up to her throat, started playing with her pendant.

'Well,' she said, looking at the pendant awkwardly, 'haven't you spoken of your family, your sister?'

'My sister's no more concerned with me than with the other members of my family. I had a falling out with her—I don't see her. Let's drop it. If I were really ill, I'd be taken care of in my building, which they're turning into a dispensary. Didn't you know?'

'It's a dump,' she said. In her agitation, she thrust her face right in mine. 'That place is contaminated. Have you forgotten about the girl on the seventh floor and how she died? I'm sure that the contagion's already everywhere.'

'No, I didn't know she was dead.'

I sat back down on the sofa; she stayed standing, not far away.

'How did she die?'

'The doctor only came after she was dead. Right after, in the middle of the night, they took away the body. The next day the whole floor was evacuated.'

'What did she die of?'

She didn't answer. I only saw her thick waist and her motionless hand, hanging in the air.

'Could you let my family know?'

'Yes, I could do that,' she said, softly. 'I think it would be a good idea. It would reassure me.'

I looked at her and started to laugh. 'You're very nice!'

'Does that make you laugh?'

'Yes; why should you still be interested in me? How can you be interested in what happens to me? It's not your job to watch over me.'

She shrugged. 'Ah, you wear me out,' she said, starting to leave.

'Please . . .'

My cry reached her only slowly; perhaps she took another step. I saw her calm shoulders stop and wait, surprisingly still; then they stopped waiting, became stolid and heavy, and took on a fathomless passivity that was communicated to the air, to myself, to everything. My hand brushed against her and traveled along her sleeve; it followed the seam, bypassed the wrists, seeking, skimming, and suddenly there was the relief of exposed embroidery: it rolled, it embedded itself, my skin in turn became something as thick and heavy as the cloth. I heard her murmur something, then speak more loudly; my eyes opened, I saw her, and suddenly I recognized the face from the photo, the brilliant paper face. 'What?' she said. Then I grabbed her, shook her, carried along by the wish to see her be separated from herself, be separated from me, and become something else, something different. She fell. On the ground she let herself go, she was crazy—she grabbed me, pushed me back, and suddenly smothered me in arms of steel. That contact, drier and harder than the wood of the floor, that breathing, mixed with mine, in which I was breathless, the closeness to that disorder which, coming out of me, pressed an identical body against my own—all of this, in an ever brighter light streaming from the window, as if day had

98

waited for this moment to break, blew me away. I saw and felt everything: <u>inert,</u> I took part in her rage; tearless, I was her spasms and sobs; I absorbed, I drank to the point of nausea this false hatred of myself, this illusory estrangement that strove for aggressive intimacy. Suddenly, she broke down in fear; she opened her eyes. What did I have in my arms? Another being, another life, a good-bye to nothing? Always this same obvious look: nothing had changed. I stood while she slipped through the air as if she were passing through coils, and then I fell back on the sofa. For a moment I lost sight of her. And yet she hadn't moved, as I saw when I re-opened my eyes. She slowly wiped the palm of her hand across her eyes, and from time to time looked at me with still expressionless eyes. Mechanically she picked up the phone and began to dial.

'What are you doing,' I said hurriedly. 'Who are you noti-fying?'

'I feel sorry for you. I can't let you run around like this.'

Nevertheless she put down the receiver.

'Who did you want to call? How do you know that number?'

'Do you realize you're completely crazy? Don't start again,' she said, raising her voice. 'Don't give me that . . . maniacal look.'

I was taken aback.

'It bothers you, doesn't it, if I look at you. So you feel it too? It's terrible, I can't get over it.'

She kept on giving me what she called that maniacal look.

'I discovered it a little while ago—we look alike. We resem-ble each other amazingly, insanely, so that we could be taken for one another. We're the same. And you feel it too. My gaze bothers you, because it's your gaze: it's you you're looking at.'

'Be quiet,' she murmured.

'That's how it is; you can't blame me. We should merge. If we're distinguishable, it can only be through <u>subterfuges</u>, painful tricks, but a fleeting identity is constantly passing between us—which makes my presence false and yours null and void. That's why I can't touch you.'

'Be quiet.'

'I have to talk, I'm suffocating. There's no mystery—it's as if we know each other too well. You could say we've lived together for thousands of years, an eternity, a calm eternity, without accidents, without confinement, which little by little eliminated the space between us. We're too close.'

'Stop!' she shouted. 'We're completely different. I have absolutely nothing in common with you.'

'Yes you do. Our faces look alike, our thoughts are the same. With you I don't exist—I exist twice.'

'Our faces . . .'

'Yes, our faces. It's the worst of all, it's intolerable. Come here.'

I led her into the studio and shoved her brusquely in front of the mirror. Her face was next to mine, our heads were touching, and her eyes, fixed on mine, became troubled. Little by little the resemblance appeared before us. The mirror's world was taken over by the similarity; it was conspicuous everywhere, it reigned and dominated with contempt, with the serenity of an inaccessible presence. And I saw by her wild look that she herself recognized the resemblance, understanding it without being able to slip away; from now on she'd be endlessly haunted by it, as by the inescapable proximity of the law.

She slowly covered her face with her hands and walked blindly into the shop. I was still right next to her. She raised her head and looked at me quietly. The tears welling up in her eyes made them even kinder and more calm; tears filled her eyes and drowned them; they overflowed but didn't spill over. When they started to flow I left.

\* \* \*

In the square I wanted to throw myself into the crowd. A number of people were still waiting in little groups, random groups that I broke up just by passing through. The noonday sun had come out, but the background of this noon was dark. Cars passed slowly. A bus pulled up by the trees and all the little groups formed a continuous line that moved forward in an orderly fashion. The conductor, standing on the back platform, started to shout: each time, someone was designated, chosen. Those still waiting delegated that person to leave for them. The waiting started again. A man with a brown cap, his jacket carefully buttoned to the collar, looked at me from time to time. By the uniform I thought I recognized one of the couriers from city hall. 'I've been waiting for half an hour,' he said. 'I'll never have the time to get back to my place. It's no good.' I nodded. 'I haven't seen you around lately. Have you been sick?' — 'I'm on sick leave.' — 'A lot of people have been missing lately.' Another bus stopped with a shrieking of metal and the smell of tar; all the passengers were told to get off, and they formed a second line parallel to the first. This led to protests, and the policemen laughed: it wasn't their problem. Then I thought I heard someone say, in a low voice, a word that came from the dawn of time and that froze me in my tracks: Sabotage. I didn't turn my head, I didn't dare look at anybody, above all I couldn't turn to whomever, once this word had been spoken, this accusing murmur that put everything in question and which itself was so close to the forbidden that it almost wasn't possible to hear it in a group. Sabotage, Sabotage. My voice? I was paralyzed when I heard my own voice echo this obscenity. An obscenity, a stain. How had this happened? In the name of whom, against whom was it speaking? As an accomplice of the law? As its accuser? Its executioner? 'Silence, please!' said the cop, but his call to order was weak. He was helpless against this inarticulate cry that could very well destroy him. Around me a space opened up, people must have stepped aside, they didn't look at me, they didn't have the right, they waited fearfully, as if everyone ran the risk of becoming guilty. What to do? Where to go? 'Hey, wait a minute,' someone yelled at me. With my elbow I pushed him back, he turned to the person next to him; I saw this stupid obstacle, this presence of a principle that didn't want to give way. 'All right, calm down,' said the policeman. 'This gets to you after a while,' said my colleague, touching my elbow in a friendly and complicitous way, but at the same time he winked to the guy behind him. I recognized the nice boy style: from the usher to the highest commissioner we were all like that, indulgent, understanding, clarifying everything, reading things backwards and turning the worst rule violations into normal acts.

I left. I walked in street after street until I was dropping with fatigue. Just as I was reaching my neighborhood I ran into a police roadblock. Police were everywhere, at small street intersections, in front of cafés, around the square. People, waiting in three lines, presented themselves to the checkpoint police who, sitting outside behind tables, looked, listened, and made decisions. I gathered that, in principle, only the residents of the neighborhood had the right to pass; I thought, then, that this formality would not pose a problem. The inspector looked at me, then at my card. 'He's a civil servant,' he said, handing the card to his helper. Both of them were dressed like anyone else in the crowd, they spoke listlessly, passionlessly, and what they said didn't seem so bad, but it took my breath away. 'Why doesn't your card have a stamp?' He twisted the card as if he wanted to turn it into worthless cardboard. Suddenly he noticed my silence. 'Let's see—you work at city hall, Henri Sorge, twenty-four years old, you live at . . . Why hasn't your card been stamped?' The problem spread to the next table, where another inspector started to look at us, interrupting his work, so that the silence seemed even more prominent. My questioner, politely raising his voice, explained that all the people in the neighborhood had received the order to be vaccinated within four days. The deadline had passed the day before; as a civil servant, I was entitled to be treated by the medical service at city hall and, under these circumstances . . . he turned to his colleague with a questioning look. 'Certainly,' the other one said. 'Under these circumstances, your card should have the verification stamp—right here, see?' He showed me where with his finger. *I was sick, so I didn't go to the office on those days.* 'So,' he said with his policeman voice, 'you won't talk?' *I was sick, so I didn't go to the office on those days.* He looked at me with a hardness that robbed me of any hope of reaching him other than by mental words; his look was dust, summer dust. 'Why won't you answer?' asked the other, nicely. But he was called away to another table, so I lost his help. 'We're going to check your identity. You can wait at the police station.'

In the waiting room I couldn't make anything out, there was cold smoke circulating in the air. I only saw a policeman hand a package to a man sitting right next to me: bread and cheese. Stealthily the man offered me a chunk of bread. 'Shop-keeper? Engineer? Professor?' He whispered without looking at me, hastily tearing at his bread; his haste, the combination of anxiety and hunger, nauseated me. 'I'm a concierge,' he said. The policeman, passing nearby, looked at me for a second and then called a skinny, ragged boy, apparently very young, who was sitting alone on a bench; both of them left. A half-dozen men without caps or jackets were thrown into the room at that point, driven in by a shower of billy club blows; confined to a corner they lay there, curled up or stretched out. 'It seems I've violated the rule on furnished rooms,' said the man, turning away quickly. 'There are a few in my build-ing. The renters come and go, but the regulations are always followed. They arrested the manager yesterday, and yet he's experienced: he manages maybe fifty buildings. Aren't you eating?' He grabbed the piece of bread I was still holding and turned to someone else. A little later, I noticed that they had taken him away; just then I was called in by the captain.

'Your house is a real Noah's ark,' he said jovially to the concierge. 'Here's your card, Mr. Sorge,' he said, looking at me as if he wanted to burn my features into his memory for his own benefit.

The concierge, his face red, winked, probably to let me know that things were working out for him. Near the door, I recognized an underling from the clinic. Outside, people were hurrying.

The fog, thinner but damper than the morning's, relieved the police station's stale air, even though it seemed a continu-ation of that atmosphere, so that, finding it again in the street, I had the impression that I saw the fog come out along with us. On the steps it appeared below us as a cloud whose origin was the shops of the impoverished neighborhood; it had a consistency so thick that to plunge into it, it seemed, was to enter a particularly bright and real area. The market was empty. The narrow street descended silently into the fog; the merchants, who usually called customers to their stalls with piercing and sometimes menacing voices, were gone. The little stores were closed. An urchin, coming out of a side street, clomped along on his clogs. A little further on, I saw a motionless woman, her back against the shutters of a store, her hands in the pockets of a huge apron. Two other women, slipping in front of us, suddenly pushed open a door and disappeared. The street seemed to come to life. In front of a café that had a huge official poster on its windows my companion stopped, whistled, and shook the door, with no results. A few steps further on we came to another door which, half open, revealed the entry of a hallway; at the back, I made out two women illuminated by an oil lamp. 'Tobacco?' he asked them. They stuck their hands into a big bag and slowly hoisted heavy cuts of meat. My companion cursed. The farther down we went, the more people there were on the street. Right on the sidewalk some of the sellers stopped people and forced them to look into their bags. Everybody cut in front of everybody else. Buyers and sellers emerged form the fog only for a second and went back in so quickly, then appearing again so quickly, that one had the impression that with every step one was being hassled by the same elusive person who was always demanding the same thing, was always offering the same thing, without waiting for an answer. At the end of the street, five or six policemen, standing around a streetlight, their backs turned to the clandestine market, watched the women go by on the other side. They watched them, but because of the fog they probably didn't see them. They themselves were only visible from a certain distance because of the weak electric light that illuminated them, immobile, numb from the cold, and obstinately faithful to their task, which seemed to be to shine like the lights of a distant reef. We took a shortcut down Washhouse Street. Here all the houses seemed empty, the public washhouse had been abandoned, the water was stagnant. The air had been replaced by a sickly cold condensation that made itself felt in the shoulders more than in the mouth. My companion was almost running.

I reached the building with relief; I only wanted, at any cost, to find shelter in my room. But my satisfaction disappeared immediately. In the entryway there was a crowd of people, dozens of them—and also in the concierge's rooms, on the steps, on the second floor. And the odor was intolerable. It had gotten past the door, I smelled it behind the wall—what a disgrace! It was like a rallying cry, the premeditation of blind forces. Should I open the window? Outside the fog was coming up like coal water. In the hallway I heard, almost all night, coming and going, the breathing of winded men; on the other side of the partition there was walking, and scraping furniture. I lay down; the covers had the smell of cheap disinfectant, of carbolic acid. I saw the sickness come from afar and wander around the room; I was cold. What could the symptoms of the disease be? A kind of typhus? I wanted to write, I took hold of the notebook on the table, but suddenly the light went down to a thin red filament. Above, below, everywhere, they had stopped walking. There wasn't a twitch on the other side of the partition. The darkness was total. Suddenly, what a racket! It came from somewhere in the neighborhood, over by the avenue. I threw back the covers. I heard some muffled sounds, coming from the same location, a series of muted explosions. Then suddenly an enormous light appeared in front of me. Nearby, a flat, cold light, more terrible than fire—yes, a painting of fire. I stared at it, I walked slowly toward it, it resisted, in the end it stuck to the window. In the distance, behind the trees, an enormous stain arose; it took over the night, even its darkest corners. With the window open the inferno started to crackle, but in a calm way, as if, in order to feed it, someone was methodically breaking twigs. Nobody was at a window; there wasn't a sound. No wind. Instead, a heavy stillness, a massive summer choking on itself. In vain I waited for the howling of sirens. When I thought I heard them, it was like a distant memory, the echo of an echo. No doubt the rescue service was busy elsewhere. But had anyone even cried Fire here? Maybe I was the only one looking at the blaze—maybe that was already too much, looking was forbidden. I hung on to the railing. Above the trees there were large whitish flakes; bits of debris floated up to the house. At times the crackling became stronger, like the bursting of stones. Everything seemed about to go up in a single blast, the conflagration would become a paroxysm of rage, aggression—challenging everyone. But little by little the calm droning started up again; the fire was only a spool slowly and endlessly turning—it was patience and stupor. How could you stand it? It burned alone.

I sat on my bed for hours without moving. In the end the room became so intensely bright that I thought the fire was in the house. A little later I saw a harassing, violent daylight, an insane sun. I became extremely agitated because of this confusion: I felt a strong need to act, I wanted to go everywhere. Finally, I thought of my neighbor who had lived on the other side of the partition and who now . . . A memory of death. I was certain that I'd find her if I ran quickly into the apartment, and everything would be all right. I opened the door with such assurance that, once inside, when I found myself facing a man drinking and looking at me over his cup, I grasped that he was really the one I had come to see, in this devastated room that would become one with my room when I moved out. My confusion intensified. The room had barely been cleaned up; the floor was still littered with rubble; pieces of an iron bed were piled in the corner. The man, sitting back against the wall, had the repellant appearance of someone being transformed by a sickness; the beard, the tangled hair, the skin—he had to be very sick. I realized I was crazy for coming in.

'My body needs to drink,' he said. 'At night, when I can get up, I walk and I drink. After walking, I burrow under the covers, I sweat, then I drink. Then I walk again.'

He poured some kind of herb tea from a pitcher.

'Are you feverish?'

'Yes. It's a cunning sickness! First, the attacks are violent but short; then they're weaker but longer. Finally, the fever never goes away. My name's Dorte,' he added.

'Dorte?' I looked at him with the feeling that I knew not only his name but his face. He too looked like a statue, but a crumpled one. I was frightened to see how his face had been ravaged by the swelling.

'Why do you want to see me?' he said. 'I'm worn out.'

'I'm sorry; I'll leave. I came in simply by accident.'

'You're the one who works in administration?'

'Yes, I live next door.'

I started to leave; I was upset, impatient. I'd have liked to have done a thousand things, been in a hundred different places—write for example, make him speak and write his words for a long time, and mine as well, what was happening right now, the room. I saw everything with an extraordinary clarity, a terrible clarity, without a single shadow, I wrote it (and at the same time everything that was happening outside). It was as if all of history in every sense had passed through me. I was stifling. I tried to open the window. 'Don't open it,' he shouted, 'I'm all sweaty.' He was shivering, he seemed about to have an attack. —'Are you sick? Do you want me to call someone?' He breathed noisily for a few seconds.

'Why are you roaming around the room? You come in, you go out.'

'Calm down. It's true, I did come in a little suddenly. But one of my friends lived here just a few weeks ago. I came in without thinking.'

'Why did you come in last night?'

'Last night?'

'Yes, you broke in, you're spying on me, you're looking at me.'

'I'm not spying on anyone; I don't know you. Bouxx mentioned your name once, that's all.'

'I've been crushed under a rock; I'm trying to get back up. And you're sitting on the rock giving me advice.'

'I'm sorry for bursting in and making your fever worse. But it was an accident. As for last night . . .'

'Last night it was the same. You burst in all of a sudden and then left again. If you're curious about my illness, then let me reassure you: it's of no concern to anyone but myself.'

'Why should your illness . . . Listen, ideas like that couldn't be further from my mind. What exactly are you getting at?'

'You're an educated man,' he said more calmly. 'I don't suppose you let a few cases of raging fever upset you. Still, it's true that sick people are coming here by the dozen. Which could be cause for concern, the way things are these days.'

'You mean an epidemic is starting?'

'Epidemic! There's a certain tone in your voice when you say that word,' he said, straightening up. 'You don't believe in it, I suppose. You don't take this calamity seriously.'

'I don't know.'

2) open shed; hut

'Why are you smiling? Are you on to something? Because of this damn fever I'm really isolated. I can hardly get up. Yes, I did tell you that I get up and go for walks. That did happen, but before. Now I can only sit on my bed—you see, like this.'

I was alarmed to see him start to throw the covers back in order to turn over and let his legs dangle from the side of the bed. He moved around like someone half paralyzed. But at the same time he pulled off his roll with a dexterity which, given his weight and huge size, showed that he still had a lot of strength and flexibility.

'I've gotten thin,' he said, taking hold of his legs which seemed, on the contrary, extremely swollen to the point of deformity. 'Do you think I'm in bad shape? Give me your honest opinion,' he added, giving me a sidelong glance.

'You'd do better to lie back down. A moment ago you were sweating. And I'm almost cold. So lie back down.'

'You're cold? With the sun like that, it's warm enough. Maybe you're not feeling very well. Really, yourself . . . Why are you living in this place?'

'I'll probably leave soon.' I watched with disgust as he put his foot on the ground, then raised it, then put it down a little further on, leaving a whole series of little wet marks on the floor—it was an activity that seemed to give him a lot of pleasure, as if he had found the equivalent of going for a real walk. 'Have you been vaccinated?' I asked suddenly.

'Vaccinated? No, why?'

'But everybody should be vaccinated! What a joint! And they call this a dispensary! Well, it's no surprise. I should know what to expect in this nuthouse.'

'So? Why are you so angry?'

'Are you a friend of Bouxx?'

'Yes, he's a buddy of mine. But it looks to me like you're really getting angry.'

'Everybody exaggerates in this place. Maybe you don't know that the hygiene agency has set up a general plan to protect the population. Everybody works, the police arrest you at any street corner, neither lateness nor negligence is tolerated. And in this hovel that they've purposely transformed into a spe-cialized institution, because it's in the middle of the danger, they make fun of the required measures and they ignore the deadlines. They pile people up, and that's it.'

'In fact I've heard of this vaccine. They must dream about it here, as elsewhere. But the place is overcrowded and not organized yet. Look at this room. And how you were shouting! You seem to be afraid of something.' He stopped and tried to pull the covers over his knees but only managed to disrupt the bed. 'Yes, I'm starting to get cold,' he said in a hoarse voice. 'Finally you take all this sickness talk seriously, too. Do you think things are really going that badly?'

'I've no idea. I'm not an expert. All I know is that general measures have been stipulated and that the public interest demands that they be applied.'

'Yes, it's really starting to get bad. You think I should have been vaccinated?'

'Sure.'

'Help me lie back down.' I went up to him, but he stayed motionless, his eyes on his enormous feet, a veritable Colossus of Rhodes. 'Does my fever make vaccination impossible or too dangerous?' he asked, timidly. 'I suppose they're taking care of me as well as they can, given their interest in me here. Such negligence can't be explained. What do you think? Maybe these public measures aren't very important, they're for show—they're of interest to healthy people. But there are certainly other things to do for sick people.'

'You're adroitly defending your friends,' I said, even though his very slow and awkward speech also seemed fairly clumsy. 'On your part it's natural, it comes from your broad outlook. Still, as far as you're concerned the only reasonable measure would be your immediate evacuation—by leaving you with these other sick people, in your current state of weakness, they're dangerously exposing you to the risk of going from one disease to another.'

'What do you mean? You seem to be insinuating something.' He waited a moment. 'You're telling me that, because they've left me here, that means I'm already . . . Have you heard someone talking about it? Do you think I'm infected?'

'Not at all, I haven't said anything of the sort. I've just given you my opinion.'

'Yes, I know—you give advice freely. And you like to inter-rogate, and you're spying on me. Well, rest assured, my sick-ness is suspicious. Look at this.'

He pulled up his shirt: his chest sprouted clumps of scrag-gly hair which gave the impression not of overabundance but of destitution. Aside from that I didn't see anything abnormal.

'Lie back down. Bouxx told me about your bouts of fever, nothing more. You're being childish.'

He glanced intently, almost greedily, inside his shirt.

'You saw it,' he said in a new, confidential tone. With his finger he showed me, along the sides of his chest, I don't know what—maybe some red streaks.

'What is it?' I asked, a little too quickly.

In a flash he lay back down, demonstrating a disgusting agility. Then, pulling the sheet up to his chin as if he were afraid of being stripped bare against his wishes, he glared at me in defiance.

'Does that scare you,' he said, 'is it suspicious?'

I wanted to slap him. What playacting! And now he didn't say anything, on purpose. I was becoming terribly impatient; I was afraid I wouldn't be able to wait any longer.

'This all comes out of your head, like my visit last night. You don't even believe it yourself.'

'Last night you howled, you came in like a crazy man, slamming the door. Luckily I had my lighter. If you wanted to frighten me, you succeeded. I spent the rest of the night trembling.'

'What a fantasy! Last night the fire kept me awake three-quarters of the time. Your fever's playing tricks on you. And why me?'

'I had the time to observe you: you were staring at the flame from my lighter with an incredible intensity, as if you wanted to drink it, consume it, as if to make me understand that it wouldn't last long. When you came in a little while ago, I recognized you immediately.'

'Yes, I'd also seen you before. But I've probably seen you on the stairs. In any case, I'm not an apparition, I'm not trying to scare you, nor am I investigating you. In my opinion you're trying to scare yourself by talking about epidemics and contagions.'

'You don't believe in the seriousness of the epidemic?'

I shook my head.

'You don't think I'm really suffering from it?'

'No, no.'

He sort of grimaced and, suddenly pulling down the sheet, showed me his side along which I saw red and purplish spots.

'I've had enough of your act,' I said, running for the door.

'Stay,' he said, very humbly. 'Just one minute.'

'What good is all this nonsense? Why are you saying I came in during the night? It's playacting.'

'A sick man's jokes, very stupid jokes. Remember, I more or less can't sleep, I spend whole days without any rest. I'm beside myself, it's the fever.'

'Don't you get the feeling sometimes that something's pushing you, it's propelling you forward, that everything's burning, that it's always going faster, and yet not fast enough? Not fast enough!'

'Sit down. You're going in circles, making me dizzy. No, I don't feel that. Rather I'm in a grave, under a rock, whatever. From what I've heard, you're in contact with the ruling circles. Maybe they find it disadvantageous to recognize that the plague has appeared and that it threatens a large part of the country. So you should be aware of these numbers: yesterday, just in this building, they counted fifty serious cases, real, verified cases. In the poorer sections, there could be hundreds, maybe a thousand.'

'The plague?'

'No doubt it's not exactly that, but for the people it's the plague.'

'Those are lies. Besides, nowadays they have drastic means of combating all these infections: we've got great scientists who've invented new treatments. And then the truth is probably completely different: it's a show, I've heard, a plan to justify certain administrative measures. Why do you claim that the government is silencing talk about the epidemic? It's not trying to suppress it at all; on the contrary, the newspapers go on about it at great length.'

'Does it bother you that I call the government into question?'

1) direction
2) loving pas
3) often ahead

'You repeat all the chatter that's going around the neighborhood. They're sick ideas, bad for you of all people.'

'Maybe it would be disadvantageous for the State,' he said, gazing at me with the fierce look of a sick man, 'to see the plague turn everyone into an abject wreck, a vector of infection; regrettable for it to see every house become a purulent hovel, and the country sink into a swamp. What do you think? Are you a good citizen?'

'Sure, I'm a good citizen: I serve the State with all my energy.'

'Well, that's not my case; I'm not a good citizen, I'm suspect.'

'Why? Not at all.'

'My sickness is suspect.'

'You're playing with words,' I said with difficulty.

'Come closer, I want to tell you something—' and he grabbed my arm with his enormous hand, whose wet touch I felt through the cloth. 'Am I really sick?' he said, half aloud. 'I don't deny it, I don't affirm it, I don't say anything, it's a secret. But I'm suspect. Think carefully about that. I've managed to become suspect. And there are thousands of suspects here now, people against whom the State protects itself with roadblocks, by force. People who escape, who can no longer be recognized, who can no longer be treated like everybody else. We're outlaws.'

'Don't talk so fast. Where did you get such ideas? It's all morbidly pretentious talk, and totally unreal. You aren't outlaws, you're sick people. And, on the contrary, as sick people, the government is especially concerned about you. It will help you with its best doctors, allow you to take advantage of its most modern institutions. Perhaps it has taken some brutal health measures, but the common good demanded it, it's doing what it thinks best.'

'Sure it's sneaky, but we're sneaky too. I've been driven to despair, but now despair has become a weapon, a terrible weapon: the stone is rising up. The more it crushes me, the stronger I am. Yes, you're right, sit on top of me—you have to, do it.'

'Be quiet,' I shouted. 'Who gave you these ideas? It's not possible: you've found them written on the ground, on walls, you've stolen them from me, you're deforming them, you're not up to their level, you're turning them into a sick man's scrawl. But wait. I think I told Bouxx something similar—what? Something about sickness; whatever. So you others, you want to use this public misfortune as a pretext to create disorder and thwart the law? You dream of developing your organizations? So the dispensary is a sham? This is all archaic and comical. Soon the dispensary will be closed, your organizations liquidated. Bouxx is chaos leading you to the slaughterhouse.'

'But the sick exist!' he cried. 'I'm sick!'

'What?' I barely heard him. What a look he had—a grubby, livid appearance; disgusting. 'What drove you to despair? What difference does your despair make, your sickness? You're not the first sick person. You'll be cared for, cured, you'll start working again. Or . . .'

'Or?'

'Let's drop it. You made me really furious with your melodrama. But after all I'm sick too.'

'Maybe we won't die,' he said. 'It's a sickness that can do you in in a few hours, but sometimes it also progresses very slowly. So you see, I'm rotting. We'll be like the earth, we'll be free.'

'Enough,' I cried. 'That's mysticism.'

I bumped into someone on the stairs and ran outside. In the street I must have kept running. But soon the smoke clogged my throat. Yes, the fire. Still, the street was tranquil, the houses were intact. I crossed the little square. On the avenue the air was breathable, the humidity and freshness of the trees could be felt. Only the absence of daylight was stifling. With the streetlights out, this wide avenue became a tunnel from which light escaped at both ends. In the middle of the street, I stumbled over a pile of boulders and burnt wood; all the way across it torn-up cobblestones made a kind of abandoned quarry on which the little flame of a lantern flickered. I felt someone watching. To the side, behind some rubble, his face covered with grease or mud, someone was staring at me like an owl. As I approached he got up, his mouth pinched in childish sucking, his hand disappearing into his jacket. Suddenly he let fly and I thought he'd thrown a stone—and indeed I felt a jolt that made me stumble. Whatever it was it rolled and bounced, and he got away. It must have been his ball. Then there was a stampede, a rush; in the echoing silence there was the sound of running, as if, hidden behind the barricade, a dozen kids fled in every direction into the alleys. I ran after them. Only for a short time, probably; halfway down the street I found myself surrounded by smoke. It enveloped me so quickly I already felt it all around me, behind me if I turned back, and always thicker and more asphyxiating in the direction I was headed. I had to shut my eyes, I turned around aimlessly, I couldn't breathe. Still, I fell fairly gently, without completely passing out, for I could sense where some people were walking, and I had the impression that they had surrounded me. One of them kicked me in the back. I jerked. I could make them out: a little group was examining me and waiting calmly for me to stop coughing and spitting. My eyes were full of tears. 'It's the smoke,' I said, smiling at the boy kneeling next to me. He put a handkerchief in my hand. As soon as I started to get up he got up too, as if he wanted to carry out the movement in my place. Then he took off; the others were already running. Then terrible shrieks of a whistle and yelling cut right through me. I was sitting on the curb, holding the bit of cloth in my hand, and police surrounded me, observing me. I looked at them. Did I make a gesture? Try to stand up? I was thrown on the ground, flat on my stomach, and the more I tried to turn over the more they kicked at me with their heels, raining the blows with lightning speed. One policeman threw himself on my back. Then, what I was expecting happened: there was a burning at my neck, a rock-hard hammering relentlessly pounding me against the pavement. I breathed shallowly. One of them must have held me by the shoulders; another wiped my forehead. 'Is that better?' he asked. 'It'll be OK now.' I looked at him; I was tempted to smile at him. Then I saw he was holding my card in his hand, my identity card which must have revealed my position as a civil servant. I had just recognized this piece of paper when my stomach heaved: yes, there was an abyss there, a boundless surging of bile, and I opened my mouth, with bitterness, to let it go. As soon as I started to vomit they released me and stepped back; I vomited endlessly, uncontrollably, my head hanging over the side-walk, and they ran, I heard them in the distance: they were fleeing. I wiped myself with the piece of cloth. 'Animals,' I choked out, 'cowards, animals.' But, getting up again, I saw the indecent little puddle in front of me. Now I too turned quickly away, shuddering; I got out of there fast, as if the puddle could have given me cholera.

# 6

*recover health*

'Come up quickly,' the cleaning lady yelled at me. 'What are you doing outside?'

I stood stock still; it was when the floor crackled, when there was a sliding void, that I felt myself pushed backward. My back to the wall, I looked at the two of them, and they observed my face, my breathing, my stained clothes. I mumbled something. But exhaustion was stronger: the memory of blows, of nausea, everything was pulling me down. 'Wait—don't come closer.' Stretched out on the bed, I noticed that they were keeping their distance. When my stepfather started to pick up the phone, I tried to get him to calm down.

'Can you walk?' he asked. 'Louise will get your suitcase ready.'

He looked around almost timidly. The room, the slovenliness, the smell—yes, the smell above all—seemed to make him feel faint.

'Stay where you are,' I said to Louise, who was heading for the clothes closet. 'You'd best take him away. Sick people are being crammed into the building.'

'Yes, things don't seem to be going very well around here. Isn't the telephone working?' he said, shaking the receiver. 'It's time you left. Near Joblin there's a convalescent home, it's like you're in the country. It's very comfortable—you'll have a nice stay out there.'

'In the country?'

'You'll see, it's perfect. There's a big building, a park, you couldn't ask for more.'

'I'm sorry,' I said, 'it's too late now.'

My eyes were on fire. I picked up a glass of water, I was so shaky I didn't dare drink.

'What's wrong with you?' asked Louise, coming up to me.

'Don't move; don't touch me. Everything's contaminated here, dirty.'

'Drink some.' Obstinately, she pushed the glass at my mouth.

'The water's . . . not even boiled. So *you* drink it,' I said, throwing the water at her. 'Leave me alone—get out.'

After a moment I put the glass down.

'It's better not to wait. I think I'm sick, too.'

'What!' said Louise. 'Where were you just now?'

'How do you feel?'

'How do I feel . . . Fever, nausea,' I said, looking at my shoes.

'A high fever?'

'How do I know? I'm cold, sweating. You saw it, I can't stand on my feet.'

'But have they done tests?'

He looked at me with his seriousness, his spirit of truth. I tore off my vest and shirt.

'You want proof? Here!' I shouted, showing the marks left by the blows, the stains left by my black and dishonored blood. I myself looked at these blotches in horror. 'Now get out. You're killing me.'

'Wait a minute,' he said to Louise. 'I'm going down to see the director.'

'Should I pack his suitcase?'

'If you touch anything here I'll . . . I'll jump out the window.'

She pulled up the stool and stared at me for a long time. 'How dirty you've gotten,' she said, almost softly. Yes, I was dressed sordidly; my clothes were rumpled and torn; and those disgusting stains. 'Don't leave me,' I said. It was as if her face reappeared, a pale, haggard face, and her dress, as always, somebody else's dress on its last legs. Where had it come from? Why this sad way of dressing, this self-punishment that was keeping her in the shadows? There was one young woman I never saw—and she was the one who overwhelmed me—my sister. Everything was so exhausting!

'What's going to happen now? Do you think I've got the fever? You want to feel my hand? I'm burning up, aren't I? Wipe yourself off—no, not with this rag, I think it's contaminated. I think the sweat is contagious.' She dried off each one of her fingers. 'You can leave if you're scared. Listen,' I said, looking at the hand she had rested on my arm, and which I feebly brushed aside, 'I just had a strange feeling. Your hand, I had the impression that it belonged to another world, that it was something that I didn't know, that it was completely different. Yes, it's strange. Would you like to put it there again for a second? No, don't do it, don't come close. I'm asking you . . . how do you see me right now? What am I to you? When we were younger you persecuted me—you wanted to make me a beggar. You remember? More than once you took my bread and threw it in the dirt, or else you shoved me under the bed, throwing garbage, filth, at me. All the same, it was strange. Now your wish has come true, I've become unclean. Did you know that this morning, a few minutes before you arrived, the police found me in the street and beat me up? Yesterday they held me at the police station. And do you smell this odor? It's drifted throughout the house—what do you think it is? It's like it came out of the grave. You'd better get out. Louise!'

'I'm here.'

'I'm not as . . . weak as you think. My insignificance has disappointed you. But from me you expected . . . you were expecting, yes, so what were you expecting?' We looked at each other. 'I understand a lot of things, I know a lot about them; in a sense, I know everything. You yourself can't see exactly what you are, or what you want. You're too caught up in the past; you're like a ghost.' I grabbed her by the arm. 'Should I tell you something about the family? Come closer, I can't shout it from the rooftop. Don't be afraid. I've always admired you, Louise. You've influenced me so much, you're so closed, so <u>voracious</u>; and you're faithful. I don't think I've ever seen you laugh. It's because . . . hold still, please don't move.' She pushed herself back against the wall; I looked at the bit of cloth I'd torn off. 'You're right,' I murmured, 'one has to be careful.'

After a bit she came back and knelt down. I started to tremble.

'You're a . . . you're really an extraordinary person. You too understand everything. I'd like to tell you something. At the office, I have a co-worker, his name is . . . You'll see him in the registry room, he's tall and thin, his left arm is half paralyzed.

I think he's had minor seizures. Have you ever been to city hall? Naturally, of course you have. I've only got a very small position there, it's almost ridiculous; I'm a sub-nothing, whatever. Just to serve the State, to give the law its warmth, its light, its life, to go with it from person to person, indefinitely, when you think it's possible—that's all you need. That's what's most high—outside of that, nothing counts, and besides there's nothing, that's right, nothing. Kid, just promise me you'll go and take a walk in the street, wander around. Please, do it, find an avenue, look at the passersby, the buildings. Hit the streets and look around: do that from time to time, please, it's very important, do it for me.'

'Why are you talking like this?' she whispered. 'Are you feeling really sick?'

'I don't know. Don't you find this place sinister? And this neighborhood . . .'

'But you're not going to stay. In an hour, we'll be gone. Let me pack your suitcase.'

'You think so? Where will I go? Tell me, Louise, what do you know about this epidemic?'

She stood up, then sat back down on the stool.

'I know they're talking about it,' she said haltingly. 'There've been cases, but it's not too serious.'

'They're talking about it? What is it, some kind of typhus?'

'They're taking preventive measures above all,' she said, looking around the room. 'Did the doctor tell you something?'

'The doctor! And that's all, they don't say anything else? Thousands of people have it, tens of thousands are at risk; a whole region is starting to die. And in your circles they only talk about cases, and preventive measures! It's vile, cowardly— besides, they're doing it on purpose.'

'Thousands, really?'

'Yes, thousands; are you blind? When you came into this neighborhood, did everything seem normal? Is it normal that half the city's been closed off; that we're locked up in it like in a prison; that the stores are closed? Is it normal that the police jump on you and beat you up; that houses are set on fire; that whole districts are burning and the firemen don't budge? Have you breathed the air in these streets? It's like black water, stagnant with filth and misery. How did you get the authorization to come here?'

'I don't know, he . . .'

'Yes, of course. So what's he doing? What's he plotting? Go find him. I've decided not to leave.'

I held her back. I looked at her steadily, I stared at the material of her dress. It was a kind of black silk, shiny in areas, dull in others; it wasn't a piece of clothing, but rather a stain, something she had soaked up and which was now seeping out, something that had neither form nor color, something that looked like that big mildew blot on the wall. And even thinking that it would go away gave me a feeling of wrongdoing, of guilt. I was betraying—what? A dress? You can laugh about it, but it was enough to wear me out; I no longer wanted to talk about it. And I barely noticed it when he came back; I didn't hold it against him. I knew he was taking my place, that he was my living, working part: he was my health. It had to be. Even the whispering with Louise didn't bother me.

'He'd better lie down,' he said suddenly. 'Do you want to help him? I'm going to try to get hold of someone.'

'I'm not leaving?'

'Ah,' he said, turning around and coming up to me, seemingly on tiptoe. 'Everything's taken care of.'

'How?'

'The director has decided that you should leave as soon as possible. There are a few papers that have to be taken care of for your transfer out of this zone. But first, as far as the epidemic goes, you can relax: you're certainly healthy.'

'I'm going to leave? When?'

'Today, for sure. This afternoon.'

'How does he know I'm healthy? He never examined me, he isn't even a doctor. He's only looking out for himself.'

'Be reasonable. These stories about all the sicknesses, you've got to understand, aren't serious. There's no epidemic, there never was one.'

'Are you really stating that? Would you be willing to testify about it, to . . . write it down?'

'But why? All right, if you really want me to—why not?'

'Would you write it, here, on this paper, it doesn't matter where.'

'Are you the one who's written these statements: "I am a good citizen, I serve" . . . ?'

'That's me. Now, would you write this: "After studying reports and consulting with experts, I certify that there is no epidemic in the Western sector, nor in any section of the city, nor in any other part of the country"?'

'That's it? You want me to sign it? What are you going to do with this document?'

I kept it in my hand, I didn't read it, and yet what a change! The letters lit up, sparkled: upon them a thousand other signs lit up, phrases of all kinds, shameful, despotic turns of phrase, the embellishments of a drunk, the screams of a wild animal, and out of this orgy the law formed a perfect and definitive sentence, an irrefutable firmament for all.

'Are you all right? What's the matter?'

'Yes,' I said, 'this text has just burned my fingers. Now it's fading. But I won't let it go; I'll keep it like a talisman; it'll be a talisman against me, a proof that will always demonstrate my error.'

'That's a lot for a joke. Come on, don't torment yourself now with this paper—give it to me instead.'

'Oh—can't you drop that tone for just a moment? Do you think I attach the least importance to your papers? I can tear it up, crumple it into a ball. Why is there always such hypocrisy in the administration? They advise civil servants to be frank and good-natured. They should be transparent, like windowpanes; yet they're only icy, with the decorum, the ceremonies, the formalities through which a spirit of comprehension endlessly meanders, one that's always just short of its goal. Or rather . . .'

'It's true, that's a very accurate remark, well put. So, no beating around the bush between us? That's what you want? A heart to heart talk? Fine, but some other time. Today we have to work out your departure.'

'No,' I said, 'just a few minutes more. I've been waiting for you for too long. First of all, do you know that your police harassed me, that yesterday I was held for several hours at the station, that the whole sector is in a state of siege, that we've got the reign of the police—that the residents are hounded, or worse yet, left to themselves, without supplies, without protection, without aid? In my case, after beating me until I was sick, the police took off and left me like a plague victim on the street. My card's gone, they confiscated it, stole it. So where am I now? What do you call this state of affairs?'

'You were struck by the police? Under what circumstances? Why didn't you tell me about it?'

'I am telling you about it, I haven't stopped telling you about it. But there is no epidemic—isn't that so? So there's no disorder, no strike, no fires. And I suppose there's no agitation?'

He was motionless for a moment, as if my impatience had stunned him.

'No,' he said, 'I don't want to irritate you more, but there isn't any. This whole vocabulary is inappropriate. Where did you pick it up?'

'From no one,' I said. 'But what do these bruises mean, and that smoke over there, do you see it? And all these people who are moving constantly, who are filling up the building, who are homeless?'

He stood for another few seconds with a doubtful look, and then sat down on a stool. He looked at me oddly without talking.

'Is it true,' he asked, 'that you let your acquaintances know about your plan to resign? Didn't you, during discussions with them, bring up grievances like those you've just mentioned? Would you like to try to recall what you could have said or done along these lines?'

'Why have you chosen precisely this moment to interrogate me?'

'But you're the one who asked for it. Don't you recall— heart to heart! Heart to heart! And this is no interrogation. Just answer yes or no, and that'll be it.'

'How did these rumors reach you?'

'Oh, come on! If you talk at the office, you aren't talking into the void. There's always someone who does a report on chatter, that's all. It's no tragedy.'

2) sarcastic

'I didn't mention these things at the office, I swear it.'

'All right, very well. That puts me at ease, so I can speak frankly. I've always appreciated your frame of mind, your cases of conscience, your seriousness, above all your seriousness. Without seriousness cases of conscience are bad. Well, if I brought up these stories now, precisely now, it wasn't to embarrass you, nor was it out of family curiosity. Only—and I can tell you this—for the last few days there have been serious signs of crisis in our departments, and harsh measures are under way. You can imagine what's going on: dossiers are being inspected, revised, gone over with a fine-tooth comb; we worry about the least little irregularity. And above all, and make note of this, because it's our latest idea, everyone, from the most important person down to the most minor, is being asked to sign a kind of profession of faith, a theoretical declaration.'

'A declaration? What kind of declaration?'

He looked at me with an insistent gentleness, an enveloping and sly benevolence which gave me the impression that not only was he next to me, but that he was also on the other side, in front, behind—and even in the other room, where I heard Louise pacing, it was him again, going back and forth.

'It's a simple formula. I can write it down: it's very short. Here it is: "I pledge to uphold legal authority and to act in conformity with it. I will cause it to be respected through my example, and I will defend it at all times. I hold it to be indestructible. I have faith in its sovereignty." It's bureaucratese,' he said sardonically.

'But why these precautions? What's going on?'

'You know the saying: problems never end. It's not the first or the last shock. And after all, it's also necessary at certain times for the administration to monitor itself. Do I have to explain that? It's justifiable and normal.'

'But you wouldn't be lying to me, by any chance? Aren't you just trying to impress me and scare me?'

He looked at me again, with his friendly and sly smile.

'You sure are suspicious and underhanded! You're not a civil servant for nothing. Do you want to know a secret? Yes, I had the idea for this oath, I'm the author. What do you think of it? Did you pay attention to certain details—did you notice this little contradiction: "I will defend it, I hold it to be indestructible." Ha ha! What do you think?'

He laughed in a strange, intolerable way, as if he wanted to say outright, Me, I've kept the right to laugh; woe to those who can no longer laugh about these things.

'Have you actually seen my dossier?'

'Your dossier? Of course! But you know what's in them—bundles of papers, a whole life in paper, it's of no importance. The outfit is good in that it sees the mountains of paper it produces as being totally worthless. To everyone it says, You are your own dossier; judge and decide. Now, even though we can set aside the recommendations, the secret notes, and the other authoritative documents, it's still true that we have family ties, that, when your name is mentioned, mine is too, as is . . . in the end, the whole story, you get the idea. Like it or not we're mixed up in this thing together, and conventions require that we let each other in on our little career setbacks.'

'Why are you making fun of me by putting me on an equal footing with you? I empty wastebaskets and you—you're at the top. It's mockery.'

'I'm sorry, but the law is clear: same rights, same duties, there are no subordinate roles, no *exceptio capitis*. Whoever's in the hall's already upstairs. Children are taught to sing it.'

How was he coming up with these things? I too had known about all this. I knew that everyone, from the most humble to the very greatest, had the duty always to see himself as representing in himself the entire administration, which therefore, constantly, revealed all its power, all its prestige by delegating it to or exposing it through any given individual. But it was as if this truth had melted away in the daylight; I had to look for it with the powerless memory of a dream.

'Whoever's in the grave doesn't need to come out,' I said suddenly.

'Really a fine way of putting it,' he remarked. 'The old writings still hold good. No, you know, you let yourself be brought down by your health problems. You've had sick leaves, you've felt yourself going downhill. With all your free time, you've been able to visit first one person, then another.

You've become upset; you've set off in search of something, as if you hadn't already received everything. And then what happened? In the end, you get dizzy, you think history has left you, that it's rolling along without you, you start judging, speaking, and even writing with the amazement of a man who's always chasing after his own shoes.'

He repeated once more the word 'writing' in a nonchalant tone, as if he had let it drop unawares. Suddenly the allusion hit me—I recalled the draft of a letter written on that terrible day; for a moment, I lost my composure.

'But you can't take that letter into account. I didn't mail it. A draft, not even that, two or three sentences without beginning or end, written just to use my pen.'

'So! That's it: a schoolboy exercise. I understood that as soon as I laid eyes on it—just some ink stains. You know, when one tries out a new pen one uses phrases of a certain kind, series of ludicrous words, grammar examples. Still, in the future, be careful—choose less conspicuous expressions for your compendium.'

'Where did that paper go? Who came and took it from my own desk, in my office?'

'I did a little inquiry into your vacation homework. I wanted to know if you had sent it. Well, things are always simple. Chance! Not even—things happen that way. The guilty party's one of your acquaintances. I think he had worked with you; when he put his papers in order, he mixed yours in by mistake, and he took it with him. Then the next day, when he was showing a dossier to Iche, the sheet suddenly appeared. To everyone's surprise, your handwriting was recognized. One thing led to another, and it got into the circuit.'

'Which acquaintance?'

'I don't know his name: thin, sickly.'

'That paralytic; I suspected as much. He rummaged around in my desk: he did it on purpose.'

'Well, the poor boy—the incident was certainly no more pleasant for him than it was for you. You can imagine the scene: the grave Iche, punctual, methodical, always working to increase productivity, a man who literally doesn't exist outside of his duties. There he is, leafing page by page through the dossier, discussing, taking notes, and as always he's dazzling in his knowledge and decisiveness, all his secretaries are around him, his new typist is stiff with admiration—and then crash! Right in the middle of the numbers drops your little prank, your incredible farce, straight from the clouds.' He took the paper out of his pocket and started looking it over with an actor's greediness. 'Yes, it's really funny: "Sir, I can no longer be a part of your department. I request that I be freed of all work and obligation. Starting on the ——, I will regain my freedom."'

I tried to grab the paper out of his hand: we struggled silently.

'Give that back: it belongs to me. Get out of here!' I screamed at Louise who came running from the next room. It was as if her presence risked complicating the situation by coming between a text that was already difficult to follow and me. 'Maybe this seems funny to you,' I said, defying him, 'but, even if it is ridiculous, I'm less tempted to laugh when I see fire, violence, and endless hardship behind these words—a whole avenue filled with coffins.'

Yes, I defied him, but far from being offended, he observed me with a sympathy that lit up, that silently shone, without cunning or malice, like a gentle glance. He smoothed out the paper and put it on the little table.

'What gave you this idea of quitting?' I gestured noncommitally. 'You know,' he said, very softly, 'you're wrong to think that your acts and projects aren't appreciated. What each person does is useful to all, and everyone has great prospects. Your voice belongs to the people. Maybe you bothered us with your inkwell fantasies, but so what—we won't lose them, we'll follow them for as long as necessary in order to appreciate their value and get some good out of them. If I laughed at your ravings it wasn't out of a lack of respect—they have their good side, it's refreshing, you can laugh about it. Here,' he said, holding the paper, 'the sheet's here, it has certain words on it, a series of clear phrases, it expresses concisely a serious decision, one that can even shake the heavens, and yet it signifies nothing. Yes, have a look, there's nothing there, it doesn't exist. Really, when I think about Iche at work lining up texts of granite, advancing with his whole crew to a rock-solid prominence and then suddenly falling on this void . . . Sorry, but it's funny—the eternal tables, the sacrosanct objects, reforms and decrees, and then this: smoke, a stain, a moth-hole. What do you think? What a circus—it's entertaining.'

He looked at me—yes, it was terrible, it made you sweat— with a kind of gratitude.

'It's not drawn up according to the rules, maybe it's stupid,' I said, 'but . . .' He encouraged me with his chin. 'Why are you acting nice?' I stammered. 'Why are you being so clever with me? You knew it from the beginning . . .'

'What?'

'Instead . . .'

I felt the need to annihilate this kindness blowing over me like a hurricane; I wanted to crush it to find deep down within some residue of cruelty, hypocrisy, and cowardly contempt. Oh—it was all so cowardly. This scrap of paper was obviously as valuable as the most beautiful piece of legal writing; by not sending it I hadn't suppressed it, but rather I had made it definitive by eliminating the possibility of any response or refusal by my directors. That was the only way I was able to really free myself from all these goings-on, to the extent that it depended on me and in that it was my work, and mine alone.

'Maybe it was childish,' I said, 'but even though it'll cost me dearly and, still not knowing why it's become inevitable, I've got to tell you again: I still am a child, and, as you've put it, from now on I'll let my shoes run off by themselves.'

When I looked at him his eyes were gleaming, as if he had just downed a glass of liquor.

'Right,' he said, as if my protest were only a digression. 'You're a serious boy, your decision could only be serious. That's just what gives it its spice.' He stopped abruptly. 'What are you getting at? What you're doing goes against the statutes and customs,' he went on, starting to speak more quickly. 'Surely you know that labor is strictly regulated, that any job change is subject to official approval and is only allowed for important reasons or on the initiative of the supervisory commissions. That's the general rule. As for the members of the central administration, whatever they are, they have special obligations. They're both more and less free, since they are often sent on job missions outside the administration, and yet, even if they spend their whole career there, they are always considered, paid, and promoted according to the criteria of their original position. Besides, it's not a question of status or contract. The life for which we've struggled obliges us at all times to consider ourselves either at work or on leave from work; it ties us, for life and through life, to the task we've assumed. That's why there isn't, strictly speaking, any difference between work and the one who carries it out: to live, to go on living, is to give oneself over to the task without reserve, constantly. Arrangements like this make for the honor of our condition, since they permit us to escape from the abject life that would be our lot if, tethered to a job as to an alien activity, we were condemned to live without expressing profoundly, through the most minor activities of life, our identification with work.'

It seemed that he was reading, but he was reading it in me; he drew these thoughts faultlessly from me, so that he was expressing them mechanically and indifferently, with the ease and light contempt of a man who mouths words. But I would have brought them forth in all sincerity, with an ever more laborious effort, with a feverish fear of having words fail me, and with the time neither to doubt it nor to believe it.

'Listen,' he said, going back to his ordinary way of talking, 'we're in agreement on this: your resignation isn't just mischief. It couldn't be more serious, but it won't change a thing. So don't you think it would be better for both of us to go back to our usual way of doing things, without wasting too much time singing that same old song about the obvious—

'Two and two make four
The stick's got two ends
The alley cat at the door
Is no more a cur than men!'

'I understand that all this seems tiresome,' I said with difficulty. 'It's tiring for me too.'

'So, it's agreed? We'll drop all this? And you won't regret not going back to it and not expressing all you have to say? It's good to talk, it's bad, whatever. But only half expressing yourself . . . it's suspicious, it's despotism. I've often experienced it recently, since the upheaval. You've got to realize that this whole thing is very serious. It's a matter of breaking, for good, the framework and doing away with the walls that separate those who administer from the things that they administer. You know what goes on already: in any job, there's a representative of the administration; behind every worker, there's a delegate who incarnates in flesh and bone the reason for his labor. In principle, the delegate is there to bring technical or moral aid, but also, well, to control the activities and permit us to use them better. It all works, more or less. The system has its weaknesses; in the end I buckled down to redo the organization, from the bottom up. I've been examining the value of some of the outside co-workers. From morning till night I chat with them, I get bogged down in gossip to see if these people can listen, and at the same time to see if my words are still worth listening to—to see if I haven't already gotten rusty, if I'm only good for liquidation. Well, I always note strange things. I talk to them about the weather—why? Because it's easier, I don't want to get bored, it's a common topic. But almost everybody thinks I'm playing a game: they get scared, flustered, they blame themselves, they tell fantastic stories. By the way, do you often leave papers lying around like the one I found on this table? What did you write? "I am a good citizen, I serve the State with all my strength"—is that it? Naturally I have nothing to add. It's patriotic, it's good. But doesn't it shock you? No? In the end it's a question of taste. And do you think it's useful? Wouldn't you prefer to write, I'm not a terribly good citizen, I willingly see measures taken in the general interest as a hassle, a methodical and deliberate work stoppage as a strike; I make beautiful declarations of my dedication to the State, but . . . Oh, I forgot to tell you that, during these endless sessions, I got to know one of your friends. A big, good-looking young woman who works with a member of the Department of Trade, I think . . . She's naive, nice. And even . . . if I can tell you something, you'll see the kind of mixed-up situation we constantly have to face. This young woman isn't married . . . yes, well, it's all a little delicate, but don't get upset, especially since the circumstances alone caused her to play a role she hadn't been assigned. In short, it turned out that you were living practically next door to each other. She'd met you a number of times, you'd been to see her in her little shop, you'd gotten along fairly well together. No,' he said, gazing at me cautiously, 'I swear that she had not been given any mission having to do with you. There was no premeditation, I can assure you of that. But naturally, the low-key relations you two had nevertheless linked you with her, you became part of her story, she had to take an interest in you, and besides it turned out well: in your condition you were upsetting everyone, and especially your poor mother, who wanted to know every day what you had done, and would gladly have tied you down so as not to lose sight of you. So, when I was shown your dossier I had her come in and, as usual, in order to have better relations with her, and to make sure that we were using words in the same way, I started to hold forth—I told her just about anything, an anecdote from my youth. When I was twenty, I worked in a print shop. I wasn't a technician, but I kept track of the condition of the machines, the pace of work. It was a fairly big operation where textbooks, brochures, even disciplinary notices for schools were printed. Among the workers in the shop there was one I liked a lot: he was fairly old, he was experienced, he'd taken part in many things and willingly discussed the organization of the work. What he said was accurate or at least instructive. Unfortunately, he had been hit by a car and suffered from neuritis: on some days he worked with difficulty, he suffered, and the cramps and spasms, which he refused to acknowledge, made him almost a cripple. So he couldn't do anything, he messed up his machine, he swore, you couldn't hear anything but him; I spent all my time standing behind him, nudging him in the right direction, or repairing his equipment. Alas, things went from bad to worse and finally, to my great regret, he had to be made to retire. That was my story. I asked the young lady what she thought of it; by that I meant, Did this story please you? Were you touched by it, do you sense the narrative intentions I put into it? Well, my boy, her response was typical: "You were the one who sabotaged the machine, because his work was no longer satisfactory and because he talked too much." That's how their minds work. They can't take a story seriously anymore; they transpose it, dissect it, draw a lesson from it. Sure, I was the saboteur, but so what? The anecdote existed nonetheless, something that I had given her as a gift, without any ulterior motive, because I'm a person just as she is and because when I saw her I recalled my youth and my years as an apprentice, years during which I saw older men stumble and disappear, at precisely my age now. What can I tell you? I don't blame her because she was right, and if she had only appreciated the purely historical side of my tale, its aesthetic value, I would have said to myself, Little fool, sentimental little goose. But listen, this is the strangest part. As you've figured out, my goal was to make her speak against you; I had to, my duty was to get a sense of the plausibility of all the stories circulating about you. But what happened? My insipid words began to foam, as if they were fermenting. She discovered something in them, and she was fascinated. I can say that I know how to recognize this kind of swirling from a distance, I follow its phases, it's a total crisis whose outcome I'm also familiar with: a thousand avowals of carelessness, of complicity, a thoughtlessness which suddenly exposes and denounces itself on the basis of an infinite number of proofs, too much proof. For your friend, because of unfortunate circumstances, this went especially far, so far that, no doubt suddenly seeing herself in a hopeless situation, what did she do? She threw out your name. So, I said to myself, *finally*—and I got ready to jot down some remarkable details. I was waiting for them, I formulated them in advance; in a way I was enjoying them, when . . . Yes, that's exactly how capricious speech is. Instead of damning you, the poor thing, from the depths of her distress, did just the opposite. She only saw your name as a way of commending herself to me, a connection, a bit of luck. You were no longer the suspect she was supposed to ruin; you'd become the only one who could make her innocent. What can

I say? After disappointments like this, you learn to be patient and you discover how long history—even if it is ended— really is, and how slowly it passes. It's like a dream.'

I couldn't look at him, and still, I knew, it was now or never that my glance could penetrate his facade. Why did he use all his frankness to display what was most frightening about it, to show that this frankness, which was so great, was an indecent disguise, and that the soundest understanding was only the mask of an always hidden face? Why try to make me recognize in universal confidence and solidarity the return of an endless betrayal, in his own benevolence a perpetual suspicion? And his fog of words, this dust thrown everywhere, which you couldn't see but which you breathed— why did it only lead to sordid scenes, informers' stories?

'Informers?' he asked.

'Yes, the police,' I stammered, showing my bruised side.

'The police,' he repeated, looking at me with growing surprise, a kind of anxiety, as if by looking at me he had become aware for the first time of what they represented, as if he saw them, by seeing me, as abjection and crime. 'What do you mean? Haven't they disappeared? Can you find them again somewhere? Haven't the prisons been opened so that those who go there are in contact in an innocent way with their offense, which is located outside them and erected like a building? Aren't they made unaware of their offense's guilty intimacy, so that they can come out, reconciled as soon as they're there and already outside the walls through which they enter only to discover that they're free, that there is no inside to what had seemed to them a crime, out of which they have come? And the police,' he added, looking around disconcertedly, 'can someone be so close to them, be so mixed up with them as to freeze things when they look like that, so that they'll be maintained indefinitely as hideous and violent power, instead of being capable of participating in universal evolution? Perhaps the police—how distant this word is; doesn't it come from the depths of the sea?—yes, perhaps they're low-down for those who look at them from below, but when one has a less fragmentary idea of the truth this impression is transformed and for he who sees all, the police are no more, they've disappeared, they're the overturned image one never sees, required by the uprightness of all things.'

'I've already heard this justification; I've inherited it. But I can't accept this inheritance any longer. There's too much hypocrisy. You've thrown too much dust: the air has become unbreathable.'

He thought for a moment.

'Why did you use that turn of phrase, that "you"? Who is it, this "you"?'

'It's the State,' I said. 'It's you.'

'Beware of hypocrisy,' he said, in a serious tone of voice. Then he leaned over the table and took the paper, lying next to my letter of resignation, on which he had written the loyalty oath. 'I hadn't thought I would bring up this question with you now, but we've come so far, and it's preferable not to return to this discussion every day. Would you sign here?' He handed me the sheet.

'No,' I said, and gave it back to him.

'Why? Aren't you in agreement with the oath?'

I nodded yes.

'The oath's not important,' I said.

'Do you have objections to offer the government? Do you have differing opinions?'

'I don't know; I don't think so.'

'If you're hoping for reforms,' he said in a conciliatory way, 'don't hesitate to propose them; they don't scare us. In the old days regimes were afraid of new measures, because movement into the future threatened them. But we aren't afraid of anything like that: we are the future, the future's been made, and our lives illuminate it.'

That was when I gave in to temptation.

'Don't you think,' I said, 'that our regime will be like the others, that one day it'll collapse? And don't you think that it might happen soon?'

He looked at me and stood up; I sank back into the cushions—no doubt he saw this flinching, this defensive move against a foreseen blow. He just laughed.

'Like the others?' he repeated, stretching strenuously. 'Sure, maybe—but as the truth they prepared and didn't know, as the affirmation they sought in their ruin. How could it end,' he said in his doctrinal tone, so irritating and exhausting since he got his authority from me, 'how could it end, if it's the one that gives meaning to all the regimes that have ended, and if, in its absence, it would no longer be possible to imagine that something could end? In some ways it itself is finished, it's found its end, it's put an end to everything, and itself. Yes, from this point of view you're right but I'm not scandalized: one can't associate it too much with ideas of death, stoppage, or the fall; but its stability is what expresses death, and its endless duration is its fall.'

He paced, softly scraping the floor with one shoe. I thought of the attack that the newspapers had spoken too much of for it not to be imaginary.

'You can't obliterate everything,' I said. 'You aren't a law professor speaking in class—even if you are immersed in history and feel it so profoundly that everything that happens is, for you, immediately transformed into the law. But I see the sick, the strikes, the riots in the street. I can't suppress them: I myself am sick; I know what the verb "to end" means.'

He turned around and smiled.

'No, maybe that's exactly what you don't know yet. You need events, you'd like the sun to disappear. I keep asking myself what these events are that people miss. Everything necessary for my enlightenment has happened, and if nothing more happens, it's because nothing that's happening adds to the truth in which I move. Maybe there will still be a lot of historic dates, strikes, like you say, earthquakes, upheavals of all kinds; it's also possible that the years to come will be empty. What difference does it make—because what counts isn't that I'm walking around in your room right now, or that I'm working in my office, as I should be doing, and from now on wars and revolutions will have neither more nor less importance than my little daily habits. What counts instead is that with every step I take I can recall, from beginning to end, the movement, filled with hardship and triumph, which permits all of us to say the last word by justifying the first.'

'Why are you talking like this to me now?' I said, watching him pace back and forth slowly, always with one shoe lightly scraping the floor. 'What did you come to do? What I decide or don't decide means nothing to you. You aren't moved by personal feelings, you suppress them. You don't like me, and I don't like you . . .' I stopped. And what if my real father were there? If the tomb as well had only been a farce? First he would have nodded his head and looked at me confidently for a long time without offending me with all this verbiage; he would have ended up taking my arm and saying, well, now, let's go! 'Louise!' I called suddenly.

'Your sister has gone out.'

'I've got a fever. She left? When?'

'A few moments ago. She went to notify one of my colleagues who will facilitate your transfer.'

'And why are you staying?'

'I'm going to leave too.'

'And those?' I said, indicating the papers.

'Do whatever you like. The government in any case will make a decision.'

'And if I refuse?'

'Your refusal will be formally recorded.'

'And what comes next then, what'll be the penalty?'

'There cannot and there will not be any. You will stay in government service, and the government will use you within the framework that you've chosen.'

'But I've resigned! I'm sticking with my letter.'

'We won't forget that. In the past there have been people who started work and then quit with a sickly fickleness, feeling they were free because, as tiny fragments, they could move around within their shells—they hadn't yet fully matured and adhered to the walls. And then there was a time when this return of an anachronistic spirit was repressed: those who fell short of their tasks were condemned. But today condemnation is no more, because there are no more lapses. The inside and the outside correspond: the most intimate decisions are immediately integrated into the forms of public usefulness from which they are inseparable.'

'And still, you're there! You circle around me, vertiginously, to convince me: I should sign this, tear up that, swear an oath of loyalty. So everything isn't for the best?'

'No, everything isn't for the best, but for you and for you alone. For the State will know how to use your insubordination, and not only will it take advantage of it, but you, in opposition and revolt, will be its delegate and representative as fully as you would have been in your office, following the law. The only change is that you want change and there won't be any. What you'd like to call destruction of the State will always appear to you really as service to the State. What you'll do to escape the law will still be the force of the law for you. And when the State decides to annihilate you, you'll know that this annihilation doesn't sanction your error, doesn't give you, before history, the vain arrogance of men in revolt, but rather that it makes you one of these modest and correct servants on the dust of whom rests the good of all—and your good as well.'

'Get out,' I said weakly.

'I'll go, but my leaving won't change anything. You could take my place and I yours. Maybe you're already in my place.'

'Out,' I repeated.

'Good-bye. I think I can get you a car by the end of the afternoon. It'll come up to the door and stop. And don't forget,' he said, suddenly returning to his former style, 'I'm a good citizen, I serve the State! That's the motto!'

I felt a wave of spit coming up in my mouth, but he had left. Almost at the same moment, Bouxx came into the room. He saw all the papers spread out on the little table and, without hesitating, stuck out his hand to grab them. I started to move, but our glances met and he did what he wanted. He was wearing his boots, crude-looking things which went halfway up his leg, making him look massive and coarse. I was extremely tired. 'Very good,' he said, 'write, keep on writing!' I answered with a shrug. I would have liked to get him out of there. He had replaced the other so quickly, and with such an extreme lack of consideration, that I was having a hard time separating the two. And his presence wore me out too: there was something crushing, mountainous, in his huge body— the equivalent of my fatigue, in stone and earth.

'Rough day,' he said, showing me his filthy boots covered with cinders and soot. 'It seems you're not feeling well?'

'You don't seem surprised,' I said, pointing to the papers.

'Why? Because of that? I figured out a long time ago why you torture yourself. You were struggling; you didn't want to see that you were condemning what you held most dear. But logic did away with it; clarity, pushed all the way, denounced itself.'

'What did you figure out?' I asked, looking at him wearily.

'For a long time I've been on your trail. Do you remember our first meeting? From that time on, I've known you and I've understood your behavior. I've gotten information about you. You're a case.'

'A case?'

'Yes,' he said, nodding his head.

'And why are you so keenly interested in this case? Can you tell me?'

'Yes, I can tell you; your question doesn't bother me. It's true I first had plans for you of a certain kind, disreputable ones. I'm talking about views that the ruling class mentality would call immoral when attributing them to its adversaries, and historical when attributing them to itself. You know, since I've returned I've worked here and there, in clinics, most often in subordinate positions, but I've also sometimes filled in for former colleagues: medical circles are less subject than others to official pressure. It was at the clinic that I first noticed you. You had just had an attack. You were walking calmly down the hall. Why did you make an impression on me, even disturb me? I don't know. Maybe it was your way of walking and looking. Yes, you looked at the things around you in a striking way: you seemed to adhere to them. Wait— even now, in the way you're looking at me, I see the same expression. It's strange, it's as if your gaze has attached itself to mine, is about to touch it. I noticed this once in a person who was blacking out: when he was coming to, his eyes opened and clung to objects. Have you had epileptic sei- zures?' I shook my head. After this meeting, I asked who you were. Your name was a surprise, and little by little I became convinced that our paths had crossed for a reason. So I made inquiries. I got information on your job, your sickness. I learned a lot about your family situation and I also figured a lot out. Yes, in the end I went too far. A case, I said to myself, an almost irrational potential for disorder and upheaval. Would it be possible for the oldest story to start up again and this time be directed and be of use? This notion was somewhat troubling, and it pursued me. I wasn't really sure yet what I wanted; I prowled around you, I tested you, I couldn't make up my mind. You were the one who finally opened my eyes; you were tempting me. And that too is strange. In a story like this, my role was to become your tempter. But you were the temptation for me, because you showed me what I was looking for. I saw the matter clearly when you saw right through me: all I was planning was revealed to me. But you locked me into my projects and, from then on, they were destroyed—for the simple reason that, as soon as you looked beyond your terror, you realized what I could get you to do, and then it was no longer possible for you to do it. You got out of the whole business and went back to yourself. Maybe it was my fault, maybe I could have acted more prudently, more silently, more intimately, by mimicking to a greater extent the patience and maturity of time. It hardly matters—what does matter is that you've never stopped understanding everything, that your fever itself knew everything and that I've always been its servant, its instrument. And I wanted nothing more than to hunt you down.'

'Why all this rehashing?' I said, with an ever growing sense of weariness. 'These are doctor's stories. You've been conditioned by your job; you're constantly driven back to the very profession from which you've been expelled—precisely because you can no longer practice it.'

'What do you mean?' he asked, becoming animated. 'Is that another joke? Why are your jokes always so disagreeable and offensive? On the contrary, yes, this recapitulation was necessary, because it's all in the past. Now I want to be frank with you. I came, precisely, to propose an open collaboration, a real common labor. Listen,' he said, as if he wanted to cut me off, in order to pass more successfully as having thoughts different from my own, 'don't answer, wait. I need you, and that's the truth. I once explained to you everything that had already been done, how long groups had been at work, in what ways they were acting, all our positions. You can't imagine, and no one can imagine, to what extent the mountain has been undermined: I myself am only a link in only one chain, while there are a thousand chains getting together and secretly linking up in order to create a force capable of nullifying all the others.'

'Why do you need me?'

'I need you . . . ,' he repeated with a suddenly self-conscious look. 'I can tell you that we have support, agents, in all circles, on all levels of your wonderful administration from top to bottom. But I don't need another agent. Besides, you're sick, immobilized.'

'A hostage?'

'Yes,' he said, suddenly excited, 'maybe a hostage. I'd like to hold on to you, keep you in this room and come up here from time to time. Oh—I'm not speaking lightly, I've observed you for a long time. I have quite a few documents in my drawers that have to do with you. You're not an enemy of the law, and still you want to leave the law—that's extremely important. Your resignation in itself doesn't interest me. I've known hundreds of civil servants who've betrayed what they serve. But, precisely, you aren't betraying; you're tied to the law and you're no longer serving it. I look at you, and on your face I see everything I hate—the benevolence, the spirit of comprehension, mixed with the most humiliating irony, including this happy, detached, almost dead gaze, the very one I have to borrow in order to see you. How offensive it all is. But you don't offend anybody. On the contrary, I get pleasure, a feeling of peace, from contemplating what's hurt me for so long. Seeing you, I can no longer be hurt. You enlighten me, you don't burn me. You really are the one I'm looking for.'

He looked at me avidly, maybe for a few seconds. Then, seeing that I wasn't answering, he threw himself on my bed, half kneeling, half sitting, his knee coming up with the boot right next to my face. What struck me was that his exaltation, which seemed almost insane, was linked in me to an extreme fatigue, as if I had to witness, after being crushed way down, the vertiginous elevation he was offering. From his proffered dream—which, according to him, was expansion, success, reconciliation—I could only know the asphyxiating mass which, like his weight, was paralyzing me. And then his humility was too great, he unconsciously humiliated himself, he believed himself to be dignified with servility, the obedience of a beaten animal, and not even that: he was nothing but the carcass of a beaten horse. I moved aside, and doing so I saw that he was asleep. Then I pulled my arm away, and he slumped over. His leather jacket gave off a stench that brought back to me the smell of the whole building. He seemed exhausted. I thought of his too slow and too quick blood, of which he was wary. He claimed it was his master and that it had just now mastered him. His sleep was so strange! He was putting me to sleep; it was the room's sleep, the building's sleep, it was my own. What time was it, anyway? Suddenly he sat up, looked at me, and then stood. 'I'm exhausted,' he said in a lugubrious voice. He was standing and looking at the window in a drowsy way. 'I'm going to have some coffee.' He was still motionless, inert, but little by little he seemed to wake up. I caught him listening. 'You hear it?' he asked. In fact I did hear a muffled cry, a kind of vicious cough that couldn't become distinct.

'It's your friend. I already heard him a little while ago.'

He listened some more and seemed annoyed, in a bad mood.

'I'm going to make him be quiet. He whines like a dog.'

'What's wrong with him?' I asked, after he had pounded the partition rapidly and irregularly a number of times, which stopped the groaning. He shrugged and went back to the middle of the room. 'But what are you going to do with all these sick people? You can't just hit the wall to make them be quiet. And you—if they lock you up, and close the dispensary?'

'This dispensary, here? Why would they close it?'

'The police are on the lookout for you, you know that.'

'The police? Why would they come? First of all, where are they? They don't want to come, I swear it. They're not even in the area. It's not their day.'

'Sooner or later they'll come, they always come. You just don't get it. They know the situation better than you, and it doesn't frighten them.'

'Sure, they know. Statistics talk. The time has come for evil to show itself. The Control Commissions are giving us the wherewithal to open four new Centers. Soon we may need a first-aid station on every street. No one is interested in being tricky anymore.'

'What are you saying? But . . . you're here! There's something crazy about you, Bouxx. If they're letting you do it, it's even worse! Don't you understand that if they're supporting you it's to destroy you—their help will ruin you, and besides, they're not helping you, it only looks that way. What means do you have at your disposal? What measures can you take? You'll go under and be swept away. You'll be ruined; we'll all be. What are you going to do with me?'

'Do you want to leave?'

'They're supposed to send a car. Did you know about that?'

'Staying in this place is not, of course, a very appealing idea.'

'What you're saying is unpleasant. I'm not responsible for that decision. If I'm evacuated under orders, I can only obey.'

'As you like.' He gathered the papers together and looked at them with indifference, almost insolently. 'Your departure is essential, of course. Your family very much wants to see you go, no doubt about that.'

'Why do you say that? Did you figure that out? Did you receive different orders?' He kept leafing through the papers but clearly not reading them. 'Come on, be a friend. Why did you imply that I'm not supposed to go? How do you know?'

'Nothing, I've no idea.'

'To hell with it,' I said, withdrawing farther back in the room.

He stepped forward.

'If you want to stay, it's easy: I'll sign a statement to the effect that you're . . . sick, contagious. From that moment on, no one will have the right to make you leave, not even the highest authority.'

'But that's an abuse of power. Or . . . tell me the truth. I demand that you tell me. It's inhuman the way you're acting; your reticence is vile.'

'I'm not holding you back. I'll only sign with your consent.'

We fell silent. Behind the partition Dorte had started coughing again; it was a really revolting, unclean cough, one that was stifling itself.

'What are the symptoms of this illness?' He shrugged, which meant: I'm not a real doctor, you yourself said so, but which also perhaps meant: Above all, don't start worrying about the symptoms, you know enough about them, we all know enough. 'Look at that,' I said.

My flesh now had a slightly reddened look; it was both repulsive and enticing. His hands went down along my sides, in the most expert way, as a nurse's would do; suddenly I had a stab of pain when he touched my thigh, which had seemed fine before.

'The police,' I said in a low voice, my ears buzzing. 'They beat me up this morning.'

He looked at my face for quite a while, then gave me a number of sharp, light slaps on the cheeks. 'Don't move your eyes. We'll do a poultice. What's that?' Getting up, he had discovered the sheet of paper I was clutching in my hand. 'Show it to me!' He tried to grab it. 'Wait a minute!' I said, pushing him away. Then, under the covers, I read the paper again.

'Do you know what this is? My stepfather's trick to reassure me, a written declaration stating that there is no epidemic, that I'm not in any danger!'

'It's from your stepfather?' He bumped into me trying to take it away. I hit him.

'You're going too far,' I said, drily. 'Besides, there's nothing more than what I've read: "I certify . . ."'

'I'd like to see his handwriting.'

'Like anybody's, everybody's, my own.' From a distance I showed it to him. 'Do you know why I'm keeping this paper? Maybe you'll laugh. It's a talisman.'

'A talisman? To protect you from the plague?'

'Suppose,' I said, 'that you were a doctor and that you were trying to treat me by telling me crazy stories, and let's suppose you were really engaged in an illegal activity, that you wanted to get your hands on me, that this country was falling apart, that the sickness was your accomplice. Let's suppose that you're some kind of a nut, that you've got two faces. Aren't you in fact sick if you're hoping to succeed in fighting against the State? And if you are sick, isn't everything you claim to be doing fog, the sign of your stalemate? But if you really are abnormal, in other words a stranger to the State, then the State itself is only a trap, a pack of lies, sheer hypocrisy, and then you're right, you're struggling for what is just, for oppressed and wretched truth. But if you are right, you are only the instrument of the State, its servant, zealous but disowned, who suffers this disowning by order of the law, in order to let it live and triumph. And if you *are* this servant, then you are also mine, you serve me, you care for me, and it makes no difference whether you do it as a real doctor or as an unqualified one or as a madman looking to me to guarantee his dreams. I'm hanging from a nail and that nail is the truth. Now I'm being strangled, and nobody's going to get me down, not you or anybody else. That's what this paper keeps telling me.'

'Do you really take me for a maniac?'

'I'm swinging, hoping to tear out the nail, that's all. Do you understand?' I said, pointing to the partition. I had never heard a cough like it; it was cracked, as if on a false note, and sickly, as if sickness, and not the sick person, had let itself go.

He stood, thinking, in front of the wall. 'I've known him for twenty years,' he said. 'I don't have a better friend. And now, what is he? A carcass on a bed!"

'And if I stay, what'll happen to me?'

'Don't worry about it. I'll come to see you from time to time. Everything will be fine. For the moment,' he said, after hesitating a second, 'I ask only one thing. When you want to write, write, and it doesn't matter what—everything that comes into your head, even trivia.'

I looked at him.

'You'd better watch out, Bouxx, I'm warning you, you'd better watch out.'

He waved good-bye and opened the door.

'Try to sleep. The nurse will come later.'

# 7

I felt sweat trickling on my hand, yet my skin was barely wet; it was even cold. Still, it was a fiery hot day. I got up and sat on the side of the bed. My leg hurt if I stretched it out; bending it pulled on the abscess and caused a shooting pain, but the swelling seemed to have gone down. I collected my sandals. The sun had reached the sixth groove on the floor; the tapping continued. Three taps, then three; one tap, then five. It was as if an animal was silently scratching on the other side or gnawing at the plaster. Five taps, then two; one tap, then five. It could be anything: a dying fly—but flies whirled around, they stuck to each other, little flies, gnats, really, who formed a flying mass in the sunshine—we were urged to kill them. With my sandal I crudely slapped the wall. Suddenly the wall responded: one tap, one tap; one tap, one tap. *Ha ha!* I knew he was hitting it with the corner of his lighter. *Ha ha!* He found it funny; the wall was laughing. A little while ago, the wall had said, *I'm getting up.* I took the stick and tapped softly: the picture was before my eyes, I saw the five lines of capital letters, I heard them like a light burning in my head, like the inflammation of my abscess. And the wall itself was more sensitive than my leg, and not only the wall, but all the partitions, every object, every part of the floor, it tapped for hours, during the day, at night, endlessly, with a furtive discretion that confused it with everything that cracked, walked, flew, so that there was no longer a single noise, or a moment of silence, that was not already a word. The daylight had reached the seventh groove; I stretched out again. The pain also started tapping on the inside of my thigh, dully, with deliberate jolts: four slow taps, then a very short tap; another slow, then five quick ones. P. E.: perhaps pestilence. Over the entire circumference the flesh was harder than rock; it was a real shell, the numbness of whatever caused the most suffering. The pain at this spot was virtually identical to that of a bandage, so much so that the worse it got, the more one had the impression that one was recovering, but also the opposite: the more numb it got, the more it hurt. In any case, the fever was burning there now. I got up. During the night the blinds had fallen and the sun covered the window and occupied the whole room. Something there had become intolerable. The heat? Yes, the heat, but also that light: it had the stupor and patience of water, it flowed as soon as one gave it an opening, it filtered through when there was no aperture: for hours, days, centuries, it was spreading, it was water. *What are you doing?* the wall asked. I got closer, I looked at the wall and followed with my finger the contour of the stain: it was spreading upward now, it seemed more visible, but above all wetter, greasier. *I'm looking at the stain,* I tapped softly. I imagined him as he must have been, pressed against the partition to the point of seeming to inhabit it, watching it, holding his head against it. *So?—Bigger.* Immediately, the wall laughed happily: *Ha ha! Ha ha,* two little dry taps that were repeated for a number of seconds. I threw myself on the bed. In the distance, water echoed; for the entire day there had been silence with the noise of water, cups, saucers, sometimes a shout. I wrapped myself in the covers and looked at the partition. Finally I saw almost legibly, as if series of words had been put up on posters, *In all buildings, if a person suffers from fever and has spots or swelling on any part of his body* . . . The text suddenly went out; the alarm sounded; I gathered that I had read directly the usual tapping of the wall. The nurse was coming up the steps: it was easy to recognize, it was always the same, rhythmless, bearing down the same way on right, then left, on left, then right, but nevertheless too heavy, awkward: her shoes must have been too big. 'Why haven't you gotten up?'—'My leg hurts too much.' She bent over the swelling. Her blouse was stiff, as if starched over her own rigidity. She opened the window with her skeleton key, pulled up the blinds, and let in some air by opening the fanlight. 'That shouldn't keep you from going out,' she said, 'on the contrary.' Right away the wall got going: *Again?* I put my hat on and knocked *Silence,*

146

*silence,* but my hand had barely stopped when I began again to hear tapping so agile, frail, and yet tenacious that I made it out even behind my own rapping. *A walk,* I said. Then the wall came up with something else: it repeated *Look, look.* It repeated it perhaps ten times and for each word it hit fifty times.

\* \* \*

Bouxx couldn't grasp that I didn't need to write: the events were recorded, were written, and they made a story by the simple fact that I was there. Everything then was so clear and rapid or, on the other hand, everything became very slow; every moment the end appeared, but the end had come a long time ago as well. I went to the window—what could you see? Nothing; where there were houses, maybe a dark mass; no windows were lit up. I went back to the bed, but it threw me out. I lay down on the floor. I saw the street clearly. Ten, maybe twenty buildings were closed—some because suffering had already gotten in, the others because they didn't want to let it come in. And always passersby, the alignment of houses, sidewalks; I had even seen flowers at some of the windows. People kept walking past each other, they walked without seeing, and yet they saw everything; at the least suspect sign, a bandaged leg or an armband, they stepped aside. I couldn't stay on the floor. I knew that if I walked, he would hear me. In the almost total darkness, it was enough to walk around the furniture ten times to get dizzy; throughout the day forty or fifty times around were necessary, and then you had to think about dizziness. I was trying to doze off. His mouse-scratching always aggravated me in my half-sleep. Really, it was no longer tapping, but rubbing, the beating of wings; at night, worn out, he must have been resigned to rubbing his fist on the wall. *What?* I asked. *—Have you heard?* What could he hear? The fever victims in the building? They were delirious, screaming when their wounds were dressed, in other words around nine o'clock and around five. But almost every night he had heard howling, terrifying cries, coming from nearby streets. Three days ago, during a walk, while we were passing a closed building, a window opened and a woman cried out three times, 'To death!' It was a small house that surely had no other tenant; the tone had seemed as surprising as the words—neither an insult, nor hatred, but a simple voice, neutral, resigned, as if this woman were inviting herself to die. *To death, to death, to death,* the wall was now repeating the cry, with its own secret and expressionless tone. It lasted until the stick hit the wall again, then it calmed down. I tried to count the noises: in the house there was no sound, neither cough, nor door, nor water. Silence, a silence like the one in a train when the noise makes everyone be quiet, but here one listened for noise in vain, and only a larger silence, one harder to uncover, came from outside. I imagined where the closest street went: behind my head. On the right the empty lots, on the left the street, the square, the avenue. In the distance, there was perhaps the vague rolling sound of trucks.

I sat up: he had started drumming. *The grave. —Where? —They're working there. —Be quiet.* It was probably in the direction of the empty lot where he often claimed to hear the noise of excavation, but I could make out only the same background silence. So, nothing, except maybe a slight stamping. He must have been hearing the sound of cars. No doubt in the distance trucks were rolling, heavy ones, or a long line of them. The noise wasn't continuous; it approached, went away, disappeared; from time to time a vehicle seemed to stop, started up, stopped again, while the others were rushing forward. It sounded like garbage collectors. Suddenly I had the impression that all the doors in the building were opening. Someone jumped out of bed above me. Sick people started coughing and whimpering. And now, clearly, a truck had come into the street, its racket was getting closer, making the walls shake, and suddenly it stopped. I couldn't see anything through the window; the hall door wouldn't open. I heard sliding noises, the sounds of feet, on the street people were working with care, things were being moved, dragged along. I sat on the stool, not wanting to hear. And indeed the silence soon returned, but soon gave way again, this time to a terrible rumbling that was spreading everywhere, covering the whole city. I heard it smash into us, it enveloped me, hit me. I of course knew it was rain, a storm, but it was so eloquent, so full of warnings and threats that it didn't allow a moment of respite: it was hunting me down, driving me crazy. When I lay down again the noise had become peaceful; it was raining gently. Dorte asked if I had heard the convoy. *What convoy?* He repeated the question, and then was silent.

\* \* \*

The abscess kept burning more fiercely. And more and more it had the look and lack of sensitivity of a plaster. During the walk I saw a man run; coming out of an adjacent street, he ran along the avenue; he was wrapped in a blanket. Nobody tried to stop him. At the intersection he fell; two or three passersby wanted to help. But after letting them come close he lunged at them, howling. With nothing to do but read Bouxx's writings, I felt the sickness burn; there was a living nail deep in the abscess and when I read, the nail drove deeper; when I continued, it turned into a screw. And still I forced myself to read. There were pages and pages of reports, a pile of proud insanity. Why was he sending me all these commentaries? To know how I felt? To get me to write? To inflame me more? I felt it couldn't go on much longer; if the burning kept plaguing me, I'd have to run, too; I'd go just about anywhere; I'd throw myself in the river. The burning was covering my whole body, it was at my fingertips, on my neck, it was drying me out, but that wasn't its real goal. What it really wanted was to get to my eyes and affect my gaze, which it made so bitter and burning that I was no longer able to raise or lower my eyelids, and it read. The burning read, joyous and attentive, the words of Bouxx—and it didn't miss a sign—in their carefully formed and shaped schoolmaster's handwriting: 'I am an insulted man. This does not mean that someone has insulted me. No, I have suffered an insult. Anyone can hurt me, everyone's a burden to me, and if I have recourse to reprisals the person I choose is necessarily the one most in the wrong. I don't look for whoever is responsible. Some are more guilty than others, but everyone is immensely guilty. It's not necessary to single out institutions, individuals, and laws. Destroying an administration is an empty and insignificant act; but dishonoring a public figure makes him forever my ally.' I knew that these words were, in a sense, written by me, I was reading them and I saw them as shameful, but I understood them and approved of them; that's why he was forcing me to read them. On another page, there were statistics: four new Centers; twenty-one newly evacuated buildings, fifty-seven isolated, forty-three because of suspicious cases, fourteen because the tenants had been in contact with contagious patients. Why all these numbers? Was he giving me them to scare me? To make them irrefutable, to have me accept them since I was the only authority that remained? I understood why I was being taken on exhausting walks: I was supposed to see the closed houses with their guards, the officially sanctioned barriers; I had to see the whole neighborhood, which seemed run through by a sordid fire which with every advance was poisoning the air and devastating the day. There were, to be sure, passersby in the streets, but it was still a desert, a space as empty as a legally closed zone, a region where those who passed were no longer capable of producing the reality of a true population. All this—so that my gaze could make it legitimate; so that the lethal measures authorized by the epidemic could be made public: things had been so transformed now that going into the street was like wading into mud, into the solitude of filthy water. I threw down the papers: I wanted to drink—anything, even disinfectant. The glass too was marked with greasy spots; my fingers left marks on the sheets, on the wall. Maybe it was the fever; it seemed that a kind of grease was coming out of my body; when I examined my leg I didn't dare touch it, it looked like stone: the skin was nauseatingly pale, it seemed as if an enormous pressure was weighing down on the flesh in order to transform it—a strange pressure that reminded me of something, something that referred back to long ago and was as heavy as a memory, as all of the past. Then I felt it, looking was too much, my glance threw acid on the burn, made it retract. Perhaps it was the contact with the air, or even the daylight. The day had made the sickness visible; suffering it was no longer enough, you still had to see it, it took up the whole room, it was pulling me out of myself, the whole room was hurting me—more than hurting me, doing something more intolerable, something that was stirring me up and filling me with enthusiasm. *Are you sick?* But the wall went on not answering; only the big formless stain was expressing itself, the stain that was like Dorte's inscription, the proof of his presence, the result of the labor of his fever and sweat. True, it seemed bigger, it was sending out its blotches; I ran up to pass my hand over it; I tapped again, I knew he wasn't sleeping. If that's the way he wants it. . . . I started walking again. Maybe the room was too empty, the walls too white; and then it opened too directly onto the outdoors, that's why I couldn't stand still. I had asked for engravings I could look at, in order to rest, and all he had been willing to give me had been a photograph showing himself, Dorte, and twenty other men, all with a strange look which seemed almost comical, yet fearfully true. Bouxx alone was recognizable. He seemed neither younger nor changed and, because of that, in a suit that made him a completely different person with nothing in common with the one I knew, he became a fantastic, unbelievable being, almost a hero. The others, grouped closely together in two rows, looked like prisoners, or sick people, or even like workers in the same office, but they all had the same subdued appearance, a subterranean look with something <u>devious.</u> Dorte could be the one on the left, immediately behind Bouxx. *Dorte?* What was he doing? Not a sound came from his room, he wasn't coughing; sometimes he whimpered. At that point I would have liked to have heard him howl or just speak. There was no talking in that room; at least I didn't hear any, and the nurse rushed through. I was distraught at the idea that something might have happened to him, as if his were the only real presence in the whole house. I looked at his spot, his wall, which he had strewn with intelligent signs. From the papers I chose the posters that were put up everywhere in the streets, and which had become a <u>litany </u>for me. I spread them across the wall. *Every isolated building is under the surveillance of two or more caretakers whose job is to provide communication with the outside. Any building in which the medical authorities have noted suspicious cases will be isolated for a period of one week.*

*If the progress of the disease reveals the presence of a contagious illness the building will be evacuated immediately. Noncontaminated persons who have been living in a building placed under an evacuation order will be observed at a Center for a period of one week. —Only authorized persons will be given access to isolated buildings. Under no circumstances will the inhabitants of these buildings be authorized to leave. —Previous legal measures are suspended until further notice.* I heard someone running in the corridor below. I felt strangely ill, which seemed to be connected with my reading, but I wasn't able to understand how. I went to the window that couldn't be opened; there was no air. I knelt down and breathed in a little of the outside air through the slots. On the other side of the courtyard, directly facing me, I made out the white bulk of a bed that seemed empty. Nevertheless after a few moments a shadow, something thick, came to add to the thickness of the glass. I waved to it. The shadow was motionless. Seeing the small shape I had the impression that it was a man kneeling on the bed, or perhaps a child, but it was big and almost deformed. Using one of the sheets of paper I rubbed at the thick coating on the windows, and, after scraping it with my nail, I managed to make the glass somewhat transparent. The individual didn't move, but clearly he saw me and was watching me. With signs I tried to get him to scrape his windowpane as well. Suddenly my opposite number became extremely agitated: he moved up and down very quickly, covering the entire expanse of the window. He crawled, then jumped up; at one point his shadow sprang up in a remarkable way to the very top of the casement, and then it started up its dance once more. The spectacle was overwhelming. I was terrified, and threw myself on the bed. The feeling that this scene was going on behind my back, that what I had just seen was still visible, gave me convulsions; I fell on the ground. Still, a little later I calmed down: the fact that I was lying on the floor and smelling the dust was strangely agreeable; I breathed softly; my agitation was again under control. Crawling, I came up to the window. Lights had been turned on in various windows. All these apartments must have housed the administrative services of the dispensary, and I had the impression that *corruption; decomposition*

Bouxx was living on the fourth floor, on the other side of the building, since the block in which we were confined was now receiving only the sick. The room across from me was still dark. I stayed squatting until the nightlight was turned on.

I decided to write to Bouxx while I was splashing water on my face. The light was so weak I could hardly write. The whole time I felt the extent to which the humiliating nature of my existence went beyond the humiliation of everyone else, because in my case I had to read, write, and reflect. I understood everything. 'I've read your writing. You didn't ask me for advice, but for a few days I've wanted to tell you this: you write too much. You're superstitious about what's written. You're too preoccupied with commentaries, orders, and reports. And your phrases lack a certain precision. They're ignorant copies, a learned language that tends to revive old examples that don't apply very well to what's going on now. In this way the past seems to be coming back, but only as a ridiculous prophecy that turns everything one tries to do into an illusion. As far as I'm concerned, the situation is becoming intolerable. Sickness is always a sad affair, but when it has such a degrading character it itself becomes ridiculous. Maybe you've forgotten that I understand everything that's going on. I perceive everything, just remember that; that's why I can't hold on long. I'm ashamed. The odor is more or less tolerable in this room. But go into the hallways: there's putrefaction; you'd think horses were rotting in every room. It's not in the air; it's something dishonorable. And please, spare me from having to go into the streets tomorrow. I don't want to run the risk any more of being exposed to people who get out of the way because I look or smell bad. Whole streets are rotting. The terror is too much. And are you still authorizing some of the butchers to sell their meat? It's madness. Listen, you can't go on humiliating unfortunates who are worse than mud, even if it is to cure them. I can assure you that curing through humiliation is the worst part of the story. When you understand everything, like I do, it's hell.' I lay down, but I got restless again. I saw the poor guy jumping, going down. He must have been wearing a shirt. Was he suffering? Why did seeing me get him all worked up? Or was this really something more abject, planned out? In my half-sleep I distinctly heard gunshots. The nightlight was still on. A gunshot went off, muffled in this distance: it could have come from the empty lots. But then there was a series of shots, quite nearby. It was so intense that my area seemed to be the target, and I even thought I heard the plaster on the wall in back disintegrating. I thought the authorities were finally waking up. I would have liked to get up, go and see, shout out, hit the door, but I didn't get up. In the morning I again felt an extreme discomfort. I smelled my hand, my jacket. In front of me a little white spot shone; it seemed that my eyes had been trained on it since I woke up. This brightness was resting on the wall, but not like a spot: it was moving, it broke away from the partition to take shape in the air. Now I watched it anxiously. A little later the sound of voices came from the next room. Then someone went out. I ran into the hallway and tried to look through a slit. I lay back down. Little by little the dangerous character of the white blotch became obvious: I felt a searing light; now it was a tooth, a shard so obscenely sharp that it made me start up the business from the day before again. Then I came out of my torpor and decided that this mark corresponded to the clear spot on the window. The sun was coming through it; it seemed the wall was buzzing. *Dorte?* An infinitely soft sound came as a response, the noise of a drop of water falling, then another. —'Are you *sick?* You *scared* me!' No more noise of water. I imagined it was going back to its place in the wall. *Answer.* I had the feeling that a reservoir was waiting to be filled: you had to wait hours for a single drop; for these two drops, all the time he had been keeping silent for so many days. Suddenly, the tapping started again, in a disordered but distinct way. *Paralysis.* —'Was that *Bouxx?*' But silence returned. Both of us heard the nurse's footsteps. She entered with a canteen full of coffee and a bucket of water. The odor she brought into the room from the outside was so strong, so disgusting, that her effort to make me drink a fluid that also had the taste of a bad pharmaceutical product was an absurd challenge. When I made it clear that I wouldn't drink, her hands stretched out to take the cup and exposed themselves in front of me; I was struck by their size, their roughness. They had a special look; what kind of work had they gotten themselves into? Better not to ask. They took the cup and came up slowly before my eyes, as if, up to now held in reserve in a case, they had purposely come out of it in order to be seen only once in a special way. That was when I realized that she almost always wore gloves; perhaps I saw her for the first time when her hands were bare. She went away to open the fanlight. I barely heard her behind my back.

'Why aren't they taking care of me? My leg is burning.' —'I can make compresses for you.' —'I couldn't care less about your compresses. I'm suffering. Do you know what that means, suffering, suffering! I'm constantly sick.' I think she put a little water that stank of creosote on my face. She straightened the bed. 'How can you stand these odors?' But without even glancing at me she continued to move around, staring at things blankly, neither indulgent nor severe, with a cold aura accompanied by a stale stench. 'Why do you have this job? Why don't you run away?' Maybe she shrugged. She turned around and got together the things she had brought. —'Wouldn't you like me to leave some coffee?' I looked at her, indicated no, but just when the door was closing I let out a cry and called for her. 'Who's living over there, in the room facing mine?' —'Where?' —'On the other side of the court-yard.' I knelt down on the bed. She went to the window and looked out for a fairly long time. I saw her half bent over, her big shoes going almost halfway up her leg: they were like the boots one saw on miners out West. 'It's a room for the dogs,' she said, turning around. —'Dogs! What are they doing there? For observation?' She made a slight gesture. I could barely wait for her to leave, so I could get up and run to the window. Behind the window there was the same white bulk which seemed to be a bed; it took up the entire space of the room. A cloth had been hung from the window latch, or maybe from a chair. The room seemed empty. I knew they had given the order to get rid of all animals, and those still running around were being hunted down and wiped out. Still, a few days ago, during one of our first walks, right on the avenue, we came upon forty big dogs. They were on leashes

held by people who took up the whole width of the street.
They were huge creatures and their fur was shaved, which
revealed a white, sickly skin, the caricature of a woman's.
Without barking or even growling they walked at the feet of
their masters and let out an immense collective noise. They
ignored the passersby on either side, who had to jump up onto
the sidewalk to give them room. Maybe they didn't even see
them—they walked blindly, giving the impression of monstrous abscesses, brought together for a short walk before
going back to their kennels. It was certainly hard to stand; the
odor was something else, an intimate, insinuating smell, as if
what was sweetest and most bland had suddenly taken on a
stifling intensity. At the time I felt an extraordinary loathing,
and now the loathing was across from me, in a room like mine.
I sat there waiting, my eyes fixed on the room and on the
courtyard. I told myself that if I ever heard those dogs barking I
wouldn't be able to stand it: the worst would happen. In the
end, looking more closely at the daylight three fingers wide
that I had opened up on the windowpane, I saw that it resembled an inscription, which, via the opening, seemed to give the
same name to everything I saw.

\* \* \*

Almost intact, the two houses let out a black smoke which
caused a motionless bunch to gather all over the street, a kind
of lugubrious crowd that didn't want to leave. The people
looked at it, and if I had counted them there would have been
twenty, maybe thirty—but they didn't really form a mob,
because they were careful to stay separate from one another.
Between each of them there was the width of a corridor, and
some tried to disappear outright by hiding their faces behind
a handkerchief. I felt she was lingering, which she shouldn't
have been. She wasn't really looking at the two houses that
had burned, but straight in front of her. The first buildings,
although no doubt inhabited, were the deadest: their windows were closed, their balconies abandoned. Many windows
were covered with pieces of cloth or paper, as if to stop up the
smallest opening. Beyond the burned hulks guards were
watching us, one standing in the doorway of a crude little

sentry box, the others in the street, each with a billy club in his hand. Further on all the houses had been marked, and they led the street into a desert. I noticed that a few people were speaking, and nothing was stranger, since they were talking without looking at each other, without getting closer, at an infinite distance from one another, as if the words were only the complement of a neutral presence. The result was that their noise resembled Dorte's wall tapping. I recalled almost analogous statements by Dorte. It seemed that the people who had torched the houses were tenants of the building across the street; it was a fairly big place whose ground floor was occupied by a clothing store. They must have been convinced that the sickness was smoldering behind windows from which they were separated merely by the street and, rather than waiting for an evacuation order, they had thrown in a few cans of gasoline. Very quickly their neighbors were in an inferno. 'You have to burn all these shacks,' said someone, half aloud. —'Yes, it's better to burn it all.' Everyone started repeating this, softly. It was like a watchword smoldering in the ashes, a dead word made to look brilliant by the fire. It was as if the odor of smoke, the bitter smell that blew in our direction, was refreshing: it kept us from breathing in the sickness, and so it became what was purest in the atmosphere. The guards motioned us to move along. Soon a number of people got going. A guard came up, holding his weapon under his arm. He's the one, they said, who maintained law and order the other night when he prevented tenants under quarantine from leaving their burning houses. Still, everyone believed that, in spite of the gunfire, a number of them had gotten out and were running around in the area.

The guard stopped ten meters away and shouted at us. At that moment I saw what she was staring at—it was the street sign, which said West Street. Above the sign someone had drawn a black circle and a white circle, signs that indicated that the street contained evacuated and isolated buildings. On the rough plaster, painted in red, was the word 'silence.' She must have noticed that we were alone, but she paid no attention to the guard's voice, a voice which seemed to me to be indicating the suspicion that, if we were standing around in this area, it was because we we were connected with these contaminated houses. Almost every tree along the avenue had a poster, but almost every one of them had been torn; huge flaps of paper, wet and dirty, were hanging there. One poster was still intact: although not large, I saw it from a distance because it had the diagonal colored line that indicated an official message. Perhaps it was recent, but nobody came up to read it. *To the guards of Washhouse Street. In Washhouse Street, where all buildings have been evacuated, with the exception of two quarantined houses, the guards of these two houses, along with a number of others, have not only pillaged the empty buildings, which had nevertheless been sealed, but have robbed and murdered the tenants of the still occupied buildings. In the course of an inspection the cadavers of two women have been found, one shot with a revolver, the other strangled by means of a rag placed in the throat. It has been determined after examination that these women were suffering from a severe and contagious disease, so that all those who came near them have been exposed to a serious risk of infection.* 'What are you doing?' she said. 'Come on!' In the last lines, the guards were warned of the risk they were running, and the risk they were forcing the general population to run, by not going as soon as possible to a dispensary. I knew she didn't want me to talk in the street. So I kept trailing after her at a fair distance, since it seemed that with every step the pain in my leg was about to become much worse. I was expecting a violent spasm. It was when we arrived, just in front of the former concierge's lodge, that I blacked out. They took me into a little room where I made out a young man dressed in a white coat, who was taking cotton pads and dirty linen from a basin and throwing them into a pail.

Through the cloudy air he thrust his fingers under my eyelids and then went away. I saw her standing near me, her arms shoved deep into the pockets of her raincoat, and on the other side he was making signs with his hands and sometimes quickly moving them up to his mouth. He repeated the word 'prison' a number of times, in a dogmatic, reverberating voice, and she was clearly watching the word on his lips. She was looking at him as if the word had a visible and brilliant form, as brilliant as the word 'fire' was a little while ago for the people on the street. 'The prison's going to be evacuated,' he suddenly declared in a thundering voice. 'It's superobvious: there's no more salubrious building in the whole country.' —'Yes,' she said, in a muffled voice. That was when I noticed how much of her face had become visible: even her neck was jutting out of the raincoat, and it reached up to her head in such a strange and conspicuous way that when she brought her hands up it was clear that she had the feeling that she was showing too much of herself and that her hands were there to sense what was going on. Without ceasing to look in front of her, she undid her raincoat, but then something stopped her and, pulling on her belt buckle, she wrapped herself up tightly again. 'It's a decisive stage in our organization,' he roared. He passed in front of me and took a notebook from the table, a kind of small double-entry ledger. She turned slowly to follow him with her eyes, but he said to her in a nervous voice, 'Look,' and she came up with such a sudden movement that I was thrown backwards. He threw me an irritated glance. 'Ah,' he said, 'there've been fourteen unexpected arrivals; they've been placed for the time being in the smaller room,' and he leaned over to point out where they were on the building map affixed to the wall. The young woman took a flask from one of the shelves. 'This?' she asked. A mild odor of mint spirits rose up from the glass they handed me. I grumbled about my leg. She in turn looked at the map on which a large number of little flags had been stuck. 'And his room?' Both of them turned toward the wall. I complained loudly about my leg. —'Is it really bad? Let me see.' He took a red flask and a cotton pad, and practically splashed the liquid on; he then cleaned it skillfully from wherever it had trickled—onto my clothes, onto the floor. She watched him with a strange look. The fire spread rapidly to my stomach and chest, with a nastiness whose presence I could feel under the burn: the pain was tolerable, but this hostility that came out of the bottle and purposely cut me to the core was not. I struggled. He kept on pouring. 'Is that enough?' he asked, squeezing a bandage on my leg that I tried to wave away, thinking that, in the fresh air, under everyone's eyes, the pain would not be so dangerously locked up within me. 'There you go,' he said, giving me a little slap on the shoulder. I looked at him, and suddenly the man in the shirt, running in the street among passersby who didn't dare touch him, seemed to come out of Bouxx's photograph. He certainly was one of those young men; he had the same grubby look, the same agitation that couldn't be contained; at a certain point the suffering made him jump out of bed and, barefoot, blew him outside with the blanket he had torn off his bed; barefoot, but I had noticed that his left foot was bandaged around the ankle with the cloth winding its way up around his leg. 'The prisoners will be taken care of!' he shouted, leading me to the door. He pushed me toward it, but I kept on looking at him: on his neck he had a whole chain of swollen, encrusted boils; his eyelids were red around the edges. What a little punk—even younger and more sickly than I was! With a self-important voice, he again yelled, 'Jeanne, don't forget those fourteen!' She smiled at him over my shoulder.

I was convinced that they were going to put a number of sick people in my room. From the noise it seemed they never stopped moving in and out. They put them in with Dorte. Some must have been put in Bouxx's old apartment. The floor became very noisy, and the smell got so strong it came into my entrance hall. The uproar ended in the evening. But soon there were new arrivals, twenty, thirty, maybe more: I counted more than fifteen in the courtyard where they were being provisionally held, some lying down, most of them squatting or standing. Fifteen others followed; I heard them, and I sensed something that was slovenly and hostile about them: they didn't seem particularly sick—they were big solid guys. And still, every time the walking started up again in the street, in the courtyard, in the hallways, I felt the sickness mounting, I felt my burns inflame, and any hope of curbing the pain, which revived after every lull, was driven away by an even darker pain, which came out of ever deeper hiding places. Where were they coming from? It was as if all those carefully guarded houses were coming back into contact with the outside, as if the dikes had burst and water flowed, calmly and alone. No doubt about it, it was going badly. They must have been piling them up in the antechambers, in the corridors, against the doors, against my door; sometimes I even imagined they were in my room, either because of their ever-closer breathing which was coming through the partition, because of their grunting, or above all because of their way of scurrying on the floor as if they had all been tied together; they seemed constantly to be gaining ground and occupying the tiniest available spaces. Fairly late, the young woman came in. Since there was no electricity I didn't understand how she was able to appear before me, standing, her face lit with its expressionless light, while she held out something I couldn't see. She lowered a flashlight and I took the glass, which I then put down so that I could look at her. 'So drink,' she said, 'I'm in a hurry.' I looked at her; her face was sallow. —'Are they going to put sick people in this room?' —'No.' I drank the liquid and handed back the glass. While she was taking it I put my hand on her glove and slowly aimed the flashlight toward the top of her face; she let me do it. Her face shown and became even more gray: the gray of cement. —'What's going on? Things are going badly, aren't they?' She stepped back, perhaps to see me better, but the instant she stepped away something she wanted to avoid settled on the immobility of her features, made them even more immobile: something that seemed to correspond to my own fear. 'It's going very badly!' I said, and I knew that what I had before my eyes was more empty and more sterile than any fear—and more humiliating, too. She gestured with her head. 'Where are these people coming from?' —'Shh, be quiet.' She repeated 'shh' in a dry voice. —'Where are they coming from? They're not serious cases, are they?' —'No.' —'But why have they brought them here?' —'I've no idea. How's your leg?' I looked for her behind this point of light that was driving her back into the shadows, and while I was looking at her large shoulders and the lower part of her face, which was also large and rough, my burning changed into a burn of shame: it became something that was poor and humiliating. 'Yes,' I said, 'your assistant did as he liked with me; that's all right, it's fine. Who is that guy?' —'You have to take it out on someone,' she said. —'Thanks, I understand. Who is this underling? I've met him before.' —'His name is Roste, David

Roste,' she said coldly. —'Roste?' The light illuminated the hallway door. I saw that she had put her raincoat on over her jacket. 'There's nothing else to eat?' —'No,' she said. 'I gave you a tranquilizer. Good night.'

In spite of the tranquilizer I stayed awake. I wasn't in pain. I would have liked to suffer more. The more I thought about this Roste the more I saw him descending with me into the fog, plunging into empty streets, and, overcome with fear, running through the mist. So he was nothing but an underling and now he was shouting, his voice was thunder. The word 'prison' was, when it came from him, something that belonged to him alone, a monumental piece of information that only he could understand. But what he said didn't tell me anything. I knew prison better than he did, I had visited the offices. I had an acquaintance there, Kraff, who showed me, through the window, the dining hall with its tables; he also showed me the old buildings which he constantly watched from his armchair. How many times had I gone there? Fairly often over a year, I was surprised to realize. Kraff had a great sinecure there, and he didn't miss the four fingers it had cost him. Once I saw him raise his hand in front of his eyes, gaze at it for a long time almost lovingly, and—even though it was horrible to look at less because of the missing fingers than because of the one that remained, a kind of white thread, incredibly long and thin, a malevolent and pitiless index finger—give it a real salute and kiss it. He had a huge, well-lit office, which looked out on the prisoners' courtyard. The buildings were absolutely superb—the most modern in a neighborhood where there were a lot of shabby streets. A little farther on there was a public park for children, a very beautiful one, with huge trees, a lake, lawns, and a little zoo. From the prison you could see the park: it was a splendid view. Kraff's accident went back two or three years. The administrative services had just been moved, and the prison was still empty. Only about fifty old inmates were still in the former prison which had not yet been demolished, but which was slated to be the following year: in the end they kept on using it, because the cells served various disciplinary purposes. Kraff found the new construction too lavish, and I too, now that I thought about it, had the feeling when I went in that it was different from other buildings only in its comfort, luxury, and good, practical organization. Kraff bitterly called it the sanatorium. Everything that happened in the prison, and everything that happened to the prisoners, was known by Kraff, and noted in his Diary. In order to be better informed, he paid the guards; he was suspected of being charged with a mission of special surveillance, even though his work had to do only with the registry office—but this reputation as an informer perhaps made him want to deserve it. His Diary became famous. He read passages to all his visitors, to his colleagues, and even to the office boys. He had read many pages to me as well, and all his stories about vicious prisoners seemed alike, but he never tired of them, for, as he said, what they go through is more concealed and more extraordinary than we can imagine. He claimed that many offenders got themselves punished to prolong their stay and that the guards knew this: they only feared attack from new inmates and those serving the end of their sentences—the new ones because they wanted to be free, and the old ones because they no longer wanted to be. This Kraff was a maniac. He would have gladly shared the cell of an inmate to get to know him better and be in his group. Deep down his situation humiliated him. His accident transformed him. When he found he was jammed between the door and the elevator cage he let out such a scream that all of city hall heard him, which in any case saved his life, because the elevator operator immediately cut the current. What was he doing now? Just then I could see his hand, I saw him as clearly as if he had been in the room, and yet I never thought about him. And the prison? Why did Roste talk of it in that triumphant way? What did he know about it? Be careful, I said to myself, you're fooling yourself, you want to stop seeing clearly. I didn't fall asleep. The tranquilizer wasn't much good. The next morning I couldn't get up.

\* \* \*

Around noon, worn out by the heat and anxiety, I got dressed. The morning could have been twenty years long, it could

have been unchanged for centuries—even if it had summoned the worst hours of the worst days, I couldn't have
been in a more miserable state. There was no one in the
corridor. Blankets, bags. All the people must have been in the
dining hall. I pushed Dorte's door open so forcefully that I
struck someone standing behind it. As I expected, there were
about fifteen in the room: eight in the beds, the rest lying on
the ground. Dorte, in his usual place, was dozing. I was
frightened by the change in his face—and even more so a
moment later when he opened his eyes. Having stared at me
for a while—and I got the feeling that he thought I was
hideous and I myself, because of that, was scared of him—he
rose up, crawled forward in his bed, pulled out his enormous
arm and tried to throw back the covers. His gesture terrified
me. Motionless for a moment, he gave me a troubled glance,
then looked at the floor; his body then hesitated slightly and
fell back. I had a horrible feeling. I would have liked to go,
but the bad air and the discomfort had stunned me. Almost
lying at my feet, an old man fixed his eyes on me. Next to the
window another person, his face resting on his knees, observed me with a certain curiosity. Suddenly I grasped to
what extent I had thought the epidemic would remain foreign
to me, or that the calamity, containing an element of exag-
geration, could have terrifying effects only to the extent that
one lingered to see it, if one didn't have the strength to go
beyond it in order to recognize its true nature. Now I was
suffocating. The certainty that my abscessed leg would end
up paralyzed, like his arm—this certainty was written on
everything, on his colorless face, on my livid hand, on my
door that was still open because I could no longer be spared
the contagion. I must have fallen onto his bed. This didn't
take long. I heard him say a few words; alert, I held my head
in my hands; then he let out that scream, an abject, piercing
scream. His head was thrown almost all the way back and I
could see only his chin and the lip mumbling something or
other. 'Dorte!' I screamed. I shouted as loud as he did; I stood
up. At this point something crazy happened. I was standing
and looking at all these people who were staring at me in a
tired and sleepy way; I would have liked to beat them, kill

them, rouse them out of their torpor and make them take part
in what was going on. I must have moved in an unexpected
way. It was then that he lunged at my hand and bit it. Somehow I knew it before he did it, before the pain had worked its
way up to my shoulder. I foresaw it with a feeling of horror as
soon as he got up, and perhaps I was waiting for something
worse, for him to grab my throat and strangle me. For a
second, two seconds, he sank his teeth in with such a furious
decisiveness that I fell on the bed, blind with pain. I didn't
lose consciousness, for I heard a kind of sob or hiccup that
shook me; I sensed that he was trying to get away a little as if
to give me room. A little later he punched me lightly three or
four times in a friendly way; then he murmured something. I
stood up; I kept on squeezing my thumb with all my strength,
pressing it against me, so that he must have looked at it too,
with a timid, scared glance, like a girl, as if what he had just
done was extreme and reprehensible, but inevitable. And
when he raised his eyes to look at me in turn, I saw that he
was so calm, his glance was so lively—and almost glowing—
that I was struck by the idea that his biting me was more
insane than I had thought. I heard him explain that his pain
was sometimes so great that he would tear and bite the covers, and sometimes his own hand; I heard this, and at the
same time he kept on looking at me with the greatest calmness, with a strange expression of satisfied vanity. 'It's bleeding,' I said inanely, showing the bulge of my thumb. He considered the wound, looking embarrassed. 'You should have it
bandaged right away,' he said. I got up; an icy momentum
swept me along. He shouted again, yes, a new scream, as
piercing, as abject as the first, at least as I heard it in the
stairway and then below, where I entered the infirmary. The
assistant ran a little electric flame over my palm, which stung
me in the joint of my shoulder; he worked slowly and conscientiously. 'Open your mouth,' he said when he had finished
the bandage. I saw his gaze oscillating under his red eyelids; it
then trained its suspicion on the upper part of my face. 'He
went out,' he said to his little helper, whom he had called for
assistance. 'How? You shouldn't be going out now—the sanitary conditions are terrible.' —'The door was open.' —'Well,

even when the door's open. And you say that, because you
were suffering, you did this to your hand? Didn't you realize
you were hurting yourself?' —'No,' I said, 'it's not me, it's a
sick person I had gone to see.' —'A sick person?' —'Yes, you
must know him: Dorte!' —'Dorte.' He repeated the name,
lowering his eyes. At this point the burning that the cauter-
ization had lessened started to hit me: I felt a desire to shove
him and say foolish and challenging things that would put
him on the spot. —'Where's Bouxx? I'd like to see him.' He
didn't seem to hear me, but suddenly he looked at me with an
air of astonished superiority, almost with amusement; he was
so little, but he was puffing himself up. 'So he doesn't come
here?' —'No,' he said, in a pitying way, 'not often!' As I left
the infirmary, the helper had me wait at the bottom of the
stairs. A whole gang was coming down, maybe thirty or forty
men, mostly apparently very young; sure, their color was bad,
they were in a sorry state, but you could hardly call them
sick. One of them called the little helper; she ran over and
shouted at me to go back to my room—she'd come later.
From the door, I showed the dressing to Dorte. The whole
room struck me as a furnace of fever and disease. It was an
overheated basement, a grave; and all these half-asleep people
who seemed to be indulging in a perpetual coma—where did
they come from?

'Where did all these people come from?'

He gave me a tired look, smiling slightly.

'Tell me,' he whispered, 'how do I seem? I've changed a lot!'

'There are too many people,' I said, looking around the
room.

'So come here! My right side can't move any more; all this
is lifeless. I've got the impression, yes, you understand, I feel
as if half my body is made out of brick: a mason is in there
working, building a wall. Is it possible?'

'If you're really paralyzed, you mustn't be suffering much
any more,' I remarked drily.

'Yes I am, when the wall collapses: then everything caves in,
breaks apart. Life comes back.' He examined me. 'You look . . .'

'Yes, I don't feel very well either.'

'You don't look bad.'

He kept on looking at me with difficulty. He seemed disconcerted and extremely tired besides; I would have liked to finish him off.

'I don't find you all that different. You've gotten to the end of the sickness; you're wearing it out.'

'You think so?'

He reflected. He made an extraordinary effort to stay awake. From time to time he grimaced. 'I don't have a fever any more,' he said with a furtive smile. But suddenly he looked at me out of the corner of his eye with an unsavory sharpness: behind his face I now saw a nasty lucidity that wanted to come up from deep in his enormous body and say its piece. But words didn't come out; he made a snoring noise that had nothing to do with his mouth, but rather with his chest and stomach. His open mouth waited and, receiving only formless fragments, threw them back in disgust. Suddenly, he said distinctly, 'The sickness doesn't always develop in the same way,' and then satisfied, he looked at me pointedly, then faltered, and finally lost me. I turned around; the door was still half open. 'Don't leave. And that?' he murmured, looking at my hand. —'Roste is taking care of it.' —'Roste?' —'Yes, the doctor downstairs.' He started coughing then, or maybe he was breathing noisily; it was as if he had too much air inside and had to get it out quickly. When he was finished, he seemed to come out of his despondency.

'That's it! Now the mason can calmly get back to work on his wall,' he said jovially. 'He doesn't work very fast, it's true. Nowadays the sick don't hang around long: three days, two, one night. Some families have been wiped out in half a day.'

'I've heard of cases like that.'

'Why is it only a few moments for some, and for the old timers weeks, months, maybe more? And which is worse, which is better? They say the critical moment is three in the afternoon. Did you know that?'

'What do you mean by the old timers?'

'The pioneers, those who contracted the illness early, before the full development of the epidemic. Did they tell you the story of Roste's family, his sister and mother?'

'No, I'm not very interested in Roste.'

'Really; you don't like him? Because of his vanity? You find him impertinent?'

'Be careful, you'll get tired.'

'No, if I stop, I'll lose the thread. Listen, it happened some time ago, in the late afternoon: the two women, who had gone to do some shopping in the neighborhood, came back fairly late. According to the young woman who was their lodger, both of them were in very good health. During the meal, the food Roste's sister was eating had a bad taste. Everything had too much seasoning, she was thirsty, and, when dinner was over, she fell into a light sleep. But when she woke up she felt better and started tidying up the apartment. While she was working she got very itchy—she couldn't stop scratching her knee and her leg: suddenly she let out a scream and showed the others a string of red spots along her thigh. As soon as she noticed this it was as if she were dead. Her mother, seeing the girl in this condition, ran through the apartment like a madwoman, screaming and gesticulating, no longer aware of the sick woman, the neighbors, or herself. The lodger went out to look for help. What happened when she was gone? When she came back, after having called the dispensary, a fire had started in the apartment and the building was burning. Had the mother, in her madness, wanted to die with her daughter—or had the daughter, waking up and suffering too intensely, set fire to her clothes? Anything could have happened.'

'And this happened to Roste's family?'

'The lodger's living here,' he went on, snickering, 'she could tell you the story. Since then Roste has become a hero, a legendary character. He has contempt for all the others who don't die in such an exceptional way. So what do you think? I wonder,' he added, looking at me insidiously, 'if those who use the sickness, as you say—those who make it last and survive, who have the strength to carry it within themselves and to make it tenacious enough to contaminate everything else—don't they count just as much as the others who go down and die in a few hours?'

'What!'

'Yes, terrifying people, drawing them into the sickness by

making them fear it, that's impressive, that's a feat, but it's a drama with no future. The sickness also has to live, you understand—the illness has to work deep down, slowly, endlessly, it has to have the time to transform what it touches, to turn everyone into a tomb and keep the tomb open. It has to be! That's how history gets infected.'

He was getting carried away, he raised himself up on his bed, and yet all his phrases were old hat as far as I was concerned—he had weighed the terms long ago, when he was in good health, and he was repeating them now because there was nothing else in his head. And all this time my hand was on fire!

'I'm suffering horribly. Good God, why did you bite me? I'll end up setting this dump on fire too! And, with the shape you're in, you keep on quibbling about fantasies? Do you really think this epidemic is going to change the course of things? Do you believe, because you're sick, that the world will be overwhelmed?'

'Yes,' he said lugubriously.

'I'm sorry, but, uh, why are you allowing yourself to be treated? Why are they treating you?'

He gave me a horrified look, and, through it, I could more or less read this: 'But they're not taking such good care of us; they're letting us croak!'

'The care is part of the disease,' he said timidly.

The sickness contaminates the law when the law cares for the sick—yes, he must have been thinking of maxims like this. I started pacing in front of the bed. Ah, nobody knows what it's like to burn! A kind of lava was coming up my arm: fire, metallic fire, a thousand times more terrible than the fire that was burning all these buildings.

'You have a strange look,' he murmured.

'What about my look? Just say it: I'm infected to the hilt, I'll go the way you're going. And afterward? There'll be millions of sick people, cadavers, cripples, insane, you'll have come a long way! What will have changed? You're trying to console yourself with superstitions. You think you can be done with the law. But the law benefits from your sick and your mass graves. You're degrading yourself for absolutely nothing. And I, because I know it, am even more vile than you.'

I gathered that he was making a great effort to keep me from coming and going; he was following me with his eyes; I was making him dizzy.

'Where's Bouxx?' I asked, stopping.

Disconcerted, he shook his head. I observed him; his expression reminded me of something: he looked at me with respect, yes, with fervor, with veneration, and at the same time he seemed to be making fun of me. 'But what's going to happen to me?' I thought.

'Is it true,' he asked, 'that he's impressed by you?'

'No, I don't impress him; I hope not. Why do you ask that?'

'Because I'm impressed by you too. And Bouxx is a very strong man, very sly, and, mark you, crazy. No one will ever get the better of him.'

'You have that much confidence in what he's done?'

'For me he's a kind of dog,' he said dreamily. 'Like a dog, he can't stay still, he's fantastic, he upsets everything, he looks, he prowls around, and suddenly he's asleep because, don't forget, his blood can sleep. In prison he slept for weeks; even standing he slept.'

'In prison?'

'Yes.'

'So Bouxx was in prison?'

'No doubt about that. Didn't you know? Otherwise how would I have known him? We shared a cell. Haven't you ever been in prison?'

'No. It never even occurred to me that I could go.'

'I've spent a third of my life there. I spent half my time in a cell. In those days cell time was spent at the bottom of a vast cement pit, which was divided into small cubicles. It was a real grave, long and narrow; the bottom was very tight; the two sides went almost straight up and opened at the top.'

'Hold on. I don't want to know all these details.'

But the words flowed from his mouth; it seemed he had to empty an ocean, to send out the thousands of little streams that were coming together from all the points of his life, streams that were hastily seeking an outlet for their trickling black water. His eyes closed now on his memories; he looked very much like an old man—exactly like the old man lying near me who, with part of his cape covering his head, was sententiously observing me. The word 'sick,' I thought, was not really appropriate to describe Dorte, at least not all the time.

'The partitions separating the cubicles were thin, but each cubicle was separated by a space; to communicate with our neighbors, to be heard, we had to knock fairly hard—and be heard also by our guards above who, in any case, didn't try to silence us, but rather wanted to listen in and report what we were saying.'

'Why were you in prison?'

'Because of technical things, a rule violation. I had been accused of clandestinely assembling, in my garage, new automobiles for factories, which could evade the production limits that way.'

'You spent ten years in prison for that?'

'No,' he said, 'not exactly. It doesn't matter. What's important is not to know why you go to prison, but why you stay there. Yes, sure, for someone who finds himself locked up there, freedom is offered at some point, often right away. But what's the price? Work, incessant work, beyond normal hours, for hours and then extra hours, sometimes all night, all day; who could stand a system like that? And whoever wants to get out of it must rely on the indulgence of the surveillance organization. Then people will close their eyes—but that costs plenty. Finally you end up in the police, so that you're always connected with the prison, but with its most degrading side—with a prison you can never get out of.'

'Aren't you exaggerating? And that's where you got to know Bouxx?'

'Bouxx from the first relentlessly opposed those willing to accept the advantages of that kind of reprieve. With his talent for intrigue, he hunted them down, persecuted them, annihilated them. He ended up establishing a real organization, and that experience was decisive for all of us. For when the State tries to tear people out of prison and forcefully drag them to freedom, that means that prison is a threat to it and that by jumping in you endanger the State.'

'You think so? Just now, you asked me ironically if I'd been

171

in prison. No, I don't know it as you do; but I can talk to you about it too. I entered a number of times, since I had dealings in the administrative section with a person named Kraff. For him the little scenes that you've just evoked could be explained in a completely different way—as common violations of morality, as there always are in these circles.'

'Why not? They're very isolated circles,' he said, with a tone of proud condescension.

'No, not really isolated. I'm afraid that you're deluding yourself, unfortunately—and that everything you've said is of very little importance. You think it clever to burrow into your cells—but what have you done? Nothing but conform to the wishes of the State, for its dearest wish was to keep you in prison, because you committed a crime, and to make you stay there freely, because this winning of freedom was the real point of your detention. Besides, were you and Bouxx really in prison? It's possible; it's all the same to me. In any case, that's no reason to act so superior.'

'That's big talk! I don't think you've missed much in life.'

'I'm not speaking to denigrate. But you don't see things as they are. You don't see everything. I see everything.'

'It's true, we don't see everything. That's why our strength is so great.'

'Wait a minute; you don't sound so friendly! Wouldn't you like to speak clearly now? A little while ago, when you bit me, did you do it without wanting to, because you were sick, or for another reason—out of bitterness?'

He gave me a shrewd look.

'But I didn't really bite you. I pressed your hand like this,' and with an extraordinarily quick movement he grabbed my good hand and raised it to his lips. It was as if I had been struck by lightning. I mechanically pulled away my hand, which I rubbed on the blanket; I looked at it with the impression that his cold, acerbic, acidic, yes, biting, mouth was still on it. 'You see,' he went on in a thick voice, his mouth open: 'no more teeth. I don't hate you at all. I miss not being able to communicate through the partition; we were, in a way, cell mates. And then you come to see me now, in spite of the sickness. Your visit does me good; since your return I've had no more attacks, and I talk a lot. Really,' he said, looking at me with a hint of impertinence, 'why did you come back?'

I glanced down at my hand. Had he really wanted to kiss it? He had mimed something, an act, the act of eating, of biting or kissing.

'I don't know. I must have given in to anxiety. Since yesterday, the building's truly been flooded. Has there really been a new wave of sickness? Or are some areas being evacuated? Do you know?'

'When you came in, I thought you had come because the end . . . I had the feeling that the moment had arrived. I hadn't expected to see you, and you came forward in such an imposing, triumphant way! One had the impression that just by moving your chin you were going to settle our lot, cover over and seal the grave. What expressiveness, what a glorious manner! Perhaps at that moment I held it against you: the insolence had seemed too much, it wounded my conviction that these things should go on simply, in perfect equality. And in any case, don't forget, you're not the conqueror.'

'But,' I said, watching my hands tremble, 'if you didn't recognize me right away, then who did you take me for?'

'But I recognized you easily.' He looked at me again. 'I think it was your air of health that overwhelmed me. Opening my eyes, I saw your radiant appearance: it was so unexpected! I had only these characters before me, and suddenly I saw your face, your dazzling gaze. It was a strange moment.'

'Did I really seem in such good health?'

'Terribly.'

He blinked his eyes and then closed them. How sad and humiliated I felt! It was still difficult to say why. At the same time I felt better; my wrist was going numb. I decided to leave, thinking with irritation about the little helper who, instead of watching me, had gone off with the gang members.

'Yet another brick,' he said, grimacing, without opening his eyes.

'Still talking about your mason?' I asked with a certain annoyance.

'He works as well as he can,' he remarked, smiling. 'Maybe he's too conscientious: he's always touching up, he comes back to the same place, the wall never seems smooth enough. I feel, when there's a certain hesitation, that he's about to move a stone. Oh!' he yelled. 'Oh, oh!'

He sat up, his eyes bulging, staring at me fiercely, and his cry, even though I had foreseen it, drove me back so powerfully that I kicked the old man. Besides, he calmed down soon enough.

'In my room I rarely hear you cry out,' I said, coming closer.

'It's because I'm rarely awake. These accidents happen when I'm half awake. And then, I help it along. All I have to do is move slightly for the work to succeed. I too play my little role.'

He wants to impress me, I thought; he thinks he's better because he's sick.

'On this sheet,' he started up again, looking at the wall, 'the length of time it takes has been calculated fairly precisely. The second part can go very quickly. When it passes the vertebrae, it comes together all at once; the whole mass of stone fits precisely between the already prepared joints. One has to be very careful or else the whole construction ends up in pieces.'

'And if everything goes well?'

'Well,' he said gaily, 'you can imagine what happens.'

'You get better,' I said nastily, 'you get better like a lot of others. None of them seem all that sick.'

'I don't know. Some of them have it bad,' he whispered. 'A few have just gotten out of the cells. — Hey, Abran, the young man who's lying near you . . .'

To whom was he speaking? Unable to turn, he looked at people at random—perhaps at a huge man, very dark, a peasant from the South, who, curled up on his mattress, seemed done for; right next to him a sick man—half crushed by the other—was slipping into the void: his brick-red hand, which I saw lying on the blanket, was grasping his other, bandaged, one. Why had Dorte surprised and even shocked me when he spoke to these people, as if we had agreed to leave them out of our conversation, or at least as if that were self-evident? And now all of them were staring at him fixedly and tensely, some with an unpleasant expression. I gathered that the person he had spoken to was the patriarch with the cape. This man, after sitting up, was stiff, his face expressionless, as it sometimes happens with very old people; he was probably listening. Finally silence reigned. A fair amount of time passed. Since we had started paying attention to them, the atmosphere had become even more oppressive, more laden with sickly odors which seemed to have nothing to do with the heat, with the pile-up of bodies, with the barely noticeable tar of disinfectants. You had the feeling that something quite small was rotting in a corner and yet you couldn't inhale it: an odor so humble, so base, that I had the sensation of sniffing it on the ground, squatting and looking for it, my hands and face on the dust of the grooves. I walked to the middle of the room. 'I'll come back as soon as I can,' I said, looking at no one. My door was wide open. Walking in, I clearly saw the extent of the misfortune I would have to recognize. For my eyes would not close: I knew too many things. It was the worst humiliation. I fell onto my bed; I chased away the little helper with her tin plates and her food. I scared her; small, fat, degenerate, she was vile. At a certain point I heard a noise behind the partition; I thought queasily that people would start talking or whimpering. Toward evening I decided to write to Bouxx. This temptation to write was dangerous, and no one knew that better than me. But the hours were so long, so dead, that I couldn't be satisfied just jotting an account: that could all be summed up in a single sentence, which was always the same and never sufficed.

'I know that you're very busy. Nevertheless, please read these lines. I've led a calm and regular life in the service of the State, troubled occasionally by my poor health. Now, I witness with horror your efforts to change the course of events. It's not that I blame you; I feel sympathy for you, and your madness soothes me. Alas, it puts you to work for everything you condemn.

'I'd like to be useful to you and demonstrate the very greatest loyalty. But you're blind, you're charging into the abyss. How can I open your eyes? You're fighting in the ranks of your enemies and I myself deceive you when I persuade you of my candor. If I tell you the truth, you will give up the struggle. If I allow you to be hopeful, you will be wrong about the struggle. Please understand: everything that you get from me is, for you, only a lie—because I'm the truth.

'I'd like to convince you of this: you're on the wrong track when you attack the offices, the administration, all the visible apparatus of the State. They don't count. If you do away with them, you do away with nothing. If you replace them with others, you replace them with the same. And, beyond that, their only goal is the public good: in order to act well they'll always be in agreement with you. I assure you: there's nothing mysterious in the offices; there are none of those little secrets that were the petty privilege of the old administrations which trouble the supplicant and make him think that behind the façade there's something essential going on to which he'll never have access. Anyone can always take everything into account. Administration, classification, decision making, all goes on in broad daylight, and perfect equality means that at every moment the whole State inhabits the bodies and minds of those who turn to it. The State is everywhere. Everyone feels it, sees it, everyone feels it live through him. In the offices it's represented rather than present. It's found there with its official features, and appearances are certainly not in short supply: historical buildings, institutions, civil servants, tables, filing cabinets, the smallest thing takes on a particular dignity. Indeed it's there that those looking for the center can flatter themselves upon having found it. But that is only the center. Having reached it, it's grasped in no more than an indirect way, through unimportant markers like mottoes above doors, the uniforms of ushers, etc.; it evaporates for whoever's not outside it. For those at home there, the offices vanish; they really exist only in the eyes of their attackers. Thus the empty feeling one gets there, which is not due exclusively to the somewhat sad and solemn appearance of the rooms, over which glides the hesitant gleam of the past. In every room there's a constant coming and going of the most serious working people, an extraordinary buzzing of activity, everyone's busy, and yet the visitor is struck by something sad and useless, as if everyone were yawning in idleness and boredom.

'I'd like you to reflect on these false appearances. Everything the administration does to give the laws a tangible reality—decrees, rules, measures of all kinds—sometimes seems to be a misleading manifestation of the power in which everyone participates. It's as if thinking unjustifiably deforms spontaneous feelings. It's well known that the laws acquire their true value in this way; they are laws only thanks to this. But a disagreeable feeling of hidden activity, of intervention after the fact, remains. When the government, in order to give official approval to the definitive right, recognized by everyone, to know everything, delegates agents who keep individuals informed, or when it puts posters on walls and prints its principal decisions in newspapers, then, in the eyes of every citizen possessing tacit knowledge, fairly petty revelations—on the scale of the means available—seem rather to conceal measures of intimidation. And the law, far from being the meeting place where everyone feels called to the common spirit, is no more than the personal and foreign warning addressed to us by a civil servant who has resolved for some reason to treat us as enemies.

'This apparent deviation cannot be taken seriously. The prestige of the State, the love we have for it and above all our absolute adherence to it, maintained through reservations and rebellions, links every mind and doesn't allow the mind to see the tiniest crack in the immense edifice from which it is inseparable. No one can distinguish the regime from its manifestations, for the law is not haphazardly revealed, and its truth lies only in the collective movement which has inscribed it deep within our souls, and which causes it to emerge in the sovereign system that represents it. In practice one can always criticize, and this often happens. Civil servants are people just like anyone else; they're not at all superior to those they administer. If they were to claim special rights for themselves then we would no longer be in our native land, and we would have to keep struggling, as it was necessary to do for centuries, against a distant and dominating power. And it isn't like men who are richer in humanity than the common run of mortals to carry out duties from which they derive no advantage. They are supposed to have a more active awareness of what they are; they live less and reflect more. I know very well that that's what indicates our administrative deformation; our most inward thoughts have something about them that's ordered, objective, as if they always had to be the subject of a report or pass unrevised into an account. Hence, no doubt, this meditative and cunning appearance which distinguishes certain important men in public and also the brutal and base manners often affected by agents of enforcement as if, among the latter, reflection, instead of manifesting itself through waiting, equivocation, and delays, demanded the haste and blind rigidity of authority. The law is sly: that's the impression it gives. It circumvents, even when it strikes. It interferes everywhere, under the pretext of never withholding itself. Never able to condemn anyone, it always seems to be concealing something under the benevolence and deceit of its plans. It is clarity itself, and it is impenetrable. It is absolute truth which expresses itself straightforwardly, and it invokes the most perfidious falsehood, one which leaves no trace, outside of, and within, our hearts. But don't believe that it is always hatching plots. With all my strength I want to warn you against such an idea, one as naive as it is depraved. We are the ones who sometimes feign to believe the law capable of dark plotting, in order to alleviate the feeling of vigilance with which its loyalty encircles us. We would like to free ourselves from this feeling and be able to rest. We imagine that there is a plot, because we cannot tolerate the idea of infinitely more complex relations, founded on good faith and clarity, relations which, far from being foreign to us, express that which is closest to us and most inward.

'Now, please listen. What I am going to tell you is serious. It's not only that I'm a danger to you through my mode of being, my turn of mind, and my habits. I also have to work: I play a role, I receive orders, I carry them out. How? I can't say, because finally that isn't true. They're ideas that take hold of me, then leave me, restful phrases meant to keep me at a good distance from a situation at which I lack the courage to gaze straight on, a situation I lack the strength to undergo indefinitely. Still, they're not fables—far from it. In the times that preceded our own, such a view of things would have been the truth itself; today, it still has all the precision of a metaphor. Civil servants, to the extent that they live in offices, sign decrees, work for the maintenance of the State, make decisions that seem to us brutal or unjust—are they themselves anything more than images that no one accepts as such, but which, as long bypassed relics, nevertheless give us an idea of the mores, the political fate, and the life of the world in general?

'Think about what's so terrible. It's that I myself, in a number of ways, am only a face. A face? Can you fathom what a dangerous, <u>perfidious</u>, hopeless, way of life such a word implies? I am a mask. I act like a mask and as such I play a dishonest role in this universal fabrication which spreads, over a humanity too full of the law—like a light varnish, in order to soften the glare—a more crude and naive humanity, one that recalls the earlier stages in an evolution which, once it has arrived at its end, tries in vain to go back.'

\* \* \*

Around midnight, I again felt almost good, I had rested, I missed my supper. Even though it was very dark, I saw that the hallway was still empty and that my door was still unlocked. A little later, as I was undressing, my room was invaded by a cold, blinding light, which seemed to come from the big lamp in the courtyard. Almost at the same moment a terrible racket erupted. The dogs! I threw myself on the ground. I made them out, a dozen monsters, gigantic creatures that two men were trying to control, and which, motionless, were howling at my window. No one had ever heard howls like that: they were choking, crawling, dragging themselves along the ground; the howls were fat, blind worms, moving in the courtyard and maybe already in my room. Nothing could be more vile. They were lying in wait for me with a humble ferocity, and they were knocking themselves out spying on me. Suddenly the light was turned off. The dogs calmed down almost immediately. When I lay down I heard them barking in the street. Where were they running? Where were they being led? I thought a long time about this incident. This nocturnal dog-walking suddenly evoked a world of decay and horror in the night, a world upon which I couldn't close my eyes. Yes, I knew that there was always more disorder at night. At night houses burned; at night guards raped and murdered. At night all those who were outlaws for having fled quarantined houses, those driven insane by sickness and hiding out anywhere—in courtyards, in empty lots—the sick who, escaping their sealed houses, thought they were escaping relentless death: this whole mob of ruined people, hiding during the day, coming out at night, to find something to eat, out of insane rage and hatred of the lucky, were attacking houses, raiding, and now perhaps engaging in actual organized expeditions. The chaos kept getting worse. It was a river overflowing its banks, a wave of flotsam demanding always more flotsam, a black tide against which authoritarian forces were now being established—forces just as dark and which, after having pushed the tide past its limits, now demanded that it go back in. At that moment the end of all these wretched people appeared to me to be so obvious, in all its incredible deception, that, in order to warn them, I wanted to write, in letters of fire on the sky, the words that would have thrown light on their misery. And I really did write these words. But misery was as heavy as lead, and looking up to receive illumination was not within their power and would not even have helped them. For the power of evil in motion was such that, if this evil had started to shine in the stars, it would not have revealed anything more than an offensive mockery, a deception stronger than evil itself, something inevitable, which could be denounced but not broken off. That the decomposing dregs, the howling and running sick, the real beacons of death, beside themselves with their own insanity—that they were now being hunted, for having fled, by those who had in a way made them flee: that was really the shameful madness, the lugubrious farce. But who was responsible? Rules that were too strict could be blamed. But the rules were strict only because the sickness was merciless, so that, as a consequence of the rigorous order that had to be imposed to control the contagion—an order both pitiless and itself already suspicious, tainted, infected with sickness—every day it seemed that still more unfortunates were being thrown into danger, people who saw themselves as ruined if they were to submit to this order and condemned to a life in slime if they didn't. Many people started to fear the guards just as much as the epidemic—guards whose job it was to protect them from the plague. Some of these guards stole and murdered. Some of them lived at the expense of the houses they were protecting, taking their cut of the commissions that were charged, ransoming, taking steep bribes for clandestine escapes, slowing down the arrival of aid and doctors, and acting in general in a way that made the rules worse than the illness they were supposed to contain. Perhaps these abuses were not very frequent; they could be explained because the guards' job was very dangerous; many in fact demonstrated devotion and courage. But just a few well-known cases were enough to make people believe that every guarded house was lost, already in its death agony. In addition there were denunciations, spying, and such a horror of the sickness that it triumphed over everything, even family ties. Everyone watched their relatives, vigilant for the tragic symptoms, constantly suspecting them of having approached a sick person, bumped against a suspect, walked near an escaping man. Many disappeared, obsessed with the mere threat of denunciation. Others, fearing traps that they saw at every turn, and making the first move, organized veritable snares. In this way, let into a house by neighbors, they often caught one of the unfortunate hunted men who, in order to have a place to stay for one night, had accepted the first offer that came along, aware or not of the role he was being forced to play. If someone ran away, his disappearance hurt all his relatives, his acquaintances, his most distant friends, even those he had known in the most distant past and who might now be suspected of giving him shelter. A wave of collective denunciation gave rise to countless dramas. The health organization had urged people to stay at home as much as possible and avoid approaching one another in the street. But even in families, apartments were being divided and rooms that were too large were split; everyone was locking himself up. The family was a real penal colony. But the opposite also occurred, and if there were so many suicides it was because some mildly contaminated sick people saw in this route a way of sparing their next of kin the dangers of a sickness that went on for too long. Many of those thought to have disappeared had died in this way (unless they had been killed), and, more or less adequately buried in some corner, they became sources of infection which contributed to the spread of the epidemic in certain streets. What happened on those nights? It was communicated by dogs' howling, it was going to happen at this very moment, or soon, tomorrow. I knew where the gang of young men I saw coming down the stairs— young men who were neither sick nor in quarantine—I knew where they were headed. Not a single person who had fled, not even the most wretched, dared to go back to empty buildings in evacuated streets: they smelled death waiting for them in those places; they had fled, and their flight had turned the buildings into the dwelling places of death. They sought out a hole at the bottom of a basement, a hiding place under a stairway, a hidden spot in a house that was still inhabited. But since there weren't enough of these sanctuaries, they were allowed to wander, willingly or unwillingly, to the empty lots where, in spite of their hatred of being together, most had ended up getting together and finding refuge. Huge graves had been dug in these lots and, because of that, the only ones who came in from the outside were a few hundred household sanitation workers—that was the name they'd been given—a band of corrupt and drunken louts, driven half crazy by the job they had to do. These graves, prepared in advance, were shelter for most of the people. Dorte had sometimes spoken to me, through the partition, of people, still alive, who had been discovered there and who, he said excitedly, had been trying to bury themselves. In fact they were only escapees who'd been unlucky enough to hide in a grave that was still in service, where they had gotten mixed in with the dead—persons who, nevertheless, had only been trying to survive. For that was the tragic dilemma of their lot: these wretched dregs could not simply do without food. If the sick were satisfied with fever, the others wanted to live: and living meant coming back, no matter what, to the normal world. Inevitably, each night's violence, in order not to degenerate into instances of madness and extermination, needed to be linked complicitously, in some way, with the authorities, who were associated for me here with Bouxx's name. Such large crowds could not be left on their own, they couldn't escape control, and the more they wanted to flee the death sentence whose horror had thrown them into the graves, the more they called down on themselves the rigor of continuous surveillance. That was the work of the men I had seen leaving. From now on they were going to live there, imposing themselves on those without means, organizing risk-free expeditions to seize supplies prepared in advance, bringing them closer to life by governing them insidiously. Wasn't it a terrible farce? At the very time when this anarchic multitude, reduced to the greatest misery, felt the most hounded, when these people were condemned to live in constant flight—they nevertheless could act only with the tolerance and at the instigation of the authorities whom they had fled, who kept them alive while keeping them separate and who, at the right time, didn't hesitate to crack down furiously, both to prevent the disorder from getting out of hand and to keep people from returning to a normal life. Yes, a farce. But the farce could no longer be stopped. And the most terrible farce was that of the victims who thought they had taken the initiative. And more terrible yet was my own. And suddenly there was no more farce, but a horrifying and dominant truth that rose above everything. Who couldn't see that these young men, slated to keep this society of death alive, ran the risk of falling at some point into the grave themselves? Rather than exposing themselves to the threat of contagion, many of this group fled as well, forming a new category of the washed-up and ruined. Who couldn't see that, between those hurled into the lower depths, and those who, under orders, joined them to keep them alive, there was something in common: the anonymous possibility of ending up in the same misfortune, the same difficulty in ever getting out, and, finally, the fascination with the grave. Orders, given to some, hidden from others, changed no one's fate. The men, sent by Bouxx, who drew a line around these irresponsible masses, themselves became irresponsible by introducing a

1) sluggish

more and more ignorant responsibility which could not save
them, which saved them all the less because they themselves
didn't know who they served—for if they believed they were
on Bouxx's side and were in fact hand in glove with the trash
they watched, Bouxx, with the blindness of an offended man,
acted in the name of the law from which he wanted to be
freed. And thus all this chaos, all this madness, served the
authorities and, from their point of view, it was all for the
best. I mustn't think that, I told myself. But the night passed
with just this one idea—the rest of the night, and perhaps the
day, perhaps many days. Sometimes I asked myself, So why
am I here? I saw the messed-up bed: while I was gone a
number of blankets had clearly been taken and given to new
arrivals, or perhaps they had been carried away in the bags of
the gang and were now being used by one or another of these
ragged men curled up somewhere in a hole. That idea overwhelmed me, grabbed hold of me. The notion didn't pursue
me: it was even singularly lethargic but I was unable to push
it away, get myself away, or get it moving again. In everything
I did the idea silently remained, taking up space. And when
the nurse came in, nothing more happened. However much I
looked at her—the heat was so heavy, the light so oppressive
that with amazement I saw her approach the bed, go over to
the table, arrange the papers, as if, through the mind-deaden-
ing heat and the motionless light, entire days were passing—her silent labor just went on.

\* \* \*

One morning she asked me to get up in order to make the
bed. Sitting on a stool, I looked at her from behind: instead of
a blouse she was wearing a gray, almost colorless dress, with
heavy boots out of which her uncovered legs rose. She walked
around the room; sometimes I saw her near the water pitcher,
at other times in front of the window. Behind her head, the
trees of the avenue raised their dead leaves, and behind the
trees the houses raised their silent façades, patiently expecting the insolent, triumphant day to reveal their hidden decomposition and secret cadavers. When I looked at her, I
thought, What is she doing there? Isn't she tired of wiping

down the walls—doesn't she have anything else to do? I thought that she was rubbing the windows, that she had been rubbing them for days, tireless and inert, standing in front of this window every morning, going there every morning, then leaving again, then coming back, sometimes wearing a blouse that smelled like creosote, sometimes the faded dress that almost wasn't a dress. I got up from the stool and looked for my clothes. 'Where are my things?' For a moment she turned away from the window and gazed with indifference at my bare legs, at the bandage on my thigh, at my bare hip. I saw her flat face, her gray eyes trained on my skin; I saw her naked legs coming out of her heavy leather boots with glacial brutality. I got partly dressed; she didn't help me. I let her know that I was going into the next room. 'If you like,' she said calmly. I went into the room, blindly, and stumbled. Dorte seemed very ill. Even his left hand was swollen. He looked at me and didn't move: I got the impression he was completely paralyzed. I wanted to talk to his companions who were more indolent and apathetic than they had ever seemed before. The one they called Abran, lying on a mat, his head half covered with the cape, opened his mouth. What made his face look so strange, thin with a thinness that had nothing to do with his sunken cheeks or his dull and voracious eyes? What a hideously *old* man, I thought. He had certainly gone beyond the point where old age, without attaining the grave character of fiction, is still only a sad reality. He was already ancient. With his hand he pulled, from his chin to his chest, a thin plantlike material. It was like a few wool threads, reddish white and a little curly. He pulled on them with a maniacal movement, spreading them out, stretching them. I sat down on the side of a box. The heat was intense. There must have been hundreds of flies and insects, whose buzzing against walls, windows, and ceiling made more noise than all of the motionless people. Eventually I saw that what was paralyzing them all was neither fever, nor heat, nor sickness. It wasn't real paralysis that was robbing Dorte of his movement and leaving him only with that unstable, suspicious and arid gaze. At a certain point someone let something fall—his sandals, I think. The noise passed through the room like a breath; no one moved, but everyone was on edge; faces turned toward the window. I myself, with all my strength, was looking through the glass. Dorte, now awake, let out a few words. His voice was very confused. I gathered that he was complaining about his hand; he said he couldn't breathe, he asked for water; then he fell silent again. Around him dozens of flies were buzzing; one after another they tried to reach a little white scar above his lip, in a hairless spot; sometimes they landed at the top of his forehead, walked down his cheeks with a capricious and sly movement, got tangled up in hairs, and arrived as if by chance at the white spot, where they started to buzz. Twice I got up to chase them away, but my movements scared him. 'Dirty flies,' I said. They were very small. It seemed that no one had seen this kind before the epidemic. The body was completely black—even the wings. They made a slight sound when they hopped, a dry sound that resembled that of their own bodies when crushed. One tried the lip, then another. I looked at them as patiently as I could: they didn't move, and neither did the lip. I had the impression that the skin was cracking under my eyes, that it was drying out and yet was covered with water. Suddenly I was lifted off the ground by a terrible explosion. I fell; the building seemed to have lost its moorings; even light was shattered into rigid reflections. 'What's going on?' I tried to get up. Dorte's face was devastated, covered with gray hatching. I grabbed the pitcher and threw some water in his face; his mouth moved slowly. I dipped a rag in water and made it drip onto his mouth. He seemed to be saying Roste's name. 'We have to call Roste,' I said to the old man. The latter, lying on his back on the mat, tried to get up. But once standing, he didn't come closer, didn't even look at the sick man; instead he turned to other men who were clustered near the window. 'I'm feeling better,' said Dorte. He was breathing deeply. His face came to life a little: he was sweating, and this gave him a kind of expression. 'I'm feeling better,' he said. —'What happened?' I asked. Around me people were speaking and whispering. How many explosions were there? Two, maybe three? And yet everything still seemed about to happen. Something sinister was going on now between us. Perhaps it came from the mouth that was mindlessly repeating 'I feel better,' without anyone being interested, so much so that the word, fallen amidst indifference, wanted to get back up again, and try to join in with the other murmuring. I gathered that they were trying to blow up the old prison buildings; these were a nest of vermin that had to be removed from the vicinity of all the new construction, if the latter was to serve as a hospital center. But 'prison' here was a word left to itself, going where it wanted to, expressing what it felt like expressing. It didn't need a mouth in order to make itself heard; behind it there was face after face—all were together, crying it out, murmuring it, crushing it between their teeth. It seemed that the prisoners had refused to evacuate their cells. They had holed up in them and were crouching there stubbornly with an inertia no persuasion could reach—so much so that Bouxx, now confronting his own tactics, found himself face to face with the orders he had given long ago. They were confronting him with their stony silence, and he had to struggle against them, struggle against himself with an elementary fury that seemed to recoil before nothing, because it wanted to conquer without caring whether conquest would leave it alive or dead. I had to say the name of Bouxx out loud. And as soon as the word sounded Dorte looked at me crazily, a look full of pleading and horror. Fixed on me, his eyes didn't seem to see me where I was, but further away, on the other side of the wall, against the door, then further, beyond this room and this building, and they saw me everywhere, and they kept going further to see me again. At this point I was certain that he too heard the tide coming up, this dead, exhausted water I had been hearing for so many days; he felt it coming up slowly with the heat and the light. Blind black tide, rolling within itself rottenness, misfortune, and humiliation—even if its waters did reach us, their contact would only leave us washed up at high noon, forever exhausted, ashamed, and despairing of the glory and good faith of the day. And already, feeling that the moment the grave was closed would also be the moment of his definitive exclusion from it; feeling with horrified astonishment that after so much pain and patience, after having dug this grave in the depths of his wretched past, he was once again about to be thrown under the light of the law and this—ultimate degradation—by the action of those in whom he had placed all his faith. Feeling this defeat, he looked at me with stunned and pleading eyes, eyes which denied what was about to happen, which denied everything, and repeated, I'm feeling better, which summoned life, recovery, exactly as the law demanded, and through me filled the room with an intolerable overflow of humiliation, regret, and hope. 'We have to notify the doctor,' I said to the helpers who were getting ready to go down and get the dinner. They went. After them, those able to do so went down to the dining hall. During the meal I felt slightly better. The room was almost half empty. Nearby, the old man was chewing calmly, industriously, seriously. Now I could see where the strange nature of his thinness came from: it was because his beard itself was thin, reduced to two or three strands that had no relation whatsoever to his face, and which even now his hand was pulling and unwinding. Even though he was still eating he stood up and greeted me. He let me see first his cape, with which he covered himself against the cold, then the thick overlaid cloth strips around his legs: he showed me all this as if it were something strange which might interest me, and not in order to complain about being cold while I was stifling in the heat. And yet, by making me the witness, he seemed to be saying, 'Enjoy this, but pay attention: somebody who's been in the hole takes the cold with him.' For he too was quick to tell me that he came from over there, that he had spent a good deal of his life there, under the yoke of the law, deep in the cells, where he had been his own guard. Yes, certainly, he could only have been condemned in his own time, long ago. Many years had passed, but to hear him it seemed that prison took great pleasure in coming to light through his aged memory, that it took advantage of that memory to change into a more foreign reality, one more closed off from the daylight, one into which he himself fell with all his memories. When he talked about it he never used the word 'prison'; for him it was 'jail,' 'the hole.' Indeed, even though he spoke of it calmly, with a grave and ceremonious delivery, his language harbored a constantly repeated and dangerously sly innuendo: that, with time, prison had sunk into the earth, that it had become the grave as well as the world below into which the old man's own years had disappeared.

'What's he talking about?' said David Roste. 'He's like a broken record.' Then he shook my arm. I got up. 'What are you doing here? You shouldn't leave your room, much less go into the other ones. Didn't I already tell you that?'

'I came with the authorization of the nurse.'

'Which nurse?'

'Jeanne.'

'What?' He raised his hand to his neck.

'Dorte's in bad shape. I thought it best to let you know.'

Brusquely he went over to the bed, leaned over, and examined Dorte's face with a superior but interested look. With his gloved hand he touched his mouth. Then he poured the contents of a vial into a glass and made him drink, slowly.

'You broken record,' he said, pushing the old man off and sitting down on the box. 'Why do you always tell the same stories?'

'I've lived them,' the old man said solemnly. 'I still see it all. My memories are so vivid it's as if I'm still living those painful days.'

'They always go on about the same things,' said Roste, looking at me. 'As if they all have exactly the same story. It would certainly be difficult to distinguish what happened to them from what they've heard about.' He snapped his mouth shut contemptuously. 'You'd be better off returning to your room,' he said.

'We haven't all suffered the same things,' said Abran unctuously, 'but the stories that recount them belong to everyone, and each person recognizes things he experienced, which gives him the right to all the rest. Forgetting's not possible; the memories are too painful, and recalling them is a great sorrow. But we have to remember them, because that's what our life was, that and nothing else.'

'Listen to him,' said Roste. 'They moan, they go through a ritual of mourning, no one has ever been as miserable as they. But deep down that's all they love—replaying their litanies,

189

plunging into the ecstasy of their destitution. By themselves would they ever make the least effort to attain something better? Would they work? Yes, you start to believe that only prison suits them. That's what they like. And if they don't like it, it's worse: because, after all, what they most want is to be in solitary.'

'They're sick,' I said.

'I'm sick too,' he said, touching his cysts. I looked at him. 'Your family was hit hard, no?'

'The epidemic came out our way,' he said smugly.

'The doctor alluded to the solemn character of our stories,' said the old man, turning toward me with a cheerful look. 'Nevertheless, the saddest ceremonies resemble festivals. Our misfortunes are recalled in the grave form suited to tragic events. We can't speak of them with familiarity. We can only confide their memory to minds that have been prepared, filled with terror but also respect. No one could endure their weight alone. And it isn't even enough for all of us to gather everything inside that's most painful, in order to respond appropriately to such great misfortunes: we still must associate them with everything we feel, even apparently misplaced feelings such as joy or gratitude. Our mourning would not be great enough if it consisted only of tears and distress. Why would we refuse it any part of our lives?'

Crazy talk, I thought. Was it the thick oil spread all over his words? An obscure reference to something ungraspable that could only be conveyed by the voice of reflection? Ah— for me this language held perhaps the greatest threat: its tone was practically insane, as if it wanted to formulate for me, following normal conventions, an ignorance below ignorance, an appalling primordial activity. Yes, he wanted me to believe it: completely adjusted to being a very old man, he was capable of using only stock expressions, clichés that were indifferent to circumstances and to which one could respond only by accepting the role previously established by the liturgy. And I too had a role. My role was to intervene in the story as a perpetually absent but always implied listener. I said nothing, but everything had to be said before me. Throughout the solemn droning, as the memories of the days of anguish were repeated, as if present-day suffering were at stake, everyone was no doubt listening, but someone most high listened as well—someone who, through his attentiveness, gave these appalling ruminations a hopeful and beautiful character.

'Enough already,' cried Roste. 'Enough of the broken record! You're trash, you're less than nothing now, but that's not enough for you. You still want to prostrate yourselves before this past. It's all you think of, you adore it. It's your master.'

Even after he stopped talking he kept on gesticulating. He leaped up and nearly bumped into a young man who was virtually bending over him. I recognized the young man because of his bandaged hand. He stood close to Roste and said in a low voice, 'Why are they preventing me from leaving? Why do we have to trade one master for another?'

Roste hardly looked at him; he shrugged. 'Playacting,' he muttered, 'fake beggars.' Standing, he looked like a runt.

'Even when we seem completely lost in this painful past,' the old man said to me, 'we're still hopeful about the future: very hopeful.'

'What hope?' said the young man with the low voice. 'Hopeful about rotting in a nut house like this wretch? Hopeful about being bombed out like everybody else?'

'Even though I'm very old,' said Abran, 'jail is all I know. The cell yesterday, the grave today: I can only place all my hope in jail. How can you distinguish the depth of our misery from the hope of escaping it? Vile, horrible miseries: they make you shudder just thinking about them. You recall that we've spent our lives at the bottom of a hole. But that hole was also our shelter, and the refuge where we've been buried has little by little become a dwelling place, still uninhabitable, but spacious all the same. The hole is now this clean and well-ventilated building, which might not be so comfortable, but which has been enlarged enough to meet our needs. To speak prudently—for in our situation one can't speak clearly— it's as if our hope is something like this hole, which sometimes devours us, sometimes shelters us.'

'Is it true,' murmured the injured man who kept pressing closer to Roste, not perhaps with an aggressive intent, but only to become one with his interlocutor—and Roste didn't even step aside, he was content just to turn his head away conspicuously, with an air of profound but childish contempt— 'is it true that when we got out of our cells we thought we'd live freely? Is it true that by getting out of these death dives we seemed to come out from below and find our place in a new life? For us, this building, administered by those like us, was more than the realization of our hopes, it was a blessing that went beyond hope, grace that constantly gave us everything. And now? We can only await orders: orders directed against us, against others? Who will explain it? The building is still a prison, you'll say. Sure, but a prison that's a broken promise, a hope that's become a curse, a stifling disappointment.'

'Well,' said the old man, 'you're plainly opening up your heart to us, and energetically telling us what you think. But the strength with which you express your grievances also shows that they're not entirely well founded. Gratitude and effusiveness are conveyed by your words, which are a categorical indictment of our life here. You claim that you miss the freedom of the cockroach who can flatten himself between two boards. But as soon as you groan and rear up, it's because, along with your claustrophobia, you have the feeling of a lighter and happier life, in the name of which you're protesting, and in the end your recriminations change into forgiveness. The promise hasn't been fulfilled, but it hasn't disappeared, either. It shines on when everything else fades out. It's there when everything else has disappeared. Oh, my dear friends, I don't know what our lamentations mean, and perhaps we're wasting our words. Our distress is certainly immense, and even though I'm old it seems I haven't lived long enough to taste all the bitterness and eat my fill. Could someone get us out of this? I hesitate to think so. Someone? Like you or me? Let me, in my misery, smile at such an unreasonable thought. You are all my witnesses: if necessary, you will attest to the fact that I haven't appealed to anyone without due cause, that I haven't asked to be released from my burden, and that, always in complete agreement with my misfortune, I've only wanted to go ever further down into the grave.'

'Enough!' screamed Roste. 'Get out of here. What a farcical ceremony!' He raised his hand to his throat. The old man calmly went back to his mat, and the others drifted away. 'It's a simple ceremony,' he said, snickering nervously. 'The details of the dialogues change, but they always turn around the same words. At certain points they raise their voices, one of them replies to another, what has to be said goes along with what's supposedly hidden. What do they want? What are they thinking? Nothing, there's not a single thought there. It's a farce, pure and simple.'

'A ceremony?' I asked. 'You're sure? Have you already heard these things?'

'A thousand times,' he said with a contemptuous look. 'Maniacs all repeat themselves. Have you noticed? You repeat yourself, too.'

But he was repeating phrases too: I seemed to be hearing Bouxx. You little gnome, I thought, if I wanted to I could reduce you to nothing.

'Can it be believed,' I said, turning my gaze on him, 'that they are so totally uninterested in the activities undertaken on their behalf?'

He looked at me with a shrewd cheerfulness, the cheerfulness of someone who is thinking, Here we are, what did I tell you?

'But they do think about them,' he said, suddenly serious. 'Listen, let's drop it.'

He looked at Dorte, who was also looking at him. He forced open Dorte's eyelid and leaned over the gray, almost black spot that shrouded the distrustful gaze. 'What a disease,' he murmured. 'It's all right, old man, it's all right. In a little while I'll have someone give you a shot.' From the door he yelled at me with his worn voice, 'And you, go back to your room. Enough chit-chat for today!'

\* \* \*

As soon as he left I sat back down. It was like the end of an intermission. The tide was coming up, we knew it. It was coming up, and, although no one was its accomplice, even though the air brought us, in the midst of the whirling insects, only light and heat, there was no one who could miss the slight dampness. Anyone could already see for himself the traces of water coming up in the streets, along houses, on walls. Could it really happen? I asked myself. Did . . . Everything now was peaceful and silent. It was nap time. The old man had pulled his cape down to his nose; the others slept with their mouths open. Everyone was asleep. Still, every single one of us heard a dull rumbling and, through the light and heat, had the feeling of something sweating, of a drop forming in the darkness and blindly expanding, seeking in daylight, in the glory of the day, the single crack where it could fall and become a true, indelible spot. And suddenly it seemed that the crack had been found. Dorte sat up. His arms twitched a little, and even his completely paralyzed right arm moved slightly. He sat serenely, adroitly, in his bed. He raised his head and looked at me. I came up, but he continued to stare at where I had been sitting before, on the box, with a clear and confident gaze. This went on—his eyes didn't move, and then he saw me further on, behind the wall and in my room, on my bed, my eyes trained on the spot on the wall. And still it went on—we looked at each other calmly, I before him, in the place where I was standing, he in the place where he saw me, lying in my room and staring at something on the wall. We kept looking at each other, and there was nothing calmer than the two of us, nothing more peaceful than the room and the building and the dull rumbling of the water around us. Slowly he turned on his side, slowly and skilfully, so that he could stare at the partition, and while he was stirring the ground started to move: a slight subsidence could be heard, the sound of eroding earth. When his body found a position, I saw one of his arms reach out toward the partition and touch it. He felt it and discovered the outline of a drawing which he then confidently followed. Then, just when the roar of the explosion hit, when the gaping crevice tore open beneath our feet, and the noise of collapse was ripping open a black hole around us, I saw, following the line traced by his hand on the partition, the thick, wet spot that his sweat and his furious pressure had pressed for so long through the brick and plaster onto the wall of my room. I saw it as I never had before,

contourless, coming from the bowels of the wall like a secre-
tion, resembling neither a thing nor the shadow of a thing,
flowing and extending, forming neither a head nor a hand nor
a thing, nothing but a thick and invisible streaming. And he
too must have seen it, just as I did. And he too must have
heard the tornado of the explosion. Suddenly he turned over,
sat up, his eyes fixed on mine; then he was on his feet in one
terrible bound, and, letting out a piercing scream, like the cry
of a woman, he howled, 'I am not dead, I am not dead,' and
even when my hand covered his mouth, pressing against it
and crushing it down to make him be quiet, my fingers kept
on grasping the same cry, and nothing could silence it.

# 8

In the end I went back to my room. I locked myself in. Now she started sitting on my bed, staying there for hours. And maybe she listened when I talked, but what came out was just for me. Feigning to write—that habit alone I couldn't kick. I went to the table; I didn't write with pleasure, and yet there were plenty of blackened pages, plenty of lived events; maybe I was writing all the time. What was she doing behind my back? That question wouldn't go away either. Before, at the same time of day, women would be beating the sheets, moving the furniture around, and men would be leaving for work. Nowadays there was the endless rolling noise of steps on the staircase: an up and down movement like a dream of cavalry. Yet the epidemic was dying down. Now that it was less violent, though, I noted that the violence had passed from the sickness to the sick. Even here their complaining had changed. Listening, I no longer heard screams and dire silence, but wild and impatient shouts, and, beyond that, the agitation of a barracks, as if, with life once again normal, the sick and the well were becoming more and more alike. And her? She watched over me, but very negligently, not seeing or hearing me. At this very moment, behind my back, she was looking not at me, but at the wall. And if I were to turn around, I would see her dress, discolored by rain and wash water, and her heavy men's shoes beneath her legs with their white, vegetal life; and all this was displayed, was shown, with impudent calmness, as if no one were there. And soon she would go down to get the meal, bringing the tray back up; she'd let me eat, only coming back at the beginning of the afternoon. She'd give me the medicine, she'd still do this and that, but she could have done a thousand other things, and maybe she still would; but that would do nothing to change her dress's leaden presence, its stonelike immobility; it seemed to be the crudely sculpted covering of something that may have been her body, but perhaps was even unsculpted granite. She may have been the young woman who had been present at, and had participated in, Roste's misfortunes—but I didn't know, I had never known. What difference did it make! But she went on seeing Roste, and he hated me. I hated him too, or at least I didn't like him; I don't hate anyone. This small-time character was trying to play a role. Maybe he had replaced Bouxx here, Bouxx whose activities were being carried out over wider areas, and who rarely came around, even though, as Roste told me with his usual snickering, my notes always reached him. Taciturn, arrogant, adroit, active—yes, in certain ways he resembled his teacher; but he lacked the more active and tragic spirit, the greater casualness, education. He had never understood me or tried to understand me. I only knew too well what I represented to him. But he didn't understand that I had seen through him: that's what distinguishes us, I thought. His role was to heal, to cure; the sickness was his concern—besides, attentive and zealous, he was somewhat wild. This wildness was everywhere now. I knew it was in the streets; it was like a remainder of the sickness, the cost of recovery. If a sinister movement of insatiable cruelty was arising out of the fever bouts and out of the madness induced by the pressure of too-strict rules; if that movement was being instigated by the runaways who were now re-infiltrating everyone's lives without officially coming home, then one had to see in these things the new form of the now pacified sickness: what was new and what was gone, and all that permitted it to subsist while disappearing. It became obvious to everyone that, as was always the case, the epidemic, in decline in the West, had appeared in the East; it had broken its bonds and soon would rage in areas which till now had been spared. So one got the feeling that the horror and the disorder that we had undergone were going to reappear everywhere. And those who, under the brilliant cover of the law, had up to now attributed the ravages of the plague to a crazy tolerance of misery, were in turn running the risk of sinking, outside the community, into the disease that caused the tongue to swell and the body to ignite, turning them

secretly gangrenous, transforming them into
they would have to rot. Perhaps a lot of peo
for this; perhaps the sick who came back to l
them a sulfurous, bituminous spirit that ma
give the sickness to others, as when, as happ
people were strong enough to cross the stree.., g.. .......... ..
into apartments free of sickness, fall down, die, and in dying
strike down the healthy. And who could really say that, in
other areas, cases of typhus and the plague weren't appearing? But it became obvious to me that the word 'epidemic,'
because it had become worn out here due to the unleashing
of all its consequences, could not cross borders in its present
form, nor could it regain elsewhere the same virulence. Instead it had to enter into what was, for it, a new era, hurdling
hundreds or thousands of years. If it was true that it was now
in contact with the pure domain of the law and that it was
trying to infect and paralyze it, then it had to appear, and try
to conquer, as the spirit of illegality. There were plenty of
signs of this transformation. When people, motivated by
more terrible feelings than that of injustice—this I recognized—having blinded themselves to the universal benevolence of the State, impudently throw themselves into the
depths of history, the events they set in motion easily appear
at different levels and, as crude as they are, get out of control
and stray, as myths, before the formidable gaze of he who has
understood them from the first, has lived them, and always
relives them. But neither Bouxx nor the men of this Committee he had founded seemed to be aware of the senseless conditions under which they had to act and live. I told him, I
wrote him incessantly, I wrote him again:

'You're on the wrong track, you're fighting this regime as if
it were like the others. It may be similar, but it's also very
different. It has penetrated the world so profoundly that it
can no longer be separated from it; it doesn't consist solely of
a political organization, or a social system: people, things,
and, as the proverbs say, the heavens and the earth are the
law, they obey the State because they are the State. You attack
the representatives of the State, the official types, but it would
be just as useful to attack all the inhabitants, all the houses,

then this table, this paper. You know that you'd have to ..ttack yourself. You'd have to see every grain of dust as an obstacle. Against you, everything is in complicity with what you want to overthrow.'

But how did he respond to these warnings? Sometimes crudely:

'What's our objective? Don't look for it, it's too simple. I'll consider my task almost accomplished when we've taken control of the organs of government. If I accepted your point of view for a minute I'd be locked forever in the world I want to escape.'

Sometimes more anxiously:

'Listen, I'm not a dreamer. I've spent years observing this society, nobody knows its strength better than I do. I've analyzed it, I've plumbed its history. I take all the truths into account. Before me there were other shocks. If they've all failed, even when success raised them up to the calm realm of the State, they've nevertheless left remnants of illegal forces, which are everywhere in the world. Could I have developed, in the course of a simple human life, such a great organization, such a network of activities and propaganda, of surveillance, of reprisals, if it all hadn't existed before me, hadn't developed, in the time that bears its trace, a half-sympathetic complicity? There isn't a region, a neighborhood, even in the most official centers, where the outline of a subversive organization, still unaware of itself, ignorant of its past and its goal, hasn't maintained the spirit of opposition. It's thanks to these embryos that the words "revolt," "war," "strike," "cell," still have meaning. Every factory, every block of flats has, for centuries, maintained an illegal section, which became at times an insignificant union, at others a chatterbox co-op, but which, with the most inoffensive goals, always aspired to an alternative life. I rediscovered all these forms and revived them. But naturally, all this is nothing. A State that's master of everything claims it can reabsorb its difficulties. It's happy with what disturbs it, and it's maintained through weak disorder. A limitless confidence ceaselessly reconciles the government with the citizens who offend it. There are never guilty people, only suspects. Whatever our crimes, in the end

200

we're won back by a satisfied good will that explains them. And, no doubt, all the unfortunate feelings that in the old days led to changes at the right time still exist, as strongly as ever, but now the sadness of oppression, the horror of injustice, fear, death, these are felt only as stages of a plenitude that returns us to the State where, once alienated, spirit finally rediscovers itself. Doctrines therefore have no meaning for combating the world from which they derive their truth and their force. But personally I hate ideas. I couldn't care less if I'm shown to contradict myself. I've only got a simple goal, with precise means worked out in diagrams. They claim that I don't want anything, that it's nothing to take over the material system of the State. They remind me that nothing more can happen. So be it. If that's a challenge, I accept it. Nothing will happen. So we can be sure that what comes out of our activities and our mud and our tears will go beyond the stage of things that happen.'

So he got out of it with a joke. And really, how do you answer a joke? It was written, that's all, and all I had to do was read it; I reread it; to make it true, I wrote it myself. At that point something strange happened: she must have gotten up, she came forward, I felt it. Behind my back she was looking at me, spying. I went on pretending to read and write; I heard the leaden steps, the footsteps that seemed to be doing heavy male labor while accompanied by the rustling of a dress, as if a man and a woman were walking together. She stopped right next to me. I let her look over my shoulder: I spread out the papers, I leafed through them, in her presence I let my hand write whatever she wanted. Then I couldn't take it any longer and turned around. I saw her a few steps away. For a few seconds she showed herself in a way I had never seen. Her face was entirely visible, appearing before me as if I hadn't been there, coming forward, floating, heavy, coming to meet me as something dull and extraordinarily visible, with me not there. Step by step she went back to the door, always staring at me; softly I heard her turning the latch behind her back, and then she slid into the hallway. 'Stay calm then,' she said, leaving. 'You don't frighten me. I'm going down to look for your lunch.' I waited; she didn't come back up. In a rage I waited, trying to figure out why, when alone, I was with the whole world, and why, in front of her, I was with a single person. Why did she look at me that way? Fairly late in the afternoon she came back, accompanied by the little servant. She brought sheets and blankets. She made the bed, straightened the room; then she sent the servant away. After a few minutes she stopped working and turned to the corner where I was standing next to the wall: it was brightly lit by the sun. Because of the sun I could hardly see her; I moved away, the daylight fell on her head, and I saw her prominent cheeks, her huge jaw marked by a strength that couldn't have had anything to do with her will but with an unshakable necessity, with the inevitability of stone and lead. I came up and touched her arm; one hand clutching the other, she was as rigid as a statue, a real statue from a tomb, hoisted and set up and which now, standing for the first time, could show, in broad daylight, the proud expression of a woman leaning against a tomb. There were no brilliant high-lights; instead she was drab and yet extraordinarily visible, and the shadow at her feet was moving no more than she was. I stared at that shadow. I watched it, without seeing it move or grow longer, as if daylight could have done nothing to change our relationship, or as if we had had no relationship at all. That was when, darkness having fallen—but it was as sultry as high noon—I noticed her absence and, raising my head, looked for her in the room. She was sitting on the stool. I forced her to get up and threw her on the bed. Her big male shoes bumped the wooden bed frame and fell heavily against my legs. Strictly speaking, she didn't resist. I tore off that dress. Her sturdy body, with its virile muscles, accepted the struggle; we fought, but the struggle, barbarous and seemingly unconcerned with the stakes, seemed a countersuit between two people unaware of what they want and confronting each other because they have to. Even when she stopped struggling, in the end turning toward me a little, there was neither consent nor surrender on her part, just as there had been neither refusal nor resolute resistance in her effort to push me away. At no time was she agitated, ill at ease, or demonstrative of any other feelings. But, appearing to submit to a decision made by an external will, a decision that concerned her only indirectly, and holding back her own decision, she remained calm and let me touch the dry, hard, body, whose coldness didn't even have the passivity of sleep, and which demonstrated a faithful and disdainful perspicacity, rather than any willingness.

She didn't change her activities. She cleaned the room and brought up my meals. She continued to watch over me, fulfilling duties which were were part of her job, and which were ordered by the doctor. Perhaps whole days were spent looking at her, listening to her, when she entered, walked, coming straight to the table to put down the food, or walking around the room and cleaning insignificant objects with infinite attention, bringing an excessive patience and punctuality to activities that seemed to be taking place a thousand miles away. I let her do whatever she wanted. Dishes were put in front of me and sometimes, just as my hand was sliding toward them, I thought that I was eating, that the days were passing, that something that up to then I had not known except through books, something called time, was trying to drag me along. But, on the other hand, sometimes feeling locked in a particularly airless moment in these unchanging summer days, I gave up trying to find out when this silent coming and going had started and whether we weren't still at the first day, at the moment when, looking at me strangely, she became more visible and more drab than she should have been. From time to time Roste came in. He sat down, and what he said didn't always reach me. According to him, Bouxx was starting to have a hard time. He was even encountering people among the masses who, after falling between the cracks of the law, managed to escape him as well, just as he eluded them through his desire to liberate them triumphantly. They were the wretched residue of disaster, seemingly led always again to fall into the depths of history because of a tragic weariness: the inertia of their hopes paralyzed him, and everything in them that was darkest and most dangerous for the law was no less troublesome to him in his struggle against the law. To enable them to live, he made authority erupt, exerting a power so methodical and hard that he seemed to want to

discredit all forms of power, even the lightest and most hypocritical ones: infinite reconciliation, reciprocal confidence,
the openness of duties—that's what was on the side of the
law, but illegality itself required the intransigence of rules and
the rigor of a vague and painstaking discipline. Roste's twisted
mind believed that such severe organization was necessary to
transform instinctive hostility against the state of things into
a true force. He claimed it was necessary, through a system of
impediments and obstacles, slowly to raise the stagnation
level of this vast inertia, and, without changing its passivity,
lift it higher than all the roadblocks. That's why, in our building where every sick or formerly sick person had been sub-
jected to so many orders, couldn't leave, couldn't even go
down into the courtyard, had been more or less locked in a
room, felt himself constantly under the control of either the
doctor or the sickness, nevertheless, in spite of all the rules
and surveillance, and because of the severity of the surveillance which amounted to a humiliating challenge, one had
the impression that life was more amorphous, more disordered, and more mixed up than if everyone had done as he
pleased. It must have been the same in the other asylums, in
the ordinary buildings where the guards, still in service, continued to see and repeat everything, holding inside who
knows what silent and blind swarming. Roste recognized in
all this the effects of a higher plan. But what he couldn't
know, and what I knew, was that all this authority and order
was no different from the formless devastation they were
supposedly organizing. And if Bouxx devoted most of his
energy to writing, regulating, and administering, putting in
more thought and effort than did any State commissioner, it
was because in him disorder was method and inertia was
work, such furious and inexorable work that everything he
did in the most organized way seemed the result of an aimless
passion, one more undone than done. What could he still
hope for? He didn't lack strength, or a talent for intrigue, or
the instinct for errors similar to his own, which he could
discover or produce anywhere. The truth dawned on him,
little by little: the law was present everywhere, and everywhere it appeared whatever happened gleamed with light,

while the heavy, material wheels of State became
When the police showed up; when, behind his ⟍
worker noticed the controller who was watching
could turn him in, this brutality and control didn't se
one of the unfortunate conditions usually attributed to 'torce
of circumstances,' tolerated but not engaged in by the law.
Quite the opposite: one sensed that the billy club, far from
contradicting the infinite tolerance of the State, represented
its purest spirit of understanding and also that the sneaky
spying of a traitor ready to turn you in was completely identi-
fiable with the heartfelt, right, and just gaze of truth. So
someone, beaten to a pulp, tortured, thrown into solitary,
who desperately invoked the law he knew to be infinitely
benevolent, only received more blows; and so too the police,
hearing him, started to laugh, slapping and burning him,
howling, acting like demons, for at that moment that was
their way of showing themselves to be the best and most
human. From this kind of view of things Bouxx seemed to
have drawn a strange conclusion: that his main chance was
on the side of the State organizations, and that the innumerable agents of the official organizations had to be his allies
and not his adversaries. For this reason as well the whole
system of oppression and inequality that he hated because it
was for him, precisely, the reign of universal law and nothing
else, became his own system, set up everywhere that he had
power and perfected through the methodical madness that
was tearing him apart. In this way he had established many
links with civil servants of all kinds; he had little clandestine
groups in all the areas where the State had a public presence.
It was the State's need to be, in certain places, manifest and
immutable that, he claimed, gave him the means necessary to
combat it. Any official organization had to end up sheltering
its own secret organization: the same resources served both
of them—the same papers, the same seals, sometimes the
same men, but one was illegal, the use of the regular forms
being only one more falsification, whereas the other was true
and made true everything that invoked its customs. Bouxx
must have known that his whole network, so cleverly and
meticulously constructed, was completely known to those he

wanted to take by surprise, that he had certainly benefited from the complicity of public organizations in order to establish it, but also that this complicity went in both directions, since it betrayed him as much as it served him. Everything he did and decided was known, classified, assessed; everything he thought he had discovered uncovered him and made him harmless. He was like his own spy; he sold his secrets just as soon as he bought them. That didn't bother him. He had a mania for activity that was encouraged by everything, and the more he saw himself exploited by the games of the official forces that were using him against himself, the more he resented their hypocrisy, their cowardice, and their lies, to the point of finding in his failure a new reason to fight and win.

When Roste came in, the nurse left. They looked at each other in a certain way. If men saw him with suspicion, women in general appreciated him: his violence and childishness, his idleness at work, connected with something more violent and childish in them, which let itself be seduced. One morning, after putting some bread and a cup in front of me and as I was hurriedly drinking, she stopped me in my tracks.

'I'll probably be given another job. I won't have time to come any more.'

She said this aggressively. I raised my head and almost got out of bed.

'Yes, so?' she said, laughing nervously. 'You'll have someone else to do this.'

What did she want? Her words were staggering. I couldn't understand it. Something was happening that couldn't happen. What was the matter? What had she said? Suddenly it hit me: I realized, amazed, that for all this time she had always done everything she had to do properly, except talk. Talking, really talking—I couldn't recall her ever doing it. Of course she spoke to me, but only when it was absolutely necessary, and in an impersonal tone of voice, so that once something was said it immediately stopped being said. And even that only happened, rarely, in the morning, when she came up from the dormitory after having spent the night there, or from the kitchen where she worked with the other women. But as soon as she examined me, let me eat, and helped me wash, the silence started. The eloquence of her face had worn off. I watched her doing this and that, without even being able to think: now she's doing this, now that. I didn't even think about her any more; even if for hours she had told me, down to the smallest detail, everything I saw her do, there would have been neither more nor less silence, and in the end I wasn't really sure if any given day hadn't disappeared in the monotony of tiresome chatter through which, sitting in a corner, I had followed her, step by step, listening and answering without realizing it.

'What's the matter? What do you want?' I thought that on occasion she had brought up jobs from downstairs, which kept her from working overtime—jobs, for example, like ironing or mending clothes—and that she resembled, for that reason, a narrow-minded and indifferent servant who never looks beyond her work. 'What did you say exactly?'

'I don't think I can keep coming.'

I listened to the voice: neutral, bodiless, whispering. I listened for a long time. Why couldn't she come?

She murmured, 'I don't want to. I . . . I'm not strong enough.'

She stared at the cup and the bread, not looking at me. What would happen? As if to speak again, more words came up from deep inside, wanted to break out, and this kept her from talking, made her talk, shook her, froze her in a violent, fanatical immobility. Her mouth was clamped shut; a little saliva moistened the corners.

'I can't,' she stammered. 'I can't get used to it.'

The bit of foam bubbled and dried. I took the cup and drank, slowly. 'It's physical,' she said with her way of laughing apologetically. She made a motion of wiping her lips. Her body stood out so I hardly needed to look at it. Suddenly she turned around and looked at me, mouth open a little, arms spread; her smell was coming up near the bed, no longer that of disinfectants, but a frightened, dark, miserable odor. 'It's physical,' she repeated, 'it's physical,' and while she was saying that, I started hearing, beneath the words, coming from deep in her throat, a gurgling: yes, it started with the murmuring of water, and then she screamed. I grabbed her by the

shoulders, shook her, and, through my hands, felt her screaming; she went on howling, louder and louder. Finally her
body stiffened and the howling settled on a blank, monotonous note, which expressed neither terror nor delirium, but
only a mindless moaning, a simple, inhuman force. Giving up
trying to silence her, I sat down to listen. She bowed her head
slightly and looked for the stool. 'It's over now,' she said. A
moment later she walked to the door; I thought she was
leaving, but she stopped, went to the table, looked for something, then came over with a sheet of paper. Her face was
livid, ashen; even her lips were white. I gathered she wanted
me to write something.

'Write that you want to keep me as your nurse,' and she
pushed the paper into my hand.

I looked at the totally white sheet.

'Write that you don't want any other nurse-companion.'

'What? I have to write that?'

'Yes.'

'It's really a question of replacing you?'

'It might happen.'

'Does Roste want to give you another job?' She lowered her
head. 'What good is this paper? It won't accomplish anything.'

Suddenly she shivered; her shoulders drooped and trembled.

'Yes it will,' she said in a low voice, whispering. 'It'll accomplish something. For me, it'll do . . . a lot.'

I was gripped with fear: these words came from so far
away, they still seemed so distant. I wanted to disappear, bury
myself. I heard myself ask, 'Why did you start shouting just
now?'

'I don't know.' She lifted her head and little by little her face
took on an expression of bitterness, almost hatred. 'I suddenly saw that you were there, personally,' she said with a
slight sneer. 'So write! What are you waiting for?'

She took a pencil out of her pocket and threw the tray in
my lap.

'Why do I have to request that you stay? You yourself don't
want to.'

'The situation will be _____ ar-cut.'

'I can't make you do wh\_\_ \_s beyond your strength.'

'The situation will be clearer,' she said, dreamily.

Since I wasn't moving, she grabbed the paper and pencil and started writing. Then she gave me the sheet, on which she had written, 'I would like Jeanne Galgat to continue acting as my nurse-companion, when she is available.'

'That's all?' She nodded.

I gave her back the paper. A ruse, a trick! I lay back on the bed. The light was already so heavy that the whole room seemed to be a pipe full of burning water. I thought of the day and how I was going to keep waiting for it to end. I'd stay in bed; I'd see the sun come up, merge with the overwhelming brightness of the day, and then get lower, whiter, then float, get lower still, and the torpor would become even heavier. And then, with the approach of darkness, the light which, during the day, had signified hope would still be present and would still signify hope; and the summer, day and night, would continue to shine and burn, granting neither sunset nor premonition of autumn. I heard her explain that she spent too much time here, more than she should have, that she had a lot to do in the building, that the other women were complaining about her absences, and that, if I signed the statement, she would at least be able to hold on to something; her long stopovers in the room would be better justified, and she would no longer feel in the wrong when spending time doing nothing. I listened and didn't listen to this. Half sitting on the bed, she was still holding the sheet of paper, waiting.

'An alliance,' she said suddenly in a low voice, and she grabbed me by the arm.

'What?'

'It'll be like a pact, an alliance.'

'This paper?'

'Yes, a sign that establishes that it's really me, and not somebody else, who's supposed to be here.'

I looked at her, and she examined me. How old was she? My age? That would have been strange! 'How old are you?' She stuck the pencil between my fingers. —'Sign here.' I signed. Suddenly she stood up. With an incredible expression

209

of shrewdness, pride, and satisfaction, her head held high, she looked around. As if to humiliate, she gazed triumphantly at everything here, one after another, everything: the stool, the table, the papers, me. She took off her cap; her face, with her mussed-up hair, took on a certain age, and suddenly I was struck with the idea that now she was going to start speaking, that since this morning the words had been welling up in her, harassing her, driving her crazy. She came up to the bed and knelt down. She told me she was thirty, that she was born near here, in West Street, where her parents lived. Her father was a well-off tradesman without a shop who sold meat in the markets and sometimes sold his product on the street, in working-class neighborhoods. He worked with a license, following the rules. One day . . . Now she was speaking with an expressionless volubility, as if the past, taking its turn to speak, left her no other role than that of a passive voice, unfamiliar with what it was saying. I gathered that one day her father had been accused of a minor offense, that an inspector had reported him for selling meat unfit for consumption. It was an insignificant affair which, at worst, could have led to a slight fine. But Galgat felt that he had been harmed, and he greatly exaggerated the incident. He gave up his business, left the neighborhood where he worked and, with his wife and small daughter, went out to the suburbs to get away, he said, from the decree makers. The child recalled the trip as a desperate flight to a land of trash. Perhaps they walked only a few hours, pushing their cart, going from one street to another and finally entering the debris-filled lots outside the city. But her memory played back certain recollections, saying 'that's how it was, I know': day after day of wandering, a life spent doing nothing but going through poor areas, walking past empty or ruined houses, going down, step by step, to the extreme depths of wretchedness and desertion. She remembered falling asleep a number of times, and then waking to find the cart rolling through an infinite plain piled high with rubble and junk. When she woke up for good, she was being carried; it was dark and very cold. She still had a child's memory of a long, windowless brick building, collapsing on both ends, open to the wind, and covered with water stains: it was inhabited by noisy and quarrelsome people. They found shelter there that night. Nevertheless, in this area a number of other houses were still inhabitable, since the young woman spoke of artisans calmly doing their jobs and laborers heading off every day to work: no doubt it was an outlying part of the suburb, a little town almost at the edge of the county, but still firmly linked to the built-up sections. Her father had money and he had resolved to start up his business again in these poor areas. Even if he had done nothing they could have lived fairly respectably for a time. But the father was obsessed with the idea of getting hired in a carpenter's shop. He did odd jobs and made some furniture for the family. The strange thing was that he knew almost nothing about this occupation; he had only gone into it in order to learn it and become an artisan beyond reproach. But he never learned anything: he liked discussions; even when he put two boards together he had to discuss and reason endlessly. Driving a nail led him to muddled proofs that no job was harder and that, really, no one before him had ever pounded a nail except by accident. He was talkative and taciturn, suspicious and confident. He changed his name a number of times. Galgat was probably just an assumed one. Since he talked a lot, he also spoke about politics and his vague and impetuous speeches often seemed very much out of place. According to the young woman they always led to the same remark: everyone has his peculiarities, and so each person criticizes everyone else; everybody refutes his neighbor, and his neighbor is his punishment. He himself was very good at tormenting those around him. He was unbearable to those in the neighborhood; fist-fights broke out. Perhaps two years after their flight from the city the father injured his employer, the carpenter, and had to flee. In the child's imagination these departures eventually seemed like a law, and, like everything subject to the law, they got worse when repeated. Their main feature was that they always lasted longer; their sole object was to develop, through meticulous effort, an always meaner life: to go from affluence to financial difficulties; from difficulties to poverty; from poverty to blind, crazy ruin. The man got older. Everywhere he went he wanted to start learning something new. But learning wasn't his goal. He didn't care about working. If he was interested in something, it was finding someone to talk to, to convince him that neither he nor anyone else knew anything at all about his own job. He kept this up stubbornly, constantly repeating it, even with those who cared nothing about him or his ideas. Thin, austere, graying, he spoke without paying attention to anyone else, and he must have, in the end, talked to himself or not answered when others spoke to him: he spent whole days dreaming serenely, with the expression of a man who's thinking or sleeping; then he started holding forth in a vacuum, and when someone derisively asked him why work had become so difficult, he would work himself up into a terrible rage, and finally he would invent proverbs: 'Where the past is missing, you need more than ten fingers.' 'When there's neither air nor earth, the grass that grows is called laziness.' His family was terrified: his mother fled. His death was somewhat mysterious. During one of their moves, they came back to the suburb that had been their first stop and, recognizing the half-ruined brick building where they first found shelter, Galgat went mad. Thinking that the police had gotten him, he beat his brains out against a wall. They took some precautions, it seems, when they buried him. The young woman said they lowered him into a tank where there were already some bodies, probably being held for burning. When he hit the bottom of this grave the child, who must have been about ten, felt—or later believed she felt—that the life of the old man had reached its finest moment; he had gone all the way down and had attained an honorable end; for the child, the tank somehow seemed important and comforting. After her father's death, they took her back to town and put her in an orphanage. Nine months later, she was sent away—according to her, for no reason: her conduct was excellent. One day a guard beat her, also for no reason; another time, they didn't feed her, and locked her up for a few days—she didn't know why; she had never stopped behaving correctly, and she never resisted an order. Finally, they kept on treating her more harshly, with an always more unjustified harshness, and she was expelled. 'Who was this guard?' She didn't remember, some woman. 'And there was no reason for

212

them to badger you, just you, like this?' No, there wasn't. She said this with an inflexible expression, her face proud and hard. And perhaps, unable to convince herself that her impenetrability and hostility were offenses, she sincerely saw this unjust treatment as inexplicably cruel. She was dismissed, but not left without means, since she was placed with a shopkeeper, a shoe salesman on the outskirts of town, who took her in to adopt her. She lived there peacefully, reasonably, escaping the hard discipline of common labor and learning basic things about nursing, until he asked her to change her name. She hung onto the name 'Galgat,' which probably wasn't even hers, and refused to use that of her adopted parents. After her refusal the merchant, a man named Linge, went to see her in the cubbyhole that served as her bedroom. Hearing him coming up, she grabbed a box and threw her clothes into it. The man opened the door and looked at the girl. Maybe he was only painfully astonished to think that his project had failed, whereas a tacit agreement had made it already seem a done deal—that it had failed for no justifiable reason, because of a girl's incomprehensible whim; and maybe he was only coming to ask for an explanation, in order to try to dispel the insult and repropose the name she had rejected. But, confronted with the man's silence, and with the resolve she read on his face and in his eyes, she was frightened and threw a stool at his head. Linge crumpled. The girl fled, not even taking her bundle of clothes. Now it was time for her to wander on her own. With a sure grasp of things, she went to an employment office on the West side, which, in connection with Bouxx's Committee, obtained work for people with problems. She was first employed in a paper plant, then in a pharmaceutical factory, then in a mine, and, in the end, as a health worker there. The placement agency protected and watched over her; she was more or less sheltered from any official inquiry, living beneath the laws, so to speak, in the symbolic pit of the mine, and following, through the different jobs—in each of which, out of caution, she couldn't remain— more or less the same route her father had followed, from the suburb to the tank into which he was lowered. Strangely, as she got closer to the present her life seemed more to escape her memory; she became something vague, a succession of gloomy episodes and abstract references, something mythical as well, which only applied to her because, precisely, her life didn't count. Between the time when the young woman was still working night and day in the underground passageways, driving her electric truck, and the day she stopped working, accepting the wretched life of dispensaries and asylums, through the stubborn decision to exclude, with a simple I Will Not Work, the entire heavy, external apparatus of labor, it seemed that nothing had happened—and that even these two periods, both of them hidden by the somber daylight of the epidemic, were entirely alike, so that only with difficulty could you distinguish oppression from deliverance, the sadness of servitude from the sadness of liberty. One day she went from one world to the other, and it was the same world, the same anthill. And now she was here, and neither of us could really be certain that she had really left the dark days of the mine.

The only difference, if it was one, was that she had finally decided to talk. Our relationship stayed the same, no one would have noticed the slightest change in her behavior. She put the tray on the table, and even when I told her to eat with me, she sat and ate heartily, showing neither estrangement nor familiarity; on the contrary, every one of her movements had only one meaning, which repeated, You don't bother me, and it doesn't bother me. At night she would stay if I asked her; if I didn't, she left at the appropriate time. And just as there was no rush, and still less regret, when she opened the door to leave, so too she expressed neither resistance nor eagerness whenever my hands held her back. From the day she told me her story, she gave up her bias against talking, even though our conversations were always dry and laconic. I listened, but even if I hadn't it's possible she would have spoken in the same way, with a cold, impersonal voice, in a hurry to get out whatever she had to say, yet neglecting no detail, with a meticulous integrity. Around this time, asking her about her acquaintances, about what they wanted and said, I saw that the hour of desperate decisions was at hand. Bouxx's situation was strange. Even though they had come out in the open, the illegal organizations were still unknown to the State. It was even believed, seeing how the Committee administration faced so little opposition, that the official powers, in the past so sensitive to the least little prank, had suddenly changed their methods and granted appointments to men about whom, formerly, it had been said, 'He's the scum of history, prison dregs.' Committee members' rights to administer and issue decrees were in no way contested. Now they no longer worked deep in basements but instead occupied the biggest buildings; they no longer allowed the chaos of the epidemic to rule everything, but they directly imposed themselves, with insolence, unwilling to please. They spoke neither of rights, nor of justice, nor of attaining new truths, nor of establishing interests. They could have spoken instead on behalf of shame, and invoked vileness and ignominy because these notions seemed the most human and the least compromised. But they invoked nothing. They had no time to justify themselves, and they didn't think of it. For whom would they have done so? To whom would they declare, 'We agree with you, we're fighting for your rights, we represent what you want to be,' if those who saw only the law could understand only the law's desire, and if one couldn't propose anything that would suit the others, since their solidarity was so extreme that you could never distinguish one from another or speak about one of them without implicating all the others, so extreme that it plunged them at the same time into a wild and solitary fate, one irreconcilable with general principles? No one could dispute what the Committee had accomplished during those dark days. The memories of those astonishing days, which accompanied everything it did, sufficed to distinguish it, and the air of insolence and surprise one could still breathe everywhere replaced the strongest ideas and made programs and promises appear ridiculous. The power of action seemed in this way to have been carried out, yet the enemy was not yet destroyed; but as the backdrop of soil and plague-stench dissipated, one saw, sitting in the first row and claiming sovereignty, the most wretched men. This authority in distress immediately took control of everything. No one discussed this. When they started to approach

the vast crater dug out by the plague, when the official representatives slipped on over to the Committee's headquarters,
they acted as they always did, demonstrating their traditional
hypocrisy and apparently having no other mission than that
of congratulating technicians who, in tragic circumstances,
had just demonstrated exemplary qualities. These delegates
were given a rude welcome, to be sure. Led into the streets,
they saw the empty houses, the still inhabited buildings surrounded by guards, the dispensaries crammed with young
escaped prisoners. They went to the trash dumps, and from
afar they could see the haze rising from the graves. They went
into asylums and they looked at the sick; they heard their
screams. Those who accompanied them said nothing, and
they themselves were silent. In an insult like this I recognized
Bouxx's spirit: the spirit of profound resentment which acted
in its own way. He sent them away, free, these visitors who
came from the fanciest areas, but he sent them away, after
having tied onto each one's back a heavy cadaver it would be
hard to get rid of. When he decided to show overtly that he
was in charge and that, in a zone that was subject the capricious movements of the disease, he had taken control of the
administrative apparatus, he expected a repudiation. But there
wasn't one. The officials who, in spite of the danger of contagion, stayed at their posts, thereby proving that they were
acting in common with him, aided him conscientiously. But,
instead of the hostility he'd been expecting, there was no
response from the outside. He wasn't bothered, there was no
sign of approval; they didn't pay any attention to him. The
events had opened a vacuum between the two authorities.
The wounded law, seeing that one of its organs had for some
reason been affected, went off to meditate in silence, waiting
for it to be restored. This freedom made many people drunk.
You breathed it in through the walls. But it was too vast,
ungraspable. Bouxx's decisions were carried out, he signed
papers, which took on the force of law. He brought several
men together in a room and told them, 'From now on, you
represent the Committee with such and such a responsibility.'
And these men fulfilled their responsibility and became the
representatives of the Committee. There was a huge amount

of activity. The results didn't correspond to the activity, because so often everything was lacking, but large numbers of
things were nevertheless accomplished, a lot more than any
of those who contributed to them could have hoped for. So
everyone could celebrate; and since, from one department to
the next, following the route he'd prepared, the lawless spirit
that insolently refused to justify itself spread to ever larger
zones, one could see how this false authority, which had the
vivacity and the heaviness of mercury, and which came from
the lower depths, from the gutted houses and the deserts of
streets, could end up replacing the law everywhere, destroying its prestige.

Still, they said Bouxx was locking himself more frequently
in his office at the main headquarters and, taciturn or furious,
he rarely came out of his bouts of apathy, when his blood got
the better of him. For a whole evening he insulted his main
representative on the Committee, someone named Lenz, a
first-rate man who had directed, for a time, the official opposition within the framework of the State and who took his
role to heart one day and went into exile; he was about fifty,
small, thin, feeble. The civil servants respected him a lot.
Bouxx called him the Colossus of Rhodes. It was Bouxx who,
with his inanimate majesty, deserved that name more than
anyone else, and if for a whole evening he had furiously
repeated it as an insult it was perhaps because he in fact saw
himself as a gigantic statue, a statue whose tiniest step could
have shaken the world, but who, realizing that his fearsome
movement wasn't meeting any obstacle, started to ask himself
if he wasn't still just an amorphous and inert piece of clay. He
was certainly too serious to let himself be fooled by the ease
of his usurpations. His successes were extraordinary. Who
could have foreseen such a sudden paralysis of the law? They
were ready to fight something incredible, a monster whose
infinite tentacles stretched everywhere and allowed only lim-
ited movement. But from the very first the beast pulled back;
it seemed tired and offended; it had suffered an affront, and
this humiliation could have unforeseen consequences. That
same evening, Bouxx declared, 'When I see your enthusiasm,
because the plan's been carried out, because decisions are

being followed, I think of a military leader buried in his bunker and who's still giving orders by telephone: if things go too well, if every order he gives is carried out to perfection, he'll suspect that the lines have been cut, that no one is listening and that everything seems to be working because he no longer knows what's going on. We're accomplishing everything because we're locked in a room, giving orders to the clock. So our success just demonstrates the fact that we're still in our hole, still totally impotent.' For a long time, the influence of Bouxx had been in doubt: he was accused of seeming too cultivated, of being too quick to approach the authorities, and of trying to negotiate certain embarrassing questions with them. His co-workers thought everything had been compromised as soon as someone started to talk with an official department. But he himself probably only wanted to make sure that, in the Councils of State, his decisions were being taken into account and to see whether or not they were regarded as valid or simply whether people had been upset. I imagine that, in his advance, occupying the main command posts one after the other, without meeting any more difficulties than if he had gone for a walk in an empty lot, he got dizzy and felt the need, above all, to prove to himself that all this wasn't a mirage and that, when he sat at a table and met with the Committee to decide on this or that, his decisions counted for history, that all that dramatic and extraordinary movement, all those decisive victories, amounted to more than just moves on a chessboard. And, when he was about to go to sleep, perhaps he prayed that the Committee really did exist, that the prisons had been opened, that he wasn't still a little doctor whose license had been revoked, or something even worse, and that the most terribly deceived people weren't once again victims of a system of illusions which made them work with enthusiasm for their own slavery. All the requests for aid were marvelously successful. The dispensaries were entirely re-equipped. The whole questionable population of evacuated houses was crammed into buildings, and bed-clothes, covers, and clothes were distributed; work started up again, slowly, in factories. These improvements, carried out after a few quick meetings, proved the strength of the organizations that had already slipped in everywhere, but Bouxx learned nothing from all this, since the secret network, the routes running in every direction, had been established by Bouxx himself. And he certainly could have been happy with such extensive measures, but he had wanted more: not, when he went into new offices, into new regions of control, to feel the satisfaction of seeing his accomplices agree, in other words to see himself everywhere, but to notice once, just once, an expression of anxiety on the face of someone he didn't know and who represented the opposing authority, when surprised by the appearance of one of those wretches who, it was thought for so long, had been crushed and annihilated.

One day I received a little note from Bouxx with these words: 'The events are coming soon, now everyone has to take part in the conflict.' It was then that, without anyone telling me, with Jeanne answering my questions only with her silent gaze, I understood that this whole, immense enterprise, prepared through so many vigils and so much sleep, all these unfortunates buried in pits and prisons, this lifeless explosion, this freedom flowing along roads and slowly rising to the level of the highest buildings in order to efface their miserable peeling façades, all these victories, all these hopes, unsure of themselves, were trying, in the violence of reprisals and in blood justice, to separate law from peace and to get, finally, the law to declare war. Now I knew what the drab and shabby crowds meant, crowds that took over the streets at certain times, whereas at others, at nightfall, the desert itself took possession of the most populous neighborhoods, as if its presence were as visible as the crowd it had chased away. When I heard again, at night, the popping of enormous boils; when, in the morning, in apparently randomly chosen locations, detonations first dripped, then flowed as from an eager wound that's the goal of everything flowing and giving life through thousands of veins and channels, then I could imagine the somber labor being readied by the humbled forces of the world, in order to derive from their humbling something other than concord and calm. And I questioned Jeanne about the people I knew: about the man with the injured hand, who had insulted Roste and whom she described, in his final hour, calmly lying at his night watchman's post, busy watching the factory he was supposed to be guarding burn; about Abran, the noble old man who, joining a group one day to stone a foreman, pushed him into a small shed and threw scrap metal and pieces of glass at his head; about one of the cooks from the kitchen, formerly a concierge in one of the beautiful country houses built in the green belt of the South: her husband did manual labor in some factory or other, and more regularly in a big sawmill where he helped stack the wood. One day labor disputes broke out; the man's situation was too insignificant for him to be involved in these incidents; the fact that he worked or didn't work was of no interest to anyone; he therefore continued doing one thing or another, finding, thanks to the situation, better paying jobs. The woman worked at the house and in its garden, which had a plot reserved for the use of her household; she also cared for the son of her employers, a young, very retarded man hidden in the country by his parents, who were high-level civil servants. One evening her husband didn't come back home, nor did he appear the next day or the day after that. She didn't know what had happened to him. Two days later someone from the police came to explain that, during a fight at the sawmill, her husband had attacked the assistant manager with a pickaxe and that the man had fired back at him with a revolver, in self-defense. The laborer, wounded, was in the hospital. The woman didn't believe a word of it. Perhaps she had a prejudice against the police, convinced that they always have a motive for giving one version of things rather than another, and she ascribed to their report only the vague sense of an ill omen. Perhaps as well, finding the incident incomprehensible, she couldn't admit that a laborer would end up wanting to kill someone in a fight he had nothing to do with. She refused to go to the hospital and stayed at home, waiting every evening for her husband's return. When she received the official death certificate, she didn't believe it either, or at least she had waited too long to believe it now. For six months she stayed on, and then one day she left, taking with her the young unfortunate, the son of her employers, who's still with her today. The young woman told me of these people in an emotionless tone of voice, without any spontaneity, and because talking was part of her life with me now. But, while I was listening to these coldly recounted stories, at the same time I kept hearing, exactly as if a loudspeaker had been given the job of repeating them for me and for everybody, the words written by Bouxx: *The events are coming soon, now everyone has to take part in the conflict.* These words, I knew, awaited a response, but the response was doomed to take on such a tragic and insulting meaning that no one in the world could have found the strength to get up, go to a desk and stop the loudspeaker for the few minutes needed to write it. There was, perhaps, something laughable in this rage of a man who wanted to make himself hated, and who was being smothered by declarations of love. But so many others, suffering from an insult that couldn't be erased, needed, in order to be free, to turn their enemies into enemies and their relations with them into combat; and these people, losing their cool, were ready to become wolves, ready to turn every doorway into a butcher shop, ready to set in motion the machinery of reprisals and war; and, finally, all these crimes could provoke nothing more than a redoubling of benign precautions; a situation like this couldn't have been anticipated, not even for a moment. War, I thought. But who could you fight with? Driven to despair by the memory of evil, they dreamed of war. But when it starts, it's not even war, it's only a humiliating masquerade, a grimacing desire, a new and shameful image of peace.

One morning we went out. She had been given the task of visiting buildings and already she could no longer leave me alone. Right away it got hotter. We turned away from the avenue and the houses became scarcer; the soil was almost yellow. The street became wider, it seemed to float; then it narrowed; the little wooden shops leaned against each other; the shacks with their tin roofs lost track of the road, only to sketch out alleyways that led nowhere. In places we found areas covered with bits of metal, through which the roadway itself was only a scrap of the route, but a little further on we rediscovered the street, always just as hesitant but sure of itself, thrusting between the houses under an unshakable vault of heat. I had no idea whether I was following her or if she was following me. She walked at my side, on her own, with an even step, looking neither right nor left. People crossed in front of us, others came from behind, for a moment hurrying in order to catch up. Cars pushed us up onto the sidewalk or against fences made of planks. Sometimes the noise increased, as if the entire crush of the city had come out of the neighboring roads and had been thrown up into this single street, and the passersby, by the hundreds, let themselves be swept along, flowing like streams, but with the lethargy of spent water that can't find its way. The noise and the crowd showed perfectly what a desert we were moving in, two shadows linked by the shadow of a link. No doubt it would have been more fitting if the street had been an out of the way road running through abandoned territory; it would have been less surprising if, coming out of living countries, it had penetrated into a chaos of stone, into a cold and sterile North. But it was the city with its trucks, carts, and farmers, under a cruelly sunny day, with women leaving shops in groups, slowly, aimlessly, and it was also the desert whose menacing strength came not from solitude or from the dead earth, or from anything bad in the world, but from splendor and from calm and inexhaustible life.

She stopped in front of a building that rose amid the disorder of sheds and empty courtyards. There was no one in the corridor. At the end of it, facing a poorly lit staircase, there was the lodge of the person in charge; he came out, looked at me, looked at the woman, and let us in. Neither on his part nor on the part of any of those I met in this place, and in others, was there ever any kind of doubt concerning my identity; no one asked who I was or what I had come to do; no one seemed to be amazed at my presence. He pulled papers from a cupboard and tossed them on the table; one of these papers was the list of refugees, with their names or their supposed names: more than three hundred lived in the building. Other inventories listed the number of sick, of aged, of children; the professions of able-bodied people; the amount of food available, with the address of suppliers and the names of people

charged with requisitioning; in the end there was a long list
of necessary products that were missing. While she was leafing through these papers the man didn't know what to do
with himself, nor did I; sometimes my eyes focused on names
and numbers, sometimes they turned to the dark recesses of
the room, which was lit by a weak bulb. In the back there
must have been a bed enclosed in a narrow recess; two rows
of benches obstructed the passageway; the room wasn't dirty,
but it was tiny, stained by a darkness that had lasted too long,
and it seemed to lack any means of ever being illuminated.
Jeanne walked to the door. At the first steps we were enveloped by a sweetish and acidic odor which evoked the
terrible smell of the dispensary, but it was more perfidious,
like the whispering of women's voices, heavy with suspicion
and accusation. On the landing, the man from the lodge
opened several doors, as if he wanted to make us see some
apartments, but these weren't apartments: there was a little
room, a hallway onto which opened, perhaps, other rooms.
The place was just about clean, but nothing indicated that
people could live there amid rolled-up mattresses, blankets,
piles of suitcases, as in the baggage room of a little provincial
train station: one expected to see the women, at the sound
of the whistle, gather up already wrapped and tied bundles, sling them over their shoulders, and leave. Not a word
was said when I appeared. I came in first. The six or seven
women, wearing bathrobes or coats, looked at me without
moving; they looked as if they had been placed there to wait
for someone, and it was perhaps me, perhaps someone else,
but none of their movements indicated what they thought of
such an apparition. During this time the man had entered
and tried to reach the window, but he didn't have time:
Jeanne came in next, and behind her—as if, up to this point,
she had held them aside by means of magic, and as if now her
own entry had called them out of every corner in the building—other women pressed forward, coming out of rooms on
the floor heralding others one could hear on the stairs. Soon
there were ten new people in the tiny room, ten curious and
apathetic persons, with similar faces—neither young nor old,
neither from the city nor the countryside, apparitions who

223

seemed to emanate from some abstract source, from a reserve of immobility and patience rather than from real rooms lived in by beings of flesh and bone. There was no surprise and no sign of blame on their faces, and no look of interest, either. Their insolent eyes, which _tacitly_ stated that I was not one of them, stopped with that verdict and didn't go any further. They looked at me with their passivity, with the idleness that was their reason for gazing, and this almost fanatical idleness made me fear something irreparable, one of those crazy acts whose effects can't be contained. I motioned to Jeanne that I wanted to leave. A number of children wormed their way through and were pestering me: one of them hung on my jacket; I shook him off, and he fell; but he didn't yell, didn't take his eyes off me—even falling he kept staring at me with an intrepid and satisfied expression. I cut through the crowd. On the landing, on the steps leading to the other floors, there were more people. A swarm of flies, I thought, autumn flies, obsequious and obsessive, already three-quarters worn out.

Then the street continued. Now it too was impregnated with the odor: as heavy as heat, it announced and escaped the houses, and the houses, losing their outlines, seemed to extend to infinity, everywhere there was still space. All along the street we bumped into people who had been calmly washed up on this provisional beach, convinced that, since the tide had carried them there, this location, and no other, was theirs alone. Lying down, standing, eating, sleeping, they were motionless, accepting everything, the burning light, the dust from cars, the kicks from passersby, and they looked at me with an arrogant impassiveness, threatening me, through their silence, with something crazy and irreparable. Beside me, Jeanne came back, as calm and as distant from what was about to happen as if I hadn't heard her repeating, on her own during our walk, the words from the loudspeaker: *Now! Now! Now!* Each time we came back it was like this. And still I knew that my relationship with her was changing. She kept getting colder, but this coldness was like the sign of something unavowable. Occasionally she was disgusted with me, but her repugnance was _insatiable_. She was cold, to be sure, but a cold despair, a cold hatred, a cold and closed savagery also developed next to me, in the circle traced around me; and from the two states, one living and the other dead, which, fiercely united, were constantly standing two paces from each other, I saw only the indifferent gaze cast by a spirit of fury and hunger. She was discreet, reserved: she always obeyed me, yet with an extreme indifference to orders, as if her precision was one of inattentiveness, an involuntary and unassailable gesture. Discreet, and I came up against a passive and anonymous thing, since I stood there before nothing, myself empty and stripped of everything, no longer knowing if she was there, feeling that within her someone else was hidden, one of those ferocious beings who assume a recognizable face, but with whom the you and the me come undone in a perpetually illusory dialogue.

One day she let loose and improvised some craziness. She announced that she would never again leave my room, and she forbade me to leave. She made me repeat some words that I barely heard; they went something like, 'I'll cherish and protect you: I'll watch only you.' I had to get away: she scratched my face. I huddled in a corner, and she was tearing herself apart, crying and screaming. And while I was looking at her, suddenly seeing her stiffen, half naked but rigid and impassive, as if she had only reprimanded me for some offense or other from the heights of her authority as a registered nurse, I noticed that black, thick water was dripping down her body, water like what had once before percolated through the walls. Maybe more than water: a harbinger coming from something intact yet ready to liquify, something oozing and hesitant, ascending to daylight and contaminating it, like an odor, spreading, drifting, stagnant, then coming up again like the spirit of cold, thick, black water.

This happened around noon. When the water withdrew, the room was visible again: the room, the splendor of noon, the shocked silence of flying and whirling flies. Then the days came back. She didn't watch over me any more than she had done before. But nobody came into the room, and when we left she made me slip down along the corridors and locked me in the elevator; we walked in the street, completely alone in the midst of people I didn't see. Every day these streets got more deserted. One had the impression that now only events had the right to come and go and that, if people still were there, walking and running between the locked houses, it was only the temporary disguise of events which, by dint of tenacity and ruses, had succeeded in collecting, bit by bit, enough solid substance to form a body, but one whose composure could be destroyed by the least touch. In any neighborhood a meeting like this could take place, and at any time. Every night there were executions, and during the day chaos advanced with its wild weight, focusing on anyone or anything, and endlessly hounding the object of misfortune. Who was burning? Who was looting? No one asked, because not individuals but a troop of burning and bloody things arose before the eyes of the victims, and everyone felt attacked by his own still stammering life, by confined, distant, and incredible memories, which were suddenly free and had become the revenge and the new justice of history. Every evening there were scenes of infinite devastation. At dawn, some areas awoke with the stupor of a man who has forgotten an earthquake and cannot understand why streets and houses, why everything is a vast, silent inferno. What made the stupor worse was the fact that the disorder did not establish any line of demarcation between those who spread it and those who underwent it. The best disciplined groups, those one sometimes saw, in parades, arrogantly challenging the established order with their own faultless order, let themselves go, violently struggling against each other, indulging in such extreme acts that every house became the common grave of the arsonist and his victims. Such things had less to do with debauchery than with disorder; and when small groups, breaking the rules and engaging in sedition, started randomly shooting and fighting with knives, the residents they came to slaughter suddenly recognized in their assailants the protectors to whom they owed their lives. The result was a confusion of relations and an uncertainty about the meaning of events: one couldn't see who the torches and dynamite were working for. It was insane that the nightly horrors couldn't even undermine neighborly relations. Maybe there was no feeling of real benevolence between people who had seen their houses destroyed, had been wounded, and those who robbed and wounded them; maybe the victims only wanted to hide their fear and resentment and to prolong indefinitely the fiction of human warmth; but it also turned out that the old brutality didn't bother the people who resorted to it and that, without any desire to provoke, they went on living amicably right next to those they terrorized, indifferent to what they had done and effacing the signs of their own license.

What did these empty streets mean, more peaceful and anxious than any street had ever been? What did these things mean—the executions and the destruction destroying even the ruins? An effort on the part of what was unjust to become just? A reconciliation through death? The advance of a mad dream that had escaped its own domain and was wandering, masked by a disfigured law? In normal times, what did the police do? It caught suspects, it took them, via long detours along juridical routes, to the sentence that was less a condemnation than the study of all of history in relation to the condemned, after which the latter took on an overwhelming and phenomenal reality. He saw himself locked into this history as in a prison or, on the contrary, he disappeared, vanished into thin air, and rediscovered the pure invisibility of his innocence. But today, in a single moment one was suspected, condemned, and executed, and no doubt the unfortunates, slashed or shot, received from the death penalty the very offense that this punishment enabled them to expiate. In this way, one could say that the most violent crimes secretly served as the law—a still summary law that lacked a past but was nevertheless, for the specialists, already venerable. But the vague horror the crimes inspired also proved that crime had changed sides, and that, in the severity and monstrosity of its acts, it drew a circle of suspicion and guilt around the victims.

Where is the law? What does it do? Cries like these have always been heard, even when times were good, and, even though expressing reproach or discontent, they are a tribute to its notable dignity. For it was law's dignity to hide and show itself: it hid in everyone, it showed itself through all; when you didn't see it, you knew it was there; when you saw it, you no longer knew you were yourself. That's why informing and suspicion were for so long somehow noble, and this impression of nobility overcame the contempt one also had to feel for these practices. The informers represent the unobtrusiveness of power, which liked to be present in some way behind your back: their silent progress testified to the scruples of omnipotence, and even more its resignation, its life in withdrawal, uncertain and almost close to disgrace and exile, whereas it was air and daylight and every movement in everyone's life. And if suddenly someone got hit from behind, hearing the fatal accusation Sabotage, Sabotage, he certainly felt sorrow and anxiety, but it was a sorrow not directed toward himself, but toward this power that, in order to maintain everyone's self-esteem, kept pretending to feel at the mercy of the first passerby.

Where is the law? What does it do? These screams now were terrible. I heard them in the empty streets, and that's why, in spite of the feverish crowd pressing for several hours from all sides, these streets were empty. I heard them behind the shutters of houses, and the houses were nothing more than ruins where workers, struggling to clear the rubble, threw in gasoline and placed explosives in the foundations. And what made them so tragic wasn't any accusatory roar, for who would still have dared to complain aloud and publicly display his misfortune? You didn't hear them, and that was the worst. It was as if they had been smothered: shouts in a basement, groaning behind a wall, sounds which didn't get past the lips, which refused to be heard. Whole populations saw fire and hunger coming at them, without having anything to say; without the slightest murmur, they were ready to slide into the enormous hole into which history stumbled. It was this silence that hit me like a powerful scream, and howling, choking, whispering, it drove the listener—who just once had agreed to listen—crazy. And this cry of distress was universal. I knew that those who wanted the death of the law were screaming like the others; and I knew that this petrified silence, through which some continued to express their confidence in an unshakable regime, to the point of not noticing what was going on and shrugging their shoulders when it was mentioned, which, for others, meant confusion when faced with the impossibility of knowing where justice ended and where terrorism began, where informing for the glory of the State won out, and where informing for its ruin did too—I knew that this tragic silence was still more fearsome than anyone could have believed, because it was emanating from the silent cadaver of the law itself, refusing to say why it had entered the tomb and whether it had gone down there to break open or to accept the tomb.

In those days I lived in a fever. I began to wait like the others, as if the imminent hour had refused to let its name be known to me, as to the others—as if it hadn't wanted to reveal whether it would be called the hour of punishment or the hour of justification. I lay flat, putting all my energy into not doing certain things, not writing certain words, and nobody knew the life I torched in this open-eyed sleep. I didn't look at her, and she didn't look at me; most often she went into other rooms and came back smelling of blood and burned flesh. While she was there I moved as little as possible, I only spoke if it was necessary, and she herself kept me informed about what she was doing and what the others were doing, in a perfectly peaceful and reasonable tone of voice. One evening she tore up the papers on which I had written a few words; she ground them to dust, but she did it calmly, without a hint of impatience and without saying anything. Another evening I had the greatest difficulty eating what she had brought. I hid my disgust in her presence. After she left, this disgust kept pressing harder. As if it were floating lightly in front of me, drawing me to the sink, then suddenly changing direction and leading me into the corridor, making me open the door, leading me prudently, patiently to the stairway, like an accomplice who's always about to take off, I followed it, and when I found I was in the second floor kitchen I noticed it had disappeared, leaving me helpless and forcing me to look for what I had come to do there. Finally, answering a woman's question, I asked for something to drink, preferably wine. She poured me a glass and I went back up, meeting again, in front of me, rising, throbbing, opening doors, the retching feeling that was now slightly tinged with wine and that had been my guide before. Maybe my guide wasn't sure or was having second thoughts I didn't know about: coming back into the room, I stumbled and lay on the floor, breathing dust. A little while later she came up. She lay down on the bed, which seemed strange. Then leaning over me she sniffed and said in a very contemptuous way, 'You've been drinking wine.' I didn't move. She sat back down. She was leaning forward, almost out of the chair.

'You shouldn't go out while I'm gone,' she said. 'You shouldn't go and talk with those women. You should stay there and if you need something, just ask me.'

I didn't move. She got up and mechanically started to take off her blouse, but a button got in the way and she tore the material. This tearing sound frightened me. I heard myself ask her, 'Why do I have to hide?' She half turned her back on me, examining the torn piece; with a hard tug she tore it some more. I heard myself repeating: 'Why do I have to hide? Why are you keeping me isolated?' She stepped toward me and said calmly,

'It's better that way.' And in the same calm voice, without really looking at me, continuing to pull at the piece of material, she added, 'You need a lot of peace and rest. Look at what's going on now.'

'But just a few steps . . . down to the kitchen!'

'No. Those women are stupid and mean. They don't understand what you need. Who gave you the wine?'

'I don't know; I don't remember.'

'It's that kid,' she said, hissing. 'She's spying on you, she knows everything you do and she tells, laughing about it. I won't stand for it. I'll beat her, crush her.'

'It wasn't her.'

'Yes it was,' she screamed. 'Get up! Get up!'

She grabbed me by the arm, pulled me up, looked me over from head to toe, and then started to laugh. I had the impression that the scene from the other day was going to happen again: she was trembling, her mouth was half open, and the more her mouth opened, the more her teeth clenched. I was overcome with dizziness. I wanted to get away, but she held me passionately. Two or three times she whispered: 'Now!

Now! Now!' and then, with terrible impatience, but still whispering, I heard her say,

'Now, now, I know who you are, I've discovered it, I have to announce it. Now . . .'

'Be careful,' I said.

'Now . . .' And she sat up suddenly, raised her head and with a voice that penetrated the walls, that overwhelmed the city and the sky, with such a full but calm voice, so imperious she reduced me to nothing, she screamed, 'Yes, I see you, I hear you, and I know that the Most High exists. I can celebrate him, love him. I turn toward him saying, "Listen, Lord."'

I couldn't look at her any more. I thought of the incident that had happened a few days before. Going out, I said hello to a woman and opened the door for her. She looked at me for a moment, shuddered, and then, pale, threw herself gravely at my feet, with a well-considered movement, her forehead pressed against the ground; then she got up nimbly and disappeared. After she left, I got worked up with enthusiasm. I wanted to do something extraordinary—kill myself, for example. Why? Out of joy, no doubt. But now this joy seemed unbelievable. I felt only bitterness. I was overwhelmed and frustrated.

'Couldn't you have kept that to yourself?' I said.

I was sitting on the bed; she came up and said softly, 'I can go. I'll leave the house, if you like.'

'Why did you speak? Get this: I don't assume the burden of your little secrets. I'm not responsible for them. I don't know what you said. I forgot it immediately.'

She didn't move.

'Your words mean nothing,' I said bitterly. 'Remember that. Even if they referred to something that's true, they would be worthless.'

'It'd be better if I left,' she said.

I found myself in the middle of the room. I noticed that I hadn't stopped walking, that I was still walking. I was dripping with sweat. Thick steam came in from the open window. I wanted to cross the room, but I stumbled over her heavy shoes, making a terrible racket. 'Get out of here,' I yelled, 'get out.' I was ashamed for having shouted. And I added nastily, 'I can't stand you any more. I hate your skin, your eyes, your nose. It's stronger than I am.' She was in a corner, on the bed: she didn't answer. Silently, I sat down near her.

'I'm tired,' I said after a moment. 'I've eaten almost nothing. What time do you think it is?'

Neither one of us tried to turn on the light. A little later someone knocked and yelled a name through the door. She went to open it. When she came back, she brought me something to drink, so I gathered that she had gone down to the kitchen.

'Roste asked for me,' she said.

I shuddered when I heard the name.

'Is he your friend? What's your relationship with Roste?'

She was still handing me the cup; I snatched it from her and threw it on the ground. The black stain, wet for a moment, got thicker as it slowly flowed, stretching to her feet.

'That's my business,' she said, stepping back.

'So you live with me, but you're also living with him!'

'That's my business,' she repeated, her back against the wall.

I looked at her forehead, that bowed head. I came forward, but barely had my hand brushed against her, and she screamed, 'Oh, don't touch me, don't you dare touch me,' as if she wanted to spit on me. She pushed me away with disgust, even though I was already some distance from her, she added two obscenities, and then, 'Leave me alone.' I must have tried to tell her to get out, but my lips were trembling, they trembled against my hand which little by little got wet and started to tremble as well. Suddenly, it was as if I'd been awakened, and a strange feeling went through me: a feeling of splendor, a majestic and radiant drunkenness. It was as if the day's events and words had found a place in their true region. Everything was firm and unshakable. Something so obvious transformed everything. At the same time I recognized that this wet animal hand resting against my face was hers, coming and going and, as soon as I wanted to speak, returning to my mouth.

'Now you should go to bed,' she said.

I sat up; she was sitting a little behind me, her face looking worn.

'I'm anybody,' I said, looking at her, 'remember that.'

'Yes.'

'I'll go out if I want to and I'll speak with whomever I like.'

'Yes.'

'I have no idea what happened last night, none whatsoever.'

'Yes.'

'You tried to fool me. You wanted to deceive me, I figured it out right away.'

'Yes,' she said, 'it's true. Now, come lie down.'

I stared at her hard.

'A farce, it was just a farce, a shameful joke.'

'Yes, yes, yes,' she screamed. 'I was joking, I'm still joking. What do you want? What are you going to do?'

I threw myself on her, I was choking her. 'Get out,' I said. She was in her corner, writhing and curling up. 'Leave right away, right away.' —'Yes, let me go. I wasn't joking, I swear.' She raised her eyes up to me, to my hand hanging like a shadow over her head.

'Listen to me!'

She pushed me away gently, got up, and stayed standing as if paralyzed. Then she said in a low voice, 'I'd still like to be able to change my words into jokes, because I feel their weight. But now you have to believe me. What I'm going to say is true. Take me at my word, tell me you'll believe me, swear to it.'

'Yes, I'll believe you.'

She hesitated, made a violent effort, and then lowered her head with a kind of laugh: *I know that you are the Unique, the Supreme One. Who could stay standing before you?*

I turned away so as not to meet her eyes. She remained motionless for another few seconds. Then she walked to the door. I thought she was going to leave. I was happy to be alone. She took her shoes and in fact did go into the corridor.

# 9

The next day she explained that events perhaps forced us to leave. Still, I didn't get up and I didn't eat. I didn't look at her either. I would have liked to do all this to be agreeable, but I knew I had to act as I was acting, that I had to stay in my corner, motionless and feigning death. She worked as hard as she could to persuade me to eat. She tormented me endlessly. For hours she repeated 'Eat, eat, eat,' in a monotonous and flat voice, as if this voice were the very thing she was pushing in my mouth to feed me. Even when she was overcome with fatigue and was able to doze off, she repeated in her sleep, 'Eat, come on, eat.' I didn't get any rest: I kept still with the greatest effort anyone can make.

Finally she told me, 'You can go on refusing to eat. I won't tell anyone, I won't have anyone come.' And she went to work.

I was overcome with the temptation to leave as soon as she closed the door. In the room, at the bottom of the wall, almost below the sink, there was a large pipe. It bent sharply there, and a large wet spot, the result of condensation, covered a certain area. This spot looked very dirty. At certain times the sweating was visible, and anyone noticing the slow noise of the dripping could know the precise moments in which a real droplet formed, got thicker, ran along the metal, fell, and landed on a rag. This rag was a piece of very bright red cloth. Now, I noticed, I must have been looking a lot at this piece of cloth, and, since I was alone, I kept on looking. It was a thick piece of fabric, crumpled into a thousand folds. It shone and glowed with exceptional brilliance. Maybe it wasn't really shining, for there was also a muted color that slowly came to light, and it was that dull, still hidden color that made it so dangerously visible, so that it came closer to me, was here, then went further away, into the street, walking slowly, inexplicably flirting before my eyes, then charged forward, and I saw it as material hanging by a string and blown by the wind—I saw it mixing dangerously with filth, curled up, brilliant and untouchable, in the garbage can. It waited infinitely for the faint, interrupted sweating. Then suddenly, as if impelled by an order from inside, the completely formed drop passed through the metal, quickly coalesced and grew, to the point where, now a real drop of liquid, it rested for a mysterious second and went on hanging, menacing, <u>avid</u>, frightened, over the still completely motionless red fabric. And as long as it didn't fall, even though, behind it, pushing it, there was an instinct like the sordid life of this pipe, there was still hope, and the day was still unbroken. And even when it was falling, as it was traveling with the lightness and clarity of a little bubble, it didn't seem to sense what was coming, and it was still possible to believe that what was about to happen wouldn't. But at the precise moment in which it slid into the folds and disappeared, entirely absorbed, not leaving the slightest trace, as hidden as could be, I only had to hear the noise of the water penetrating the fabric to feel that it was meeting something shamefully wet, wetter than it was, a sticky thickness, a saturated, unstanchable deposit. The sound was driving me crazy. It was the sound of a fluid going bad, losing its transparency, becoming something still wetter, secreted by a cast-off life, a cold, thick, black stain. And what made this such a dangerous situation was not that one had to wait for hours for the water to ooze, nor foresee and practically desire the fall of the tiny drop, nor even hear or feel the slow infiltration itself, but rather that with each new drop the fabric maintained the same dry and brilliant look, the same shining and unchanging red. That was the damn trick of this whole business. I couldn't get over how this insolent redness, which was locking up a stock of stagnant water in its always dry husk, was pulling me by the arm, dragging my body along, making me lean forward, intoxicating my fingers with the thought that they need only suddenly grab this piece of visible and tidy cloth in order to squeeze out its <u>latent</u> intimacy, to spurt that out and display it forever as an indelible, thick, black stain.

She came back a number of times, each time more nervous and irritated. Finally she noticed that if I didn't look at her it was because I was looking at something else, and if I didn't speak to her it was because I didn't want to be distracted from what was bothering me. It took her a while to figure this out. But as soon as she had, her face changed, she grabbed me by the ears, held me with all her strength in front of her, as if to force me to see her, shook me, pulled me from side to side, then, rushing to the sink, she grabbed a wash basin and the rag, did something I couldn't see, something revealed by an insane noise, and I saw her disappear with the basin, looking like someone who has just won a victory and gotten her revenge.

When she came back she carefully washed my face. Now she was treating me very well. And when she handed me a cup of cold coffee, I made the effort to gulp some down. Holding the cup myself, I looked at this strange, barely black liquid: I observed it, it fascinated me. But almost immediately she got impatient again, grabbed the cup I was clutching, made as if to throw it away, then examined it, training on its insides her overtaxed and distrustful gaze.

'Ah, I've had enough of you!'

She was walking around the room—fortunately she did it slowly, without making me dizzy.

'I've put up with a lot of things. But really, you can't expect me to put up with that.'

She saw on the table the papers covered with ink: she tore them to pieces with her glance, then started looking at everything around her.

'And this room! I can't look at it any more. I hope a bomb drops and cleans it up.'

With a violent kick she overturned the stool.

'All these things! They're like you! It's as if they're satisfied, because you look at them, because you look only at them. Ugh! What a scene!'

She hid her face in her hands, but suddenly, raising her eyes, she must have thought that I was defying her by continuing to look at something, for she jumped on me, buried my head under a pillow, pounded it with her fists for quite a while. I stayed like that. As if from afar, I heard laughing. 'A worm, a wimp'—this last word burst into my ear and, again, I saw her standing, her hands up against me, so close that I moved back. She too looked at the hands I had just avoided; they were as dull as plaster.

'I'm not blind,' she said, continuing to look at them. 'As soon as I approach, you step away. If I go away, you don't notice it. You never look at me or hear me. You pay less attention to me than to a rag.'

She spoke slowly, with an almost serene voice: what she was saying was beyond discussion and no longer belonged to anyone. She aimed her hand at the bed.

'Why did you come here? I could ask you for a long time. Why, right now, are you here, near me? If it's to mock me, I'm not ashamed, I take pride in it. If it's to reject me, I'm not hurt, I'm stronger. Because I don't give a damn about you, either. I know who you are and I don't give a damn about you.'

She started shouting again, and yet her voice still hit me with a sad and self-important calmness. I heard words and more words, they went past and left no other trace than mockery, indecency, desecration, the sad and cold truth of her face next to mine. 'I have no use for your feelings.' She was repeating that now, she repeated it with a pointless rage, as if whole days had passed with nothing other than this mechanical language being produced. 'I'll lock you up like a dog. No one will know anything about you, no one other than me will have seen you.'

'Let me speak,' she screamed again, pushing her face even closer to mine—and I took in her breath, I fathomed its odor, which was that of a plant coming out of the ground.

'I expect nothing from you. I've asked for nothing. I've lived without being concerned with your life. You should know that I have never, ever implored or begged you. I have never said: come, come, come!'

She let out a terrible scream: suddenly the black, abject tide came out of her and overwhelmed me. Her hair covered me, her body flowed over mine. I couldn't tell if everything was happening with words, or if, with her saliva and moist limbs, she was really drawing me into a corner of the room, into the street, into these always saturated and inundated places. My mouth was dripping. I felt her stuck against me, a foreign flesh, a dead, liquifying flesh; and the more I pushed it away, the more it collapsed and curled around me. I think in the end I spat in her face; my whole body was expiring, but she too spat in my eyes, on my cheeks, wordlessly, and I sensed the triumph in the incredible scream coming from her throat.

Her scream continued, alone, while she seemed to have disappeared. It wandered, disembodied, peaceful, a little frightened by its imprisonment in this room. Sometimes, it was nothing more than a murmur, just the thought of an open mouth, then once again it surged, overflowed the walls, covered a limitless space, driving before itself the noises of the courtyard, the house, the rumbling of a whole city. At a certain point it sat up and listened. The strong and authoritarian voice of a loudspeaker came from the street—a loudspeaker which, from a point somewhere in the street, but also from an inaccessible region, that of fire and hunger, was endlessly throwing words together. The voice broke off and was replaced by silence. Then again, further away, from deep within a still inaccessible region of threats and fear, the voice could be heard; then, after a silence, even further away, it loomed up, still desperate and immutable, still addressing anyone from the depths of death, searching for an undiscoverable and anonymous someone incapable of hearing or understanding it.

Suddenly she stood up and threw herself forward, running, with a terrible noise, and not concerned with doors or walls, as if she were in the middle of a field. But the noise went away from her and came back to her with overwhelming speed; it enveloped and gathered up everything, finally throwing it all in my direction and throwing itself on me, with the weight of an enormous, solid mass, which was also a staggering and cavernous void. I didn't move. A bitter, thick dust rose, which I breathed slowly. Being in a corner, I felt the need to flatten myself against the plaster, so as to feel it flowing around me and onto my skin. Through the sand, I reached an almost cool layer and, embedding myself a little more, I discovered, right in my chest, the stench of true wetness. 'Don't be afraid,' she said. For a moment she stayed fairly far away, almost squatting, and during this time her voice kept groping to find me, as if she had latched on to the memory of a former state of things and, in the midst of this unknown debris, was trying to force her way through. And she herself, when she came forward, seemed to extricate herself with difficulty from an unsteady location, which she really wasn't escaping, which accompanied her with its imbalance, got loose in order to follow her, and then suddenly pulled back. 'You're afraid,' she said, grabbing me roughly. I buried myself as best I could in the plaster. She kept on wobbling and moved like a livid and cadaverous odor whose contact frightened me, or she disappeared in a swirl, floating behind me in order to grab me without warning. This odor was totally threatening. She stayed there, lying down, as heavy as a corpse, contourless, overflowing, everywhere present and waiting with insidious patience to get herself breathed. And I felt that, by dint of patience, waiting, and trickery, she would end up finding a complicitous respiration; even the softness of the plaster per-meated you, and when she spoke, saying Now it's over, they didn't get us, it's over, she wasn't really speaking, she was tagging along behind her words, carrying with her a latent life, a life of earth and water; and she was patiently on the lookout for a breathing that was still to come, and that would take her in. She stayed there stubbornly, sometimes smother-ing and inundating me, as if she were mud destined to swal-low me up, sometimes leaving, and letting herself be sought and smelled out in a distance that had become the vague depths of a hollow filled with water.

When the night was over she took me into the street. But I saw clearly that the road was hesitating, apparently immobile, thrust into the disorder of smoke and dust. Then the passion of forward movement overcame it again, and it changed course, stretched out, narrowed, cloaked itself in black dust, passed next to a huge building that looked like a factory, and finally crossed a courtyard. Its destination was a small wing of a building into which, pushing me gently, it entered as well, as if now the road had become this room. 'Now you'll

240

have some peace,' she said. 'It's the isolation ward.' Just after she made me lie on one of the two beds, I saw her moving the boxes which had been blocking the hall, lifting them, turning them over, stacking them methodically against the wall. A little later, she opened the door and left. Through the glass of the door you could see an almost cloudy light that seemed to adhere to the glass, obscuring it. From there it flowed slowly to the middle of the room, and, as it got higher, I saw on the other wall countless little gray spots start swaying, getting closer to the milky zone with infinitely small movements, yet in such a massive way that the wall itself started to move. In turn, all the light got going and slid off, as if, after having watched for a long time, it now decided to finish off its prey, and it really did throw itself on it; then immediately the little spots got thicker, became tiny wingless, crawling flies, barely born and already caught in the silence of an organic digestion. She came in at that point, pushing the door open with her foot. In one hand she had a broom and a bag, in the other a washbowl. She pulled a little lamp out of the bag and hung it above me. She came and went, brought in a plank and dropped it on two sawhorses, opened the bag, and stuck her hands in. For a moment she looked at the curtain that hid a corner of the room, and then disappeared behind it; when she came out her face, neck, and arms were dripping with water. I saw her looking for something to sit down on; she was motionless, her face a little overwhelmed, her head resting on her hands, which were pulling absent-mindedly on her hair, parting it, digging into it, and from time to time putting something in her mouth. While she was doing this, her head still lowered, she let out a little cry, an upsetting, animal cry, a bark choked off by fear, and suddenly I was sure that something in her had awakened, awakened without her knowledge, an animal instinct, that of a being anxiously foreseeing the arrival of something terrifying, because she kept on calmly arranging her hair, and even when I saw her pulling pins out of her mouth, looking at the door, screaming, 'Don't come in,' I still heard the yelping that echoed in her words, and which remained as a sign no one could obliterate. She came in and looked at me. 'I'm going to the dispensary,' she said. 'Above

241

all, keep still.' She wrapped her hair in a scarf, looked at me, and left.

I didn't move. I knew that, whatever happened, I had to keep still now. That was my chance. Really, everything was calm. I heard voices buzzing outside. I thought about this new room—I had walked right in and had been pleased from the start: it looked a lot like the other one, with walls, door, and windows; also, I wasn't as hot, and I had walked right in. A little later, I was almost happy. My thoughts were so strong and peaceful that this afternoon seemed one of the best I had had for a long time. I remembered that nothing could happen and I remembered that I knew it. I knew it. This thought was extraordinarily comforting, in one fell swoop it restored everything. I'm going to get up, I thought, and clean the room up a little. It really was messed up—with the suitcase open on the floor, the table hidden under a pile of clothes, underwear, and blankets, and also, in a corner, a comb and mirror. I got up and grabbed the broom. I recall that, seeing her come in, I had hoped to see her take up the broom, since the floor tiles were covered with dust, dry mud, even straw. You could walk right in, that was obvious. I vowed to sweep a long time, carefully; when she came back she'd be amazed, since she was so tidy. At this point it occurred to me that she resembled my sister. I was near one of the sawhorses, I leaned on it, and, while I was thinking, I heard a slight noise. I completely stopped moving and didn't look anywhere; after a few moments, I started sweeping again. I swept for a fairly long time. I really went at it; I was enveloped in dust. After I made a little pile I swept it toward the boxes. I felt a little dazed, although perfectly fine. Reaching the boxes, I again distinctly heard a slight noise. I squatted near the wall, right next to the pile of sweepings. A wet, earthy smell, a mugginess that hadn't cooled down, but which had never ceased being cold, came out of this trash. I breathed it in slowly, with a strange feeling, because it was clear that I was breathing in someone's fear; I recognized the dark flavor, it was floating just above the floor and came from the same place as the noise. I had to get up, but I didn't do it and instead I collapsed onto the garbage. From then on there wasn't any doubt: something was going

242

on near the boxes. I heard a start, a slow movement, a kind of dragging. A movement? No, something much less true, a fearful and awkward effort, a hasty endeavor carried out by a single thing. So—I had to stay still, still, still, and my heart started repeating that, and I listened to it, and the more I listened the more I was afraid, because it itself was already crazy and ruined and because every beat made a terrifying sound, the suspicious sound of someone else's heart. And yet it happened: I could stay still.

When I got a grip on myself, it was still day. Things hadn't moved, but the room seemed more empty: more monumental and more crushing, but emptier; it was as if it had pulled back and was waiting a little ways back, making me do something to fill it; I had to recapture it, and I was neglecting a duty by not doing so. So what was it? Should I look at it? Soon it got away from me, and I felt myself sliding, swirling down. I couldn't move. I was covered with an earthy, almost cold slaver, which flowed in and out through my nose and mouth; it filled me and smothered me; I was already suffocating. But at that moment it withdrew. A moment later it started flowing again, it permeated, penetrated me, I breathed with it, I felt it as I felt myself. Then it withdrew. At the same time, right next to me, the noise started again, right next to me, an intermittent noise, of sand flowing and oozing, an extremely slow panting, as if someone were there, breathing, keeping himself from breathing, hidden right next to me. I wanted to open my eyes and get away, but then, horrified, I realized that my eyes were already open and were already looking at and touching and seeing what no gaze should ever have fallen upon or endured. I had to scream, howl, I tore at myself with the feeling of howling in another world.

When she came in I was still screaming, but perhaps because my scream had become deep-rooted and calm, she acted as if she didn't notice. I got up and went to the other side of the table. Behind my back the boxes were piled up. 'Why were you yelling like that?' she said, lifting up the plank. She pulled a fat watch, a revolver, and a cigarette box stuffed with papers out of a basket. 'It belongs to someone who's been injured; he gave it to me for safekeeping.' She kept

1) stolen, shy

looking at me. 'Don't stay there, all right?' and she grabbed me, reaching over the plank: her hand on my arm, examining me, looking only at me, she saw nothing. She pulled me gently and I walked to the bed. Saying nothing, she gave me something to eat. She ate too, standing, her eyes on the door, her head raised above me. I heard her say that she was on call around midnight. 'Before that, I have to rest: I absolutely have to sleep.' She put on her old raincoat and tightened the belt. 'Don't leave,' I said. Outside there was a confused racket, people went out, others were pounding violently with hammers. She got her arm loose, and her hand furtively caressed my face and stopped at my shoulder. With the other she looked for something in the pocket of her blouse. She pulled out a piece of paper, and it went up to her eyes, which became slits and shone. 'Things are on the right track,' she said. She turned the paper toward me, so that I could see the writing, and then she suddenly stopped and listened. I sat up. At the head of the bed there had been a slight noise, in about the middle of the wall. Her gaze seemed to fasten onto something, then it became inattentive and wandered. I heard her ask what day it was.

'I can hardly believe,' she said, 'that something like that could happen one day. Is it possible? Could you ever say, "from that day on . . ."'

From the expression on her face I saw that she had started listening again, that she couldn't keep from listening. But I heard nothing; it was impossible for me to hear. I myself was in this noise which was rising slowly and falling with slight jolts. I fastened onto this indefinite and blind groping—an enormous sticky stain, already hounded and encircled by the panic it was oozing—which was heading in all directions, spreading itself out, to its own horror, more and more in broad daylight. I suddenly became calm when I realized that, after attacking the wall, the noise was starting to move to my side, toward the open air. I grabbed Jeanne by the wrist.

'It's . . . it's a toad,' I stated, categorically.

She drew back a little.

'What are you saying? What did you say? Why are you talking to me about that?'

244

She tried to get up.

'Where is it?'

First she looked at me absently, then her gaze settled on my face: on my face, not on me. She remained tense, suspiciously taking in my features. Perhaps she gave a quick glance under the bed, but it was in such a sudden way that she immediately reappeared, her eyes trained on my face, with the same expression of worry and suspicion. 'I wonder what's going to happen to you,' she said. She pushed aside her raincoat. I heard the slight friction of fabric, and when she went to close the door, she was already accompanied by sounds of the night. Coming back, her hand moved to the table and put the things back in the basket. Raising her arms, she hoisted them onto the little shelf near the lamp.

'I'm going to lie down,' she said. 'I have to sleep.'

I moved next to the wall. She threw a blanket over both of us, stretched out, and lay still.

'My joy's too great,' she said in the darkness. 'I have to struggle and I don't want it to carry me away. During the day, things hold their shape. But at night you're forced to come up with thousands of plans and take on new thoughts.' Her voice hesitated for a moment. 'I'm extremely tired,' she said, and then she was quiet.

I was a little cold; I pulled up the blanket and forced myself against the wall. For a moment I thought I'd beaten the cold, but soon I was trembling. The shivers came from far away, from different points in the room, they turned me into a confused quivering and went elsewhere, without leaving me, tormenting ever vaster regions of space. Her voice too entered the world of shivering.

'Don't ever leave me,' she said. 'I didn't ask you to come, but now . . .' She got closer and jostled me roughly. 'I know that some day I'll atone for what I did. It's not important. I've given you your name, and I'm the only one who knows it.'

Her voice resonated with such intensity that I had the impression someone was calling from outside.

'What's going on,' I said, 'what's the matter?'

My voice was rough and hoarse. She sat up too and we stayed there, motionless. 'What a wretched business,' she said with a low voice. She waited a little longer, then dove under the blanket.

A moment later, I felt myself falling into a glacial abyss; I got back up: the darkness seemed to be hiding something. My hand cautiously approached the wall, but, as far out as it went it didn't run into anything solid: it helplessly groped, not really behaving like a hand in the darkness. Suddenly I realized that she had gotten up. I recalled some knocking at the door and the rocking of the mattress as her body slid into the void. I slowly looked for my sandals, and I was already getting up when my feet cramped and became harder and colder than steel. I held them in my hands: they were horribly contracted. I rubbed them and warmed them up; slowly the feeling returned and they led me across the room, passing and turning slowly around objects. I stopped in front of the table. I went back to the bed. I reached out: my fingers, going to the shelf, grasped a little box and lifted up the lamp. It lit up, feebly. I didn't move, and I held it against me; a sheet of cold light came out of it, a trap. Quickly I bent over, put it on the ground, and threw myself back near the bed, my feet together under the stool. I saw the empty space in front of me, hewn out of the shadows like a cement tomb with rough edges. I didn't move my eyes; they were riveted, bearing down on this spot. I saw it empty, naked, bottomless, its contours crisply outlined, sharp. And yet, if it were possible, one of the sides of this tank, the one near the bed, was less sharp than the others: it formed a blurry line, it rounded out, as if the outline of another shadow . . . and, God, this shadow was moving, slightly oscillating, getting wider. I dove down and crazily pushed the lamp away. Immediately, there was a cracking sound, a smooth and gaping stretching. Terrifyingly vast, the noise of heavy water lapping in a container broke all bounds, flooded up and hit the wall. I saw the bed rise up and the mass of things surrounding it, even the darkness, tip over under enormous, blind pressure, greater than any obstacle; I saw this pressure surge with a <u>bestial</u> power against things about which it knew nothing. And suddenly—who was pushing me?—I could move, and I put the lamp back in its old place. Then there was silence. A strange, amazed silence:

empty and amazed; and, after a long moment, as if this void were a reflection, a mild subsidence took place, then continued, then went on without stopping, slow and gigantic, infinite, inexorable beyond measure, to the point where I couldn't endure it, persisting to the point where everything that had been done was completely nullified, completely reduced to nothing, by a disavowal which, for *its* part, seemed a contemptuous and threatening retraction, not only of its acts, but even of its existence, and ultimately I was forced to see that there was nothing left: everything was as before.

As before, I stared at the edges of the luminous zone. As before the lamp emitted the same serene and calm light. Nothing had happened. I couldn't stand it. I got up and went into the sheet of light. I went through space. With an insane gesture I traveled through it. Then I wanted to come back but my body wouldn't move. I tried to turn my eyes but suddenly, right next to me, so close I couldn't make out its meaning, a soft clicking was going on, like the start of a slow swallowing; then a trail appeared, a vague swirling that came together from every point in infinity, and in a moment it became insanely strong: it went up in a disgusting jump, the jump of something material, frozen in its motionless life. I was sure it was going to fall on me. My head was thrown backwards. I felt, on my chest, the weight of a bladder which spread out after a violent impact and clung perfectly to my clothing. My fists swung and beat the air. I tried to shake myself loose, but the weight was enormous: I couldn't breathe, it was like a heavy tumor that had already merged with my life. Then my mouth must have opened to grab some air. There wasn't any: I gasped convulsively, but everything was greasy and sticky. I twisted and jerked with revulsion, and while I was trying to find some way out, I felt space oscillate, and I fell down, half on the floor, half on the bed.

I turned over; my body spun on itself. I followed the lamp's blinking, and my eyes moved to the greenish, motionless block, shining brightly; they looked at it without even seeing it; they skimmed over a landslide, which had flattened from its fall and was criss-crossed with crevices; the mound was more or less the color of the ground: a compact and gaping pile—a hole. But when I reached out with my hand to explore what I saw, my fingers immediately went insane, shriveling, going limp, turning over; I was stifling, I bit my skin, I looked over my hand at a pair of fascinated and terrified eyes. It was absolutely quiet, motionless, lying on the ground, it was there, I saw it, completely and not its image, as much from within as from without; I saw something flow, solidify, flow again, and nothing in it moved, its every movement was total numbness, these wrinkles, these excrescences, this surface of dry mud its crushed insides, this earthen heap its amorphous exterior, it didn't start anywhere, it didn't end anywhere, it didn't matter which side you caught it from, and once its form was half perceived it flattened out and fell back into a mass from which eyes could never get free.

I knew I could never withstand this empty look. I got up and took one step, then another. I squatted down next to the lamp. The pile took no notice of my presence. It let me approach, I came still closer, and it didn't move; I wasn't even a stranger to it, I slid up to it like no one had ever done before, and it didn't hide, it didn't turn away, didn't ask for anything, didn't take anything away. Suddenly—and this I saw—a fairly long appendage, which seemed to be demanding a separate existence, came up out of the lump; it thrust itself out and stayed there, stretching; the entire mass turned slowly with idiotic ease and without budging. I encountered two little transparent orbs, lying on top, rootless, smooth, oily, extremely smooth. They weren't looking at me; no hint or movement came from them and I myself saw them no more than if they had been my own eyes, and already I was very close to them, dangerously close—who had ever been that close? Then I felt my arm extend, slide toward the lamp, my fingers grabbed it; they enticed it over gently. I saw them approach and slowly pass in front of me; their movement became infinitely slow, they buried themselves in the ground, became embedded, then nevertheless reached a point, then stopped, and yet—how did it happen?—were already further along. Then I saw that I was alone; no one was holding me back, not an order, not a thought, not an obstacle, and I knew something was going to happen, something vile, and I saw

248

and understood everything . . . and my hand sprang up, projecting flame, while I twisted and struggled on the ground, hoping that my screams would drown out the ominous, formless noises that were merging with me.

\* \* \*

I heard her come in and I threw myself on the bed. She pulled the other mattress to the middle of the room. She must have lain down on it, but, a moment later, she wanted to touch the end of my bed: she felt for the sheet, and, through the sheet, she tried to reach for something. She did this a number of times. Even half-asleep she sent her hand in my direction. A little later, she tossed about and, from under the covers, I saw her head come up to the level of my bed and then, higher, flat as a disk, it tried to place itself in front of me, in front of where it thought I was. 'Where are you? Why did you hide when I came in?' Then she fell back heavily. When I opened my eyes again, she was standing nearby. But I didn't move. She was motionless, leaning forward a little; she was trying to shift the sheets with her gaze. But I wasn't breathing. Two or three times her gaze passed before my eyes but didn't see me. I felt the blanket slide, I couldn't hold it back, but she didn't hear. And suddenly she froze. She stood straight up, rigid, her eyes staring at me with an extraordinary rigor; her features had thickened, her jaw was bigger, her neck bulged; for a moment, her whole being distended, tried to disconnect it-self, get away, only her eyes trained on mine kept her from simply floating away; then they turned slowly and looked at me with a fascinated blankness. I tried to hide under the covers, to slide away, I curled up, but my whole upper body was exposed. She turned around halfway, but immediately threw herself in front of me, her arms swinging violently in my direction. I pulled back and tried to get away. She tore a blanket from her mattress and whipped it out a number of times, making me jump from side to side, and finally, when I was half out of the bed, she threw it at my head.

I lost my footing and fell on the floor; my limbs and body got caught up in the material. The darkness completely para-lyzed me. There was a confused silence and, under the blanket, the sound of water. My eyes got heavy. I felt I had to get back up right away. Bumping against a piece of wood, I grabbed hold of it, pulled myself up, but I knocked something over; I slid slowly. I started coming up again; the material, disagreeably rough and coarse, pulled against me; then it was the void again. My fall made me thrash violently, I struggled, jumping and jerking; I shook off the cover and trampled it. When it was loose I saw that I was lying almost flat near the bed, my head up against the box. I lay there, breathing more and more softly, my eyelids lowered, amid the soft sound of water; in the distance I made out shoes and bare legs; I looked at them, I sank down again a bit, the silence was heavy; I glimpsed the legs going away, fading, and finally becoming quite blank. I immediately recognized them and sat up. Her face also appeared; I got up, it slid through space, came up, then pulled back into a frightened distance. I buried myself under the covers. She was sitting on the mattress, her elbows on her knees and her face supported by her hands. She was looking at something in the background, behind me. Her eyes fixed on this point, she got halfway up, then went past the bed bending over; then she walked backwards holding the lamp and staring at it, touching the broken glass. She took up the broom. Everything was peaceful and quiet. She swept, looking at the ground and sending in my direction a fine black dust which sweetened the air and helped me breathe. Then she went out.

I fell into a half-sleep and heard the distant sound of little flies; an insect threw itself against the wall with little leaps, fell back, relaunched itself, fell back; on the ground, it was still buzzing heavily, it ran, dragging itself along the wall, unable to relax, releasing around itself the odor of that overabundant noise it couldn't contain. Suddenly someone violently slammed against the door; it shook and rattled; I got up, it opened, banged against the partition, and revealed two men who pushed their way into the room. 'Oh! sorry,' and when they said that they went back out as if the banging of the door had pushed them back outside; then they slowly returned to the doorway; I saw them still outside, leaning over and trying to see into the room, coming forward a bit, until they saw the dress and the raincoat on the mattress. 'So! A woman.' At this point a wild noise erupted, a blast, a tumultuous and choked-off racket. Something threw itself against their legs. I curled up and pushed myself further into the wall. I tried to get up to the window. The dog's howls shot out and smashed against me, screams, horrible, desperate groans. It threw itself flat onto the bed, howling: ah, I recognized it, I'd waited a long time for this moment, I saw its pale, hairless skin, its bloody eyes. 'You're crazy,' she howled. The dog leapt onto the covers and, now howling myself, I pushed it away with a horrible blow, using the sheet, while the barking went on down below, was stifled, became more fanatical and more distant; and even when it had faded I remained glued to the wall, feeling that it was still mixed in with the fabric, out of which hideous worms of stench kept rising.

She tried to make me drink. She came up, her arm stretched out, separated from her; I saw the glass floating in the void. She came at me again, and when the dark expanse of liquid began to tip, my mouth started sucking it up. But the glass started shaking even more, and she quickly pulled it back. I didn't move. She stayed there with her eyes trained on the lower part of my face, on my mouth which was still coming forward, still sucking, and slowly the glass came up again and I felt the bitter taste coming in a wave, wounding and stifling me. She uncovered the upper part of my body and let me breathe freely. Her hands brushed against my neck. She tried to arrange the covers and tuck in the sheet; she slid a pillow behind me. As much as I could I stayed motionless. When she had finished, she pushed me into the corner and touched me overtly, in an insistent way, as if her hand were trying to say, You see, I'm touching you. Then she sat on the stool near the bed. I heard the insect buzzing, it had landed on the wall, had reached the area of light, but stayed at the edges and its buzzing was extremely soft.

'I think,' she said, 'this place is going to be evacuated. But I'll keep taking care of you, I won't abandon you.'

The insect let out a violent, drunken noise; I saw it had a wing that was three-quarters torn off. Stuck against the wall, it was heaving powerfully.

'I'll work with all my strength,' she said, 'night and day, tirelessly.'

She stopped and looked with me at the wall. The insect was flying up very fast, letting out a somber buzz. It got to the window and stopped at the wood of the sash; it stretched its wings and they started to vibrate, endlessly, hypnotically, and this vibration made me dizzy, like hunger. Abruptly she got up.

'Please, listen to me,' she said breathlessly. 'Up to now I've behaved badly. But now I'll struggle, everything I have will be yours. Ah, I know it, I'll succeed.'

I started whistling softly. I whistled a little louder and the slight clicking of wings was set off; when she leaned over me the insect took off, whirled around, and fell backwards heavily onto the sheet. For a moment it didn't move; only one of its legs was trembling, and I saw it. Then the legs started moving slowly, and again the soft, throbbing buzzing arose, coming through the sheet. The side legs clung to the fabric, they pulled gently on the linen, moistening it, and with a single bound it turned over with such force that it lay flat and didn't move. I heard her yelling, 'I'll be your creature. You'll never, ever get away from me.' The insect was running with insane speed, constantly changing direction, dodging the same danger in front and behind. I got up to see it better; it stopped, out of breath, then took off like a shot, blindly, blindly. She threw herself on me, then fell back. I lay flat against the wall. My jaw, tight and tense, was grinding. A moment later she bumped against the stool and ran out. I opened my mouth so as not to suffocate.

When she returned, she came up mysteriously, her face distant and haggard, pressing her sleeve mechanically against her lips. She gave me an indifferent look and lay down on the mattress. A little later she went to the doorway. 'I think this is the first convoy,' she said, coming back into the room. 'I'll have to make my rounds down there.' She took a scarf and tied it around her hair. She stood over the table and looked into the mirror, silently. All of a sudden she was kneeling in front of the bed. 'I'll come back in a moment,' she whispered. 'I'll be able to overcome everything. Whatever happens, I'll follow you, I'll stay close to you. I'll live only under your gaze.' She looked at me with her pale eyes, then quickly she leaned over, and her mouth passed over me. 'Kiss me,' she hissed. 'Really kiss me. We mustn't do things halfway. Come, come,' she shouted, trying to grab me around the waist, but as her chest was starting to press mine, she broke away convulsively and jumped back. She stumbled, got back up. 'Well,' she said after a moment, 'I've done it. No one but me has ever done it.' A bright gleam came from her eyes; she took her raincoat and left. And now, I said to myself. The air was heavy. I made an effort to turn to the window but while I was moving my eyes closed. I wasn't surprised to see her again in the room; the suitcase was open on the stool; she was coming and going peacefully, straightening things up. She reached up to the shelf, gathered the injured man's things, and put them on the table. She looked at me calmly. 'Now,' she said, 'I think it's time.' She took the injured man's bag and left. I tried to get out of bed. I got caught up in the covers, it was as if they were tied around me. I pulled on them and got closer to the edge. I got ready to plunge softly, but I saw her; she was watching me from the door. She closed the door behind her without ceasing to look at me. Her eyes on mine, she walked up, approaching almost without stirring. In front of the bed she looked at me again and said in a low voice: 'I've never prayed to you. I don't think I've ever cringed in front of you. We're blameless toward each other.' She kept on hugging the bag. She started to open it.

'Now,' she said, 'we have to put an end to it.'

The covers were strangling me, I could barely look at her; her face was drifting away, disappearing. She gave the bed a sharp kick.

'Do you hear me? Am I speaking to a rock? Maybe you'll keep deceiving me, right up to the end?'

I started to shake; I couldn't move, everything was moving. She got much closer and said in a low voice, quickly, 'But I see you. You're not just something one dreams about; I've recognized you. Now I can say: he's come, he's lived near me, he's there, it's crazy, he's there. I have to do it,' she said softly. 'I can't hold on to you alive.'

I felt myself shuddering so hard I was out of breath; something insane passed through my body. I have to speak, I thought.

'Alive, you've been alive for no one but me: no one in the world, no one, no one. Couldn't you just die of it?'

I got ready to speak, I had to master my trembling, but the trembling had completely taken over, and if I opened my mouth a terrible gasp would come out.

'Now it's time. Your life has only been for me, so I'm the one who has to take it from you.'

I felt that gasp coming up from below, it was shaking me, lifting me, suffocating me.

'Nobody knows who you are, but I know, and I'm going to destroy you.'

I let out a scream, but it wasn't a word, as I had hoped: it was only a hoarse, low growl, which made her shudder and freeze, but in which she seemed eventually to perceive something, because her eyes appeared to be interrogating me, waiting, hesitating, waiting some more, but I was trembling more and when she didn't speak I could no longer hope to speak to her. Then she knelt down and pulled out the revolver. I looked at the groove over which the daylight was sliding. She too was looking at the weapon, and I knew that as long as she didn't raise her eyes I still had a little time. I stopped breathing. I kept my eyes down, didn't hear anything. Slowly the weapon came up. She looked at me and smiled. 'Well,' she said, 'good-bye.' I too tried to smile. But suddenly her face froze, and her arm jolted so violently that I jumped back against the wall, shouting,

'Now, now I'm speaking.'

René Daumal
*You've Always Been Wrong*
Translated by Thomas Vosteen

Max Jacob
*Hesitant Fire: Selected Prose of Max Jacob*
Translated and edited by Moishe Black
and Maria Green

Jean Paulhan
*Progress in Love on the Slow Side*
Translated by Christine Moneera Laennec
and Michael Syrotinski

Benjamin Péret
*Death to the Pigs, and Other Writings*
Translated by Rachel Stella and Others

Boris Vian
*Blues for a Black Cat and Other Stories*
Editied and translated by Julia Older